Praise for the long-awaited return of *New York Times* bestselling author Robert McCammon and . . .

SPEAKS THE NIGHTBIRD

"Thoughtful as well as entertaining—think *Burn, Witch, Burn* crossed with Arthur Miller's *The Crucible*. . . . The week I spent listening to the nightbird every evening between eight and eleven was a very fine one."

—Stephen King

"[This] story is as timely as today. It's about superstition, prejudice, good and evil, hatred and love. Told with matchless insight into the human soul, this novel makes for a deeply satisfying read."

—*New York Times* bestselling author Sandra Brown

"A decade's hiatus has done nothing to dull McCammon's abilities as a storyteller or a literary craftsman. . . . Will keep readers glued to the pages."

—*Denver Rocky Mountain News*

"A trial for witchcraft proves the tip of an iceberg of intrigues in this absorbing historical mystery. . . . A compulsively readable yarn. McCammon's loyal fans will find his resurfacing reason to rejoice."

—*Publishers Weekly*

"*Speaks the Nightbird* is a welcome return of a master who keeps his audience spellbound with every sentence. . . . Powerful and tense, thrilling and atmospheric . . . reads like a rocket on a witch hunt. Once you hear the Nightbird sing, you'll never be the same."

—*Clarion-Ledger* (Jackson, MS)

"Shocking and funny . . . richly imagined and genuinely compelling. . . . First-rate entertainment by a world-class storyteller. . . . McCammon is still a potent force in contemporary popular fiction."

—*Locus*

"Disturbing. . . . McCammon tells a compelling story."

—*Library Journal*

"*Speaks the Nightbird* is rendered in vivid scenes with exquisite historical detail, dropping the reader into a fictional dream."

—*ForeWord*

Critical Acclaim for Robert McCammon's
BOY'S LIFE

"Enthralling. . . . *Boy's Life* is teeming with smartly realized characters. . . . A cornucopia of bittersweet fantasy storytelling that is by far McCammon's finest book."

—*Kirkus Reviews*

"*Boy's Life* is a wonderful story of powerful emotions, marvelous images and inventive narrative . . . filled with enough adventure, joy, discovery and heartache for a dozen boys' lifetimes."

—*Houston Chronicle*

"McCammon hangs this expertly told episodic tale on the bones of a skeleton that becomes symbolic of evil doings in the quiet waters of small-town life. . . . This evocative novel is successful on more than one level. The mystery will satisfy the most finicky aficionado."

—*Publishers Weekly*

ALSO BY ROBERT MCCAMMON

Boy's Life
Swan Song
Gone South
Mystery Walk
Usher's Passing
Mine
The Wolf's Hour
Blue World
Stinger

PUBLISHED BY POCKET BOOKS

ROBERT McCAMMON

SPEAKS THE NIGHTBIRD

VOLUME II: EVIL UNVEILED

POCKET BOOKS

New York London Toronto Sydney Singapore

POCKET BOOKS, a division of Simon & Schuster, Inc.
1230 Avenue of the Americas, New York, NY 10020

This book is a work of fiction. Names, characters, places and incidents are products of the author's imagination or are used fictitiously. Any resemblance to actual events or locales or persons, living or dead, is entirely coincidental.

Copyright © 2002 by McCammon Corporation

Published by arrangement with River City Publishing

All rights reserved, including the right to reproduce this book or portions thereof in any form whatsoever. For information address River City Publishing, 1719 Mulberry Street, Montgomery, AL 36106

ISBN: 0-7434-7139-3

First Pocket Books paperback edition October 2003

10 9 8 7 6 5 4 3 2 1

POCKET and colophon are registered trademarks of Simon & Schuster, Inc.

Cover design and illustration by David Stevenson

Manufactured in the United States of America

For information regarding special discounts for bulk purchases,
please contact Simon & Schuster Special Sales at 1-800-456-6798
or business@simonandschuster.com.

*Think where man's glory most begins and ends
And say that my glory was I had such friends.*

—William Butler Yeats

SPEAKS THE NIGHTBIRD

ONE

atthew could hear the tempestuous sound of the sea. Breakers were hitting islands or exposed sandbars some distance away from the swamp that he was now negotiating with great difficulty. Ahead of him and almost at the limit of his perception was the midnight traveller—a dark, moving blotch within further darkness—who would have been totally lost to him had it not been for the faint orange moonlight, and even that meager illumination was jealously guarded by the streams of moving clouds.

The man had come this way before, that was a certainty. And more than once. His pace was swift and sure-footed, even without benefit of a lantern. Matthew was up to the task of following through the waist-high grasses and across the muck that pulled at his shoes, but it was a tough and laborious journey.

They had left Fount Royal far behind. Matthew estimated the distance at least a quarter mile from the watchman's tower, which had been easily circumvented by cutting through the pinewoods. If the watchman had been awake—and this Matthew seriously doubted—he'd been looking out to sea. Who would expect anyone in their right mind to venture out into this morass in the dead of night?

The midnight traveller had a definite purpose, one that gave speed to his step. Matthew heard something rustle off in the grass to his right; it sounded large and quite sinister, therefore he found a little extra speed himself. He discovered in the next moment, however, that his worst enemy was the swamp itself, as he walked into a shallow pond that closed about his knees and almost sent him sprawling. The mud at the pond's bottom seized his shoes and it was only with extreme tenacity that Matthew worked his way to freedom. Once out of the water he realized he could no longer detect his quarry's movement. He scanned from right to left and back again, but the darkness had truly dropped its curtain.

Still, he knew the man must be going in this general direction. He started off again, more mindful of where he was stepping. The swamp was indeed a treacherous place. The midnight traveller must surely have come out here many times to be able to navigate these dangers. Indeed, Matthew thought the man may have made a map of his route and consigned it to memory.

After three or four minutes, Matthew was yet unable to spy any movement in the darkness. He glanced back and saw that his course had taken him around a headland. A black line of pines and swamp oaks stood between his current position and the watchman's tower, which was probably the greater part of a mile behind. Beyond him was only more swamp. He debated whether to turn back or forge on. Everything out here was only greater and lesser shades of dark, so what was the point? He did continue on a few paces, though, and again paused to scan the horizon. Mosquitoes hummed about his ears, hungry for blood. Frogs croaked in the rushes. Of another human, however, there was not a sign.

What was there to bring a person out here? This was wild desolation, hardly a civilized soul standing between his footprints and the city of Charles Town. So what did the midnight traveller seek to accomplish?

Matthew looked up at the banners of stars. The sky was so huge and the horizon so wide that it was fearsome. The sea, too, was a dark continent. Standing on this coast with the unknown world at his back, he felt more than a little distress, as if his equilibrium and very place on earth were challenged by such immensity. He understood at that moment the need for men to build towns and cities and surround them with walls—not only to keep out the threat of Indians and wild beasts, but to maintain the illusion of control in a world that was too large to be tamed.

His contemplation was suddenly broken. Out at sea, two lights blinked in quick succession.

Matthew had been about to turn his face toward Fount Royal again, but now he stood motionless. A few seconds went by. Then, once again, the two lights blinked.

What followed next gave his heart a jolt. Not fifty yards from where Matthew was standing, a lighted lantern appeared and was uplifted. The lantern swung back and forth, and then disappeared—concealed, Matthew suspected, by the midnight traveller's cloak. The man must have either crouched down to strike a match and flame the candle, or done it within the cloak's folds. Whatever and however, a signal had been answered.

Matthew lowered himself into the protection of the marsh grass, so that just his eyes were above it. He desired a closer view, and began to move quietly and carefully toward where the lantern had been revealed. It came to mind that if he stepped on a venomous reptile in his present posture, its fangs would strike a most valuable area. He got to within thirty feet of the dark-cloaked man and was forced to stop when the cover of the high grass ended. The man was standing on a stretch of hard-packed sand, just a few yards short of the Atlantic's foamy waves. He was waiting, his face aimed toward the ocean and his lantern hidden in the cloak.

Matthew also waited. Presently, after the passage of perhaps ten minutes during which the man paced back and forth but never left his station, Matthew was aware of a shape emerging from the darkness of the sea. Only when it was about to make landfall did Matthew make out an oarboat, painted either black or dark blue. There were three men aboard, all of whom also wore night-hued clothing. Two of the men jumped out into the surf and pulled the oarboat to shore.

Matthew realized the boat must have come from a larger vessel some distance away. His thought was: *I have found the Spanish spy.*

"Greetin's!" the man who had remained in the oarboat called, his accent as far from being Spanish as Gravesend was from Valencia. He stepped down onto the sand. "How goes it?"

The midnight traveller answered, but his voice was so low Matthew heard only a murmur.

"Seven this trip," the oarboater said. "That oughta do you. Get 'em out!" He had delivered this command to the other two men, who began to unload what appeared to be wooden buckets. "Same place?" he asked the midnight traveller, who answered with a nod. "You're a man of habit, ain't you?"

The midnight traveller raised his lantern from the folds of his cloak and by its yellow glow Matthew saw his face in profile. "A man of *good* habit," Edward Winston said sternly.

"Cease this prattle, bury them, and be done with it!" He dropped the lantern, which had been used to show the other man that he was in no mood for dawdling.

"All right, all right!" The oarboater reached into the bottom of his craft and brought up two shovels, and then he walked up the beach to the edge of the high grass. His path brought him within fifteen feet of Matthew's concealment. He stopped at a thatch of spiny palmettos. "This where you want 'em?"

"It will do," Winston said, following.

"Bring 'em on!" the man ordered his crew. "Hurry it, we ain't got all night!" The buckets, which appeared to be sealed, were carried to the designated place. The oarboater handed the two shovels to the other men, who began to dig into the sand.

"You know where a third shovel is," Winston said. "You might employ it, Mr. Rawlings."

"I ain't no damn Injun!" Rawlings replied tartly. "I'm a chief!"

"I beg to differ. You *are* an Indian, and your chief is Mr. Danforth. I suggest you earn the coin he's paying you."

"Very *little* coin, sir! Very *little,* for this night work!"

"The faster they're buried, the sooner you may go."

"Well, why bury 'em anyway? Who the hell's comin' out here to find 'em?"

"Safe is better than sorry. Just lay one bucket aside and put the others under with no further argument."

Muttering beneath his breath, Rawlings reached carefully into the palmettos and pulled out a short-handled shovel that had been hidden there. Matthew watched as Rawlings fell to digging at rhythm with his companions. "What of the witch?" he asked Winston as he worked. "When's she gonna hang?"

"Not hang. She'll be burned at the stake. I expect it shall be within the next few days."

"You'll be cooked too then, won't you? You and Danforth both!"

"Just concern yourself with your digging," Winston said tersely. "You needn't put them deep, but make sure they're well covered."

"All right! Work on, my lads! We don't want to tarry long in this Satan's country, do we?"

Winston grunted. "Here or there, it's *all* Satan's country, isn't it?" He gave the left side of his neck a sound slap, executing some bloodsucking beastie.

It took only a few moments for a hole to be opened, six buckets secreted within it, and the sand shovelled over them. Rawlings was a master at appearing to work hard, with all the necessary facial contortions and exertions of breath, but his shovel might have been a spoon, for all the sand it moved. When the buckets were laid under, Rawlings stepped back, wiped his brow with his forearm, and said, "Well done, well done!" as if he were congratulating himself. He returned the implement to its hiding place amid the palmettos and grinned broadly at Winston, who stood nearby watching in silence. "I expect this'll be the last trip, then!"

"I think we should continue one more month," Winston said.

Rawlings's grin collapsed. "What need will you have of any more, if she's to be burned?"

"I'll make a need. Tell Mr. Danforth I shall be here at the hour."

"As you please, your majesty!" Rawlings gave Winston an exaggerated comical bow and the two other men laughed. "Any other communications to the realm?"

"Our business is concluded." Winston said coldly. He picked up by its wire handle the seventh bucket that had been laid aside, and then he abruptly turned toward Matthew—who instantly ducked down and pressed himself against the earth—and began to walk through the grass.

"I've never seen a burnin' before!" Rawlings called after him. "Make sure you take it all in, so's you can describe it to me!" Winston didn't respond, but kept on walking. His course, Matthew was relieved to see, took him along a diagonal line perhaps ten or twelve feet to Matthew's west. Then Winston had gone past, holding the lantern low under his cloak to shed some light on where he was stepping. Matthew presumed he would extinguish the candle long before he got within view of the watchman's tower.

"That tight-assed prig! I could lay him out with my little finger!" Rawlings boasted to his companions after Winston had departed.

"You could lay him out with your bloody *breath!*" one of the others said, and the third man guffawed.

"Right you are, at that! Come on, let's cast off this damned shingle! Thank Christ we've got a fair wind for a change tonight!"

Matthew lifted his head and watched as the men returned to their oarboat. They pushed it off the beach, Rawlings clambered over the side first and then the other men, the oars were taken up—though not by the big chief—and the vessel moved out through the lathery surf. It was quickly taken by the darkness.

Matthew knew that if he waited long enough and kept a sharp enough eye he might see some evidence of a larger craft at anchor out there—possibly the flare of a match lighting a pipe, or a stain of mooncolor on a billowing sail. He did not, however, have the time or the inclination.

Suffice it to know that an oarboat was not a vessel suitable for a sea voyage.

He looked in the direction Winston had gone, back toward Fount Royal. Satisfied that he was alone, Matthew got up from his defensive posture and immediately went on the offensive. He found the disturbed area beside the palmettos where the buckets had been buried, and—two painful palmetto-spike stabs later—gripped his hand on the concealed shovel.

As Winston had specified, the buckets were not buried very deeply. All Matthew desired was one. The bucket he chose was of common construction, its lid sealed with a coating of dried tar, and of weight Matthew estimated between seven and eight pounds. He used the shovel again to fill the cavity, then returned it to the palmettos and set off for Fount Royal with the bucket in his possession.

The way back was no less difficult than his previous journey. It came to him that he was most likely locked out of Bidwell's mansion and would have to ring the bell to gain entrance; did he wish to let anyone in the household see him with this bucket in hand? Whatever game Winston was up to, Matthew didn't want to tip the man that his table had been overturned. He trusted Mrs. Nettles to a point, but in his opinion the jury was still out on everyone in the damned town. So: what to do with the bucket?

He had an idea, but it would mean trusting one person implicitly. Two persons, if Goode's wife should be counted. He was eager to learn the bucket's contents, and most likely Goode would have an implement to force it open.

With a great degree of thankfulness Matthew put the swamp at his back, negotiated the pinewoods to avoid the watchtower, and shortly thereafter stood before John Goode's door. Upon it he rapped as quietly as he thought possible, though the sound to his ears was alarmingly loud and must have awakened every slave in the quarters. To his chagrin, he had to knock a second time—and harder—before a light blotched the window's covering of stretched oilskin cloth.

The door opened. A candle was pushed out, and above it was Goode's sleepy-eyed face. He'd been prepared to be less than courteous to whoever had come knocking at such an hour, but when he saw first the white skin and then who wore it he put himself together. "Oh . . . yes suh?"

"I have something that needs looking at." Matthew held up the bucket. "May I enter?"

Of course he was not to be denied. "What is it?" May asked from their pallet of a bed as Goode brought Matthew in and closed the door. "Nothin' that concerns you, woman," he said as he lit a second candle from the first. "Go back to sleep, now." She rolled over, pulling a threadbare covering up to her neck.

Goode put the two candles on the table and Matthew set the bucket down between them. "I followed a certain gentleman out to the swamp just a while ago," Matthew explained. "I won't go into the particulars, but he has more of these buried out there. I want to see what's in it."

Goode ran his fingers around the tar-sealed lid. He picked up the bucket and turned it so its bottom was in the light. There, burnt by a brand into the wood, was the letter K and beneath that the letters *CT*. "Maker's mark," he said. "From a cooper in Charles Town, 'pears to be." He looked around for a tool and put his hand on a stout knife. Then he began chipping the tar away as Matthew watched in eager anticipation. When enough of the seal had been broken, Goode slid the blade under the lid and worked it up. In another moment the lid came loose, and Goode lifted it off.

Before sight was made of what the bucket concealed, smell gave its testimony. "Whoo!" Goode said, wrinkling his nose. Matthew put the sharp odor as being of a brimstone quality, with interminglings of pine oil and freshly cooked tar. Indeed, what the bucket held looked to be thick black paint.

"Might I borrow your blade?" Matthew asked, and with it he stirred the foul-smelling concoction. As he did, yellow streaks of sulphur appeared. He was beginning to fathom what he might be confronted with, and it was not a pretty picture. "Do you have a pan we might put some of this in? A spoon, as well?"

Goode, true to his name, supplied an iron pan and a wooden ladle. Matthew put a single dip of the stuff into the pan, just enough to cover its bottom. "All right," Matthew said. "Let us see what we have." He picked up one of the candles and lowered its flame into the pan.

As soon as the wick made contact, the substance caught fire. It was a blue-tinged flame, and burned so hot both Matthew and Goode had to draw back. There were small pops and cracklings as more flammable additives in the mixture ignited. Matthew picked up the pan and took it to the hearth so that the fumes might be drawn upward. Even with so little an amount, the heat on his hand was considerable.

"That's the Devil's own brew, ain't it?" Goode said.

"No, it's made by men," Matthew answered. "Diabolical chemists, perhaps. It's called 'infernal fire,' and it has a long history of being used in classical naval warfare. The Greeks made bombs from it and shot them from catapults."

"The Greeks? What're you goin' on about? Uh . . . beggin' your pardon, suh."

"Oh, it's all right. I think the use of this material is very clear. Our swamp-travelling gentleman has a zest for fire."

"Suh?"

"Our gentleman," Matthew said, watching the flames continue to burn brightly in the pan, "likes to see houses alight. With this chemical, he is sure of setting fire to even damp wood. I expect he might paint it on the walls and floor with a brush. Then the stuff is touched off at several strategic places . . . and the firemen will inevitably be too late."

"You mean . . ." The truth of the matter was dawning on Goode. "The man's been usin' this to burn down houses?"

"Exactly. His last strike was against the schoolhouse." Matthew set the pan down in the fireplace's ashes. "Why he would wish to do so, I have no idea. But the fact that this bucket was fashioned in Charles Town and was brought by sea bodes ill for his loyalty."

"Brought by sea?" He stared long and hard at Matthew. "You know who the man be, don't you?"

"I do, but I'm unprepared to speak the name." Matthew returned to the table and pushed the lid down firmly on the bucket once more. "I have a request to make. Will you hold this in safekeeping for a short time?"

Goode regarded the bucket with trepidation. "It won't blow us up, will it?"

"No, it needs a flame to ignite. Just keep it closed and away from fire. You might wrap it up and treat it with the same care you treat your violin."

"Yes suh," he said uncertainly. "Only thing be, I don't believe nobody ever got blowed up from fiddle music."

At the door, Matthew cautioned, "Not a word to anyone about this. As far as you should be concerned, I was never here."

Goode had picked up both candles to remove them from the immediate vicinity of such destructive power.

"Yes suh. Uh . . . you'll be comin' back to *get* this here thing, won't you?"

"I will. I expect I'll need it very soon." But not until he determined exactly why Edward Winston was burning down his employer's town, he might have added.

"The sooner I'll like it," Goode said, already looking for a piece of burlap with which to wrap the offensive visitor.

Matthew left Goode's house and walked to the mansion, which was a relatively short distance but a world away from the slave quarters. He knew he should get to sleep quickly, as there was much to do at daylight. But he knew also that sleep was going to be difficult in the few hours of dark that remained, because his mind would twist this new revelation into every possible shape in an attempt to understand it. Banished now from his thoughts was the equine lust of Seth Hazelton; the crimes of Edward Winston loomed far larger, for the man had set those fires and willingly ascribed them—as did Bidwell and everyone else—to Rachel's pact with the Devil.

Matthew had every intention of going to the door and ringing the bell to gain entry if necessary, but between intention and deed he shifted his course a few degrees and soon found himself standing again on the grassy bank of the spring. He sat down, pulled his knees up to his chin, and stared out across the smooth water, his mind turbulent with questions of what was and what might be.

Presently he decided to stretch out, and lying on his back in the grass he looked up at the streams of stars that showed between the moving clouds. His last conscious thought before he drifted to sleep was of Rachel in the darkness of her cage; of Rachel, whose life depended on his actions in the hours that remained.

Of Rachel.

TWO ◆

A chorus of roosters crowed like triumphant horns. Matthew opened his eyes to a rose-colored light. Above him, the sky was pale pink and dappled with purple-edged clouds. He sat up, drawing in the sweet air of what seemed the first true morning of May.

Someone began ringing a bell, and then a second higher-toned bell added its voice. Matthew got to his feet. He heard a man's joyous shout from further along Harmony Street, and then Matthew saw perhaps the most beautiful sight of his life: the sun, a golden fireball, was rising over the sea. This was the sun of creation, and its mere touch had the force to waken the earth. Matthew lifted his face toward the light as a third bell chimed. Two birds began to chirp in one of the oaks that stood around the spring. Tendrils of low-lying mist still clung to the ground, but they were pitiful and short-fated relatives to the massive thunderclouds that had so long held dominion. Matthew stood breathing the air as if he'd forgotten what springtime smelled like, as indeed he had: not the wet, foul stagnance of a swamp, but the clean soft breeze that brought the promise of new beginnings.

If ever there had been a morning to put Satan to flight, this was the one. Matthew stretched his arms up toward the sky to loosen the tight muscles in his back, though it could certainly be said that sleeping outdoors in the grass was preferable to grappling with Somnus in the gaol. He watched the sunlight strengthening across the roofs, yards, and fields of Fount Royal, the mist in full retreat. Of course the clear weather might only last one day before the rain returned, but he dared think nature's pendulum had swung in Bidwell's favor.

He had business this morning with the master of Fount Royal. He left the spring and walked to the mansion, the shutters of which had already been opened to the air. He found the entrance unlatched, and as he considered himself somewhat more than a visitor he opened it without ringing the bell and proceeded up the stairs to look in on the magistrate.

Woodward was still asleep, though either Mrs. Nettles or one of the other servants had already entered to crack the shutters of his room. Matthew approached the bed and stood beside it, looking at the magistrate. Woodward's mouth was partway open, the sound of his breathing like the faint scraping together of rusted iron wheels in a mechanism that was near failure. Brown bloodstains on the pillow behind his head marked the administrations of Dr. Shields's lancet last night, a task that was becoming a nocturnal ritual. A plaster medicated with some kind of nose-searing ointment bad been pressed upon Woodward's bare chest, and grease glistened on the magistrate's upper lip and around his green-crusted nostrils. On the bedside table, three candles that had burned down to stubs indicated that

Woodward had attempted more reading of the documents last night, and the documents themselves had spilled off the bed and lay now on the floor.

Matthew set about picking up the papers, carefully arranging them in proper sequence, and when he was done he returned them to the wooden box. The portion that Matthew had taken to his room and read yesterday evening had not delivered any further insights, much to his disappointment. He stared at Woodward's face, at the way the yellow-tinged flesh stretched over the skull, at the pale purple eyelids through which could be seen the protrusions of the orbs. A spiderwork of tiny red blood vessels had appeared on either side of Woodward's nose. The man seemed to have become thinner since Matthew last saw him, though this was due possibly to the change of light. He appeared much older too, the lines upon his face cut deeper by suffering. The blotches on his scalp had darkened as the flesh paled. There was a terrible fragility about him now, something breakable as a clay cup. Looking upon the magistrate in this condition frightened Matthew, yet he was compelled to observe.

He had seen the mask of Death before. He knew it was now before him, clasping on to the magistrate's face. The skin was being shrunken, the skull sharpened for its imminent emergence. A dagger of panic pierced him and twisted in his guts. He wished to shake Woodward awake, to pull him to his feet and make him walk, talk, dance . . . anything to banish this sickness. But, no . . . the magistrate needed his rest. He needed to sleep long and hard, with the benefit of the ointments and the bloodletting. And now there was good reason to hope for the best, with the freshened air and the sun's appearance! Yes, it was best to let the magistrate sleep until he awakened on his own, no matter how long, and let nature work its medicine.

Matthew reached out and gently touched Woodward's right hand. Instantly he drew back, because even though the magistrate's flesh was hot there was yet a moist waxy sensation to it that greatly disturbed him. Woodward made a soft moaning sound, and his eyelids fluttered but he didn't awaken. Matthew backed to the door, the panic dagger still jabbing at his stomach, and then he went quietly out into the hallway.

Downstairs, he followed the noise of cutlery scraping a plate and found Bidwell at the feasting table attacking a breakfast of corncakes, fried potatoes, and hambone marrow. "Ah, here is the clerk this fine, God-lit morning!" Bidwell said before he stuffed his mouth. He wore a peacock-blue suit, a lace-ruffled shirt, and one of his most elaborately combed and curled wigs. He washed the food down with a drink of apple beer and nodded toward the place that had been set for Matthew. "Sit down and feed yourself!"

Matthew accepted the invitation. Bidwell shoved a platter of corncakes in his direction and Matthew speared two of them with his knife. The marrow platter followed.

"Mrs. Nettles told me you weren't in your room when she knocked." Bidwell continued to eat as he talked, which resulted in half-chewed food spilling from his mouth. "Where were you?"

"Out," Matthew answered.

"*Out,*" Bidwell said, with a note of sarcasm. "Yes, I know you were out. But out where, and doing what?"

"I went outside when I saw the schoolhouse on fire. I stayed out the rest of the night."

"Oh, that's why you look so poorly then!" He started to stab a fried potato with his knife, but paused in mid-thrust. "Wait a moment." His eyes narrowed. "What mischief have you been up to?"

"Mischief? You presume the worst, I think."

"You may think, but I *know*. Whose barn have you been poking around in this time?"

Matthew looked him in the eyes. "I went back to the blacksmith's barn, of course."

There was a deadly quiet. Then Bidwell laughed. His knife came down into the potato; he claimed it from the platter and shoved the rest of the charred tubers toward Matthew. "Oh, you're full of spite today, aren't you? Well, I know you may be a young fool but you are not fool enough to go back to Hazelton's place! No sirrah! That man would put a pole to your backside!"

"Not unless I was a mare," Matthew said quietly, taking a bite of a corncake.

"What?"

"I said . . . I would do well to beware. Hazelton, I mean."

"Yes, and that's the smartest thing I've heard leave your lips!" Bidwell spent a moment eating again, as if food would be outlawed by the King on the morrow, before he spoke. "Your back. How is it?"

"A little painful. Otherwise, all right."

"Well, eat up. A full belly dulls all pain. That's what my father used to tell me, when I was your age. Of course, by the time I was your age I was working on the docks fourteen hours a day, and if I could steal a pear I was as happy as a lord." He paused to quaff from his tankard. "Have you ever worked a whole day in your life?"

"Physical work, you mean?"

"What other kind of work is there for a young man? Yes, I mean physical! Have you ever sweated to move a pile of heavy crates twenty feet because the bastard in charge says you'll do it or else? Have you ever pulled a rope until your hands bled, your shoulders cracked, and you cried like a baby but you knew you had to keep pulling? Have you ever gotten on your knees and scrubbed the deck of a ship with a brush, and then gotten down and scrubbed it again when that bastard in charge spat on it? Well? Have you?"

"No," Matthew said.

"Ha!" Bidwell nodded, grinning. "I have. Many times! And I'm damned proud of it, too! You know why? Because it made me a man. And you know who that bastard in charge was? My father. Yes, my father, rest his soul." He stabbed a chunk of potato with a force that Matthew thought might send the knife through the plate and table both. When Bidwell chewed it, his teeth ground together.

"Your father sounds like a hard taskmaster," Matthew said.

"My father," Bidwell replied, "came up from London's dirt, just as I did. My first memory of him was the smell of the river. And he knew those docks and those ships. He started out as a cargo handler, but he had a gift for working wood and he could lay a hull patch with the best who ever lived. That's how the yard started. One ship here, another there. Then more and more, and soon he had his own drydock. Yes, he was a hard taskmaster, but just as hard on himself as on anyone else."

"You inherited your business from him, then?"

"*Inherited?*" Bidwell cast a scornful glance. "I inherited nothing from him but misery! My father was inspecting a hulk for salvage—something he'd done dozens of times before—when a section of rotten planks gave way and he fell through. His knees were shattered. Gangrene set in and to save his life the surgeon took both his legs. I was nineteen years old, and suddenly I was responsible for my invalid father, my mother, and two younger sisters, one of whom was sickly to the point of emaciation. Well, it quickly became clear to me that though my father was a hard taskmaster he was a sorry bookkeeper. The records of income and debts were abysmal, if they existed at all. And here came the creditors, who presumed the yard would be sold now that my father was confined to his bed."

"But you didn't sell it?" Matthew asked.

"Oh, I sold it all right. To the highest bidder. I had no choice, the records being as they were. My father raged like a tiger. He called me a fool and a weakling, and vowed he would hate me to his grave and beyond for destroying his business." Bidwell paused to swig from the tankard. "But I paid off the debtors and settled all accounts. I put food on our table and bought medicine for my sister, and I found I had a small amount of money left. There was a small marine carpentry shop that advertised for investors, as they were expanding their workplace. I decided to put every last shilling I had into it, so I might have some influence over the decisions. My family name was already known, of course. The greatest problem I first faced was in raising more money to put into the business, which I did by laboring at other jobs and also by some bluffing at the gaming tables. Then there were the small-thinkers to be gotten rid of, those men who let caution be their rulers and so never dared to win for fear of losing."

Bidwell chewed on bone marrow, his eyes hooded. "One of those men, unfortunately, had his name above the workplace door. He was too concerned with inches, while I thought in terms of leagues. He saw marine carpentry, while I saw shipbuilding. Thus—though he was thirty years older than me, and had built the shop from its beginnings—I knew the pasture belonged to him, but the future was mine. I set out to procure business that I knew he would not condone. I prepared profit statements and cost predictions, down to the last timber and nail, which I then presented to a meeting of the craftsmen. My question to them was: did they wish to take a risk of a great future under my guidance, or did they wish to continue their current plodding path under Mr. Kellingsworth? Two of them voted to throw me out the door. The other four—including the master drafts-man—voted to take on the new work."

"And Mr. Kellingsworth?" Matthew raised his eyebrows. "I'm sure he had something to say?"

"At first he was mute with anger. Then . . . I think he was relieved, because he didn't want the mantle of responsibility. He wanted a quiet life far removed from the specter of fail-ure that haunted his successes." Bidwell nodded. "Yes, I think he'd been searching for a way to that pasture for a long time, but he needed a push. I gave it to him, along with a very decent buyout settlement and a percentage of future income . . . to decrease with the passage of time, of course. But my name was on the placard above the door. My name and my name only. That was the starting of it."

"I expect your father was proud of you."

Bidwell was silent, staring at nothing though his eyes were fierce. "One of the first things I purchased with my profits was a pair of wooden legs," he said. "The finest wooden legs that could be made in all of England. I took them to him. He looked at them. I said I would help him learn to walk. I said I would hire a specialist to teach him." Bidwell's tongue emerged, and he slowly licked his upper lip. "He said . . . he would not wear them if I had bought him a pair of real legs and could bind them solid again. He said I could take them to the Devil, because that is where a traitor was destined to burn." Bidwell pulled in a long breath and let it go. "And those were the final words he ever spoke to me."

Though he didn't particularly care for Bidwell, Matthew couldn't help but feel little sad for him. "I'm sorry."

"*Sorry?*" Bidwell snapped. "Why?" He thrust his food-streaked chin forward. "Sorry because I'm a success? A self-made man? Sorry because I am rich, that I have built this house and this town and there is more building yet to be done? Because Fount Royal will become a center of maritime trade? Or because at long last the weather has cleared and the spirits of my citizens will rise accordingly?" He jabbed another piece of potato with his knife and pushed it into his mouth. "I think," he said as he chewed, "that the only thing you're sorry for is the impending execution of that damned witch, because you won't be able to get up her skirt!" A wicked thought struck him and made his eyes glint. "Ah ha! Perhaps *that's* where you were all night! Were you in the gaol with her? I wouldn't doubt it! Preacher Jerusalem told me about you striking him yesterday!" He gave a dark grin. "What, did a blow upon the preacher earn you a blow from the witch?"

Matthew slowly put down his knife and spoon. Flames were burning behind his face, but he said coldly, "Preacher Jerusalem has his own intents toward Rachel. You may think as you please, but be aware that he has put a ring through your nose."

"Oh yes, of course he has! And she hasn't put a ring through *yours,* I suppose? Or perhaps she has put her kiss of approval on your balls, is that it? I can see her now, on her knees, and you up close against those bars! Oh, that's a precious sight!"

"I had a precious sight of my own last night!" Matthew said, the flames beginning to burn through his self-control. "When I went out to the—" He stopped himself before the words could flow. He'd been on the verge of telling Bidwell about Winston's escapade and the buckets of infernal fire, but he was not going to be goaded to spill his knowledge before he was ready. He stared down at his plate, a muscle working in his jaw.

"I never met a young man so full of pepper and manure as you," Bidwell went on, calmer now but oblivious to what Matthew had been about to say. "If it were up to you, my town would be a witch's haven, wouldn't it? You'd even defy your own poor, sick master to save that woman's flesh from the fire! I think you ought to get to a monastery up there in Charles Town and become a monk to save your soul. Either that, or go to a bawdy-house and fuck the doxies 'til your eyeballs blow out."

"Mr. Rawlings," Matthew said, his voice strained.

"*Who?*"

"Mr. Rawlings," he repeated, realizing he had set one foot into the morass. "Do you know that name?"

"No. Why should I?"

"Mr. Danforth," Matthew said. "Do you know *that* name?"

Bidwell scratched his chin. "Yes, I do. Oliver Danforth is the harbormaster in Charles Town. I have had some trouble with him, in getting supplies through. What of him?"

"Someone mentioned the name," Matthew explained. "I hadn't met anyone by that name, so I wondered who he might be."

"Who mentioned him?"

Matthew saw ahead of him a maze taking shape, and he must quickly negotiate out of it. "Mr. Paine," he said. "It was before I went into the gaol."

"Nicholas, eh?" Bidwell frowned. "That's odd."

"Is it?" Matthew's heart gave a thump.

"Yes. Nicholas can't stand the sight of Oliver Danforth.

They've had some arguments over the supply situation, therefore I've been sending Edward to deal with him. Nicholas goes along too, to protect Edward from harm on the road, but Edward is far better a diplomat. I don't understand why Nicholas should be talking about Danforth to *you*."

"It wasn't to me, exactly. It was a name I overheard."

"Oh, you have big ears too, is that it?" Bidwell grunted and finished off his drink. "I should have guessed!"

"Mr. Winston seems a valuable and loyal man," Matthew ventured. "Has he been with you very long?"

"Eight years. Now what're all these questions about?"

"My curiosity, that's all."

"Well for Christ's sake, rein it in! I've had enough of it!" He pushed himself up from his seat in preparation to leave.

"Please indulge me just a minute longer," Matthew said, also standing up. "I swear before God I won't bother you with any further questions if you'll just answer a few more."

"Why? What is you wish to know about Edward?"

"Not about Mr. Winston. About the spring."

Bidwell looked as if he wasn't sure whether to laugh or cry. "The *spring?* Have you lost your senses altogether?"

"The spring," Matthew repeated firmly. "I'd like to know how it came to be found, and when."

"You're serious, aren't you? Lord, you really are!" Bidwell started to blast at Matthew, but all the air seemed to leave him before he could gather himself. "You have worn me out," he admitted. "You have absolutely tattered my rag."

"Humor me, as it is such a beautiful morning," Matthew said steadfastly. "I repeat my promise not to plague you again, if you'll tell me how you came to find the spring."

Bidwell laughed quietly and shook his head. "All right, then. You must know that, in addition to royally funded explorers, there are men for hire who will carry out private explorations for individuals or companies. It was one of these that I contracted to find a settlement area with a fresh water source at least forty miles south of Charles Town. I stressed the fact that access to the sea was needed, yet a direct seafront was not necessary. I could drain a marsh, therefore the presence of such was tolerable. I also needed an abundance of hardwood and an area defensible from pirates and Indian raiders. When the proper place was found—*this* place—I presented the findings and my plans to the royal court, whereupon I waited two months for a grant to purchase the land."

"It was given readily?" Matthew asked. "Or did anyone attempt to block the grant?"

"Word had gotten to Charles Town. A coalition of their paid magpies swooped in and tried to dissuade the transaction, but I was already ahead of them. I had greased so many palms I could be called an oil pot, and I even added free giltwork to the yacht of the colonial administrator so he might turn heads on his jaunts up and down the Thames."

"But you hadn't visited this area before you made the purchase?"

"No, I trusted Aronzel Hearn. The man I'd hired." Bidwell took his snuffbox from his coat pocket, opened it, and noisily sniffed a pinch. "I saw a map, of course. It suited my needs, that's all I had to know."

"What of the spring?"

"*What of it,* boy?" Bidwell's patience was fraying like a rope rubbing splintered wood.

"I know the land was mapped," Matthew said, "but what of the spring? Did Hearn take a sounding of it? How deep is it, and from where does the water come?"

"It comes from . . . I don't know. Somewhere." Bidwell

took another sniff. "I do know there are other smaller springs out in the wilderness. Solomon Stiles has seen them, and drunk from them, on his hunting trips. I suppose they're all connected underground. As far as the depth is concerned . . ." He stopped, with his snuff-pinched fingers poised near his nostrils. "Now that's strange," he said.

"What is?"

"Speaking of the spring like this. I remember someone else asking me similar questions."

At once Matthew's bloodhound sense came to full alert. "Who was it?"

"It was . . . a surveyor who came to town. Perhaps a year or so after we began building. He was mapping the road between Charles Town and here, and wished to map Fount Royal as well. I recall he was interested in the depth of the spring."

"So he took a sounding?"

"Yes, he did. He'd been set upon by Indians several miles from our gate. The savages had stolen all his instruments, therefore I had Hazelton fashion him a rope with a sounding weight tied at the end. I also had a raft built for him, that he might take his measurements from various areas of the fount."

"Ah," Matthew said quietly, his mouth dry. "A surveyor without instruments. Do you know if he discovered the spring's depth?"

"As I remember, the deepest point was found to be some forty feet."

"Was this surveyor travelling alone?"

"He was alone. On horseback. I recall he told me he had left the savages playing with his bag, and he felt lucky to escape with his hair. He had a full beard too, so I expect they might have sheared his face off to get it."

"A beard," Matthew said. "Was he young or old? Tall or short? Fat or thin?"

Bidwell stared blankly at him. "Your mind is as addled as a cockroach, isn't it? What the bloody hell does it matter?"

"I would really like to know," Matthew persisted. "What was his height?"

"Well . . . taller than me, I suppose. I don't remember much about him but the beard."

"What color was it?"

"I think . . . dark brown. There might have been some gray in it." He scowled. "You don't expect me to fully remember a man who passed through here four years ago, do you? And what's the point of these foolish questions?"

"Where did he stay?" Matthew asked, oblivious to Bidwell's rising ire. "Here in the house?"

"I offered him a room. As I recall, he refused and asked for the loan of a tent. He spent two or possibly three nights sleeping outside. I believe it was early September, and certainly warm enough."

"Let me guess where the tent was pitched," Matthew said. "Was it beside the spring?"

"I think it might have been. What of it?" Bidwell cocked his head to one side, flakes of snuff around his nostrils.

"I am working on a theory," Matthew answered.

Bidwell giggled; it sounded like a woman's laugh, it was so quick and high-pitched, and Bidwell instantly put his hand to his mouth and flushed crimson. "A theory," he said, about to laugh again; in fact, he was straining so hard to hold back his merriment that his jowls and corncake-stuffed belly quivered. "By God, we must have our daily theories, mustn't we?"

"Laugh if you like, but answer this: for whom was the surveyor working?"

"For whom? Why . . . one moment, I have a *theory!*" Bidwell widened his eyes in mockery. "I believe he must have been working for the Council of Lands and Plantations! There *is* such an administrative body, you know!"

"He told you he was working for this council, then?"

"Damn it, boy!" Bidwell shouted, the mighty schooner of his patience smashing out its belly on the rocks. "I've had enough of this!" He stalked past Matthew and out of the banquet room.

Matthew instantly followed him. "Please, sir!" he said as Bidwell walked to the staircase. "It's important! Did this surveyor tell you his name?"

"Pah!" Bidwell replied, starting up the steps. "You're as crazy as a loon!"

"His name! Can you recall it?"

Bidwell stopped, realizing he could not shake the flea that gave him such a maddening itch. He looked back at Matthew, his eyes ablaze. "No, I do not! Winston walked him about the town! Go ask him and leave me be! I swear, you could set Satan himself running for sanctuary!" He jabbed a finger toward the younger man. "But you won't ruin this glorious day for me, no sirrah you won't! The sun is out, praise God, and as soon as that damned witch is ashes this town will grow again! So go march to the gaol and tell her that Robert Bidwell has never failed, *never,* and will never *be* a failure!"

A figure suddenly appeared at the top of the stairs. Matthew saw him first, of course, and Matthew's astonished expression made Bidwell jerk his head around.

Woodward braced himself against the wall, his flesh near the same hue as his pap-stained cotton nightgown. A sheen of sweat glistened on his sallow face, and his eyes were red-rimmed and weak with pain.

"Magistrate!" Bidwell climbed the risers to lend a supporting arm. "I thought you were sleeping!"

"I *was,*" he said hoarsely, though speaking with any volume caused his throat grievous suffering. "Who can sleep . . . during a duel of cannons?"

"I apologize, sir. Your clerk has roused my bad manners yet again."

The magistrate stared down into Matthew's face, and at once Matthew knew what had been important enough to force him from his bed.

"My deliberations are done," Woodward said. "Come prepare a quill and paper."

"You mean . . . you mean . . ." Bidwell could hardly contain himself. "You have reached your decision?"

"Come up, Matthew," Woodward repeated, and then to Bidwell, "Will you help me to my bed, please?"

Bidwell might have bodily lifted the magistrate and carried him, but decorum prevailed. Matthew ascended the stairs, and together he and the master of Fount Royal took Woodward along the hallway to his room. Once settled in bed again and propped up on the blood-spotted pillow, Woodward said, "Thank you, Mr. Bidwell. You may depart."

"If you don't mind, I would like to stay and hear the decree." Bidwell had already closed the door and claimed a position next to the bed.

"I *do* mind, sir. Until the decree is read to the accused"— Woodward paused to gasp a breath—"it is the court's business. It would not be seemly otherwise."

"Yes but—"

"Depart," Woodward said. "Your presence delays our work." He glanced irritably at Matthew, who stood at the foot of the bed. "The quill and paper! *Now!*" Matthew turned away to get the document box that also held sheets of clean paper, the quill, and the inkjar.

Bidwell went to the door, but before he left he had to try once again. "Tell me this, then: should I have the stake cut and planted?"

Woodward squeezed his eyes shut at Bidwell's dogged disregard for propriety. Then he opened them and said tersely, "Sir . . . you may accompany Matthew to read my decree to the accused. Now please . . . leave us."

"All right, then. I'm going."

"And . . . Mr. Bidwell . . . please refrain from dawdling in the hall."

"My word on it as a gentleman. I shall be waiting downstairs." Bidwell left the room and closed the door.

Woodward stared out the window at the gold-tinged sun-illumed morning. It was going to be beautiful today, he thought. A more lovely morning than he'd seen in the better part of a month. "Date the decree," he told Matthew, though it was hardly necessary.

Matthew sat upon the stool beside the bed, using the document box as a makeshift writing table propped on his knees. He dipped the quill into the ink and wrote at the top of the paper *May Seventeenth, Sixteen-Ninety-Nine.*

"Ready it," Woodward prodded, his eyes fixed on the outside world.

Matthew scribed the preface, which he had done enough times in enough different circumstances to know the correct wording. It took him a few moments and a few dips of the quill: *By Decree of the Right Honorable King's Appointed Magistrate Isaac Temple Woodward on This Day in the Settlement of Fount Royal, Carolina Colony, Concerning the Accusations of Murder and Witchcraft to Be Detailed As Follows Against the Defendant, a Woman Citizen Known Hereby As Rachel Howarth . . .*

He had to stop to work out a kink in his writing hand. "Go on," Woodward said. "It must be done."

Matthew had an ashen taste in his mouth. He dipped the quill again, and this time he spoke the words aloud as he wrote them: "On the Charge of the Murder of the Reverend Burlton Grove, I Find the Aforesaid Defendant—" He paused once more, his quill poised to record the magistrate's decree. The flesh of his face seemed to have drawn tight beyond endurance, and a heat burned in his skull.

Suddenly Woodward snapped his fingers. Matthew looked at him quizzically, and when the magistrate put a finger to his lips and then motioned toward the door Matthew realized what he was trying to communicate. Matthew quietly put aside his writing materials and the document box, got up from the stool, went to the door, and quickly opened it.

Bidwell was down on one knee in the hallway, busily buffing his right shoe with his peacock-blue sleeve. He turned his head and looked at Matthew, lifting his eyebrows as if to ask why the clerk had emerged so stealthily from the magistrate's room.

"Gentleman, my ass!" Woodward hissed under his breath.

"I thought you were going downstairs to wait," Matthew reminded the man, who now ferociously buffed his shoetop and then heaved himself up to his feet with an air of indignance.

"Did I say I would *race* there? I saw a blemish on my shoe!"

"The blemish is on your vow, sir!" Woodward said, with a measure of fire that belied his watery constitution.

"Very well, then! I'm going." Bidwell reached up and adjusted his wig, which had become somewhat tilted during his ascent from the floor. "Can you blame me for wanting to know? I've waited so long for it!"

"You can wait a little longer, then." Woodward motioned him away. "Matthew, close the door." Matthew resettled himself, with the box on his knees and the writing materials and paper before him.

"Read it again," Woodward said.

"Yes, sir." Matthew took a deep breath. "On the Charge of the Murder of the Reverend Burlton Grove, I Find the Aforesaid Defendant—"

"Guilty," came the whispered answer. "With a stipulation. That the defendant did not actually commit the murder . . . but caused it to be committed by her words, deeds, or associations."

"Sir!" Matthew said, his heart pounding. "Please! There's absolutely no evidence to—"

"Silence!" Woodward lifted himself up on his elbows, his face contorted with a mixture of anger, frustration, and pain. "I'll have no more of your second opinions, do you hear me?" He locked his gaze with Matthew's. "Scribe the next charge."

Matthew might have thrown down the quill and upset the inkjar, but he did not. He knew his duties, whether or not he agreed with the magistrate's decision. Therefore he swallowed the bitter gall in his throat, redipped the quill— that bastard weapon of blind destruction—and spoke again as he wrote: "On the Charge of the Murder of Daniel Howarth, I Find the Aforesaid Defendant—"

"Guilty, with a stipulation. The same as above." Woodward glared at him when Matthew's hand failed to make the entry. "I should like to finish this sometime today."

Matthew had no choice but to write down the decree. The heat of shame flared in his cheeks. Now, of course, he knew what the next decision must be. "On the Charge of Witchcraft . . . I Find the Aforesaid Defendant—"

"Guilty," Woodward said quickly. He closed his eyes and rested his head back down on the stained pillow, his breathing harsh. Matthew heard a rattling sound deep in the magistrate's lungs. "Scribe the preface to sentencing."

Matthew wrote it as if in a trance. *By Virtue of the Power Ascribed to Me As Colonial Magistrate, I Hereby Sentence the Aforesaid Defendant Rachel Howarth to . . .* He lifted his quill from the paper and waited.

Woodward opened his eyes and stared up at the ceiling. A moment passed, during which could be heard the singing of birds in the springtime sunlight. "Burning at the stake, as warranted by the King's law," Woodward said. "The sentence to be carried out on Monday, the twenty-second of May, sixteen-ninety-nine. In case of inclement weather . . . the earliest necessary date following." His gaze ticked toward Matthew, who had not moved. "Enter it."

Again, he was simply the unwitting flesh behind the instrument. Somehow the lines were quilled on the paper.

"Give it here." Woodward held out his hand and took the document. He squinted, reading it by the light that streamed through the window, and then he nodded with satisfaction. "The quill, please." Matthew had the presence of mind—or rather the dignity of his job—to dip the quill in the inkjar and blot the excess before he handed it over.

Woodward signed his full name and, below it, the title *Colonial Magistrate.* Ordinarily an official wax seal would be added, but the seal had been lost to that blackhearted Will Shawcombe. He then returned the paper and the quill to Matthew, who knew what was expected of him. Still moving as if enveloped in a gray haze, Matthew signed his name beneath Woodward's, along with the title *Magistrate's Clerk.*

And it was done.

"You may read it to the defendant," Woodward said, avoiding looking at his clerk's face because he knew what he would see there. "Take Bidwell with you, as he should also hear it."

Matthew realized there was no use in delaying the inevitable. He slowly stood up, his mind yet fogged, and walked to the door with the decree in hand.

"Matthew?" Woodward said, "For whatever this is worth . . . I know you must think me heartless and cruel." He hesitated, swallowing thick pus. "But the proper sentence has been given. The witch must be burned . . . for the good of everyone."

"She is innocent," Matthew managed to say, his gaze cast to the floor. "I can't prove anything yet, but I intend to keep—"

"You delude yourself . . . and it is time for delusions to cease."

Matthew turned toward the man, his eyes coldly furious. "You are *wrong,* sir," he added. "Rachel is not a witch, she's a pawn. Oh yes, all the conditions for a burning at the stake have been met, and all is in order with the law, sir, but I am damned if I'll let someone I know to be innocent lose her life on hearsay and fantasy!"

Woodward rasped, "Your task is to read the decree! No more and no less!"

"I'll read it." Matthew nodded. "Then I'll drink rum to wash my mouth out, but I will not surrender! If she burns on Monday, I have five days to prove her innocent, and by God that's what I intend to do!"

Woodward started to answer with some vinegar, but his strength failed him. "Do what you must," he said. "I can't . . . protect you from your nightbird, can I?"

"The only thing I fear is that Rachel is burned before I can prove who murdered her husband and Reverend Grove. If that happens, I don't know how I can live with myself."

"Oh, my Christ." It had been spoken as nearly a moan. Woodward closed his eyes, feeling faint. "She has you so deeply . . . and you don't even realize it."

"She has my trust, if that's what you infer."

"She has your *soul*." His eyes opened; in an instant they had become sunken and bloodshot. "I long for the moment we shall leave this place. Return to Charles Town . . . civilization and sanity. When I am cured and in good health again, we'll put all this behind us. And then . . . when you can see clearly . . . you'll understand what danger tempted you."

Matthew had to get out, because the magistrate had been reduced to babbling. He couldn't bear to see the man—so proud, so regal, and so correct—on the verge of becoming a fever-dulled imbecile. He said, "I'm going," but he still hesitated before he left the bedchamber. His tone had softened; there was no point now in harshness. "Can I get anything for you?"

Woodward drew in a suffering breath and released it. "I want . . ." he began, but his agonized throat felt in jeopardy of closing and he had to start again. "I want . . . things to be as they were . . . between us. Before we came to this wretched place. I want us to return to Charles Town . . . and go on, as if none of this ever happened." He looked hopefully at Matthew. "All right?"

Matthew stood at the window, staring out at the sunlit town. The sky was turning bright blue, though the way he felt it might have been a dismal downpour out there. He knew what the magistrate wanted him to say. He knew it would ease him, but it would be a lie. He said quietly, "I wish it might be so, sir. But you and I both know it will not be. I may be your clerk . . . I may be under your watchcare, and live in your house . . . but I am a man, sir. If I fail to fight for the truth as I see it, then what kind of man am I? Surely not the kind you have taught me to be. So . . . you ask for something I am unable to give you, Isaac."

There was a long, torturous silence. Then the magistrate spoke in his dry husk of a voice: "Leave me."

Matthew walked out, taking the hateful decree downstairs to where Bidwell was waiting.

THREE

"The magistrate has made his decree," Matthew said. Rachel, who was sitting on her bench with the coarse robe around her and the cowl shielding her face, hadn't moved when Matthew and Bidwell entered the gaol. Now she simply gave a brief nod, signifying her acknowledgment of the document that was about to be read.

"Go on, let's hear it!" Bidwell had been in such a hurry that he'd demanded they walk instead of waiting for the horses and carriage to be readied, and now he was truly champing at his bit.

Matthew stood beneath the roof hatch, which was open. He unrolled the document and began to read the preface in a calm, emotionless voice. Behind him, Bidwell paced back and forth. The master of Fount Royal abruptly stopped when Matthew reached the portion that began: "On the Charge of the Murder of the Reverend Burlton Grove . . ." Matthew could hear the man's wolfish breathing at his back. "I Find the Aforesaid Defendant Guilty."

There was a *smack* as Bidwell struck his palm with his fist in a gesture of triumph. Matthew flinched, but kept his attention focused on Rachel. She showed no reaction whatsoever. "With a Stipulation," Matthew continued. "That the Defendant Did Not Actually Commit the Murder, But Caused It to be Committed by Her Words, Deeds, or Associations."

"Yes, but it's all the same, isn't it?" Bidwell crowed. "She might as well have done it with her own hands!"

Matthew kept going by sheer force of will. "On the Charge of the Murder of Daniel Howarth, I Find the Aforesaid Defendant Guilty, With a Stipulation." At the word *guilty,* this time Rachel had given a soft cry and lowered her head. "That the Defendant Did Not Actually Commit the Murder, But Caused It to be Committed by Her Words, Deeds, or Associations."

"Excellent, excellent!" Bidwell gleefully clapped his hands together.

Matthew looked fiercely into the man's grinning face. "Would you please restrain yourself? This is not a five-pence play requiring comments from the idiots' gallery!"

Bidwell's grin only broadened. "Oh, say what you like! Just keep reading that blessed decree!"

Matthew's task—performed so many times at the magistrate's behest over criminals common and extraordinary—had become a test of endurance. He had to go on.

"On the Charge of Witchcraft," he read to Rachel, "I Find the Aforesaid Defendant . . ." and here his throat almost clenched shut to prevent him from speaking, but the horrible word had to be uttered, ". . . Guilty."

"Ah, sweet deliverance!" Bidwell all but shouted.

Rachel made no sound, but she put a trembling hand to her cowl-shrouded face as if the word—which she had known would be delivered—had been a physical blow.

"By Virtue of the Power Ascribed to Me As Colonial Magistrate," Matthew read, "I Hereby Sentence the Aforesaid Defendant Rachel Howarth to Burning at the Stake As Warranted by the King's Law. The Sentence to be Carried Out on Monday, the Twenty-Second of May, Sixteen-Ninety-Nine." When the distasteful chore was finished, he dropped the document down by his side.

"Your hours are numbered!" Bidwell said, standing behind Matthew. "Your master may have torched the schoolhouse last night, but we'll build it back!"

"I think you should leave," Matthew told him, though he was too drained to raise his voice.

"You may go to your reward knowing that all your work to destroy my town was for nothing!" Bidwell raved on. "Once you're dead, Fount Royal shall rise to fame and glory!"

Rachel gave no response to these cutting comments, if indeed she felt them through her sphere of misery.

Still Bidwell wasn't done. "This is truly the day that God made!" He couldn't help it; he had to reach out and clap Matthew on the back. "A fine job you and the magistrate have done! And an excellent decision! Now . . . I must go start the preparations! There's a stake to be cut, and by Christ's blood it'll be the best stake any damned witch was ever burned on!" He glared at Rachel through the bars. "Your master may send every demon in his barn to cause us woe between now and Monday morn, but we'll weather it! You may rely on that, witch! So tell your black-cocked dog that Robert Bidwell never failed at anything in his life and Fount Royal will be no exception! Do you hear me?" He was no longer speaking directly to Rachel now but was looking around the gaol, his voice thunderous and haughty as if he were sending a warning to the very ears of the Devil. "We shall live and thrive here, no matter what treacheries you send against us!"

His chest-beating complete, Bidwell stalked to the door but stopped when he realized Matthew had not followed. "Come along! I want you to read that decree in the streets!"

"I take my commands from the magistrate, sir. If he requires me to read it for the public, I shall, but not until he so orders it."

"I've neither the time nor inclination to wrangle with you!" Bidwell's mouth had taken on an ugly sneer. "Ohhhh . . . yes, I see why you wish to dawdle! You intend to console her! If Woodward could see this lovely scene, it would send him two steps nearer his death!"

Matthew's initial impulse was to advance upon Bidwell and strike his face so hard that what served as the man's brains might dribble from his ears, but the ensuing duel that would likely follow would provide no good purpose save work for the gravedigger and a probable misspelling of his own name on the marker. Therefore he reined in his inclination and simply glowered daggers at the man.

Bidwell laughed, which acted as a bellows to further heat Matthew's banked fires. "A tender, touching moment between the witch and her latest conquest! I swear, you'd be better off lying in the lap of Mrs. Nettles! But do as you please!" He aimed his next jibe at Rachel. "Demons, old men, or babes in the woods: it doesn't matter what flavor your suckets! Well, take your rapture, as you shall be paying dearly for it come Monday!" He turned and made his leave like the strutting bird whose gaudy blue colored his suit.

In the aftermath of Bidwell's departure, Matthew realized that words were not potent enough instruments with which to communicate his sorrow. He rolled up the document, as it would have to be placed on official file in Charles Town.

Rachel spoke, her face still shielded. "You have done what you could. For that I thank you." Her voice, though weakened and listless, yet held a full measure of dignity.

"Listen to me!" Matthew stepped forward and grasped one of the bars with his free hand. "Monday is still a distance off—"

"A small distance," she interrupted.

"A *distance*, nevertheless. The magistrate may have issued his decree, but I don't intend to stop my inquiries."

"You might as well." She stood up and pushed the cowl back from her face. "It is finished, whether you accept it or not."

"I *don't* accept it!" he shouted. "I never shall accept it!" He shut his mouth, shamed by his loss of control; he stared down at the dirty floor, searching within himself for any semblance of an articulate response. "To accept such a thing . . . means I agree with it and that is impossible. I can never, as long as I live, agree with this . . . this wrongful execution of an innocent victim."

"Matthew?" she said softly, and he looked at her. They stared at each other for a moment. Rachel approached him but stopped well short of the bars.

She said, "Go on about your life."

He found no answer.

"I am dead," Rachel told him. "Dead. When I am taken on Monday to be burned, my body will be there for the flames . . . but the woman I used to be before Daniel was murdered is no longer here. Since I was brought to this gaol, I have slipped away. I did have hope, at one point, but I hardly remember what it felt like."

"You mustn't give up hope," Matthew insisted. "If there is one more day, there is always—"

"Stop," she said firmly. "Please . . . just stop. You think

you are doing the right thing, by encouraging my spirit . . . but you are not. The time has come to embrace reality, and to put aside these . . . fantasies of my life being spared. Whoever committed these murders is too smart, Matthew. Too . . . demonic. Against such a power, I have no hope and I wish to cease this pretending. It does not prepare me for the stake, and that above all else is what I must do."

"I am close to learning something," Matthew said. "Something important, though I'm not sure yet how it relates to you. I think it *does,* though. I think I have uncovered the first strands that form a rope, and the rope will lead me to—"

"I am begging you," she whispered, and now there were tears in her eyes though her face displayed no other betrayal of emotion, "to cease this playing with Fate. You can't free me. Neither can you save my life. Do you not understand that an end has been reached?"

"An end has *not* been reached! I'm telling you, I have found—"

"You have found something that may mean something," Rachel said. "And you might study it until a year from Monday, but I can't wish for freedom any longer, Matthew. I am going to be burned, and I must—I *must*—spend the time I have left in prayer and preparation." She looked up at the sunlight that streamed through the hatch, and at the cloudless azure sky beyond. "When they come for me . . . I'll be afraid, but I can't let them see it. Not Green, not Paine . . . especially not Bidwell. I can't allow myself to cry, or to scream and thrash. I don't want them sitting in Van Gundy's tavern, boasting over how they broke me. Laughing and drinking and saying how at the end I begged for mercy. I will not. If there is a God in Heaven, He will seal my mouth on that morning. They may cage me and strip me, dirty me and call me witch . . .

but they will not make me into a shrieking animal. Not even on the stake." Her eyes met Matthew's again. "I have a single wish. Will you grant it?"

"If it's possible."

"It is. I wish you to walk out of here and not return."

Matthew hadn't known what to expect, but this request was as painful—and as startling—as a slap across the face.

Rachel watched him intently. When he failed to respond, she said, "It is more than a wish, it is a demand. I want you to put this place behind you. As I said before: go on about your life." Still he couldn't summon an answer. Rachel came forward two more paces and touched his hand that gripped the bar. "Thank you for your belief in me," she said, her face close to his. "Thank you for *listening*. But it's over now. Please understand that, and accept it."

Matthew found his voice, though it was near perished. "How can I go on about my life, knowing such injustice was done?"

She gave him a faint, wry smile. "Injustice is done somewhere every day. It is a fact of living. If you don't already know that to be true, you are much less worldly than I thought." She sighed, and let her hand fall away from his. "Go away, Matthew. You've done your best."

"No, I haven't."

"You *have*. If you need me to release you from some imagined obligation to me . . . there." Rachel waved her hand past his face. "You are released."

"I cannot just walk out of here like that," he said.

"You have no choice." Again, she levelled her gaze at him. "Go on, now. Leave me alone." She turned away and went back to her bench.

"I will not give up," Matthew said. "*You* may . . . but *I* swear I won't."

Rachel sat down and leaned over toward her waterbowl. She cupped her hand into it and brought water to her mouth.

"I won't," he repeated. "Do you hear me?" She pulled her hood over her head, shrouding her face once more, and withdrew into her mansion of solitude.

Matthew realized he might stand here as long as he pleased, but Rachel had removed herself to a sanctum that only she could inhabit. He suspected it was the place of reflection—perhaps of the memories of happier times—that had kept her mind from cracking during the long hours of her imprisonment. He realized also, with a twist of anguish, that he was no longer welcome in her company. She did not wish to be distracted from her inner dialogue with Death.

It was indeed time to leave her. Still he lingered, watching her immobile figure. He hoped she might say something again to him, but she was silent. After a few moments he went to the door. There was no movement or response from Rachel. He started to speak once more, but he knew not what to say. *Goodbye* seemed the only proper word, yet he was loath to utter it. He walked out into the cruel sunlight.

Shortly the smell of charred wood drifted to his nostrils, and he paused at the pile of blackened ruins. There was hardly anything left to attest that it had ever been a school-house. All four walls were gone, and the roof had fallen in. He wondered if somewhere in the debris might be the wire handle of what had been a bucket.

Matthew had almost told Rachel about his findings of last night, but he'd decided not to for the same reason he'd decided to withhold the information from Bidwell: for the moment, the secret was best kept locked in his own vault.

He needed an answer to the question of *why* Winston was spiriting infernal fire from Charles Town and using it to set flame to Bidwell's dream. He also needed from Winston further details—if the man could supply them—of the so-called surveyor who'd come to Fount Royal. Therefore his mission this morning was clear: to find Edward Winston.

He inquired from the first person he saw—a pipe-smoking farmer carrying a flasket of yellow grain—as to the location of Winston's house, and was informed that the dwelling stood on Harmony Street just shy of the cemetery. Matthew started off to his destination, walking at a brisk pace.

The house did stand within a stone's toss of the first row of grave markers. Matthew noted that the shutters were sealed, indicating that Winston must be out. It was by no means a large dwelling, and probably only held two or three rooms. The house had been painted white at some point in the past but the whitewash had worn off, leaving a mottled appearance to the walls. It occurred to Matthew that—unlike Bidwell's mansion and some of the sturdier farmhouses—Winston's abode had an air of shoddy impermanence akin to that found in the slave quarters. Matthew continued up the walk, which was made of packed sand and hammer-crushed oyster shells, and knocked soundly at the door.

There was but a short wait. "Who is it?" came Winston's voice—rough-edged and perhaps a bit slurred—from within the house.

"Matthew Corbett. May I please speak with you?"

"Concerning what?" This time he was making an obvious effort to disguise what might be termed an unbalanced condition. "The witch?"

"No, sir. Concerning a surveyor who came to Fount Royal four years ago." Silence fell. "Mr. Bidwell has told me you walked the man around," Matthew pressed on. "I'd like to know what you might recall of him."

"I . . . have no recollection of such a man. If you'll forgive me now . . . I have some ledger business to attend to."

Matthew doubted that Winston had any business other than drinking and plotting more conflagrations. "I do have some information pertaining to Rachel Howarth. Might you want to see the magistrate's decision? I've just come from reading it to her."

Almost at once there was the sound of a latch being undone. The door opened a few inches, enough for a slice of sunlight to enter the house and fall upon Winston's haggard, unshaven face. "The decision?" he said, squinting in the glare. "You have it with you?"

"I do." Matthew held up the rolled document. "May I come in?"

Winston hesitated, but Matthew knew the die had been cast. The door was opened wide enough to admit Matthew and then closed again at his back.

Within the small front room, two candles burned on a wicker table. Beside the candles, and set before the bench that Winston had been occupying, was a squat blue bottle and a wooden tankard. Up until this moment Matthew had thought Winston to be—judging from his usual neatness of appearance and his precise manners—a paradigm of efficiency, but Matthew's opinion suddenly suffered a sharp reversal.

The room might have sickened a pig. On the floor lay scattered shirts, stockings, and breeches that Winston had not bothered to pick up. The smell of damp and musty cloth—coupled with body odor from some of the gamier articles—was somewhat less than appealing. Also littering the floor were crumpled balls of paper, spilled tobacco, a broken clay pipe here and there, a few books whose bindings had come unstitched, and sundry other items that had outlived their use but not been consigned to a proper garbage pit. Even the narrow little hearth was near choked with cold ashes and bits of trash. In fact, it might be within bounds to say that the entire room resembled a garbage pit, and Matthew shuddered to think what Winston's bedchamber might conceal. A bucket of sulphurous chemicals might be the least noxious of it.

Nearby stood the desk that Winston had recovered from the gaol. Now Matthew understood why it had been so thoroughly cleaned out when Winston had it carted over, as its surface was a jumbled mess of more crumpled and ink-splattered papers, a number of candles melted down to stubs, and a disorderly pile of ledger books. Matthew was surprised that Winston had been able to lay his hands on a clean sheaf of paper and an unspilled inkjar in this rat's nest. It occurred to him, in his brief but telling inspection, that all Winston's business with Bidwell was done at the mansion because Winston wished not to reveal his living conditions—and possibly the condition of his mental affairs—to his employer.

Winston was pouring liquid from the blue bottle into his tankard. He wore a long gray nightshirt that bore evidence of many poor repatchings, as well as several small scorched holes that told Matthew the man's control of fire did not extend to power over a spilled pipe. "So," Winston said. "The decree's been made, eh?" He downed some of his pleasure, which Matthew assumed was either hard cider or rum. "Bring it over here and spread it out."

Matthew did, but he kept a hand on the document, as it was his charge. Winston leaned over and read the ornate handwriting. "No surprises there, I see. She's to be burned on Monday, then?"

"Yes."

"High time. She should've gone to the stake a month ago; we'd all be the better for it."

Matthew rolled the decree up again. He cast a disdainful eye about his surroundings. "Do you always live in this fashion?"

Winston had been about to drink again, but the tankard's ascent paused. "No," he said with sarcasm. "My servants have been called away. Ordinarily I have a footman, a parlor wench, and a chamberpot scrubber." The tankard went to his mouth and he wiped his lips with the back of his hand. "You may go now, Sir Reverence."

Matthew smiled slightly, but his face was tight. *Sir Reverence* was gutter slang for human excrement. "You must have had a late night," he said.

"A late night?" Winston's eyebrows went up. "Meaning what?"

"Meaning . . . a late night. I had assumed you were an early riser, and therefore must have been working into the small hours."

"Working." He nodded. "Yes. I'm always working." He motioned toward the ledger-laden desk. "See there? Managing his money. His pence and guineas and dog dollars. His ins and outs. That's what I do."

"You don't sound particularly proud of your accomplishments for Mr. Bidwell," Matthew ventured. "He must rely on your services quite a lot, doesn't he?"

Winston stared at Matthew, his bloodshot eyes wary. "You may go now," he repeated, with a more ominous inflection.

"I shall. But Mr. Bidwell himself suggested I find you and ask about the surveyor. As you were the one who escorted the man around, I hoped that—"

"A *surveyor?* I hardly remember the man!" Again Winston quaffed from the tankard, and this time the gleaming residue trickled down his chin. "What was it? Four years ago?"

"Or thereabouts."

"Go on, get out!" Winston sneered. "I don't have time for your foolishness!"

Matthew took a deep breath. "Yes, you do," he answered.

"What? By God, will I have to throw you out of here?"

Matthew said quietly, "I know about your nocturnal activities."

The hand of God might have come down to stop time and still all sounds.

Matthew went on, taking advantage of the moment. "In addition, I have one of the six buckets that Mr. Rawlings and the others buried. Therefore it's no use to go out tonight and move them. The seventh bucket you took away is hidden here somewhere, I presume?"

The hand of God was a mighty instrument. It had turned Edward Winston into a gape-mouthed statue. In another few seconds, however, the tankard slipped from Winston's grasp and crashed to the floor.

"I presume it is," Matthew said. "You used a brush to paint the chemicals on the walls of the houses you set afire, am I correct? It does seem to be a potent concoction."

Winston did not move, did not speak, and hardly appeared to be breathing. The color of his face and the somber *grisard* of his nightshirt were one and the same.

Matthew spent a moment looking around the littered room before he spoke again. "This is what I believe," he said. "That on one of your supply trips to Charles Town with Nicholas Paine, you approached someone of authority there. Possibly Mr. Danforth, the harbormaster, but possibly someone with more interest in seeing that Fount Royal never grows to Bidwell's ambition. I suspect you might have sent Mr. Paine on some errand or another while you made this contact. He doesn't know, does he?"

Matthew hadn't expected Winston to reply, therefore he was not disappointed. "I don't think he knows," Matthew said. "I think this is your intrigue alone. You volunteered to take advantage of Rachel Howarth's plight and set numerous fires to empty houses, thus speeding along the process of emptying more. Am I so far correct?" Winston slowly sank down upon his bench, his mouth still open.

"The problem was that you needed an incendiary to ignite in wet weather." Matthew prodded some discarded clothes with the toe of his right shoe. "The buckets of chemicals had to be mixed in Charles Town and secreted here by ship. The crew must have had some rough voyages, I'd suspect. But Mr. Rawlings must be making a profit for his risk. I would think *you* are making a profit for your risk as well. Or perhaps you've been promised a position in Charles Town after Fount Royal fails?"

Winston lifted a hand and put it to his forehead, his eyes glassy with shock.

"It is to your credit that you don't mar your dignity with denials," Matthew offered. "I *am* curious, though. Bidwell tells me you've been in his employ for eight years. Why did you turn against him?"

Now both hands were pressed to Winston's face. He breathed raggedly, his shoulders slumped.

"I have seen enough of human nature to have an idea." Matthew went to the cluttered desk and opened one of the ledger books. He flipped through the pages as he spoke. "You know more than anyone else how much Bidwell is worth. You see his wealth on display, you see his plans for the future, and you see . . . your own existence, which according to the way you live is at a low flux. So I would venture to say this revolves around your own perceived misery. Did they promise you a mansion in Charles Town? A statue in your honor? What exactly *did* they promise, Mr. Winston?"

Winston reached with a feeble hand for the blue bottle, brought it to his mouth, and took a long swallow of courage. When he lowered the bottle, he blinked away tears and said, "Money."

"Considerably more than Bidwell was paying you, yes?"

"More than . . . I could hope to earn in two lifetimes." Again he drank copiously from the bottle. "You don't know what it's like, working for him. Being around him . . . and all that he has. He spends on wigs alone every year an amount I might live on as a prince. And the clothes and food! If you knew the numbers, you would understand and be sickened as I am by the man's philosophy: not a shilling more for a servant's needs, but spare no expense for the master's desires!"

"I won't defend him, but I will say that such is the right of a master."

"It is the right of *no* man!" Winston said heatedly. "I have an education, I am literate, and I consider myself reasonably bright! But I might as well be a slave, as far as he's concerned! I might even be the better for it!" He laughed harshly. "At least Bidwell cares enough about Goode to have bought him a fiddle!"

"The difference is that Goode is a slave and you're a free man. You can choose your employer. Then again . . ." Matthew nodded. "I suppose you *have*."

"Oh, be as smug as you please!" Winston turned upon Matthew an expression of the deepest disgust. "Look at my house, and look at his! Then look in the ledgers and see who directs the course of his monies! *I* do! He pretends to be such a sterling businessman, but in fact he is skilled at two things: intimidation and bluster. I ought to be a partner in his enterprises, for what I've encouraged! But it has been clearly and plainly shown to me by his actions that Bidwell takes good opinions and presents them as his own."

He held up a finger to mark his point. "Now, failed ventures . . . that's a different cart. Failure is always the fault of someone else . . . someone who invariably deserves to be banished from the kingdom. I have seen it happen. When Fount Royal fails—and it will, regardless of how many houses I flamed and how long the witch roasts on her stake—he will begin to fire his cannons of blame at every possible target. Including this one." He thumped his chest with his fist. "Do you think I should sit at his beck and call and await a further slide into poverty? *No.* For your information—and whatever you choose to do with it—I did not do the approaching. They approached *me,* when Paine and I were on separate tasks in Charles Town. At first I refused . . . but they sweetened their offer with a house and a position on the Shipping Council. It was my idea to set the fires."

"And a clever idea it was," Matthew said. "You hid behind Rachel Howarth's skirts and the Devil's shadow. Did it not trouble you in the least that these fires were ascribed to her?"

"No," he answered without hesitation. "If you'll read that document you hold, you'll find there's no charge there concerning the setting of fires. She fashioned the poppets, committed the murders, and consorted with Satan of her own accord. I simply used the situation to my benefit."

"*Simply?*" Matthew echoed. "I don't think there's anything simpleminded about you, Mr. Winston. I think *coldly* might be a better word."

"As you please." Winston offered a bitter smile. "I have learned from Bidwell that one fights fire with fire and ice with ice." His eyes narrowed. "So. You have a bucket. I presume you were hiding out there?" He waited for Matthew to nod. "Who else knows?"

"If you are considering violence as a solution, you might think otherwise. Someone else *does* know, but your secret is in no current danger."

Winston frowned. "What, then? Aren't you going to go running to Bidwell and tell him?"

"No, I'm not. As you've pointed out, the fires were incidental in the charges against Madam Howarth. I am hunting a smarter—and colder—fox than you."

"Pardon my dulled wits, but what are you talking about?"

"Your grievance against Bidwell is not my concern. Whatever you choose to do from this point is not of interest to me, either. As long as there are no future conflagrations, I might add."

Winston let go a sigh of relief. "Sir," he said, "I bow gratefully before your mercy."

"My mercy has a price. I wish to know about the surveyor."

"The surveyor," Winston repeated. He rubbed his temples with both hands. "I tell you . . . I can hardly recall the man. Why do you care to know about him, anyway?"

"My interest is a personal matter. Do you remember his name?"

"No. Wait . . . give me a moment . . ." He closed his eyes, obviously trying his best to concentrate. "I think . . . it was Spencer . . . Spicer . . . something similar to that, at least." His eyes opened.

"The man was bearded?"

"Yes . . . a heavy beard. And he wore a hat."

"A tricorn?"

"No. It was . . . a loose-brimmed shade hat. Much like any farmer or traveller might wear. I remember . . . his clothing was rustic, as well."

"You took him walking around Fount Royal. How much time would you say you spent with him?"

Winston shrugged. "The better part of an afternoon, I suppose."

"Do you recall his description?"

"A beard and a hat," Winston said. "That's all I can remember."

"And probably all you were meant to remember."

Winston gave him a questioning look. "What does this concern?"

"It concerns the manipulation of memory," Matthew answered. "Something I think my fox knows a great deal about."

"If you are making sense, I am unable to follow it."

"I believe I have information enough. Thank you for your time." Matthew started toward the door, and Winston stood up.

"Please!" Winston's voice held a note of urgency. "If you were in my position . . . what would you do? Remain here—and await the end—or go to Charles Town and try to salvage what I can of a future?"

"A difficult question," Matthew said after a short consideration. "I would agree that your present is precarious, and since you have neither love nor loyalty for Bidwell you might as well seek your fortune elsewhere. However . . . as much a dog you think Bidwell to be, your masters in Charles Town are probably mongrels of similar breed. You might have known that, judging from the voracity with which they have eaten your soul. So . . . flip a coin, and good luck to you."

Matthew turned his back and left Edward Winston standing forlorn and alone in the midst of his self-made chaos.

FOUR

His thoughts still clouded by Winston's betrayal, Matthew was ascending the stairs to look in upon the magistrate when he almost collided with Mrs. Nettles, who was descending with a tray upon which sat a bowl of pap.

"How is he?" Matthew asked.

"Not verra well," she said, her voice low. "He's havin' some trouble even swallowin' the mush."

Matthew nodded grimly. "I have my doubts about whether the bloodletting is doing any good."

"I've seen it do wonders, though. That afflicted blood's got to be rid of."

"I hope you're right. I'm not sure his condition isn't being hastened by all this bleeding." He started to slide past her up the stairs, which was a precarious maneuver due to her formidable size and the lack of a railing.

"Just a moment, sir!" she said. "You have a visitor."

"A *visitor?* Who?"

"The child," she said. "Violet Adams. She's in the library, waitin' for you."

"Oh?" Matthew instantly went back down the stairs and entered the library. His quick entrance startled the little girl, who was standing before the open window studying a bishop she had picked up from the chessboard. She jumped and backed away from him like a cornered deer.

"Forgive me," Matthew said in a calming tone. He showed one palm in a non-threatening gesture, while he held the rolled-up decree at his side. "I should have announced myself."

She just stared at him, her body rigid as if she might either decide to flee past him or leap through the window. On this occasion she definitely was not groomed for a court appearance. Her light brown hair was loose about her shoulders and in need of washing, her tan-and-red-checked shift was held together with patches, and her shoes were near worn through.

"You've been waiting for me?" Matthew asked. She nodded. "I presume this is not an errand on behalf of your father and mother?"

"No sir," she answered. "They sent me to fetch some water."

Matthew looked down and saw two empty buckets on the floor. "I see. But you decided to come here first?"

"Yes sir."

"For what reason?"

Violet carefully placed the chesspiece back in its proper place on the board. "What are these, sir? Are they toys?"

"It's a game called chess. The pieces have different patterns of movement across the board."

"Ohhhh." She seemed much impressed. "Like knuckles 'n' stones, 'ceptin' you play that in the dirt."

"I imagine so, yes."

"They're pretty," she said. "Did Mr. Bidwell carve 'em?"

"I doubt it."

She continued staring at the chessboard. The tic of her upper lip had returned. "Last night," she said, "a rat got in my bed." Matthew didn't quite know how to respond to this matter-of-fact statement, so he said nothing.

"It got all tangled up in the beddin's," she went on. "It couldn't get out, and I could feel it down at my feet, thrashin'. I couldn't get loose, neither. Both of us were tryin' to get out. Then my papa come in and I was scared I was gonna get bit so I was screamin'. So he grabbed it up in the sheet and hit it with a candlestick, and then my mama started screamin' 'cause there was blood everywhere and that sheet was ruined."

"I'm sorry," Matthew said. "It must have been traumatic." Especially for a child of her sensitive nature, he might have added.

"Trau—*what*, sir?"

"I meant it must have been a fearsome experience."

"Yes sir." She nodded, and now she picked up a pawn and studied it in the sunlight. "The thing about it, though . . . is that . . . near mornin', I started rememberin' somethin'. About that man's voice I heard singin' in the Hamilton house."

Matthew's heart suddenly lodged in his throat. "Remembering what?"

"Whose voice it was." She put down the pawn and lifted her eyes to his. "It's still a fog . . . and thinkin' about it makes my head hurt somethin' awful, but . . . I recollected what he was singin'." She took a breath and began to softly sing, in a sweet and clear timbre: "*Come out, come out, my dames and dandies. Come out, come out, and taste my candies . . .*"

"The ratcatcher," Matthew said. In his mind he heard Linch singing that same macabre song during the massacre of rats at the gaol.

"Yes sir. It was Mr. Linch's voice I heard, from that room back there."

Matthew stared intensely into the child's eyes. "Tell me this, Violet: how did you know it was Linch's voice? Had you ever heard that song before?"

"One time he come to kill a nest of rats my papa found. They were all big ones, and black as night. Mr. Linch came and brought his potions and his sticker, and that was what he was singin' when he was waitin' for the rats to get drunk."

"Did you tell anyone else about this? Your mother and father?"

"No sir. They don't like for me to talk of it."

"Then you shouldn't tell them you've been here to see me, either."

"No sir, I wouldn't dare. I'd get a terrible whippin'."

"You ought to get your water and go home, then," Matthew said. "But one more thing: when you entered the Hamilton house, do you remember *smelling* anything? Like a very bad odor?" He was thinking of the decaying carcass. "Or did you see or hear a dog?"

Violet shook her head. "No sir, none of that. Why?"

"Well . . ." Matthew reached down to the chessboard and traded positions between the king's knight and the king's bishop. "If you were to describe this board and the pieces upon it to someone not in this room, how would you do so?"

She shrugged. "I suppose . . . that it's a wooden board with light and dark squares and some pieces in position on it."

"Would you say the game is ready to be played?"

"I don't know, sir. I would say . . . it is, but then again I don't know the particulars."

"Yes." He smiled slightly. "And it is the *particulars* that make all the difference. I want to thank you for coming to tell me what you've remembered. I know this has been very difficult for you."

"Yes sir. But my mama says when the witch is burnt up my head won't pain me no more." She picked up the two buckets. "May I ask you somethin' now, sir?"'

"You may."

"Why do you suppose Mr. Linch was back there in the dark, singin' like that?"

"I don't know," he answered.

"I thought on it all this mornin'." She stared out the window, the yellow sunlight coloring her face. "It made my head ache so bad I almost cried, but it seemed like somethin' I had to keep thinkin' on." Violet didn't speak for a moment, but Matthew could tell from the set of her jaw that she had come to an important conclusion. "I think . . . Mr. Linch must be a friend of Satan's. That's what I think."

"You might possibly be right. Do you know where I might find Mr. Linch?"

An expression of alarm tightened her face. "You're not going to *tell* him, are you?"

"No. I promise it. I would just like to know where he lives."

She hesitated for a few seconds, but she knew he would find out anyway. "At the end of Industry Street. He lives in the very last house."

"Thank you."

"I don't know if I was right to come here," she said, frowning. "I mean to say . . . if Mr. Linch is a friend of the Devil, shouldn't he be called to account for it?"

"He'll be called for an accounting," Matthew said. "You may depend on that." He touched her shoulder. "You *were* right to come. Go ahead, now. Get your water."

"Yes sir." Violet left the library with her buckets in tow, and a moment later Matthew stood at the window watching her walk to the spring. Then, his mind aflame with this new information, he hurried upstairs to look in on the magistrate.

He found Woodward sleeping again, which was probably for the best. The magistrate's face sparkled with sweat, and when Matthew approached the bed he could feel the man's fever long before he placed his fingers to Woodward's hot forehead.

The magistrate stirred. His mouth opened, yet his eyes remained sealed. *"Hurting,"* he said, in that tormented whisper. *"Ann . . . he's hurting . . ."*

Matthew drew his hand back. The tips of his fingers felt as if he had held them over a forge. Matthew placed the rolled-up decree atop the dresser and then picked up the box that held the remainder of the court documents so that he might continue reading through them tonight. For now, though, he had other things to do. He went to his room, put the document box on the table beside his bed, splashed water in his face from his shaving bowl to revive his flagging energies, and then was again out the door.

It had become a truly magnificent day. The sky was bright blue and cloudless and the sun was gorgeously warm. A light breeze was blowing from the west, and in it Matthew could detect the fragrances of wild honeysuckle, pine sap, and the rich aroma of fulsome earth. He might have sat down upon the bank of the spring to enjoy the warmth, as he saw several citizens doing, but he had a task ahead of him that granted no freedom of time for simple pleasures.

On his way along Industry Street—which he was beginning to know quite well—he passed Exodus Jerusalem's camp. Actually, he heard the bluster of Jerusalem's preaching before he got there and he marvelled that the breeze didn't become a hot and malodorous tempest in this quarter of Fount Royal. Jerusalem's sister—and by that term Matthew didn't know whether the preacher meant by blood or by indecent patronage—was scrubbing clothes in a washpot next to the wagon, while the young nephew—and here it was best to make no mental comment—was lying on a quilt in the shade nearby, picking the petals off a yellow flower and tossing them idly aside. The black-garbed master of ceremonies, however, was hard at work; he stood upon an overturned crate, orating and gesticulating for a somber crowd of two men and a woman.

Matthew stared straight ahead, hoping to invoke invisibility as he slipped past Jerusalem's field of view, but he knew it was not to be. "Ah!" came the sky-ripping shout. "Ah, there walketh a sinner! Right there! Look, everyone! Look how he doth scurry like a thief in broad daylight!"

What Jerusalem called scurrying Matthew called picking up his pace. He dared not pause to deflect Jerusalem's hook, for then he would be nattered to holes by this pseudo-holy imbecile. Therefore he kept a constant course, even though the preacher began to rant and rave in a fashion that made Matthew's blood start to boil: "Yes, look at him and thy looketh upon the pride of a witch's bed! Oh, did thou not all know the vile truth? Well, it is as plain as the writ of God across the soul of a righteous man! That sinner yonder hath actually struck me—*struck* me, I sayeth!—in defense of that wanton sorceress he so dearly yearneth to protect! And not just protect! Gentle flock, if thou but kneweth the cravings in that sinner's mind concerning the dark woman, thou might falleth to thy knees in the frenzy of madness! He wisheth the flesh of her body be gripped in his hands, her mouth open to his abominable needs, her every orifice a receptacle of his goatly lusts! And there he goeth, the blind wretched beast, scurrying away from the word of God lest it scorcheth some light into his eyes and maketh him see the path to Damnation upon which he rusheth to travel!"

The only path upon which Matthew rusheth was the one leading away from Exodus Jerusalem. It occurred to him, as he gladly left the preacher's caterwaulings behind, that the gentle flock would probably cough up some coins to hear more on the subject of orifices, receptacles, and goatly lusts, which was probably at the heart of it the whole reason for their attendance today. Matthew had to admit that Jerusalem had a talent at painting horny pictures. For now, though—until, dreadfully, he had to come back this way—his attention was focused on finding the ratcatcher's domicile.

He passed the Hamilton house and Violet's home, and continued by a large weed-choked field where a split-rail fence had fallen to disrepair. Further on, what appeared to be an attempt at an apple orchard was stubbled with dwarfed and twisted trees that seemed to be begging for the mercy of an axe. On the opposite side of Industry Street, the feeble trees of another unfortunate planting drooped in apparent pain, their few remaining leaves blotched with brown and ochre sores. In this area of Fount Royal, the sun might be shining but there was definitely no rejoicing of nature.

Matthew saw that Bidwell's orchards had suffered greatly during the long period of storms. The coarse, sandy earth had been washed away to such an extent that some trees seemed more exposed roots than branches, and what branches there were had shrivelled and malformed in their piteous reach for sunlight. Here and there some kind of knobby-looking thing had sprouted, but it was more green mold than edible product. This display of blighted agriculture seemed to stretch on and on like a preview of the harvests of Hell, and Matthew could readily understand how Bidwell and the citizens might ascribe the devastation not to natural causes but to a demonic purpose.

As Matthew continued walking between the miserable fields he reflected on the possibility that, in addition to the havoc wreaked by the deluge, this climate and soil might not be suited to sustain the types of crops that Bidwell was trying to grow. Of course Bidwell was trying to produce something that would earn him money and attention from the home country, but it might be that apples, for instance, were doomed in this swamp air. Likewise doomed was whatever those green molded things were. It might be, then, that a suitable cash crop for Fount Royal was yet to be planted, and Bidwell could benefit from the advice of a professional botanist. Yet a botanist would command a sizeable fee, and Matthew thought that if Winston was correct about Bidwell's combination of stinginess and swollen self-worth—and there was no reason to doubt it—then the master of Fount Royal was apt to consider himself as much an expert on growing crops as in building ships.

Presently Matthew came to the last dwelling on Industry Street, beyond which stood the fortress wall.

If the ratcatcher desired to live apart from other human beings, he could only have created a more suitable abode by digging a hole in the earth and covering it with a mudcaked roof. The house—if it might be distinguished by such a term—made Winston's shack appear the brother of Bidwell's mansion. Brush had been allowed to grow up around it, all but obscuring it from view. Vines gripped the gray clapboards and ivy grew abundant on the roof. The house's four windows were sealed by unpainted and badly weathered shutters, and Matthew thought it was a wonder the rains hadn't broken the poor place down to the ground entirely.

Matthew made his way to the door over a bare yard still treacherous with mud. Over the door Linch had hung three large rat skeletons from leather cords, as if to announce his trade to the world—whatever portion of the world cared to come to this place, that is. But then again, perhaps those three rats had given him such a fight Linch felt the need to mount them as trophies. Matthew swallowed his disgust, balled up his fist, and knocked at the door.

He waited, but there was no response. Matthew knocked again, and this time called, "Mr. Linch? May I speak with you, please?" Still there was no answer. The ratcatcher was out, probably pursuing some long-tailed dame or dandy.

Matthew had come a distance to see the man, and he despised the thought of making a second trip. He might wait for Linch, he decided, though there was no telling when the ratcatcher would return. He knocked a third time, just to know he had, and then he put his hand on the door's crude latch. He paused, weighing his sense of morality as concerning entering a man's home unbidden.

Pulling his hand back, he stepped away from the door and stood looking at the latch with his hands on his hips. What was the right thing to do? He glanced up Industry Street the way he'd come. There was no sign of a living soul. Of course, the *right* thing was to leave and return at a later time. The *necessary* thing . . . now that was a horse pulling a different cart.

But he wasn't sure he *wanted* to enter Linch's sanctum. If a place ever smelled like dead rats, he was sure this one did. And those skeletons did not speak well of what else might be on display in there. Matthew looked again down

Industry Street. Still no sign of anyone. If he wanted a chance to explore the ratcatcher's quarters, this was definitely the moment.

He took a deep breath. Trespassing upon a house was far different than intruding upon a barn . . . or was it? He didn't care to debate the distinction.

He quickly lifted the latch, before he could think better of it, and pushed the door open. It went smoothly, on oiled hinges. And by the sunlight that entered the house Matthew saw a very strange thing.

He stood at the threshold, peering in and wondering if he had lost his senses. Or at least his sense of order. This revelation took him inside. He looked around, his curiosity now well and truly piqued.

There was a desk and a sleeping pallet, a hearth and a shelf of cooking utensils. There was a chair and beside it a table on which sat a lantern. Nearby were a half-dozen candles wrapped up in oiled paper. A chamberpot was placed at the foot of the pallet. Two pairs of dirty shoes were lined up side-by-side next to the hearth, which was perfectly devoid of ashes. A broom leaned against the wall, ready for work.

And this was what so completely astounded Matthew: Linch's dwelling was the absolute picture of neatness.

The pallet had been made, its bedding tight and precise. The chamberpot was spotless. So too were the cooking pots and utensils. The lantern's glass bore not a trace of candle-soot. The floor and walls had been recently scrubbed, and the house still smelled of pinetar soap. Matthew thought he might have eaten off that floor and not tasted a grain of dirt. Everything was so orderly that it put a scare into Matthew even more than the terrible chaos of Winston's home, for the single reason that—like Winston had been—the rat-catcher was not who he appeared to be.

"Well," Matthew said, and his voice trembled. He looked once more toward town, but thankfully Industry Street was still empty. Then he continued his examination of this place that seemed to be a hovel from without but within was the epitome of . . . might the word Matthew was searching for be *control?*

This was one of the damnedest things he'd ever seen. The only bad note in the house was the foursome of dirty shoes, and Matthew thought those were part of Linch's ratcatching costume. He decided to add a pound to his penny of intrusion and therefore opened a trunk, finding within it more clothes—shirts, breeches, and stockings, all of them clean and perfectly folded.

Beside the lantern and the candles was a small ivory box. Matthew opened it and discovered matches and a flint, the matches all lined up like obedient soldiers. In a larger box that occupied a corner Matthew discovered a supply of salted beef, ears of corn, a pot of flour and a pot of grain, a bottle of rum and a bottle of wine, and various other foodstuffs. Upon the desk was a clay pipe and a carefully wrapped packet of tobacco. There was also an inkpot, a quill, and some papers ready to be written upon. He slid open the desk's top drawer, and found a second inkpot and a stack of paper, a leather wallet and . . . wonder of wonders . . . a book.

It was a thin volume, but a well-read and well-travelled tome, from the wear and tear of the binding. Matthew gently opened it to the title page—which threatened to fall out between his fingers—and received another puzzlement. The book's title, faded as it was, read *A Pharaoh's Life, or Concerning Fanciful Events in Ancient Egypt.*

Matthew knew that Egyptian culture, known through the travails of Moses in the Holy Bible, was a source of great fascination to a certain segment of the English and

European populace—mainly, those gentry who had the time and inclination to indulge in theories and discourse on what that mysterious civilization might have been like. He could have expected a book of this nature to adorn Bidwell's library, simply for the show of it, but never touched; it was absolutely incredible that the ratcatcher might have an interest in the life of a pharaoh, however fancifully described. Matthew would have paged through the book to get an idea of its contents, but as the leaves were so fragile he decided to forgo that particular exploration. It was enough for now to know that Gwinett Linch was not the man he presented himself to be.

But if not . . . then who *was* he?

Matthew closed the book and made sure it was exactly in the position it had been when he'd touched it, as he had the feeling that Linch would know if it had been moved a hair's width. He picked up the wallet, unfolded it, and found inside a small object wrapped in brown cotton cloth and secured with knotted twine. Matthew's interest was further sharpened. The problem, however, was not the undoing of the twine but in the redoing of it. Was it worth the time and effort?

He decided it was.

He carefully untied the cord, noting the structure of the knot. Then he opened the cloth.

It was a piece of jewelry: a circular gold brooch, but missing its clasping pin. Picking up the item, he held it into the sunlight . . . and stared with amazement into the blazing dark blue depths of a sapphire that was near the size of his thumbnail.

The hairs stood up on the back of his neck. He twisted his head around, his eyes widening, but the doorway was empty.

Linch—or the man who called himself Linch—was not there. From where he stood, Matthew could see no one approaching. But he was certain that if Linch found him with this fabulous jewel in his hand, his life would be as short as that of a belly-gashed rat on the bloody blade of that sticker.

Time to go. Time to get out, while he could.

First, though, to wrap the brooch up once more, return it to the wallet and replace the wallet exactly—*exactly*—as it had been. His hands were shaking, as precision was a demanding taskmaster. When the wallet was correctly positioned, Matthew slid the drawer shut and stepped back, wiping his moist palms on his hips.

There were other drawers he might have wished to go through, and he might have desired to inspect the underside of Linch's pallet and further explore the house, but it would be daring Fate. He retreated to the door and was about to shut it when he realized with a shock that he had smeared across the otherwise-pristine floor a small amount of mud from the sodden yard.

He bent down, attempting to get the debris up with his hand. He succeeded somewhat but there was still a telltale streak. No doubt of it: Linch was going to know his sanctum had been violated.

A bell began ringing in the distance. Matthew, still working at removing the stain of his presence by spittle and elbow-grease, realized it was the watchman at the gate signaling an arrival. He had done the best he could do. A little grime on the floor would pall before the gore that would flow if Linch found him here. He stood up, went out, pulled the door shut, and dropped its latch.

As Matthew started walking back along Industry Street, the signal bell ceased. He assumed that the new arrival had been allowed into Fount Royal. Would that it was a doctor whose method was more medicine and less bloodletting!

The sun warmed his face and the breeze blew softly at his back. Yet Matthew had never felt as if he walked a darker or colder path. The sapphire in that brooch had to be worth a small fortune, therefore why was Linch stabbing rats for a living? And why did he go to such effort to disguise his true nature, which appeared to be a preference for order and control, behind a facade of filthiness? It seemed to Matthew that Linch even wished his house to look absolutely decrepit from the outside and had gone to some lengths to make it so.

This pit of deceit was deeper than he'd expected. But what did it have to do with Rachel? Linch was obviously a learned, intelligent man who could write with a quill and read books of theoretical substance; he was also quite well off financially, judging from the sapphire brooch. Why in the world was he acting such a wretched part?

And then there was the singing to consider. Had Violet gone into the Hamilton house or not? If she had, why didn't she notice the disagreeable odor of that dead dog? And if she had not gone in, then what strange power had made her believe she *had?* No, no; it was confusing to even his disciplined mind. The most troubling things about Violet's supposed entrance into the house were her sighting of the white-haired imp and her memory of the six gold buttons on Satan's cloak. Those details she shared with Buckner and Garrick were damnable evidence against Rachel. But what about the rat-catcher singing in that dark room where Matthew had found the bitch and her pups? One might say Violet had imagined it, but then could one not infer that she'd imagined the whole incident? But she could not imagine details that had already been supplied by Buckner and Garrick!

So: if Violet *had* entered the house, why was the ratcatcher singing back there in the dark? And if she had *not* entered the house, why—and how—did she fervently believe she had, and from where did those details of the white-haired imp and the six gold buttons come?

He was thinking so furiously on these questions that he failed to gird his wits for his return engagement with Exodus Jerusalem, but he found that the preacher's tongue had ceased its salivation over orifices. Indeed, Jerusalem, the trio of audience, and the so-called sister and the so-called nephew had departed and were nowhere to be seen. Matthew was soon aware, however, of a *balhaloo* in progress on Harmony Street. He saw four covered wagons and fifteen or twenty townspeople thronged about them. A lean gray-bearded man wearing a green tricorn sat at the reins of the first wagon's team and was engaged in conversation with Bidwell. Matthew also saw Winston standing behind his master; the cur had gone to some effort to shave and dress in clean clothes to make a presentable picture, and he was speaking to a young blond-haired man who appeared to be a companion to the wagon driver.

Matthew approached a farmer standing nearby. "May I ask what's going on?"

"The maskers have come," the man, who had perhaps three teeth in his head, answered.

"Maskers? You mean *actors?*"

"That's right. They come every year and show a play. Weren't expected 'til midsummer, though."

Matthew was amazed at the tenacity of a travelling actors' troupe to negotiate the bone-jarring road between here and Charles Town. He recalled a book on the English theater he'd seen in Bidwell's library, and realized Bidwell had engineered a yearly entertainment—a midsummer festival, so to speak—for his citizenry.

"Now we'll have a fine time!" the farmer said, grinning that cavernous mouth. "A witch-burnin' in the morn and a play in the eve!"

Matthew did not reply. He observed that the gray-bearded man, who appeared to be the troupe's leader, seemed to be asking instructions or directions from Bidwell. The master of Fount Royal conferred for a moment with Winston, whose outward mannerisms gave no inkling that he was anything but a loyal servant. Then, the conference done, Bidwell spoke again to the bearded man and motioned westward along Industry Street. Matthew realized Bidwell must be telling the man where the actors might set up their camp. He would have paid an admission fee to hear the thoughts of Exodus Jerusalem when the preacher learned his neighbors would be thespians. Then again, Jerusalem might make some extra coins by giving the players acting lessons.

Matthew went on his way, avoiding contact with Bidwell and the scoundrel in his shadow. He paused for a short while at the spring, watching the golden sunlight ripple on the water's surface. It entered his mind to go to the gaol and look in on Rachel; in fact, he felt an urgent need to see her, but with a considerable effort of willpower he declined. She had made it clear she did not want his presence there, and as much as it pained him, he must respect her wishes.

He returned to the house, found Mrs. Nettles, and asked if he might have some lunch. After a quick repast of corn soup and buttered bread, he ascended the stairs to his room and settled in a chair by the open window to contemplate his findings and to finish reading through the documents.

He could not shake the feeling, as he read the answers to the questions he had posed, that a revelation was close at hand. He only dimly heard the singing of birds and sensed the warmth of the sun, as all his attention was focused on these responses. There had to be something in here—something small, something overlooked—that might be a key to prove Rachel's innocence. As he read, however, he was distracted by two things: first, the bellringing and braying voice of a public crier announcing the magistrate's decree even in the slave quarters; and second, the sound of an axe chopping timber in the woods between the mansion and the tidewater swamp.

Matthew reached the end of the documents. He had found nothing. He realized he was looking for a shadow that may or may not exist, and to find it—if it was discoverable—he must concentrate on reading between the lines. He ran a weary hand over his face, and began once more from the beginning.

FIVE

Lanterns glowed across Fount Royal, and the stars shone down.

Isaac Woodward inhabited a realm that lay somewhere between twilight and Tartarus. The agony of his swollen throat had spread now through his every nerve and fiber, and the act of breathing seemed itself a defiance toward the will of God. His flesh was slick with sweat and sore with fever. Sleep would fall upon him like a heavy shroud, bearing him into blessed insensibility, but while he was awake his vision was as blurred as a candle behind soot-filmed glass. In spite of all these torments, however, the worst was that he was keenly aware of his condition. The deterioration of his body had not yet reached his mind, and thus he had sense enough to realize he was perilously close to the grave's edge.

"Will you help me turn him over?" Dr. Shields asked Matthew and Mrs. Nettles.

Matthew hesitated, his own face pallid in the light from a double candleholder to which was fixed a circle of reflective mirror. "What are you going to do?"

Dr. Shields pushed his spectacles up on the bridge of his nose. "The afflicted blood is pooling in his body," he answered. "It must be moved. Stirred up from its stagnant ponds, if you will."

"Stirred up? How? By more bleeding?"

"No. I think at this point the lancet will not perform its necessary function."

"How, then?" Matthew insisted.

"Mrs. Nettles," the doctor said curtly, "if you'll please assist me?"

"Yes sir." She took hold of Woodward's arm and leg on one side and Shields took the opposite side.

"All right, then. Turn him toward me," Shields instructed. "Magistrate, can you help us at all?"

"I shall try," Woodward whispered.

Together, the doctor and Mrs. Nettles repositioned Woodward so he lay on his stomach. Matthew was torn about whether to give a hand, for he feared what Dr. Shields had decided to do. The magistrate gave a single groan during the procedure, but otherwise bore the pain and indignity like a gentleman.

"Very well." Dr. Shields looked across the bed at Mrs. Nettles. "I shall have to lift his gown up, as his back must be bared."

"What procedure is this?" Matthew asked. "I demand to know!"

"For your information, young man, it is a time-tested procedure to move the blood within the body. It involves heat and a vacuum effect. Mrs. Nettles, would you remove yourself, please? For the sake of decorum?"

"Shall I wait outside?"

"No, that won't be necessary. I shall call if you're needed." He paused while Mrs. Nettles left the room, and when the door was again closed he said to Woodward, "I am going to pull your gown up to your shoulders, Isaac. Whatever help you may give me is much appreciated."

"Yes," came the muffled reply. "Do what is needed."

The doctor went about the business of exposing Woodward's buttocks and back. Matthew saw that at the base of the magistrate's spine was a bed sore about two inches in diameter, bright red at its center and outlined with yellow infection. A second, smaller, but no less malignant sore had opened on the back of Woodward's right thigh.

Dr. Shields opened his bag, brought out a pair of supple deerskin gloves, and began to put them on. "If your stomach is weak," he said quietly to Matthew, "you should follow Mrs. Nettles. I need no further complications."

"My stomach is fine," Matthew lied. "What . . . is the procedure?"

The doctor reached into the bag again and brought out a small glass sphere, its surface marred only by a circular opening with a pronounced curved rim. The rim, Matthew saw with sickened fascination, had been discolored dark brown by the application of fire. "As I said before . . . heat and vacuum." From the pocket of his tan waistcoat he produced the fragrant piece of sassafras root, which he deftly pushed to the magistrate's lips. "Isaac, there will be some pain involved, and we wish your tongue not to be injured." Woodward accepted the tongue-guard and sank his teeth into the accustomed grooves. "Young man, will you hold the candles, please?"

Matthew picked up the double candlestick from the table beside Woodward's bed. Dr. Shields leaned forward and stroked the sphere's rim from one flame to the other in a circular motion, all the time staring into Matthew's eyes in order to gauge his nerves. As he continued to heat the rim, Shields said, "Magistrate, I am going to apply a blister cup to your back. The first of six. I regret the sensation, but the afflicted blood will be caused to rise to the surface from the internal organs and that is our purpose. Are you ready, sir?"

Woodward nodded, his eyes squeezed tightly shut. Shields held the cup's opening directly over the flames for perhaps five seconds. Then, rapidly and without hesitation, he pressed the hot glass rim down upon Woodward's white flesh a few inches upward from the virulent bedsore.

There was a small noise—a snake's hiss, perhaps—and the cup clamped tightly as the heated air within compressed itself. An instant after the hideous contact was made, Woodward cried out around the sassafras root and his body shivered in a spasm of pure, animal pain.

"Steady," Shields said, speaking to both the magistrate and his clerk. "Let nature do its work."

Matthew could see that already the flesh caught within the blister cup was swelling and reddening. Dr. Shields had brought a second cup from his bag, and again let the flames lick its cruel rim. After the procedure of heating the air inside the cup, the glass was pressed to Woodward's back with predictable and—at least to Matthew—spine-crawling result.

By the time the third cup was affixed, the flesh within the first had gone through the stages of red to scarlet and now was blood-gorged and turning brown like a maliferous poison mushroom.

Shields had the fourth cup in his gloved hand. He offered it to the candle flames. "We shall see a play directly, I understand," he said, his voice divorced from his actions. "The citizens do enjoy the maskers every year."

Matthew didn't answer. He was watching the first brown

mushroom of flesh becoming still darker, and the other two following the path of swollen discoloration.

"Usually," the doctor went on, "they don't arrive until the middle of July or so. I understand from Mr. Brightman—he's the leader of the company—that two towns they customarily play in were decimated by sickness, and a third had vanished altogether. That accounts for their early arrival this year. It's a thing to be thankful for, though, because we need a pleasant diversion." He pressed the fourth blister cup onto Woodward's back, and the magistrate trembled but held back a moan. "My wife and I used to enjoy the theater in Boston," Shields said as he prepared the fifth implement. "A play in the afternoon . . . a beaker of wine . . . a concert on the Commons." He smiled faintly. "Those were wonderful times."

Matthew had recovered his composure enough to ask the question that at this point naturally presented itself. "Why did you leave Boston?"

The doctor waited until the fifth cup was attached before he replied. "Well . . . let us say I needed a challenge. Or perhaps . . . there was something I wished to accomplish."

"And have you? Accomplished it, I mean?"

Shields stared at the rim of the sixth cup as he moved it between the flames, and Matthew saw the fire reflected in his spectacles. "No," he said. "Not yet."

"This involves Fount Royal, I presume? And your infirmary?"

"It involves . . . what it involves." Shields glanced quickly into Matthew's eyes and then away again. "You *do* have a fetish for questions, don't you?"

If this remark was designed to seal Matthew's mouth and turn aside his curiosity, it had the opposite effect. "Only for questions that go unanswered."

"Touché," the doctor said, and he pressed the sixth blister cup firmly onto Woodward's back. Again the magistrate trembled with pain but was steadfastly silent. "All right, then: I left Boston because my practise was failing there. The city has a glut of doctors, as well as lawyers and ministers. There must be a dozen physicians alone, not to mention the herbalists and faith-healers! So I decided that for a space of time I would leave Boston—and my wife, whose sewing enterprise is actually doing quite well—and offer my services elsewhere."

"Fount Royal is a long distance from Boston," Matthew said.

"Oh, I didn't come directly here. I lived for a month in New York, spent a summer in Philadelphia, and lived in other smaller places. I always seemed to be heading southward." He began peeling off his deerskin gloves. "You may put the candles down now."

Matthew returned the double candlestick to the table. He had seen—though he certainly didn't let his eyes linger on the sight, or his imagination linger on what the sensation must be—that the flesh gripped by the first two cups had become hideous, blood-swollen ebony blisters. The others were following the gruesome pattern.

"We shall let the blood rise for a time." Dr. Shields put the gloves into his bag. "This procedure breaks up the stagnant pools within his body, you see."

Matthew saw nothing but grotesque swellings. He dared not dwell on what pressures were inflicted within the magistrate's suffering bones. To keep his mind from wandering in that painful direction, he asked, "Do you plan on staying in Fount Royal very much longer?"

"No, I don't think so. Bidwell pays me a fee, and he has certainly built a fine infirmary for my use, but . . . I do miss my wife. And Boston, too. So as soon as the town is progressing again, the population healthy and growing, I shall seek to find a replacement for myself."

"And what then would be the accomplishment you crave, sir?"

Dr. Shields cocked his head to one side, a hint of a smile on his mouth but his owlish eyes stony. "You're a regular goat amid a briar patch, aren't you?"

"I pride myself on being persistent, if that's your meaning."

"No, that is *not* my meaning, but I'll answer that rather meddlesome question in spite of my reluctance to add pine knots to your fire. My accomplishment—my *hoped-for* accomplishment, that is—would be twofold: one, to aid in the construction of a settlement that would grow into a city; and two, to have my name forevermore on the title of Fount Royal's infirmary. I plan on remaining here long enough to see both those things come to pass." He reached out and gently grasped the first blister cup between thumb and forefinger, checking its suction. "The influence of Rachel Howarth," he said, "was an unfortunate interruption in the forward motion of Fount Royal. But as soon as her ashes are buried—or scattered or whatever Bidwell's going to do with them—we shall put an end to our calamities. As the weather has turned for the better, the swamp vapors have been banished. Soon we shall see an increase in the population, both by people coming in from elsewhere and by healthy babies being born. Within a year, I think Fount Royal will be back to where it was before this ugly incident ever happened. I shall do my best to aid that growth, leave my mark and name for posterity, and return to Boston and my wife. *And,* of course, the comfort and culture of the city."

"Admirable aims," Matthew said. "I expect having your

name on the mast of an infirmary would help your standing in Boston, as well."

"It would. A letter from Bidwell stating that fact and his appreciation for my services could secure me a place in a medical partnership that ordinarily I might be denied."

Matthew was about to ask if Bidwell knew what the doctor intended when there was a knock at the door. Shields said, "Who is it, please?"

"Nicholas," came the reply. "I wanted to look in on the magistrate."

Instantly Matthew sensed a change in Dr. Shields's demeanor. It was nothing radical, but remarkable nevertheless. The doctor's face seemed to tighten; indeed, his entire body went taut as if an unseen hand had gripped him around the back of his neck. When Shields answered, even his voice had sharpened. "The magistrate is indisposed at the moment."

"Oh . . . well, then. I'll return later."

"Wait!" Woodward had removed the sassafras root from his mouth, and was whispering in Matthew's direction. "Ask Mr. Paine to come in, please."

Matthew went to the door and stopped Paine before he reached the stairs. When Paine entered the room, Matthew watched the doctor's face and saw that Shields refused to even cast a glance at his fellow citizen.

"How is he?" Paine inquired, standing at the door.

"As I said, indisposed," Shields replied, with a distinct chill. "You can see for yourself."

Paine flinched a little at the sight of the six glass cups and the ebony blisters they had drawn, but he came around to Matthew's side of the bed for a view of the magistrate's face. "Good evening," he said, with as much of a smile as he could summon. "I see . . . Dr. Shields is taking care of you. How are you feeling?"

"I have felt . . . much superior," Woodward said.

"I'm sure." Paine's smile faltered. "I wanted to tell you . . . that I approve heartily of your decree, sir. Also that your efforts—and the efforts of your clerk, of course—have been nothing short of commendable."

"My thanks," Woodward replied, his eyes heavy-lidded.

"Might I get you anything?"

"You might *leave,*" Shields said. "You're taxing him."

"Oh. I'm sorry. I don't wish to do any harm."

"No harm." Woodward gasped for a breath, a green crust around his nostrils. "I appreciate . . . your taking . . . time and effort . . . to come and see me."

"I also wanted to tell you, sir, that the stake has been cut. I understand Mr. Bidwell hasn't yet decided where the execution shall take place, but the likelihood is in one of the unused fields on Industry Street."

"Yes." Woodward swallowed thickly. "That would do."

Shields grasped the first blister cup and popped it free. Woodward winced and bit his lower lip. "I think you should depart now," the doctor said to Paine. "Unless you'd like to give a hand in this procedure?"

"Uh . . . yes, I'd best be going." Paine, for all his manly experiences, appeared to Matthew to be a little green around the gills. "Magistrate, I'll look in on you at a later time." He glanced at Matthew with a pained expression of commiseration and took a step toward the door.

"Mr. Paine?" Woodward whispered. "Please . . . may I ask you something?"

"Yes, surely." Paine returned to the bedside and stood close, leaning toward the magistrate, the better to hear him clearly.

Shields removed the second blister cup. Again Woodward winced, and now his eyes were wet. He said, "We share . . . a commonality."

"We do, sir?"

"Your wife. Died of fits, I understand. I wanted you to know . . . my son . . . perished of fits . . . suffered by the plague. Was your wife . . . also plague-stricken?"

Dr. Shields's hand had seized the third blister cup, but had not yet removed it.

Nicholas Paine stared into Woodward's face. Matthew saw a pulse beating at Paine's temple. "I fear you're mistaken, sir," Paine said, in a strangely hollow voice. "I have never been married."

"Dr. Shields told me," Woodward went on, with an effort. "I know . . . such things are difficult to speak of. Believe me, I do know."

"Dr. Shields," Paine repeated, "told you."

"Yes. That she suffered fits until she died. And that . . . possibly it was the plague."

Shields removed the third cup and placed it almost noiselessly into his bag.

Paine licked his lower lip. "I'm sorry," he said, "but I fear Dr. Shields is just as mistaken as—" He chose that instant to look into the doctor's face, and Matthew was a witness to what next occurred.

Something passed between Paine and Shields. It was something intangible, yet absolutely horrific. For the briefest of seconds Matthew saw the doctor's eyes blaze with a hatred that defied all reason and logic, and Paine actually drew back as if from a threatening physical presence. Matthew also realized that he'd witnessed very little direct communication between Dr. Shields and Paine. It dawned on Matthew that it was the doctor who preferred to keep his distance from Paine, yet the feeling had been so well disguised that Paine might not even have been aware of a void between them.

However, now an ugly animosity was clearly revealed if only for that fleeting second. Paine perhaps recognized it for the first time, and his mouth opened as if he might exclaim or protest against it. Yet in the next heartbeat Paine's face froze as tightly as the doctor's and whatever he might have said remained unborn.

Shields held the dark bond between them for only a second or two longer, and then he very calmly returned his attention to his patient. He removed the fourth blister cup, and into the bag it went.

Matthew looked questioningly at Paine, but the other man had blanched and would not meet his gaze. Matthew realized a piece of information had been delivered from Dr. Shields to Paine in that brief hateful glare, and whatever it was had almost buckled Paine's knees.

"My wife," Paine's voice was choked with emotion. "My wife."

"My son . . . died," Woodward said, oblivious to the drama. "Fits. From the plague. Pardon my asking you . . . but I wished you to know . . . you were not alone in your grief."

"Grief," Paine repeated. Shadows lay in his eye sockets, and his face appeared to have become more gaunt and aged by five years in as many seconds. "Yes," he said quietly. "Grief."

Dr. Shields pulled the fifth blister cup free, none too gently, and Woodward winced.

"I should . . . tell you about my wife," Paine offered, his face turned toward the window. "She did perish from fits. But not caused by the plague. No." He shook his head. "Hunger was the killer. Hunger . . . and crushing despair. We were very young, you see. Very poor. We had a baby girl who was sick, as well. And I was sick in the mind . . . and very desperate."

No one spoke. Even the magistrate, in his cloudy realm on the edge of delirium, realized Paine had dropped his mask of sturdy self-control and was revealing heart's blood and fractured bones.

"I think I understand this," Paine said, though that strange remark itself was a puzzle to Matthew. "I am . . . quite overcome . . . but I must tell you . . . all of you . . . that I never intended . . . the result of what happened. As I said, I was young . . . I was brash, and I was frightened. My wife and my child needed food and medicine. I had nothing . . . but an ability I had learned from hunting cruel and violent men." He was silent for a time, during which Dr. Shields stared intently at the sixth blister cup but made no attempt at removing it.

"I did not fire the first shot," Paine went on, his voice tired and heavy. "I was first struck myself. In the leg. But you must know that already. Something I had been taught by the older men . . . during my career at sea . . . was that once a weapon—pistol or rapier—was aimed at you, you fired or slashed back with grievous intent. That was our creed, and it served to keep us—most of us—among the living. It was a natural reaction, learned by watching other men die wallowing in their own blood. That was why I could not—*could* not—spare Quentin Summers in our duel. How can a man be taught the ways of a wolf and then live among sheep? Especially . . . when there is hunger and need involved . . . and the specter of death knocking at the door."

Matthew's curiosity had ignited from a flame to a bonfire and he yearned to ask Paine exactly what he was talking about, but something of the moment seemed almost sacred in its self-revelation, in its picture of a proud man giving up his pride to the overwhelming desire for confession and—perhaps—sanctuary from past misdeeds. Therefore he felt it small of himself to speak and break this spell of soul-broaching.

Paine walked to the window and looked out over the lantern-spangled town. On Industry Street, two fires some distance apart marked the camps of Exodus Jerusalem and the newly arrived maskers. Through the warm night wafted the faint sound of laughter and the trilling of a recorder from Van Gundy's tavern. "My compliments," Paine said, his face still averted. "I presume my wound left a trail. Is that what you followed?"

Dr. Shields at last freed the ebony flesh under the sixth blister cup. He put the implement into his bag, followed by the sassafras root. Then, slowly and methodically, he began to close the bag by its buttons and loops.

"Are you not going to answer me?" Paine asked. "Or is this a torture by silence?"

"I think," the doctor said with grit in his voice, "that the time has come for you to depart."

"Depart? What game are you playing at?"

"No game. I assure you . . . no game." Shields pressed a finger to one of the six horrid black swellings that protruded from Woodward's back. "Ah, yes. Quite firm now. We have drawn the stagnant blood upward from the organs, you see?" He glanced at Matthew, then away. "This procedure has a cleansing effect, and we should see some improvement in the magistrate's condition by morning."

"And if not?" Matthew had to ask.

"If not . . . then there is the next step."

"Which is?"

"Again applying the cups," Shields said, "and then bleeding the blisters." Matthew instantly regretted his inquiry. The thought of those swellings being burst by a lancet was almost too much to consider.

Shields lowered the magistrate's gown. "You should endeavor to sleep on your stomach tonight, Isaac. I know your position is less than comfortable, but I'm afraid it's necessary."

"I shall endure it," Woodward rasped, drifting even now toward sleep again.

"Good. I'll have Mrs. Nettles send a servant with a cold compress for your fever. In the morning we shall—"

"Shields, what do you want of me?" Paine interrupted, this time daring to face the other man. Moisture glistened on Paine's forehead and cheeks.

The doctor lifted his eyebrows. "I've already told you, sir. I wish you to *depart*."

"Are you going to hold this over my head for the rest of my life?"

Shields did not answer, but stared fixedly through his spectacle lenses at his antagonist. So damning was this wordless accusation that Paine was forced at length to drop his gaze to the floorboards. Then, abruptly, Paine turned toward the door and slinked out in the manner of the wolf he had proclaimed himself to be—yet, however, a wolf whose tail had been shorn off by an unexpected blade.

In the wake of Paine's departure; Dr. Shields let free a breath he'd been hoarding. "Well," he said, and behind the lenses his magnified eyes appeared stunned by the rapid turn of events. He blinked slowly several times, as if clearing his mind as well as his vision. "What was I saying? Oh . . . in the morning we shall administer a colonic and apply fresh plasters. Then we shall proceed as necessary." He took a handkerchief from inside his jacket and mopped his brow. "Is it hot in here to you?"

"No, sir," Matthew said. "The temperature seems very regular." He now saw his opportunity. "May I ask what your exchange with Mr. Paine concerned?"

"I will have Mrs. Nettles look in on the magistrate from time to time tonight," the doctor said. "You might keep yourself aware, also. I will be ready to come if any emergency presents itself." He placed a reassuring hand on Woodward's shoulder. "I'm going to leave now, Isaac. Just rest and be of good spirits. Tomorrow we might have you up and walking for some exercise." From the magistrate there was no reply, because he had already fallen asleep.

"Good night," Shields said to Matthew and, taking his bag with him, he left the bedchamber.

Matthew was after him like a shot. "One moment, sir!" he called in the hallway, but to be such a small-framed man Dr. Shields suddenly had the stride of a racehorse. Just before the doctor reached the stairs, Matthew said, "If you refuse to tell me, I shall find out on my own."

This statement caused an immediate reaction. Dr. Shields halted in his tracks, spun around with furious speed, and advanced on Matthew as if to strike the clerk a blow. By the Mars-orange glow of the hallway's lantern, Shields's face was a Hellish, sweating rictus with bared and clenched teeth, his eyes drawn into narrow slits that made him appear a stranger to the man Matthew had seen only seconds before. To compound this transformation, Shields gripped the front of Matthew's shirt with one hand and forced his back solidly and painfully into the wall.

"You *listen!*" Shields hissed. His hand tightened, twisting the fabric it clenched. "You do not—I repeat, do *not*—have the right to interfere in my business. What transpired between Paine and myself tonight will remain just that: between him and me. No one else. Certainly not *you*. Do you understand me, boy?" Shields gave Matthew a violent shake to underscore his vehemence. *"Answer!"*

In spite of the fact that he towered over the doctor,

Matthew was stricken with fright. "Yes, sir," Matthew said. "I do understand."

"You'd better, or by God you'll wish you had!" Shields held Matthew pressed up against the wall for a few seconds longer—an eternity to Matthew—and then the doctor's hand left his shirt. Without a further word, Shields walked away and descended the stairs.

Matthew was left severely confused and no less severely scared. The doctor might have been a brother to Will Shawcombe, for all that rough treatment. As he straightened his shirt and tried to steady his nerves, Matthew realized something truly treacherous was going on between Shields and Paine; indeed, the violence induced from Shields spoke volumes about the doctor's mental state. What had all that been, about wounds and weapons and Paine's deceased wife? *I presume my wound left a trail,* Paine had said. *Is that what you followed?*

Whatever the problem was, it had to do with Paine's past—which seemed more infamous now than ever. But Matthew was faced with so many puzzles to untangle concerning Rachel's plight—and such a short time to untangle them—that this new situation seemed more of a sideshow than a compelling attraction. He didn't believe the strife between the two men had anything to do with Rachel, whereas, for instance, Gwinett Linch's voice singing in the darkness of the Hamilton house while Satan laid an ultimatum at the feet of Violet Adams most certainly did.

Therefore, though he might fervently desire to know more about the relationship he'd witnessed tonight, he felt pressed by time to keep his focus on proving Rachel's innocence and let old griefs fall by the wayside. For now, at least.

He looked in once more on the magistrate and waited for the servant girl to come with the cold compress. Matthew thanked her, bade her go, and himself applied the compress—a water-soaked cotton cloth, to be accurate—to the sleeping man's face and on the back of his neck where the fever seemed most heated. Afterward, Matthew went downstairs and found Mrs. Nettles closing the shutters for the night. He asked if he might have a pot of tea and some biscuits, and was soon thereafter in possession of a tray with both. He took the moment to inquire of Mrs. Nettles what she knew about the ratcatcher, but she could supply nothing other than the facts that Linch kept to himself, and though he was sorely needed he was something of a pariah because of the nature of his craft. Matthew also asked—in a most casual way—if Mrs. Nettles had ever detected a tension between Dr. Shields and Nicholas Paine, or knew of anything that might be a cause of trouble in their dealings with each other.

Mrs. Nettles answered that she knew of no trouble, but that she was aware of a certain chill emanating from the good doctor regarding Mr. Paine. By contrast, she said, Dr. Shields acted warmly toward Mr. Winston and Mr. Bidwell, but it was apparent to her that the doctor would rather not share the same room in which Mr. Paine was present. It was nothing so dramatic that anyone else might notice, but in her opinion Dr. Shields had a marked distaste for the man.

"Thank you," Matthew said. "Oh . . . one more thing. Who arrived first in Fount Royal? Mr. Paine or the doctor?"

"Mr. Paine did," she replied. "It was . . . oh, more'n a month or two a'fore Dr. Shields came." She knew there must be a valid reason for these questions. "Does this concern Rachel Howarth?"

"No, I don't believe so. It's only an observation I needed verified."

"Oh, I swan it's more'n that!" She offered him a sly smile. "You canna' leave a thread undone, can ya?"

"I might find employment as a weaver of rugs, if that's what you mean."

"Ha!" She gave a rough bark of a laugh. "Yes, I 'spect you might!" However, her smile vanished and her countenance darkened until she had reached her customary grim composure. "It's all up for Madam Howarth then, is that the basket?"

"The lid has not yet been closed," Matthew said.

"Meanin' what?"

"Meaning that the execution flame has not yet been lighted . . . and that I have some reading to do. Excuse me and good night." Matthew took his tray of tea and biscuits upstairs to his room, where he poured himself a cup and sat down next to the open window, his lantern burning on its sill. For the third time he took the documents from their protective box and began reading through them, starting at the beginning.

By now he might have recited the testimony by heart. Still he felt—or, rather, ardently *hoped*—that something in the thicket of words might leap out at him like a directional signpost, signaling the next step in his exploration. He drank from his cup of tea and chewed on a biscuit. Bidwell had taken his own repast at Van Gundy's tavern, as Matthew had discovered from Dr. Shields, who had earlier seen Bidwell hoisting a tankard with Winston and several other men in a general air of merry celebration.

He finished—for the third time—Jeremiah Buckner's account and paused to rub his eyes. He felt in need of a tankard himself, yet strong drink would weaken his resolve and blur his sight. Oh, for a night of pure sleep untouched by the thought of Rachel afire on the stake!

Or even a night untouched by the thought of Rachel. Period.

He recalled what the magistrate had said: *Helping her. Finding the truth. Being of service. Whatever and however you choose to phrase it . . . Rachel Howarth is your nightbird, Matthew.* Perhaps the magistrate was right, but not in the sinister way he had meant it.

Matthew closed his eyes for a moment to rest them. Then he opened them, drank some more tea to fortify himself, and continued his reading. Now he was venturing into the testimony of Elias Garrick, and the man's recollection of the night he had awakened and— *Wait,* he thought. *That was odd.*

He read again over the section he had just digested. *That night I was feelin' poorly, and I waked up to go outside and spew what was makin' me ill. It was silent. Everythin' was silent, like the whole world was afeared to breathe.*

Matthew sat up from his slouched position in the chair. He reached out and pulled the lantern nearer. Then he turned back through the pages until he found the beginning of Jeremiah Buckner's testimony.

And there it was.

Me and Patience went to bed just like usual that night. She put out the lamp. Then . . . I don't know how long it was later . . . I heard my name spoke. I opened my eyes. Everythin' was dark, and silent. I waited, a'listenin'. Just silent, like there was nothin' else in the whole world makin' a sound but my breathin'. Then . . . I heard my name spoke again, and I looked at the foot of the bed and seen her.

With an eager hand, Matthew turned to the beginning of Violet Adams's testimony, as she recounted entering the Hamilton house. He put a finger on the line of importance, his heart starting to slam hard in his chest.

There wasn't nary a noise. It was silent, like . . . it was just me breathin' and that was the only sound.

Three witnesses.

Three testimonies.

But the same word: *silent.*

And that about breathing being the only sound . . . what possible coincidence could that be? Also the repeated phrase *whole world* by both Buckner and Garrick . . . it defied reason to think both men would speak the exact same words.

Unless . . . without knowing it . . . all three of the witnesses had been told what to say.

Matthew felt a chill skitter up his spine. The hairs on the back of his neck moved. He realized he had just had a glimpse of the shadow he sought.

It was a terrifying realization. Because the shadow was larger and darker and more strangely powerful than he had dared believe. The shadow had been standing behind Jeremiah Buckner, Elias Garrick, and Violet Adams there in the gaol, all the time they'd been giving their accounts.

"My God," Matthew whispered, his eyes wide. Because he had realized the shadow was in their minds, directing their words, emotions, and counterfeit memories. The three witnesses were no more than flesh-and-blood puppets, constructed by the hand of an evil beyond Matthew's imagining.

One hand. The same hand. A hand that sewed six gold buttons on a Satanic cloak. That created a white-haired imp, a leathery lizard-like manbeast, and a bizarre creature that had a male penis and female breasts. The same hand had created these scenes of sickening depravity, had painted them on the very air to display to Buckner, Garrick, Violet, and probably other citizens, who had fled for their sanity. For that's what the scenes were: air-paintings. Or, rather, paintings that came to life inside the minds that were spelled to accept them as truth.

That was why Buckner could not recall where he'd put his cane, which he was unable to get around without, or whether he had worn a coat outside in the cold February air, or whether he had taken his shoes off when he'd climbed back into bed.

That was why Garrick could not recall what clothes he had worn outside to go spew, or whether he had put on shoes or boots, or what pattern the six gold buttons were arranged in though he clearly noted their number.

That was why Violet Adams had not noticed the reek of a decaying dog's carcass, or the fact that the Hamilton house was overrun by canines.

Not one of the three witnesses had actually witnessed anything but these mental paintings, constructed by a shadowy hand that had emphasized some details for the purpose of shock and disgust—the kind of details that would make for damning court testimony—but had omitted other details of a more commonplace nature.

Except for the pattern of gold buttons on the cloak, Matthew thought. That was where the shadowy hand had been . . . the only word Matthew could think of was *precious*.

The hand had made the oversight of not detailing the arrangement of buttons for Buckner or Garrick, but had attempted to make up for it by providing that detail to Violet, who collected buttons and therefore might be more observant as to their pattern.

It occurred to Matthew that the shadowy hand might have placed the poppets under the floor of Rachel's house, and then painted the dream by which Cara Grunewald had seen an item of importance hidden there. He would have liked to have spoken to Madam Grunewald, to learn if, when she'd gone to sleep that night, everything was silent, as if the whole world was feared to breathe.

Matthew turned through the pages to another point he recalled of Garrick's account. It was when he had challenged Garrick concerning the arrangement of the six gold buttons, and had pressed his question to the man's obviously confused agitation.

Garrick's response had been a whispered *It was a silent town. Silent. The whole world, afeared to breathe.*

Matthew realized that what he had heard was Garrick repeating a phrase supplied to him by the owner of the shadowy hand. Garrick had been unable to answer the question, and had unwittingly fixed on that somnambulistic phrase in a moment of great stress because it was one of the clearest things he *did* remember.

And now there was the question of Linch's voice, singing in the dark at the Hamilton house. If Violet had not actually set foot in the house, how could she have heard the ratcatcher singing his grotesque ditty from the back room?

Matthew put aside the documents and finished his cup of tea, staring out the window toward the slaves' quarters and the darkness beyond. He might have decided that Violet had been dreaming the involvement of Linch as well as the rest of it, but his own exploration of Linch's dwelling told Matthew the ratcatcher had concealed the secrets of his identity behind a cleverly constructed front.

Linch was literate and obviously cunning. Was it possible his was the shadowy hand that had guided the three witnesses?

But *why?* And *how?* By what form of sorcery had Linch—or whomever—caused three individuals to see similar apparitions and believe without a doubt they had been viewing reality? It had to be black magic, of a sort. Not the kind popularly associated with Satan, but the kind that evolves from a corrupt and twisted human mentality. But also a mentality that was well ordered and precise, as Linch's must be.

Matthew couldn't understand how Linch, or anyone else, might have done it.

Such a thing—the guiding of three minds toward a common fiction—seemed to be absolutely impossible. Nevertheless, Matthew was certain that was exactly what had occurred.

And what of the question of motive? Why go to such lengths—and such incredible risk—to paint Rachel as being a servant of the Devil? It had to be much more than simply covering the tracks that led away from the murders of Reverend Grove and Daniel Howarth. In fact, those killings seemed to Matthew to have been committed to add weight of suspicion upon Rachel.

So the point was to create a witch, Matthew thought. Rachel was already disliked by many of the citizens before Grove was murdered. Her dark beauty could not have aided her popularity among the other women, and her Portuguese heritage reminded the men of how close the Spanish territory lay to their farmland. She had a tongue, a willful spirit, and courage that ruffled the feathers of the church-guarding hens. Therefore Rachel was from the beginning a perfect candidate.

Matthew chewed on another biscuit. He looked at the stars that glittered above the ocean, and at the candle that burned within the lantern's glass. The light of understanding was what he sought, yet it was a difficult illumination to unveil.

Why create a witch? What possible reason was there for it? To hurt Bidwell? Was all this engineered by the jealous ravens of Charles Town to destroy Fount Royal before it could grow to rivalry?

If that were so, wouldn't Winston have known Rachel was innocent? Or had the Charles Town elders planted another traitor or two within Fount Royal's midst and for the sake of security not informed Winston?

And then there was the question of the mysterious surveyor, and what might lie in the mud at the fount's bottom. It struck him that tomorrow night—very late, after the last lantern had gone out and the final celebrants swept from Van Gundy's tavern—he might try his strength at some underwater swimming.

Though the tea was certainly sturdy enough, Matthew still felt weariness pulling at him. It was his mind that needed rest just as much—if not more so—than his body. He needed to climb into bed, sleep until dawn, and awaken ready for a fresh appraisal of what he suspected, what he knew, and what he had yet to learn.

Matthew relieved himself at the chamberpot, then undressed and lay down upon the bed. He left the lantern burning, as his realization of the shadowy hand's strange and compelling power had made him somewhat less than easy with the dark.

He tossed and turned in the first bout of what would be a nightlong grappling with the hot gearwheels of his brain. At last, though, he relaxed enough to sleep for a time, and except for the occasional barking of a mongrel the town was ruled by silence.

Six

Upon awakening at first light and the rooster chorale, Matthew hurriedly pulled on his breeches and crossed the hall to look in on the magistrate.

Woodward was still sleeping on his stomach, his breathing harsh but steady. Matthew was curious as to the state of the blisters on Woodward's back, and so carefully lifted the gown to view them.

Instantly he wished he had not. The blisters had flattened into ugly ebony bruises surrounded by circles of mottled flesh. Streaks of red ran underneath the skin, attesting to the pressures that the magistrate's body had endured. It occurred to Matthew that this procedure of heat and blister cups was more suited for the torture chamber than the sickbed. He lowered Woodward's gown again, then dipped a cloth into the bowl of water that sat atop the dresser and spent a moment wiping away the green crust that had accumulated around the magistrate's nostrils. The magistrate's face was damp and swollen, the fever radiating from him like the calidity from a bellows-coaxed blaze.

"What . . ." Woodward whispered, his eyelids fluttering. "What is the day?"

"Thursday, sir."

"I must . . . get up . . . and about. Can you help me?"

"I don't think it's wise to get up quite yet, sir. Possibly later in the day."

"Nonsense. I . . . shall miss court . . . if I don't get up." Matthew felt something as keen as an icy dagger pierce his guts. "They . . . already think me . . . lax in my duties," Woodward continued. "They think . . . I am more fond . . . of the rumpot . . . than the gavel. Yes, I saw Mendenhall yesterday. That peacock. Laughing at me . . . behind his hand. What day is it, did you say?"

"Thursday." Matthew's voice was hushed.

"I . . . have a larceny trial to hear. This morning. Where are my boots?"

"Sir?" Matthew said. "I fear . . . that court has been postponed for the day."

Woodward was quiet. Then, "Postponed?"

"Yes, sir. The weather being so bad." Even as he spoke it, he could hear birds singing in the trees around the spring.

"Ahhhhh, the weather," Woodward whispered. His eyes had never fully opened, but remained hidden behind the fever-inflamed lids. "Then I shall stay indoors today," he said. "Shall light a fire . . . drink a hot rum."

"Yes, sir, I think that would be best."

Woodward said something that was more gibberish than language, as if he were losing control over even his speech, but then he spoke clearly enough for Matthew to make out the words, "My back. Pains me."

"It will be well soon. You must lie still and rest."

"A bottle," Woodward said, drowsing off once more. "Will you . . . bring me a bottle?"

"I shall, yes, sir." It seemed a small but helpful untruth. The magistrate's eyelids had ceased their war against gravity and he lay quiet again, his breathing returned to its accustomed rasp like that of a rusted hinge being slowly worked back and forth.

Matthew finished his task of carefully cleaning Woodward's nostrils. When he left the room, he was stricken in the middle of the hallway by what might have been a crushing weight suddenly applied to his shoulders. At the same time, the icy dagger that had entered his entrails seemed to twist toward his heart. He stood short of his own door, one hand clasped to his mouth and above it his eyes wide and brimming with tears.

He was trembling, and wished to make it cease but could not. A sensation of utter powerlessness had come upon him, a sensation of being a leaf stripped from a tree in a high wind and blown through a terrifying altitude of lightning and rain.

He had realized that every day—every *hour*—brought the magistrate closer to death. It was not now a question of whether the magistrate *might* die, but *when*. Matthew was sure this bleeding-and-blistering treatment was not sufficient; indeed, he doubted the ability of Dr. Shields to heal a man who was only half as ill as the magistrate. If Woodward could be gotten to Charles Town, to the attentions of the urban doctors who commanded fully equipped infirmaries and a benefit of medicines, then there was a chance—be it however diminished—that he might be cured of this savage malady.

Yet Matthew knew that no one here would volunteer to carry Woodward the long distance to Charles Town, especially if it meant denigrating the abilities of their own doctor. If he undertook to convey Woodward there, he would lose at the very least two vital days from his investigation, and by the time he returned here Rachel would likely be a black smudge on a charred stake. Woodward might not be his father, it was true, but the man had served in as near that capacity as was humanly possible, saving him from the drear almshouse and setting him on a path of purpose. Did he not, then, owe the magistrate at least *something?*

He might persuade Winston to take Woodward to Charles Town, under threat of revealing the incriminating bucket, but should such a disloyal dog be trusted with a man's life? Winston could as well leave his charge on the side of the road for the animals to eat, and never return.

No, not Winston. But . . . would Nicholas Paine be willing to do the job?

It was a spark, but it might kindle a flame. Matthew pulled himself together, wiped his eyes clear with the back of his hand, and continued into his room. There he shaved, cleaned his teeth, and finished dressing. Downstairs, he found Bidwell clad in a lime-green suit at the bountiful breakfast table, the foxtail of his wig tied with an emerald-hued ribbon.

"Sit down, sit down!" Bidwell offered, his mood jovial because the day promised to be as sunwarmed and beautiful as the one before. "Come have breakfast, but please let us announce a truce on the subject of theories."

"I haven't time for breakfast," Matthew said. "I am on my way to—"

"Oh, of *course* you have time! Come sit down and at least eat a blood sausage!" Bidwell indicated the platter heaped with sausages, but their color was so similar to the ebon collapsed blisters on the magistrate's back that Matthew couldn't have swallowed one if it had been shot into his throat from a pistol. "Or, here, have a pickled melon!"

"No, thank you. I am on my way to see Mr. Paine. Can you tell me where he lives?"

"To see Nicholas? Why?" Bidwell speared a segment of pickled melon with his knife and slid it into his mouth.

"Some business I wish to discuss."

"What business?" Bidwell now was truly suspicious. "Any business you have with him is also business with me."

"All right, then!" Matthew had reached his zenith of frustration. "I wish to ask him to take the magistrate to Charles Town! I want him placed in an infirmary there!"

Bidwell cut a blood sausage in two and chewed thoughtfully on half of it. "So you don't trust Dr. Shields's method of treatment? Is that what you're saying?"

"It is."

"I'll have you know," and here Bidwell aimed his knife at Matthew, "that Ben is just as good a doctor as any of those quacks in Charles Town." He frowned, knowing that hadn't come out as he'd intended. "I mean to say, he's an *able* practitioner. Without his treatment, I'll grant you that the magistrate would have been deceased days ago!"

"It's the days hence I'm concerned about. The magistrate is showing no improvement at all. Just now he was speaking to me in delirium!"

Bidwell pushed his knife into the second half of sausage and guided the greasy black thing into his mouth. "You should by all means be on your way, then," he said as he chewed. "Not to see Nicholas, but to visit the witch."

"Why should I wish to do that?"

"Well, isn't it *obvious?* One day after the decree is delivered, and the magistrate lies at death's door? Your skirt has placed a curse on him, boy!"

"That's nonsense!" Matthew said. "The magistrate's condition has worsened because of this excessive bloodletting!

And also because he was required to sit in that cold gaol for hours when he should have been in bed resting!"

"Oh, ho! His sickness is now *my* fault, is that it? You cast about for blame from everyone except that to whom it rightly belongs! Besides . . . if *you* hadn't pulled your stunt with Seth Hazelton, the witch's case would have been heard in the public meetinghouse—which has a very comfortable hearth, I might add. So if you wish to blame anyone, go speak to a mirror!"

"All I wish to do is find the house of Nicholas Paine," Matthew said, his cheeks flushed and his teeth gritted. "I don't care to argue with you, for that is like trying to out-bray a jackass. Will you direct me to his house, or not?"

Bidwell busied himself by stirring the scrambled eggs on his plate. "I am Nicholas's employer, and I direct his comings and goings," he said. "Nicholas will not go to Charles Town. He is needed here to help with the preparations."

"By God!" Matthew shouted, with such force that Bidwell jumped in his chair. "Would you deny the magistrate a chance at *living?*"

"Calm your vigor," Bidwell warned. A servant girl peeked in from the kitchen and then quickly drew her head back. "I will not be shouted at in my own house. If you wish to spend time hollering down the walls at the gaol, I might arrange it for you."

"Isaac needs better medical attention than what he's getting," Matthew insisted. "He needs to be taken to Charles Town *immediately.* This morning, if possible."

"And I say you're wrong. I'd also say that the trip to Charles Town might well kill the poor wretch. But . . . if you're so willing to gallop in that direction, you should load him on a wagon and take him yourself. I will even make you a loan of a wagon and two horses, if you will sign a note of agreement."

Matthew had stood listening to this with his face downcast, staring at the floor. Now he drew in a deep breath, his cheeks mottled with red, and he walked purposefully to the end of the table. Something in his pace or demeanor alerted Bidwell to danger, because the man started to push his chair back and rise to his feet—but before he could, Matthew had reached Bidwell's side and with one sweep of his arm sent the breakfast platters off the table to the floor in a horrendous echoing crash.

As Bidwell struggled to stand up, his distended belly jiggling and his face dark with rage, Matthew clamped a hand on his right shoulder and bore down with all his weight, at the same time thrusting his face into Bidwell's.

"That man you call a *wretch*," Matthew said, in what was barely more than an ominous whisper, "has served you with all of his heart and soul." Matthew's eyes blazed with a fire that promised to scorch Bidwell to a cinder, and the master of Fount Royal was for the moment transfixed. "That man you call a *wretch* lies dying because he has served you so well. And you, sir, for all of your wealth, fine clothes, and pufferies, are not worthy to clean the magistrate's boots with your dung-dripping tongue."

Bidwell suddenly laughed, which made Matthew draw back.

"Is *that* the worst insult you can construct?" Bidwell lifted his eyebrows. "Boy, you are a rank amateur! On the matter of the boots, however, I'll have you recollect that they are *not* the magistrate's. Indeed, every item of your own clothing was supplied by me. You came to this town nearnaked, the both of you. So remember that I clothed you, fed you, and housed you, while you are flinging insults in my face." He noted the presence of Mrs. Nettles from the corner of his eye, and he turned his head toward her and said, "All's well, Mrs. Nettles. Our young guest has shown his tail, that's—"

The noise of the front door bursting open interrupted him. "What the bloody *hell?*" he said, and now he brushed Matthew's hand aside and hoisted himself to his feet.

Edward Winston came into the dining room. But it was a different Winston than Matthew had seen; this one was breathing hard, as if he'd been running, and his face was drawn and pale in the aftermath of what seemed a terrible shock.

"What's the matter?" Bidwell asked. "You look as if you've—"

"It's Nicholas!" Winston put a hand up to his forehead and appeared to be fighting a faint.

"What about him? Talk *sense,* man!"

"Nicholas . . . is dead," Winston answered. His mouth gaped, trying to form the words. "He has been murdered."

Bidwell staggered as if from a physical blow. But instantly he righted himself and his sense of control came to the forefront. "Not a word about this!" he told Mrs. Nettles. "Not to a single servant, not to *anyone!* Do you hear me?"

"Yes sir, I do." She appeared just as stunned as her master.

"Where is he?" Bidwell asked Winston. "The body, I mean?"

"His house. I just came from there."

"You're *sure* of this?"

Winston managed a grim, sickened half-smile. "Go look for yourself. I promise you won't soon forget such a sight."

"Take me there. Clerk, you come too. Remember, Mrs. Nettles: not a word about this to a single soul!"

During the walk in the early sunlight, Bidwell maintained his pace at a quick clip for a man of his size. Several citizens called a morning greeting, which Bidwell had the presence of mind to answer in as carefree a voice as he could manage. It was only when one farmer tried to stop him to talk about the forthcoming execution that Bidwell snapped at the man like a dog at a worrisome flea. Then Bidwell, Winston, and Matthew reached the whitewashed dwelling of Nicholas Paine, which stood on Harmony Street four houses northward of Winston's shuttered pigsty.

Paine's house was also shuttered. Winston's pace slowed as they neared the closed door, and finally he stopped altogether.

"Come along!" Bidwell said. "What's wrong with you?"

"I . . . would rather stay out here."

"Come along, I said!"

"*No,*" Winston answered defiantly. "By God, I'm not going in there again!"

Bidwell stared at him openmouthed, thunderstruck by this show of impudence. Matthew walked past both men, lifted the door's latch, and pushed the door open. As he did, Winston turned his face and walked away a few strides.

Matthew's first impression was of the copious reek of blood. Secondly, he was aware of the buzzing of flies at work. Thirdly, he saw the body in the slanting rays of vermilion light that entered between the shutter slats.

Fourthly, his gorge rose and if he had eaten any breakfast he surely would have expelled it.

"Oh . . . my Jesus," Bidwell said softly, behind him. Then Bidwell was overcome by the picture. He hurried outside and around the house to vomit up his blood sausage and pickled melon where he would not be seen by any passing citizen.

Matthew stepped across the threshold and closed the

door to block this sight from view of the street. He stood with his back against the door, the fresh sunlight reflecting off the huge pool of blood that surrounded the chair in which Paine was sitting. Indeed, it appeared that every drop had flowed from the man's veins onto the floor, and the corpse had taken on a waxy sallow color. Matthew saw that Paine had been tied in an upright position, ropes binding his arms behind him and his ankles to the chair legs. His shoes and stockings had been removed, and his ankles and feet slashed to sever the arteries. Likewise slashed were the insides of both arms beginning at the elbows. Matthew shifted his position to see that the deep, vein-slicing cuts continued down the forearms to the wrists. He moved a little closer to the corpse, careful that he not step into the crimson sea of gore.

Paine's head was tilted backward. In his mouth was stuffed a yellow cloth, possibly a pair of stockings. His eyes, mercifully, were closed. Around his neck was knotted a noose. On the right side of his forehead there was a vicious black bruise, and blood had flowed from both nostrils down the white of his shirt. A dozen or more flies crawled over the gashes in Paine's corpse and supped from the bloody banquet at his feet.

The door opened and Bidwell dared enter. He held a handkerchief pressed to his mouth, his face gleaming with beads of sweat. Quickly, he closed the door at his back and stood staring numbly at all the carnage.

"Don't be sick again," Matthew warned him. "If you are, I shall be as well and it will not add to this prettiness."

"I'm all right," Bidwell croaked. "I . . . oh dear God . . . oh Christ . . . who could have done such a murder as this?"

"One man's murder is another man's execution. That's what this is. You see the hangman's noose?"

"Yes." Bidwell rapidly averted his eyes. "He . . . he's been drained of blood, hasn't he?"

"It appears his arteries have been opened, yes." Matthew walked around to the back of the body, getting as close as possible without sinking his shoes into the quagmire. He saw a red clump of blood and tissue near the crown of Paine's head. "Whoever killed him beat him first into insensibility with a blunt object," Matthew said. "He was struck on the head by someone standing behind and above him. I think that would be a requirement because otherwise Paine would be a formidable opponent."

"This is the Devil's work!" Bidwell said, his eyes glassy. "Satan himself must have done it!"

"If that is so, Satan has a clinical eye as to the flow of blood. You'll notice that Paine's throat was not slashed, as I understand was done to Reverend Grove and Daniel Howarth. Whoever murdered Paine wished him to bleed to death slowly and in excruciating fashion. I venture Paine might have regained consciousness during the procedure, and then was struck again on the forehead. If he was able to return to sensibility after that, by that time he would have been too weak to struggle."

"Ohhhh . . . my stomach. Dear God . . . I'm going to be sick again."

"Go outside, then," Matthew directed, but Bidwell lowered his head and tried to ward off the flood. Matthew looked around the room, which showed no other signs of tumult, and fixed his attention on a nearby desk. Its chair was missing, and probably was the chair in which Paine had died. On a blotter atop the desk was a sheet of paper with several lines written upon it. An inkpot was open, and on the floor lay the quill pen. A melted stub in a candlestick attested to his source of light. Matthew saw drops and smears of blood on the floor between the desk and where the chair was positioned. He walked to the desk and read the paper.

"*I, Nicholas Paine,*" he recited, "*being of sound mind and of my own free will do hereby on this date of May eighteenth, sixteen hundred and ninety- nine, confess to the murder of* . . ." And here the writing ended in a blotch of ink. "Written sometime after midnight, it seems," Matthew said. "Or close enough that Paine scribed today's date." He saw something else in the room that warranted his attention: on the bedpallet was an open trunk that had been partly packed with clothing. "He was about to leave Fount Royal, I think."

Bidwell stared with dread fascination at the corpse. "What . . . murder was he confessing?"

"An old one, I believe. Paine had some sins in his past. I think one of them caught up with him." Matthew walked to the bed to inspect the contents of the trunk. The clothes had been thrown in, evidence of intention of a hurried departure.

"You don't think the Devil had anything to do with this? Or the witch?"

"I do not. The murders of the reverend and Daniel Howarth were—as I understand their description—meant to kill quickly. This was meant to linger. Also, you'll note there are no claw marks, as in the other killings. This was done with a very sharp blade by a hand that was both vengeful and . . . shall we say . . . experienced in the craft of cutting."

"Oh my God . . . what shall we *do?*" Bidwell lifted a trembling hand to his forehead, his wig tilted to one side on his pate. "If the citizens find out about this . . . that we have another murderer among us . . . we won't have a soul in Fount Royal by the end of the day!"

"That," Matthew said, "is true. It will do no good to advertise this crime. Therefore, don't expose it."

"What do you suggest? Hiding the corpse?"

"The details, I'm sure, are better left to you. But yes, I propose wrapping the corpse in a bedsheet and disposing of it at a later date. The later, of course, the more . . . disagreeable the task will be."

"We cannot just pretend Paine has left Fount Royal! He has friends here! And he at least deserves a Christian burial!"

Matthew aimed his stare at Bidwell. "It is your choice, sir. And your responsibility. After all, you *are* his employer and you direct his comings and goings." He walked around the body again and approached the door, which Bidwell stood against. "If you'll excuse me?"

"Where are you going?" A flare of panic leaped in Bidwell's eyes. "You can't leave!"

"Yes, I can. Don't concern yourself with my speaking about this to anyone, for I vow I shall not." Except for one person, he might have added. The person he now intended to confront.

"Please . . . I need your help."

"By that, if you mean you need a pair of hands to strip the pallet, roll Paine up in the sheet, and scrub the floor with ashes and tar soap . . . then I must deny your noble request. Winston might help you, but I doubt if any amount of coercion or threat will make him cross that threshold again." Matthew smiled tightly. "Therefore . . . speaking to a man who so abhors failure . . . I sincerely hope you are successful at your present challenge. Good day to you, sir." Matthew thought he was going to have to bodily pry Bidwell away from the door, which might have been a labor fit for Hercules, but at last the master of Fount Royal moved aside.

As Matthew started to open the door, Bidwell said in a small voice, "You say . . . ashes and tar soap, then?"

"Some sand, too," Matthew advised. "Isn't that how they scrub blood off the deck of a ship?" Bidwell didn't answer, but stood looking at the corpse with his handkerchief pressed against his mouth.

Outside, the air had never smelled sweeter. Matthew closed the door again, his stomach still roiling and what felt like cold sweat down the valley of his spine. He approached Winston, who stood in the shadow of an oak tree a few yards away.

"How did you come to find him?" Matthew asked.

Winston still appeared dazed, his color not yet returned. "I . . . intended . . . to ask Nicholas to escort me to Charles Town. On the pretense of negotiating for supplies."

"After which, you intended not to return here?"

"Yes. I planned on leaving Nicholas while I went to see Danforth. Then . . . I would simply lose myself in Charles Town."

"Well, half of your intent has come to fruition," Matthew said. "You are indeed lost. Good day." He turned away from Winston and walked back along Harmony Street in the direction they'd come, as he had seen the infirmary in passing.

Presently Matthew stood before the door and pulled the bellcord. There was no response to the first pull, nor to the fifth. Matthew tried the door, found it unlatched from within, and entered the doctor's domain.

The parlor held two canaries in a gilded cage, both singing happily toward the shafts of light that filtered through the white shutters. Matthew saw another door and knocked at it, but again there was no reply. He opened it and ventured into a hallway. Ahead there were three rooms, the doors of the first two ajar. In the initial room stood the barber's chair and leather razor-sharpening strop; in the second room there was a trio of beds, all of which were neatly made and unoccupied. Matthew continued down the hallway to the third door, where he knocked once more.

When there was no response he pushed the door open and faced what appeared to be the doctor's chemistry study, judging from all the arcane bottles and beakers. The chamber held a single shuttered window through which the rays of bright sunlight streamed, though hazed by a pall of blue-tinged smoke.

Benjamin Shields sat in a chair with his back against the wall, holding a small object in a clamplike instrument in his right hand. The object was smoldering, emitting a thin smoke plume. Matthew thought the clouded air smelled of a combination of burnt peanuts and a rope that had been set afire.

The doctor's face was veiled by shadow, though stripes of contaminated light lay across the right shoulder and arm of his tan-colored suit. His spectacles had been placed atop a stack of two leatherbound books that sat on the desk to his right. His legs were crossed at the ankles, in a most casual pose. Matthew didn't speak. He watched as the doctor lifted the burning object—some kind of wrapped tobacco stick, it appeared—to his lips and pulled in a long, slow draw.

"Paine has been found," Matthew said. Just as slowly as he had drawn the smoke, the doctor released it from his mouth. It floated in a shimmering cloud through the angled sunrays.

"I thought your creed was to save lives, not take them," Matthew went on. Again, Shields drew from the stick, held it, then let the smoke dribble out.

Matthew looked around at the vessels of the doctor's craft, the glass bottles and vials and beakers. "Sir," he said, "you are as transparent as these implements. For what earthly reason did you commit such an atrocity?"

Still there was no reply.

Matthew felt as if he'd entered a tiger's den, and the tiger was playing with him like a housecat before it bared its fangs and claws and sprang at him. He kept firmly in mind the position of the door behind him. The savagery of Paine's death was undeniable, and therefore the ability of savagery lay within the man who sat not ten feet away. "May I offer a possible scenario?" Matthew asked, and continued anyway when the doctor refused to speak. "Paine committed some terrible offense against you—or your family—some years ago. Did he murder a family member? A son or a daughter?" A pause did not coax a reaction, except for a further cloud of smoke.

"Evidently he did," Matthew said. "By a gunshot wound, it seems. But Paine was wounded first, therefore I'm inclined to believe his victim was male. Paine must have had cause to find a doctor to treat his injury. Is that how you followed his trail? You searched for the doctor who treated him, and tracked Paine from that point? How many months did it take? Longer than that? *Years?*" Matthew nodded. "Yes, I'd suspect several years. Many seasons of festering hatred. It must have taken that long, for a man of healing to give himself over so completely to the urge for destruction."

Shields regarded the burning tip of his tobacco stick.

"You learned the circumstances of the death of Paine's wife," Matthew said. "But Paine, in wishing to put the past behind him, had never told anyone in Fount Royal that he'd ever been married. He must have been astounded when he realized you knew his history . . . and, Paine being an intelligent man, he also realized *why* you knew. So you went to his house sometime around midnight, is that correct? I presume you had all the ropes and blades you needed in your bag, but you probably left that outside. Did you offer to keep your silence if Paine would write a confession and immediately leave Fount Royal?"

Smoke drifted slowly through the light.

"Paine never dreamt you'd gone there to kill him. He assumed you were interested in unmasking him before Bidwell and the town, and that the confession was the whole point of it. So you let Paine sit down and begin writing, and you took the opportunity to bash him in the head with a blunt instrument. Was it something you had hidden on you or something already there?"

No response was forthcoming.

"And then came the moment you relished," Matthew said. "You *must* have relished it, to have performed it so artfully. Did you taunt him as you opened his veins? His mouth was gagged, his head near cracked, and his blood running out in streams. He must have been too weak to overturn the chair, but what would it have mattered? He probably *did* hear you taunting him as he died, though. Does that knowledge give you a feeling of great joy, sir?" Matthew raised his eyebrows. "Is this one of the happiest mornings of your life, now that the man you've sought so long and steadfastly is a blood-drained husk?"

Shields took another draw from the stick, released the smoke, and then leaned forward. Light touched his moist, perspiring face, and revealed the dark violet hollows of near-madness beneath his eyes.

"Young man," the doctor said calmly, his voice thick with constrained emotion, "I should like to tell you . . . that these baseless accusations are *extremely* ill advised. My attention should rightly be directed to the magistrate's health . . . rather than any other mental pressure. Therefore . . . if you desire the magistrate to live beyond this evening . . . what you ought to do is . . ." He paused to suck once more from the dwindling stick. ". . . is make absolutely certain I am free to treat him." He leaned back again, and the shadows claimed his countenance. "But you have already decided that, have you not? Otherwise you never would have come here alone."

Matthew watched the smoke move slowly across the room. "Yes," he said, feeling that his soul had less foundation than those miniature clouds. "I have already decided."

"An excellent . . . *splendid* decision. How goes his health this morning?"

"Badly." Matthew stared at the floor. "He's been delirious."

"Well . . . that may wax and wane. The fever, you see. I do believe the blistering will show a benefit, though. I intend to apply a colonic today, and that should aid in his recovery."

"His *recovery?*" Matthew had spoken it with a shade of mockery. "Do you honestly believe he's going to recover?"

"I honestly believe he has a chance," came the reply. "A small chance, it is true . . . but I have seen patients come back from such an adverse condition. So . . . the best we can do is continue treatment and pray that Isaac will respond."

It was insane, Matthew thought. Here he was, talking about the healing arts with a half-crazed butcher! And talking about *prayer*, to add another level of lunacy! But what choice did he have? Matthew remembered what Bidwell had said, and it had rung very true though he'd made a show of temper over it: *The trip to Charles Town might well kill the poor wretch.*

Springtime or not, the open air and the swamp humours it carried were dangerous to Woodward's remaining strength. The wagon trip over that road would be torture to him, no matter how firmly he was swaddled. In spite of how much he wished to the contrary, Matthew sincerely doubted that the magistrate would reach Charles Town alive.

So he was forced to trust this man. This doctor. This murderer. He had noted a mortar and pestle on the shelf, and he said, "Can't you mix some medicine for him? Something that would break his fever?"

"Fever does not respond to medicine as much as it responds to the movement of blood," Shields said. "And as a matter of record, the supply of medicine through Charles Town has become so pinched as to be withered. But I do have some vinegar, liverwort, and limonum. I could mix that with a cup of rum and opium and have him drink it . . . say . . . thrice daily. It might heat the blood enough to destroy the afflictions."

"At this point, anything is worth trying . . . as long as it doesn't poison him."

"I do know my chemicals, young man. You may rest assured of that."

"I won't rest," Matthew said. "And I am not assured."

"As you please." Shields continued smoking what was now only a stub. The blue clouds swirled around his face, obscuring it from scrutiny even the more.

Matthew released a long, heavy sigh. "I don't doubt you had sufficient reason to kill Paine, but you certainly seemed to enjoy the process. The hangman's noose was a bit much, don't you think?"

Shields said, "Our discussion of Isaac's treatment has ended. You may go."

"Yes, I'll go. But all that you told me of leaving Boston because your practise was suffering . . . of wanting to aid in the construction of a settlement and having your name forever emblazoned upon this infirmary . . . those were all lies, weren't they?" Matthew waited, but he knew there would be no reply. "The one true accomplishment you sought was the death of Nicholas Paine." This had not been phrased as a question, because Matthew needed no answer to what he knew to be fact.

"You will pardon me," Shields said quietly, "if I do not rise to show you out."

There was nothing more to be said, and certainly nothing more to be gained. Matthew retreated from the doctor's study, closed the door, and walked back along the hallway in a mind-numbed daze. The burning-rope smell of that tobacco stick had leeched into his nostrils. When he got outside, the first thing he did was lift his face to the sunlight and draw in a great draught of air. Then he trudged the distance to Bidwell's mansion, his head yet clouded on this clear and perfect day.

SEVEN

There was a knock at Matthew's door. "Young sir?" asked Mrs. Nettles. "Mr. Vaughan has come for ye."

"Mr. Vaughan?" He got up from his chair, where he'd been drowsing in the twilight of early evening, and opened the door. "What does he want?"

Mrs. Nettles pursed her lips, as if in a silent scold for his deficient memory. "He says he's come to escort you to his home for dinner, and that it shall be a'table at six o'clock."

"Oh, I did forget! What time is it now?"

"Near ha' past five, by the mantel clock."

"If there was ever an evening I didn't care to go out to dinner, this is it." Matthew said, rubbing his bleary eyes.

"That may be so," Mrs. Nettles said curtly, "but as much as I do nae care for Lucretia Vaughan, I am also sure some effort has been made to show you hospitality. Ye ought nae to disappoint 'em."

Matthew nodded, though he couldn't erase his frown. "Yes, you're right. Very well, then: please tell Mr. Vaughan I'll be downstairs in a few minutes."

"I shall. Oh . . . have ye seen Mr. Bidwell since mornin'?"

"No, I haven't."

"He always tells me if he's gonna attend dinner. I'm driftin' without a sea-chain, nae knowin' what he cares ta do."

"Mr. Bidwell . . . likely is wrapped up in the sorry engagement involving Mr. Paine," Matthew said. "You of all people must know how buried he becomes in his work."

"Oh, yes sir, 'tis true! But y'know, we're havin' a festival of sorts here tomorra eve. Mr. Bidwell's hostin' a dinner for some of the maskers. Even though we've suffered such a tragedy, I do need ta know what he desires a'table."

"I'm sure he'll be around sooner or later tonight."

"Mayhaps. I've told no one about the murder, sir. Just as he wished. But do you have any idea who mi' ha' done it?"

"*Not* Rachel, the Devil, or any imagined demon, if that's what you're asking. This was a man's work." He dared go no further. "Excuse me, I'd best get ready."

"Yes sir, I'll tell Mr. Vaughan."

As he hurriedly scraped a razor across the day's growth and then washed his face, Matthew steeled himself for companionship though he fervently wished only to be left alone. He had spent the day attending to the magistrate, and observing Dr. Shields as the excruciating colonic was applied. A fresh plaster had been pressed to the pine oil dressing on Woodward's chest, and the pine oil liniment had also been rubbed around his nostrils. The doctor on his first visit this morning had brought a murky amber liquid that the magistrate swallowed with great difficulty, and had administered a second dose of the potion around four o'clock. Matthew could not help but watch Dr. Shields's hands and envision their grisly work of the previous midnight.

If Matthew had been expecting rapid results, he was disappointed; for most of the day Woodward had remained in a stupor, his fever merciless; but at least the magistrate once asked Matthew if preparations for Madam Howarth's execution were proceeding, therefore he seemed to have returned from his bout with delirium.

Matthew put on a fresh shirt and buttoned it up to the neck, then left his room and went downstairs. Waiting for him was a slim, small-statured man in a gray suit, white stockings, and polished square-toed black shoes. On his head was a brown tricorn and he was holding a lantern that bore double candles. It took only a few seconds of observation for Matthew to detect the darned patches at the man's knees and the fact that his suit jacket was perhaps two sizes too large, indicating either a borrow or a barter.

"Ah, Mr. Corbett!" The man exhibited a smile that was strong enough, but something about his deep-set pale blue eyes, in a face that had a rather gaunt and skeletal appearance, suggested a watery constitution. "I am Stewart Vaughan, sir. Pleased to make your acquaintance."

Matthew shook his hand, meeting a grip that had little substance. "Good evening to you, sir. And I thank you for your invitation to dinner."

"Our gratitude that you might grace us. The ladies are waiting. Shall we go?"

Matthew followed the man, who walked with a pronounced bowlegged gait. Over the roofs of Fount Royal the sky was crimson to the west and violet to the east, the first stars gleaming in the ruddy orange directly above. The breeze was soft and warm, and crickets chirruped in the grass around the spring.

"A lovely evening, is it not?" Vaughan asked as they left Peace Street and walked along Harmony. "I feared we would all drown ere we saw Good Sol again."

"Yes, it *was* a difficult time. Thanks be to God the clouds have passed for a time."

"Thanks be to God that the witch will soon be dead! She had a hand in that deluge, I'll swear to it!"

Matthew answered with a grunt. He realized it was going to be a very long evening, and he was still measuring that phrase Vaughan had used: *The ladies are waiting.*

They passed Van Gundy's tavern, which—from the racket of its customers and the caterwauls of two aspiring musicians playing a gittern and a drum—seemed to be a place of high and potent spirits. Matthew thought that Vaughan aimed a wistful eye at the establishment as they continued on. In another moment they walked by the house of the recently deceased Nicholas Paine, and Matthew noted with interest that candlelight could be seen through the shutter slats. He envisioned Bidwell on his knees, scrubbing blood off the floor with tar soap, ashes, and sand, and cursing cruel Fate while Paine's corpse was wrapped up in a sheet and stowed beneath the pallet for future disposal. He was sure Winston had invented some reason to tell Bidwell why he'd gone to see Paine so early in the morning. If nothing else, Winston was an agile liar.

"There is the house," Vaughan said, indicating a well-lit dwelling two houses northward and across Harmony Street from Paine's. Matthew had remembered Paine's admission of having carnal relations with Lucretia Vaughan, and he could see her approaching his house with a basket of hot buns and he returning the favor by knocking at her entry with a pistol in his pocket.

Matthew saw a small sign above the door that read *Breads & Pies Baked Daily*. Then Vaughan opened the door with the announcement, "I've brought our guest!" and Matthew entered the abode.

The house smelled absolutely delicious. A fragrant bread or pie had only just been baked, but also in the house were the commingled aromas of past delights. Matthew saw that the lady Vaughan possessed an extremely neat and painstaking hand, as the floor had been swept spotless, the whitewashed walls free of any trace of hearth soot or smoke, and even the wood surfaces of the furniture smoothed and polished. Around the large stone fireplace stood a well-organized battery of skillets and cooking pots, the genteel fire burning under a pot on a jackhook. Even the cooking implements appeared to have been scrubbed clean. Adding to the pleasant, welcoming air of the house were several sprays of wildflowers set about in hammered-tin containers, and the remarkable extravagance of perhaps a dozen candles casting golden light. The supper table, which was covered with a snowy linen cloth and displayed four places readied, stood in the corner of the room opposite the hearth.

The hostess made her entrance from another door at the rear of the house, where the bedchamber likely was. "Mr. Corbett!" she said, showing a toothy smile that might have shamed the sun's glow. "How *wonderful* to have you in our home!"

"Thank you. As I told your husband, I appreciate the invitation."

"Oh, our pleasure, I assure you!" Lucretia Vaughan, in this wealth of candlelight, was indeed a handsome woman, her fine figure clad in a rose-hued gown with a lace-trimmed bodice, her light brown curls showing copper and aureate glints. Matthew could readily see how Paine could be spelled by her; to be fixed in the sights of her penetrating blue eyes was akin to the application of heat. Indeed, Matthew felt a sensation of melting before her leonine presence.

As perhaps she sensed this, she seemed to increase the power of her personality. She approached him nearer, her eyes locked with his. He caught the scent of a peach-inspired perfume. "I *know* you have many other offers to attend dinner," she said. "It is not often that we find such a sophisticated gentleman in our midst. *Stewart, leave your jacket on.* We are so very pleased you have chosen to grace our humble table with your presence." Her instruction to her husband had been like the swift stroke of a razor, not even requiring her to glance at him. Matthew was aware of Stewart standing to his left, shrugging again into the garment the man had nearly gotten out of. "Your hat is removed," Lucretia said. Stewart's hand instantly obeyed, revealing a thin thatch of blond hair.

"'Sophistication is what we yearn for in this rustic town." It seemed to Matthew that the woman had come even closer to him, though he hadn't seen her move. "I note you have buttoned your shirt to your throat. Is that the current fashion in Charles Town?"

"'Uh . . . no, I simply did it on the moment."

"Ah!" she said brightly. "Well, I'm sure it shall be fashionable in the *future*." She turned her head toward the rear doorway. "Cherise? Dearest? Our guest wishes to meet you!"

There was no response. Lucretia's smile appeared a shade frayed. Her voice rose to a higher, sharper pitch: "Cherise? You are *expected!*"

"Obviously," Stewart ventured meekly, "she's not yet ready."

The wife speared her husband with a single glance. "I shall help her *prepare*. If you'll pardon me, Mr. Corbett? Stewart, offer our guest some wine." She was through the door and gone before she'd completed her last direction.

"Wine," Stewart said. "Yes, wine! Would you care for a

taste, Mr. Corbett?" He proceeded to a round table on which was placed a rather ostentatious green glass decanter and three cuplike glasses of the same *emeraude*. Before Matthew had answered "Yes," the decanter was unstoppered and the pouring begun. Stewart passed a glass to Matthew and set in on his own with the gusto of a salt-throated sailor.

Matthew had no sooner taken his first sip of what was rather a bitter vintage when from the rear doorway two feminine voices, determined to overpower each other, rose in volume, tangled like the shrieks of harpies, and then fell to abrupt silence as if those winged horrors had dashed themselves upon jagged rocks.

Stewart cleared his throat. "I myself have never been whipped," he said. "I imagine it is a less than pleasant experience?"

"Less than pleasant," Matthew agreed, glancing now and again at the doorway as at a portal beyond which an infernal struggle raged. "But more than instructive."

"Oh yes! I would think so! You committed an injury to the blacksmith, I understand? Well, I'm sure you must have had a reason. Did you see him treating a horse with less than affection?"

"Um . . ." Matthew took a sturdier drink of wine. "No, I believe Mr. Hazelton has a strong affection for horses. It was . . . let us say . . . a matter best kept stabled."

"Yes, of course! I've no wish to pry." Stewart drank again, and after a pause of three or four interminable seconds he laughed. "Oh! *Stabled!* I get your jest!"

Lucretia emerged once more, her radiance undiminished by the wrangling that had just occurred. "My apologies," she said, still smiling. "Cherise is . . . having some difficulty with her hair. She wishes to make a good presentation, you see. She is a perfectionist, and so magnifies even small blemishes."

"Her mother's daughter," Stewart muttered, before he slid his lips into the glass.

"But what would this world be without its perfectionists?" Lucretia was addressing Matthew, and deigned not to respond to her husband's comment. "I shall tell you: it would be all dust, dirt, and utter confusion. Isn't that right, Mr. Corbett?"

"I'm sure it would be disastrous," Matthew replied, and this was enough to put a religious shine in the woman's eyes.

She made a sweeping gesture toward the table. "As Cherise may be some moments yet, we should adjourn to dinner," she announced. "Mr. Corbett, if you will sit at the place that has a pewter plate?"

There was indeed a pewter plate on the table, one of the few that Matthew had ever seen. The other plates were of the common wooden variety, which indicated to Matthew the importance the Vaughans gave to his visit. Indeed, he felt as if they must consider him royalty. He sat in the appointed chair, with Stewart seated to his left. Lucretia quickly donned an apron and went about spooning and ladling food from the cooking pots into white clay serving bowls. Presently the bowls were arranged on the table, containing green stringbeans with hogsfat, chicken stew with boiled potatoes and bacon, corncakes baked in cream, and stewed tomatoes. Along with a golden loaf of fresh fennel-seed bread, it was truly a king's feast. Matthew's glass was topped with wine, after which Lucretia took off her apron and seated herself at the head of the table, facing their guest, where by all rights of marriage and household the husband ought to be.

"I shall lead us in our thanks," Lucretia said, another affront to the duties of her husband. Matthew closed his eyes and bowed his head. The woman gave a prayer of thanksgiving that included Matthew's name and mentioned her hope that the wretched soul of Rachel Howarth find an angry God standing ready to smite her spectral skull from her shoulders after the execution stake had done its work. Then the fervent "Amen" was spoken and Matthew opened his eyes to find Cherise Vaughan standing beside him.

"Here is our lovely daughter!" Lucretia exclaimed. "Cherise, take your place."

The girl, in a white linen gown with a lace bodice and sleeves, continued to stand where she was and stare down at Matthew. She was indeed an attractive girl, perhaps sixteen or seventeen, her waves of blonde hair held fixed by a series of small wooden combs. Matthew imagined she must closely resemble her mother at that age, though her chin was longer and somewhat more square and her eyes almost as pale blue as her father's. In these eyes, however, there was no suggestion of a watery constitution; there was instead a haughty chill that Matthew instantly dropped his gaze from, lest he shiver from a December wind on this May night.

"Cherise?" Lucretia repeated, gently but firmly. "Take. Your. Place. Please."

The girl sat down—slowly, at her own command—on Matthew's right. She wasted no time in reaching out and spooning chicken stew onto her plate.

"Are you not even going to say hello to Mr. Corbett?"

"Hello," she answered, pushing the first bite of food into her cupid's-bow mouth.

"Cherise helped prepare the stew," Lucretia said. "She has been desirous to make certain it was to your liking."

"I'm sure it's excellent," Matthew answered. He spooned some of the stew onto his plate and found it as good as it appeared, then he tore off a hunk of bread and sopped it in the thick, delicious liquid.

"Mr. Corbett is a fascinating young man." This was spoken to Cherise, though Lucretia continued to gaze upon him. "Not only is he a sophisticated gentleman and a judicial apprentice from Charles Town, but he fought off that mob of killers and thieves who attacked the magistrate. Armed only with a rapier, I understand?"

Matthew accepted a helping of stewed tomatoes. He could feel three pairs of eyes upon him. Now was the moment to explain that the 'mob' consisted of one ruffian, an old crone, and an infirm geezer . . . but instead his mouth opened and what came out was, "No . . . I . . . had not even a rapier. Would you pass the corncakes, please?"

"My Lord, what a night that must have been!" Stewart was profoundly impressed. "Did you not have a weapon at *all?*"

"I . . . uh . . . used a boot to good advantage. This is an absolutely *wonderful* stew! Mr. Bidwell's cook ought to have this recipe."

"Well, our Cherise is a wonderful cook herself," Lucretia assured him. "I am currently teaching her the secrets of successful pie baking. Not an easy subject to command, I must say."

"'I'm sure it's not." Matthew offered a smile to the girl, but she was having none of it. She simply ate her food and stared straight ahead with no trace of expression except, perhaps, absolute boredom.

"And now . . . about the treasure chest full of gold coins you found." Lucretia laid her spoon and knife delicately across her plate. "You had it sent back to Charles Town, I understand?"

Here he had to draw the line. "I fear there was no treasure chest. Only a single coin."

"Yes, yes . . . of course. Only a single coin. Very well, then, I can see you are a canny guardian of information. But what can you tell us of the witch? Does she weep and wail at the prospect of burning?"

The stew he was about to swallow had suddenly sprouted thorns and lodged in his throat. "Mrs. Vaughan," he said, as politely as possible, "if you don't mind . . . I would prefer not to talk about Rachel Howarth."

Suddenly Cherise looked at him and grinned, her blue eyes gleaming. "Oh, *that* is a subject I find of interest!" Her voice was pleasingly melodic, but there was a wickedly sharp edge to it as well. "*Do* tell us about the witch, sir! Is it true she shits toadfrogs?"

"*Cherise!*" Lucretia had hissed the name, her teeth gritted and her eyes wide with alarm. Instantly her composure altered with the speed of a chameleon's color change; her smile returned, though fractured, and she looked down the table at Matthew. "Our daughter has . . . an earthy sense of humor, Mr. Corbett. You know, it is said that some of the finest, most gracious ladies have earthy senses of humor. One must not be *too* stiff and rigid in these strange times, must one?"

"Stiff and rigid," the girl said, as she pushed a tomato into her mouth and gave a gurgling little laugh. Matthew saw that Lucretia had chosen to continue eating, but red whorls had risen in her cheeks. Stewart drank down his glass of wine and reached for the decanter.

No one spoke for a time. It was then that Matthew was aware of a faint humming sound, but he couldn't place where it was coming from. "I might tell you, as a point of information," he said, to break the wintry silence, "that I am not yet a judicial apprentice. I am a magistrate's clerk, that's all."

"Ah, but you *shall* be a judicial apprentice in the near future, will you not?" Lucretia asked, beaming again. "You are young, you have a fine mind and a desire to serve. Why should you not enter the legal profession?"

"Well . . . I probably shall, at some point. But I do need much more education and experience."

"A *humble* soul!" She spoke it as if she had found the Grail itself. "Do you hear that, Cherise? The young man stands on the precipice of such political power and wealth, and he remains humble!"

"The problem with standing on a precipice," he said, "is that one might fall from a great height."

"And a *wit* as well!" Lucretia seemed near swooning with delight. "You know how wit charms you, Cherise!"

Cherise stared again into Matthew's eyes. "I desire to know more about the witch. I have heard tell she took the cock of a black goat into her mouth and sucked on it."

"Umph!" A rivulet of wine had streamed down Stewart's chin and marred his gray jacket. He had paled as his wife had reddened.

Lucretia was about to either hiss or shriek, but before she could, Matthew met the girl's stare with equal force and said calmly, "You have heard a lie, and whoever told you such a thing is not only a liar but a soul in need of a mouth-soaping."

"Billy Reed told me such a thing. Shall I find him tomorrow and tell him you're going to soap his mouth?"

"That thug's name shall not be uttered in this *house!*" The veins were standing out in Lucretia's neck. "I forbid it!"

"I *will* find Billy Reed tomorrow," Cherise went on, defiantly. "Where shall I tell him you will meet him with your soap?"

"I beg your pardon, Mr. Corbett! I beg a *thousand* pardons!" In her agitation, the woman had spilled a spoonful of corncake and cream on the front of her gown, and now she was blotting the stain with a portion of the tablecloth. "That thug is James Reed's miscreant son! He's near an imbecile, he has the ambition of a sloth . . . *and* he has wicked designs on my daughter!"

Cherise grinned—or, rather, leered—into Matthew's face. "Billy is teaching me how to milk. In the afternoons, at their barn, he shows me how to hold the member. How to slide my hand up and down . . . up and down . . . up and down . . ." She displayed the motion for him, much to his discomfort and her mother's choked gasp. "Until the cream spurts forth. And a wonderful hot cream it is, too."

Matthew didn't respond. It did occur to him that— absolutely, positively—he'd lately been hiding in the wrong barn.

"I think," Stewart said, rising unsteadily to his feet, "that the rum bottle should be unstoppered."

"For God's sake, stay away from that rum!" Lucretia hollered, oblivious now to their honored guest. "That's the cause of all our troubles! That, and your poor excuse for a carpentry shop!"

Matthew's glance at Cherise showed him she was eating her dinner with a smirk of satisfaction upon her face, which was now not nearly so lovely. He put his own spoon and knife down, his appetite having fled. Stewart was fumbling in a cupboard and Lucretia was attacking her food with a vengeance, her eyes dazed and her face as red as the stewed tomatoes. In the silence that fell, Matthew heard the strange humming sound again. He looked up.

And received a jolt.

On the ceiling directly above the table was a wasp's nest the size of Mr. Green's fist. The thing was black with wasps, all crowded together, their wings folded back along their stingers. As Matthew watched, unbelieving, he saw a minor disturbance ripple across the insects and several of them commenced that angry humming noise.

"Uh . . . Mrs. Vaughan," he said thickly. "You have . . ." He pointed upward.

"Yes, wasps. What of it?" Her manners—along with her composure, her family, and the evening—had greatly deteriorated.

Matthew realized why the nest must be there. He'd heard of such a thing, but he'd never before seen it. As he understood, a potion could be bought or made that, once applied to an indoor ceiling, enraptured wasps to build their nests on the spot.

"Insect control, I assume?" he asked.

"Of course," Lucretia said, as if any fool on earth knew that. "Wasps are jealous creatures. We suffer no mosquitoes in this house."

"None that will bite *her*, anyway," Stewart added, and then he continued suckling from the bottle.

This evening, Matthew thought, might have been termed a farce had there not been such obvious suffering from all persons involved. The mother ate her dinner as if in a stunned trance, while the daughter now set about consuming her food more with fingers than proper utensils, succeeding in smearing her mouth and chin with gleaming hogsfat. Matthew finished his wine and a last bite of the excellent stew, and then he thought he should make his exit before the girl decided he might look more appealing crowned with a serving-bowl.

"I . . . uh . . . presume I'd best go," he said. Lucretia spoke not a word, as if her inner fire had been swamped by her daughter's wanton behavior. Matthew pushed his chair back and stood up. "I wish to thank you for the dinner and the wine. Uh . . . no need to walk me back to the mansion, Mr. Vaughan."

"I wasn't plannin' on it," the man said, clutching the rum bottle to his chest.

"Mrs. Vaughan? May I . . . uh . . . take some of that delicious bread with me?"

"All you wish," she murmured, staring into space. "The rest of it, if you like."

Matthew accepted what was perhaps half a loaf. "My appreciation."

Lucretia looked up at him. Her vision cleared, as she seemed to realize that he actually was leaving. A weak smile flickered across her mouth. "Oh . . . Mr. Corbett . . . where are my manners? I thought . . . hoped . . . that after dinner . . . we might all play at *lanctie loo*."

"I fear I am without talent at card games."

"But . . . there are so *many* things I wished to converse with you about. The magistrate's condition being one. The state of affairs in Charles Town. The gardens . . . and the balls."

"I'm sorry," Matthew said. "I don't have much experience with either gardens or balls. As to the state of affairs in Charles Town, I would call them . . . somewhat less interesting than those in Fount Royal. The magistrate is still very ill, but Dr. Shields is administering a new medicine he's concocted."

"You know, of course," she said grimly, "that the witch has cursed your magistrate. For the guilty decree. I doubt he shall survive with such a curse laid on him."

Matthew felt his face tighten. "I believe differently, madam."

"Oh . . . I . . . I am being so *insensitive*. I am only repeating what I overhead Preacher Jerusalem saying this afternoon. Please forgive me, it's just that—"

"That she has a knife for a tongue," Cherise interrupted, still eating with graceless fingers. "She only apologizes when it cuts herself."

Lucretia leaned her head toward her daughter, much in the manner of a snake preparing to strike. "You may leave the table and our presence," she said coldly. "Inasmuch as you have disgraced yourself and all of us, I do hope you are happy."

"I *am* happy. I am also still hungry." She refused to budge from her place. "You know that you were brought here to *save* me, do you not?" A quick glance was darted at Matthew, as she licked her greasy fingers. "To rescue me from Fount Royal and the witless rustics my mother despises? Oh, if you are so sophisticated you must have known that already!"

"Stop her, Stewart!" Lucretia implored, her voice rising. "Make her hush!"

The man, however, tilted the bottle to his mouth and then began peeling off his suit jacket.

"Yes, it's true," Cherise said. "My mother sells them breads and pies and wishes them to choke on the crumbs. You should hear her talk about them behind their backs!"

Matthew stared down into the girl's face. *Her mother's daughter,* Stewart had said. Matthew might have recognized the streak of viciousness. The pity, he mused, was that Cherise Vaughan seemed to be highly intelligent. She had recognized, for instance, that speaking of Rachel Howarth had caused him great discomfort of a personal nature.

"I will show myself out," Matthew said to Mrs. Vaughan.

"Again, thank you for the dinner." He started toward the door, carrying the half-loaf of fennel-seed bread with him.

"Mr. Corbett? Wait, please!" Lucretia stood up, a large cream stain on the front of her gown. Again she appeared dazed, as if these verbal encounters with her daughter sapped the very life from her. "Please . . . I have a question for you."

"Yes?"

"The witch's hair," she said. "What is to become of it?"

"Her . . . *hair?* I'm sorry, I don't understand your meaning."

"The witch has such . . . shall I say . . . *attractive* hair. One might say *beautiful*, even. It is a sadness that such thick and lovely hair should be burnt up." Matthew could not have replied even if he'd wished to, so stunned was he by this direction of thinking.

But the woman continued on. "If the witch's hair should be washed . . . and then shorn off, on the morning of her execution . . . there are *many*, I would venture—who might pay for a lock of it. Think of it: the witch's hair advertised and sold as a charm of good fortune." Her countenance seemed to brighten at the very idea of it. "It might be heralded as firm evidence of God's destruction of Evil. You see my meaning now?"

Still Matthew's tongue was frozen solid.

"Yes, and I would grant you a portion of the earnings as well," she said, mistaking his amazed expression as approval. "But I think it best if you washed and cut the hair yourself, on some pretext or another, as we wouldn't wish too many fingers in our pie."

He just stood there, feeling sick. "Well?" she urged. "Can we consider ourselves in company?"

Somehow, he turned from her and got out the door. As he walked away along Harmony Street, a cold sheen of moisture on his face, he heard the woman calling him from her doorway: "Mr. Corbett? Mr. Corbett?"

And louder and more shrill: *"Mr. Corbett?"*

EİGHT

Past the house of deceased Nicholas Paine he went, past Van Gundy's tavern where the revelers made merry, past Dr. Shields's infirmary and the squalid house of Edward Winston. Matthew walked on, his head bowed and the half-loaf of fennel-seed bread in his hand, the night sky above him a field of stars and, in his mind, darkness heavy and unyielding.

He turned left onto Truth Street. Further along, the blackened ruins of Johnstone's schoolhouse secured his attention. It was a testament to the power of the infernal fire as well as a testament to the power of infernal men. He recalled how Johnstone had raged in helpless anguish that night, as the flames had burned unchecked. The schoolmaster might be bizarre—with his white face powder and his deformed knee—but it was a surety that the man had felt his teaching was a vital calling, and that the loss of the schoolhouse was a terrible tragedy. Matthew might have had his suspicions about Johnstone, but the fact that the man believed Rachel not to be a witch—and, indeed, that the entire assertion of witchcraft was built on shaky ground—gave Matthew hope for the future of education.

He went on, nearer to where he had known he was going.

And there the gaolhouse stood. He didn't hesitate, but quietly entered the darkened structure.

Though he endeavored to be quiet, his opening of the door nevertheless startled Rachel. He heard her move on her pallet of straw, as if drawing herself more tightly into a posture of self-protection. It occurred to him that, with the door still unchained, anyone might enter to taunt and jeer at her, though most persons would certainly be afeared to do so. One who would not be afeared, however, would be Preacher Jerusalem, and he imagined the snake must have made an appearance or two when no other witnesses were present.

"Rachel, it's me," he said. Before she could answer or protest his presence, he said, "I know you've wished me not to come, and I do respect your wishes . . . but I wanted to tell you I am still working on your . . . um . . . your situation. I can't yet tell you what I've found, but I believe I have made some progress." He approached her cell a few more paces before he stopped again. "That is not to say I've come to any kind of solution, or have proof of such, but I wished you to know I have you always in mind and that I won't give up. Oh . . . and I've also brought you some very excellent fennel-seed bread."

Matthew went the rest of the way and pushed the bread through the bars. In the absolute dark, he was aware only of her vague shape coming to meet him, like a figure just glimpsed in some partially remembered dream.

Without a word, Rachel took the bread. Then her other hand grasped Matthew's and she clutched it firmly against her cheek. He felt the warm wetness of tears. She made a choked sound, as if she were trying mightily to restrain a sob.

He didn't know what to say. But at this revelation of unexpected emotion his heart bled and his own eyes became damp.

"I . . . shall keep working," Matthew promised, his voice husky. "Day and night. If an answer is to be found . . . I swear I will find it."

Her response was to press her lips against the back of his hand, and then she held it once more to her tear-stained cheek. They stood in that posture. Rachel clutched to him as if she wanted nothing else in the world at that moment but the warmth—the care—of another human being. He wished to take his other hand and touch her face, but instead he curled his fingers around one of the iron bars between them.

"Thank you," she whispered. And then, perhaps overcoming with an effort of will her momentary weakness, she let go of his hand and took the bread with her back to her place in the straw.

To stay longer would be hurtful both to himself and her, for in his case it would make leaving all the more painful. He had wished her to know she was not forgotten, and that had certainly been accomplished. So he took his leave and presently was walking westward along Truth Street, his face downcast and his brow freighted with thought.

Love.

It came to him not as a stunning blow, but as a soft shadow.

Love. What was it, really? The desire to possess someone, or the desire to free them?

Matthew didn't believe he had ever been in love before. In fact, he knew he had not been. Therefore, since he had no experience, he was at a loss to clearly examine the emotion within him. It was an emotion, perhaps, that defied examination and could not be shaped to fit into any foursquare box of reason. Because of that, there was something frightening about it . . . something wild and uncontrollable, something that would not be constrained by logic.

He felt, though, that if love was the desire to possess someone, it was in reality the poor substance of self-love. It seemed to him that a greater, truer love was the desire to open a cage—be it made of iron bars or the bones of tormented injustice—and set the nightbird free.

He wasn't sure what he was thinking, or why he was thinking it. On the subjects of the Latin and French languages, English history, and legal precedents he was comfortable with his accumulated knowledge, but on this strange subject of love he was a total imbecile. And, he was sure the magistrate would say, also a misguided youth in danger of God's displeasure.

Matthew was here. So was Rachel. Satan had made a recent fictitious appearance and certainly dwelled in both the lust of Exodus Jerusalem and the depraved soul of the man who worked the poppet strings.

But where was God, in all this?

If God intended to show displeasure, it seemed to Matthew that He ought to take a little responsibility first.

Matthew was aware that these thoughts might spear his head with lightning on a cloudless night, but the paradox of Man was the fact that one might have been made in the image of God, yet it was often the most devilish of ideas that gave action and purpose to the human breed.

He returned to Bidwell's mansion, where he learned from Mrs. Nettles that the master had not yet returned from his present task. However, Dr. Shields had just left after giving Woodward a third dose of the medicine, and currently the magistrate was soundly asleep. Matthew chose a book from the library—the tome on English plays and dramatists, so that he might better acquaint himself with the craft of the maskers—and went upstairs. After looking in on Woodward to verify that he was indeed sleeping but breathing regularly, Matthew then retired to his bedchamber to rest, read, think, and await the passage of time.

In spite of what had been a very trying day, and the fact that the image of Paine's butchered corpse was still gruesomely fresh in his mind, Matthew was able to find short periods of sleep. At an hour he judged to be past midnight, he relit the lantern he had blown out upon lying down and took it with him into the hallway.

Though it was certainly late, there was still activity in the house. Bidwell's voice could be heard—muffled but insistent—coming from the upstairs study. Matthew paused outside the door, to hear who was in there with him, and caught Winston's strained reply. Paine's name was mentioned. Matthew thought it best he not be a party to the burial plans, even through the thickness of a door, and so he went on his way down the stairs, descending quietly.

A check of the mantel clock in the parlor showed the time to be thirty-eight minutes after midnight. He entered the library and unlatched the shutters so that if the door was later locked from the inside he might still gain admittance without ringing for Mrs. Nettles. Then he set off for the spring, the lantern held low at his side.

On the eastern bank, Matthew set the lamp on the ground next to a large water oak and removed his shoes, stockings, and shirt. The night was warm, but a foot slid into the water gave him a cold shock. It was going to take a sturdy measure of fortitude just to enter that pond, much less go swimming about underwater in the dark.

But that was what he had come to do, and so be it. If he could find even a portion of what he suspected might be hidden down there, he would have made great progress in solving the riddle of the surveyor's visit.

He eased into the shallows, the cold water stealing his breath. A touch of that fount's kindness upon his groin, and his stones became as true rocks. He stood in water up to his waist for a moment, his feet in the soft mud below, as he steeled himself for further immersion. Presently, though, he did become acclimated to the water and he reasoned that if turtles and frogs could accept it, then so could he. The next challenge was going ahead and sliding the rest of the way down, which he did with clenched teeth.

He moved away from the bank. Instantly he felt the bottom angling away under his feet. Three more strides, and he was up to his neck. Then two more . . . and suddenly he was treading water. Well, he thought. The time had come.

He drew a breath, held it, and submerged.

In the darkness he felt his way along the sloping bottom, his fingers gripping into the mud. As he went deeper, he was aware of the thump of his own heartbeat and the gurgle of bubbles leaving his mouth. Still the bottom continued to slope downward at perhaps an angle of thirty degrees. His hands found the edges of rocks protruding from the mud, and the soft matting of moss-like grass. Then his lungs became insistent. and he had to return to the surface to fill them.

Again he dove under. Deeper he went this time, his arms and legs propelling his progress. A pressure clamped hold of his face and began to increase as he groped his way down. On this descent he was aware of a current pulling at him from what seemed to be the northwestern quadrant of the fount. He had time to close his fists in the mud, and then he had to rise once more.

When he reached the surface, he trod water and squeezed the mud between his fingers. There was nothing but finely grained *terra liquum*. He took another breath, held it, and went down a third time.

As Matthew descended what he estimated to be more than twenty feet, he again felt the insistent pull of a definite current, stronger as he swam deeper. He reached into the sloping mud. His fingers found a flat rock—which suddenly came to life and shot away underneath him, the surprise bringing a burst of bubbles from his mouth and causing him to instantly rise.

On the surface he had to pause to steady his nerves before he dove again, though he should have expected to disturb turtles. A fourth descent allowed him to gather up two more fistfuls of mud, but in the muck was not a trace of gold or silver coinage.

He resolved on the fifth dive to stay down and search through the mud as long as possible. He filled his lungs and descended, his body beginning to protest such exertion and his mind beginning to recoil from the secrets of the dark. But he did grip several handfuls and sift through them, again without success.

After the eighth dive, Matthew came to the conclusion that he was simply muddying the water. His lungs were burning and his head felt dangerously clouded. If indeed there was a bounty of gold and silver coins down there, they existed only in a realm known by the turtles. Of course, Matthew had realized that a pirate's treasure vault would be no vault at all if just anyone—particularly a land creature like himself—could swim down and retrieve it. He had never entertained the illusion that he could—or *cared* to—reach the fount's deepest point, which he recalled Bidwell saying was some forty feet, but he'd hoped he might find an errant coin. He imagined the retrieval process would involve several skilled divers, the kind of men who were useful at scraping mollusks from the bottoms of ships while still at sea. The process might also demand the use of hooks and chains, a dense netting and a lever device, depending on how much treasure was hidden.

He had surfaced from this final dive near the center of the spring, and so he began the swim back to the shallows. He was intrigued by the current he'd felt below the level of fifteen feet or thereabouts. It had strengthened as he'd gone deeper, and Matthew wondered at the ferocity of its embrace at the forty-foot depth. Water was definitely flowing down there at the command of some unknown natural mechanism.

In another moment his feet found the mud, and he was able to stand. He waded toward the bank and the tree beside which he'd left his clothes and the lantern.

And that was when he realized his lamp was no longer there.

Instantly a bell of alarm clanged in his mind. He stood in the waist-deep water, scanning the bank for any sign of an intruder.

Then a figure stepped out from behind the tree. In each hand was a lantern, but they were held low so Matthew couldn't see the face.

"Who's there?" Matthew said, trying mightily to keep his speech from shivering as much as his body was beginning to.

The figure had a voice: "Would you care to tell me what you're up to?"

"I am swimming, Mr. Winston." Matthew continued wading toward the bank. "Is that not apparent?"

"Yes, it's apparent. My question remains valid, however."

Matthew had only a few seconds to construct a reply, so he gave it his best dash of pepper. "If you knew anything of health," he said, "which obviously you do not, because of your living habits, you would appreciate the benefit to the heart of a nocturnal swim."

"Oh, of course! Shall I fetch a wagon to help load this manure?"

"I'm sure Dr. Shields would be glad to inform you of the benefit." Matthew left the water and, dripping, approached Winston. He took the lantern that Winston offered. "I often swim at night in Charles Town," he plowed on, deepening the furrow.

"Do tell."

"I *am* telling." Matthew leaned down to pick up his shirt and blot the moisture from his face. He closed his eyes in so doing. When he opened them he realized that one of his shoes—which had both been on the ground when he'd picked up the shirt—was now missing. At the same instant he registered that Winston had taken a position behind him.

"Mr. Winston?" Matthew said, quietly but clearly. "You don't really wish to do what you're considering." From Winston there was no word or sound.

Matthew suspected that if a blow from the stout wooden heel was going to come, it would be delivered to his skull as he turned toward the other man. "Your disloyalty to your master need not deform itself into murder." Matthew blotted water from his chest and shoulders with a casual air, but inwardly he was an arrow choosing his direction of flight. "The residents might find a victim of drowning on the morrow . . . but you will know what you've done. I don't believe you to be capable of such an act." He swallowed, his heart pounding through his chest, and took the risk of looking at Winston. No blow fell. "I am not the reason for your predicament, " Matthew said. "May I please have my shoe?"

Winston sighed heavily, his head lowered, and held out his hand with the shoe in it. Matthew noted that it was offered heel-first. "You are not a killer, sir," Matthew said, after he'd accepted the shoe. "If you'd really wished to bash my head in, you never would have signalled your presence by moving the lantern. May I ask how come you to be here?"

"I . . . just left a meeting with Bidwell. He wants me to take care of disposing of Paine's corpse."

"So you came to consider the fount? I wouldn't. You might weigh the corpse down well enough, but the water supply would surely be contaminated. Unless . . . that's what you intend." Matthew had put on his shirt and was buttoning it.

"No, that's not my intention, though I *had* considered the fount for that purpose. I might wish the *town* to die, but I don't wish to cause the deaths of any citizens."

"A correction," Matthew said. "You wish not to bear the *blame* for the death of Fount Royal. Also, you wish to improve your financial and business standing with Mr. Bidwell. Yes?"

"Yes, that's right."

"Well, you're aware then that you have Mr. Bidwell stretched over a very large barrel now, don't you?"

Winston frowned. "What?"

"You and he share important knowledge he would rather not have revealed to his citizens. If I were in your position, I would make the most of it. You're adept at drawing up contracts, are you not?"

"I am."

"Then simply contract between yourself and Mr. Bidwell the task of corpse disposal. Write into it whatever you please and negotiate, realizing of course that you will most likely not get everything you feel you deserve. But I'd venture your style of living would find some improvement. And with Bidwell's signature on a contract of such . . . *delicate* nature, you need never fear losing your position with his company. In fact, you might find yourself promoted. Where is the body now? Still at the house?"

"Yes. Hidden under the pallet. Bidwell wept and moaned such that I . . . had to help him place it there."

"That was your first opportunity to negotiate terms. I hope you won't miss the next one." Matthew sat down in the grass to put on his stockings.

"Bidwell will never sign any contract that implicates him in hiding evidence of a murder!"

"Not gladly, no. But he *will* sign, Mr. Winston. Particularly if he understands that you—his trusted business manager—will take care of the problem without bringing anyone else into it. That's his greatest concern. He'll also sign when you make him understand—firmly but diplomatically, I hope—that the task will not and cannot be done without your doing it. You might emphasize that the contract with his signature upon it is a formality for your legal protection."

"Yes, that would make sense. But he'll know I might use the contract as future leverage against him!"

"Of course he will. As I said, I doubt if you'll find yourself without a position at Bidwell's firm anytime soon. He might even send you back to England on one of his ships, if that's what you want." The job of putting on his stockings and shoes done, Matthew stood up. "What *do* you want, Mr. Winston?"

"More money," Winston said. He took a moment to think. "And a fair shake. I should be rewarded for my good work. *And* I ought to get credit for the business decisions I've made that have helped pad Bidwell's pockets."

"What?" Matthew raised his eyebrows. "No mansion or statue?"

"I am a realistic man, sir. I might only push Bidwell so far."

"Oh, I think you should at least try for the mansion. If you'll excuse me now?"

"Wait!" Winston said when Matthew started to walk away. "What do you suggest I do with Paine's corpse?"

"Actually, I have no suggestion and I don't care to know what you do," Matthew replied. "My only thought is . . . the dirt beneath Paine's floor is the same dirt that fills the cemetery graves. I know you have a Bible and consider yourself a Christian."

"Yes, that is right. Oh . . . one more thing," Winston added before Matthew could turn to leave. "How are we to explain Paine's disappearance? And what shall we do to find his killer?"

"The explanation is your decision. About finding his killer . . . from what I understand, Paine dabbled with other men's wives. I'd think he had more than his share of enemies. But I am not a magistrate, sir. It is Mr. Bidwell's responsibility, as the mayor of this town, to file the case. Until then . . ." Matthew shrugged. "Good night."

"Good night," Winston said as Matthew departed. "And good swimming to you."

Matthew went directly to Bidwell's house, to the library shutters he'd unlatched, opened them, and put the lantern on the sill. Then he carefully pulled himself up through the window, taking care not to overturn the chess set on his entry. Matthew took the lantern and went upstairs to bed, disappointed that no evidence of a pirate's hoard had been found but hopeful that tomorrow—or later today, as the fact was—might show him some path through the maze of questions that confronted him.

When the rooster choir of Friday's sunrise sounded, Matthew awakened with the fading impression of a dream but one very clear image remaining in his memory: that of John Goode, talking about the coins he'd discovered and saying *May's got it in her mind we're gon' run to the Florida country.*

He rose from bed and looked out the window at the red sun on the eastern horizon. A few clouds had appeared, but they were neither dark nor pregnant with rain. They moved like stately galleons across the purple sky.

The Florida country, he thought. A Spanish realm, the link to the great—though English-despised—cities of Madrid and Barcelona. The link, also, to Rachel's Portuguese homeland.

He recalled Shawcombe's voice saying *You know them Spaniards are sittin' down there in the Florida country, not seventy leagues from here. They got spies all in the colonies, spreadin' the word that any black crow who flies from his master and gets to the Florida country can be a free man. You ever heard such a thing? Them Spaniards are promisin' the same thing to criminals, murderers, every like of John Badseed.*

Seventy leagues, Matthew thought. Roughly two hundred miles. And not simply a two-hundred-mile *jaunt*, either. What of wild animals and wild Indians? Water would be no hardship, but what of food? What of shelter, if the heavens opened their floodgates again? Such a journey would make his and the magistrate's muddy trek from Shawcombe's tavern seem an afternoon's idyll.

But evidently others had made the journey and survived,

and from much greater distances than two hundred miles. May was an elderly woman, and she had no qualms about going. Then again, it was her last hope of freedom.

Her last hope.

Matthew turned away from the window, walked to the basin of water atop his dresser, and liberally splashed his face. He wasn't sure what he'd been thinking, but—whatever it may have been—it was the most illogical, insane thought he'd ever had. He was surely no outdoorsman or leatherstocking, and also he was proud to be a British subject. So he might dismiss from his mind all traces of such errant and unwise consideration.

He shaved, put on his clothes, and crossed the hallway to look in on the magistrate. Dr. Shields's latest potion was evidently quite powerful, as Woodward still dwelled in the land of Nod. A touch of the magistrate's bare arm, however, gave Matthew reason for great joy: sometime during the night, Woodward's fever had broken.

At breakfast Matthew sat alone. He ate a dish of stirred eggs and ham, washed down with a strong cup of tea. Then he was out the door on a mission of resolve: to confront the ratcatcher in his well-ordered nest.

The morning was pleasantly warm and sunny, though a number of white-bellied clouds paraded across the sky. On Industry Street, Matthew hurried past Exodus Jerusalem's camp but neither the preacher nor his relations were in evidence. He soon came to the field where the maskers had made their camp, near the Hamilton house. Several of the thespians were sitting around a fire over which a trio of cooking pots hung. Matthew saw a burly, Falstaffian fellow smoking a churchwarden pipe while conversing with emphatic gestures to two other colleagues. A woman of equal if not greater girth was busy with needle and thread, darning a red-feathered hat, and a more slender female was at work polishing boots. Matthew knew little about the craft of acting, though he did know that all thespians were male and therefore the two women must be wives who travelled with the troupe.

"Good day, young man!" one of the actors called to him, with a lift of the hand.

"Good day to you!" Matthew answered, nodding.

In another few minutes Matthew entered the somber area of deformed orchards. It was fitting, then, that this was the locale chosen for Rachel's burning, as the justice such a travesty represented was surely misshapen. He looked at a barren brown field upon which had been erected the freshly axed execution stake. At its base, ringed by rocks, was a large firemound of pinewood timbers and pineknots. About twenty yards away from it stood another pile of wood. The field had been chosen to accommodate the festive citizens and to be certain no errant sparks could reach a roof.

At first light on Monday morning Rachel would be brought here by wagon and secured to the stake. Some kind of repugnant ceremony would take place, with Bidwell as its host. Then, after the crowd's flame had been sufficiently bellowed, torches would be laid to the firemound. More fuel would be brought over from the woodpile, to keep the temperature at a searing degree. Matthew had never witnessed an execution by burning, but he reasoned it must be a slow, messy, and excruciating business. Rachel's hair and clothes might be set aflame and her flesh roasted, but if the temperature wasn't infernal enough the real burning would take hours. It would be an all-day thing, anyway, for Matthew suspected that even a raging fire had difficulty gnawing a human body to the bones.

At what point Rachel would lose consciousness, he didn't know. Even though she wished to die with dignity and might have readied herself for the ordeal as much as humanly possible, her screams would be heard from one wall of Fount Royal to the other. It was likely Rachel would perish of asphyxiation before the fire cooked her. If she had her senses about her, she might hurry death by breathing in the flames and copious smoke. But who at that agonizing moment could do anything but wail in torment and thrash at their bonds?

Matthew assumed the fire would be kept burning throughout the night, and the citizens encouraged to witness as the witch shrank away to a grisly shade of her former self. The execution stake would dwindle too, but would be kept watered to delay its disappearance. On Tuesday morning, when there was nothing left but ashes and blackened bones, someone—Seth Hazelton, possibly—might come with a mallet to smash the skull and break the burnt skeleton into smaller fragments. It was then that Matthew could envision the swooping down of Lucretia Vaughan—armed with as many buckets, bottles, and containers as she might load upon a wagon—eager to scoop up ashes and bits of bone to sell as charms against evil. It occurred to him that her intelligence and rapacity might encourage her to enter an unholy alliance with Bidwell and Preacher Jerusalem, the former to finance and package this abomination and the latter to hawk it in towns and villages up and down the seaboard.

He had to banish such thoughts, ere they sapped the strength of his belief that an answer could be found before that awful Monday dawn.

He continued westward along Industry. Presently he saw a wisp of white smoke curling from the chimney of Linch's house. The lord of rodents was cooking his breakfast.

The shutters were wide open. Obviously Linch wasn't expecting any visitors. Matthew walked to the door, under the hanging rat skeletons, and knocked without hesitation.

A few seconds passed. Then, suddenly, the shutters of the window nearest the door were drawn closed—not hastily or loudly, but rather with quiet purpose. Matthew knocked again, with a sterner fist.

"Who is it?" came Linch's wary voice.

Matthew smiled thinly, realizing that Linch might just as easily have looked out the window to see. "Matthew Corbett. May I speak with you?"

"I'm eatin' my breakfast. Don't care for no mornin' chat."

"It should just take a minute."

"Ain't got a minute. Go 'way."

"Mr. Linch," Matthew said, "I do need to speak with you. If not now, then I'll have to persist."

"Persist all you please. I don't give a damn." There was the sound of footsteps walking away from the door. The shutters of a second window were pulled closed, followed by the shutters of a third. Then the final window was sealed with a contemptuous *thump*.

Matthew knew there was one sure way to make Linch open the door, though it was also surely a risk. He decided to take it.

"Mr. Linch?" Matthew said, standing close to the door. "What interests you so much about the Egyptian culture?"

A pot clattered to the floor within.

Matthew stepped away from the door several paces. He waited, his hands clasped behind his back. A latch was thrown with violent force. But the door was not fairly ripped from its hinges in being opened, as Matthew had expected. Instead, there was a pause.

Control, Matthew thought. *Control is Linch's religion, and he's praying to his god.* The door was opened. Slowly.

But just a crack. "Egyptian culture? What're you blatherin' about, boy?"

"You know what I mean. The book in your desk."

Again, a pause. Something about it this time was ominous.

"Ohhhhh, it was *you* come in my house and gone through my things, eh?" Now the door opened wider, and Linch's clean but unshaven face peered out. His pale, icy gray eyes were aimed at Matthew with the power of weapons, his teeth bared in a grin. "I found your shoemud on my floor. You didn't shut my trunk firm enough, either. Have to be blind not to see it was open a quarter-inch."

"You're very observant, aren't you? Does that come from catching rats?"

"It does. I see, though, I let a whorin' mother's two-legged rat creep in and nibble my cheese."

"Interesting cheese, too," Matthew said, maintaining his distance from the door. "I would never have imagined you . . . how shall I say this? . . . lived in such virtuous order, from the wreck you've allowed the exterior of your house to become. I also would never have imagined you to be a scholar of ancient Egypt."

"There is a law," Linch said, his grin still fixed and his eyes still aimed, "against enterin' a man's house without bein' invited. I believe in this town it's ten lashes. You care to tell Bidwell, or you want me to?"

"Ten lashes." Matthew frowned and shook his head. "I would surely hate to suffer ten lashes, Mr. Linch."

"Fifteen, if I can prove you thieved anythin'. And you know what? I might just be missin' a . . ."

"Sapphire brooch?" Matthew interrupted. "No, that's in the drawer where I left it." He offered Linch a tight smile.

The ratcatcher's expression did not change, though there might have been a slight narrowing of the eyes. "You're a cocksure bastard, ain't you? But you're good. I'll grant you that. You knotted the twine back well enough to fool me . . . and I ain't fooled very often."

"Oh, I think it's you who does the fooling, Mr. Linch. What is this masquerade about?"

"Masquerade? You're talkin' riddles, boy!"

"Now you just said an interesting word, Mr. Linch. You yourself are a riddle, and one I mean to solve. Why is it that you present yourself to the town as being . . . and let us be plainspoken here . . . a roughhewn and filthy dolt, when you actually are a man of literacy and good order? *Meticulous* order, I might say. And need I add the point of your obvious financial status, if indeed that brooch belongs to you?"

From Linch there was not a word nor a trace of reaction but Matthew could tell from the glint of his extraordinary eyes that the man's mind was working, grinding these words into a fine dust to be weighed and measured.

"I suspect that even your harborfront accent is shammed," Matthew went on. "Is it?"

Linch gave a low, quiet laugh. "Boy, your brainpan has been dented. If I were you, I'd either go get drunk or ask the town quack for a cup of opium."

"You are not who you pretend to be," Matthew said, defying the man's cutting stare. "Therefore . . . who are you?"

Linch paused, thinking about it. Then he licked his lower lip and said, "Come on in and we'll have us a talk."

"No, thank you. I do enjoy the sun's warmth. Oh . . . I also spoke to one of the maskers as I passed their camp. If I were to . . . suffer an accident, say . . . I'm sure the man would recall I'd been walking in this direction."

"Suffer an *accident?* What foolishness are you prattlin'?

No, come on in and I'll spell you what you care to know. Come on." Linch hooked a finger at him.

"You may spell me what I care to know right here as well as in there."

"No, I can't. 'Sides, my breakfast is coolin'. Tell you what: I'll open all the shutters and leave the door wide. That suit you?"

"Not really. I *have* noticed a dearth of neighbors in this vicinity."

"Well, either come in or not, 'cause I'm done with this chattin'." He opened the door to its widest possible degree and walked away. Soon afterward, the nearest window was opened, the shutters pushed as far as their hinges would allow. Then the next window was opened, and afterward the third and fourth.

Matthew could see Linch, wearing tan-colored breeches and a loose-fitting gray shirt, busying himself around the hearth. The interior of the house appeared just as painstakingly neat as Matthew had previously seen it. He realized that he'd begun a duel of nerves with the ratcatcher, and this challenge to come into the house was the riposte to his own first slash concerning Linch's interest in Egyptian culture.

Linch stirred something in a skillet and added what might have been spices from a jar. Then, seemingly unconcerned with Matthew, he fetched a wooden plate and spooned food onto it.

Matthew watched as Linch sat down at his desk, placed the plate before him, and began to eat with a display of mannered restraint. Matthew knew nothing was to be gained by standing out here, yet he feared entering the ratcatcher's house even with the door and every window open wide. Still . . . the challenge had been given, and must be accepted.

Slowly and cautiously, he advanced first to the doorway, where he paused to gauge Linch's reaction. The ratcatcher kept eating what looked to be a mixture of eggs, sausage, and potatoes all cooked together. Then, even more cautiously, Matthew walked into the house but stopped with the threshold less than an arm's length behind him.

Linch continued to eat, using a brown napkin to occasionally wipe his mouth. "You have the manners of a gentleman," Matthew said.

"My mother raised me right," came the reply. "You won't find me stealin' into private houses and goin' through people's belongin's."

"I presume you have an explanation for the book? And the brooch as well?"

"I do." Linch looked out the window that his desk stood before. "But why should I explain anythin' to you? It's *my* business."

"That's true enough. On the other hand, can't you understand how . . . uh . . . *strange* this appears?"

"*Strange* is one of them things in the eye of the beholder now, ain't it?" He put his spoon and knife down and turned his chair a few inches so that he was facing Matthew more directly. The movement made Matthew back away apace. Linch grinned. "I scare you, do I?"

"Yes, you do."

"Well, why should you be scared of me? What have I ever done to *you*, 'cept save your ass from bein' et up by rats there in the gaol?"

"You've done nothing to me," Matthew admitted. He was ready to deliver the next slash. "I just wonder what you may have done to Violet Adams."

To his credit—and his iron nerves—Linch only exhibited a slight frown. "Who?"

"Violet Adams. Surely you know the child and her family."

"I do. They live up the street. Cleaned some rats out for 'em not too long ago. Now what am I supposed to have done to that little girl? Pulled her dress up and poked her twat?"

"No, nothing so crude . . . or so obvious," Matthew said. "But I have reason to believe that you may have—"

Linch suddenly stood up and Matthew almost jumped out the door.

"Don't piss your breeches," Linch said, picking up his empty plate. "I'm gettin' another helpin'. You'll pardon me if I don't offer you none?"

Linch went to the hearth, spooned some more of the breakfast onto his plate, and came back to his chair. When he sat down, he turned the chair a few more inches toward Matthew so that now they almost directly faced each other. A stream of sunlight lay across Linch's chest. "Go on," he said as he ate, the plate in his lap. "You were sayin'?"

"Uh . . . yes. I was saying . . . I have reason to believe you may have defiled Violet Adams in a way other than physical."

"What other way is there?"

"Mental defilement," Matthew answered. Linch stopped chewing. Only for a space of perhaps two heartbeats, however. Then Linch was eating once more, staring at the pattern of sunlight on the floorboards between them.

Matthew's sword was aimed. It was time to strike for the heart, and see what color blood spurted out. "I believe you created a fiction in the child's mind that she had an audience with Satan in the Hamilton house. I believe you've had a hand in creating such a fiction in many people hereabouts, including Jeremiah Buckner and Elias Garrick. *And* that you planted the poppets under Rachel Howarth's floor and caused Cara Grunewald to have a 'vision' that led to their discovery."

Linch continued to eat his breakfast without haste, as if these damning words had never been uttered. When he spoke, however, his voice was . . . somehow changed, though Matthew couldn't quite explain its difference other than a subtle shift to a lower pitch.

"And just how am I supposed to have done such a thing?"

"I have no idea," Matthew said. "Unless you're a warlock, and you've learned sorcery at the Devil's knee."

Linch laughed heartily and put his plate aside. "Oh, that's rich indeed! Me a warlock! Oh, yes! Shall I shoot a fireball up your arse for you?"

"That's not necessary. If you wish to begin refuting my theory by explaining your masquerade, you may proceed."

Linch's smile faded. "And if I don't, you'll have me burnin' at the stake in place of your wench? Listen to me, boy: when you go see Dr. Shields, ask for a whole *keg* of opium."

"I'm sure Mr. Bidwell's curiosity about you will be fired just as mine was," Matthew said calmly. "Particularly after I tell him about the book and the brooch."

"You mean you haven't *already?*" Linch gave a faint, sinister smile.

"No. Mind you, the maskers saw me pass their camp."

"The *maskers!*" Linch laughed again. "Maskers have less sense than rats, boy! They pay attention to no details but lookin' at their own damned faces in mirrors!"

This had been said with contemptuous ferocity . . . and suddenly Matthew knew.

"Ahhhhh," he said. "Of course. *You* are a professional actor, aren't you?"

"I've already told you I spent some time with a circus," Linch said smoothly. "My act with trained rats. I had some dealin's with actors, much to my sorrow. I say to Hell with the whole lyin', stealin' breed. But look here." He opened the drawer and brought out the Egyptian tome and the wallet that hid the sapphire brooch. Linch placed both objects on the desktop, then removed the twine-tied brown cotton cloth from the wallet and began to untie it with nimble fingers. "I expect I *should* give you some kind of explanation, such as it is."

"It would be much appreciated." And very intriguing to see what Linch came up with, Matthew thought.

"The truth is . . . that I *am* more learned than I let on. But I ain't shammin' the accent. I was born on the breast of the Thames, and I'm proud of it." Linch had undone the twine, and now he opened the cloth and picked up the sapphire brooch between the thumb and forefinger of his right hand. He held it in the stream of sunlight, inspecting it with his pale, intense eyes. "This belonged to my mother, God rest her lovin' soul. Yes, it's worth a good piece of coin but I'd never part with it. Never. It's the only thing I've got to remember her by." He turned the brooch slightly, and light glinted from its golden edge into Matthew's face. "It's a thing of beauty, ain't it? So beautiful. Like she was. So, so beautiful." Again, the brooch was turned and again a glint of light struck Matthew's eyes.

Linch's voice had almost imperceptibly softened. "I'd never part with it. Not for any amount of money. So beautiful. So very, very beautiful."

The brooch turned . . . the light glinted . . .

"Never. For any amount of money. You see how it shines? So, so beautiful. Like she was. So, so beautiful."

The brooch . . . the light . . . the brooch . . . the light . . .

Matthew stared at the golden glint. Linch had begun to angle the brooch slowly in and out of the sun's stream, in a regular—and transfixing—pattern.

"Yes," Matthew said. "Beautiful." With a surprising amount of difficulty, he pulled his gaze away from the brooch. "I want to know about the book."

"Ahhhh, the book!" Linch slowly raised the index finger of his left hand, which again secured Matthew's attention. Linch made a small circle in the air with that finger, then slid it down to the brooch. Matthew's eyes followed its smooth descent, and suddenly he was staring once more at the light . . . the brooch . . . the light . . . the brooch . . .

"The book," Linch repeated softly. "The book, the book, the book."

"Yes, the *book,*" Matthew said, and just as he attempted to pull his gaze again from the brooch Linch held it motionless in the light for perhaps three seconds. The lack of movement now seemed as strangely compelling as the motion. Linch then began to move the brooch in and out of the light in a slow clockwise direction.

"The book." This was peculiar, Matthew thought. His voice sounded hollow, as if he were hearing himself speak from the distance of another room. "Why . . ." The brooch . . . the light . . . the brooch . . . the light. "Why Egyptian culture?"

"Fascinating," Linch said. "I find the Egyptian culture fascinating."

The brooch . . . the light . . .

"Fascinating," Linch said again, and now he too seemed

to be speaking from a distance. "How they . . . forged an empire . . . from shifting sand. Shifting sand . . . all about . . . shifting sand . . . flowing . . . softly, softly . . ."

"What?" Matthew whispered. The brooch . . . the light . . . the brooch . . .

"Shifting . . . shifting sand," Linch said.

. . . the light . . .

"Listen, Matthew. Listen."

Matthew was listening. It seemed to him that the room around him had become darkened, and the only glint of illumination came from that brooch in Linch's hand. He could hear no sound but Linch's low, sonorous voice, and he found himself waiting for the next word to be spoken.

"Listen . . . Matthew . . . the shifting sand . . . shifting . . . so so beautiful . . ."

The voice seemed to be whispering right in his ear. No, no: Linch was closer than that. Closer . . .

. . . the brooch . . . the light . . . the brooch . . .

Closer.

"Listen," came the hushed command, in a voice that Matthew now hardly recognized. "Listen . . . to the silence."

. . . the light . . . the shifting shifting sand . . . the brooch . . . the so so beautiful light . . .

"Listen, Matthew. To the silence. Every. Thing. Silent. Every. Thing. So so beautiful. The shifting shifting sand. Silent, silent. The town . . . silent. As if . . . the whole world . . . holds its breath . . ."

"Uh!" Matthew said; it was the panicked sound of a drowning swimmer, searching for air. His mouth opened wider . . . he heard himself gasp . . . a terrible noise . . .

"Silent, silent," Linch was saying, in a hushed, slow singsong voice. "Every. Thing. Silent. Every. Till—"

"No!" Matthew took a backward step and collided with

the doorframe. He jerked his eyes away from the glinting brooch, though Linch continued to turn it in and out of the sunlight. "No! You're not . . . going to . . ."

"What, Matthew?" Linch smiled, his eyes piercing through Matthew's skull to his very mind. "Not going to what?" He stood up from his chair . . . slowly . . . smoothly . . . like shifting shifting sand . . .

Matthew felt terror bloom within him unlike anything he'd ever experienced. His legs seemed weighted in iron boots. Linch was coming toward him, reaching out to grasp his arm in what seemed a strange slow-motion travesty of time. Matthew could not look away from Linch's eyes; they were the center of the whole world, and everything else was silent . . . silent . . .

He was aware that Linch's fingers were about to take hold of his sleeve.

With all the effort of will he could summon, Matthew shouted, *"No!"* into Linch's face. Linch blinked. His hand faltered, for perhaps a fraction of a second.

It was enough.

Matthew turned and fled from the house. Fled, though his eyes felt bloodshot and swollen. Fled though his legs were heavy and his throat as dry as shifting sand. Fled with silence thundering in his ears, and his lungs gasping for breath that had seemed stolen away from him only a few seconds before.

He fled along Industry Street, the warm sunlight thawing the freeze that had tightened his muscles and bones. He dared not look back. Dared not look back. Dared not.

But as he ran, putting precious distance between himself and that soft trap he had nearly been snared by, he realized the enormity and strange power of the force that Linch wielded. Such a thing was unnatural . . . monstrous . . . such a thing was *shifting sand . . . shifting . . .* sorcery and must be *silent silent* of the very Devil himself.

It was in his head. He couldn't get it out, and that further terrified him because the contamination of his mind—his most dependable resource—was utterly unthinkable.

He ran and ran, sweat on his face, and his lungs heaving.

Nine

Matthew sat, shivering in the sunlight, in the grass beside the spring.

It had been a half hour since he'd fled Linch's house, and still he suffered the effects of their encounter. He felt tired and sluggish, yet frightened to the very core of his being. Matthew thought—and thinking seemed more of an effort than ever in his life—that Linch had done to his mind what *he* had done to Linch's dwelling: entered it without permission, poked about, and left a little smear of mud to betray his presence.

Linch had without a doubt been the winner of their duel.

But—also without a doubt—Matthew now knew Linch was the owner of the shadowy hand that could reach into the human mind and create whatever fiction it pleased. Matthew considered himself intelligent and alert; if *he* had been so affected by the ratcatcher's trancing ability, how simple a task it must have been to overwhelm the more rustic and less mentally agile Buckner, Garrick, and the other targets. And indeed Matthew suspected that the persons in whose minds Linch had planted the scenes of depravity had been carefully chosen because of their receptivity to such manipulation. Linch had obviously had a great deal of experience at this bizarre craft, and most surely he could recognize certain signals that indicated whether a person was a likely candidate for manipulation. Matthew thought that in his own case, Linch had been probing his line of mental defense and had been unsuccessful in breaking the barrier. Linch would probably have never even attempted such a thing if the man hadn't been desperate.

Matthew offered his face to the sun, trying to burn out the last vestiges of shifting sand from the storehouse of memory.

Linch, Matthew believed, had underestimated Violet Adams. The child was more intelligent than her timidity let her appear. Matthew believed that the house in which she described seeing Satan and the white-haired imp was not the Hamilton house, but the house of her own mind. And back there in the dark room was the memory of Linch trancing her. Surely the man had not actually sung that song as he'd done the work, but perhaps the recollection of the event had been locked away from her and so the song—which Violet had heard when Linch had come ratcatching at her house—was an alternate key.

The question was: where and when had Violet been entranced? Matthew thought that if Buckner and Garrick could remember correctly, they might supply the fact that Linch had also come ratcatching—or simply spreading poisoned bait as a "precaution"—to their own houses. Matthew could envision Linch asking either man to step out to the barn to look at evidence of rodent infestation, and then—once away from the sight of wives or other relatives—turning upon them the full power of this strange weapon that both erased reality and constructed a lifelike fiction. What was particularly amazing to Matthew was the fact that the effects of this power might be delayed some length of time; that is, Linch had given some mental command that the fiction not be immediately recollected, but instead recalled several nights later. And the memory of being entranced was erased from the mind altogether . . . except in the case of Violet Adams, whose mind had begun to sing to her in Linch's voice.

It was the damnedest thing he'd ever heard of. Surely it was some form of sorcery! But it was real and it was here and it was the reason Rachel was going to be burned on Monday morning.

And what could he do about it?

Nothing, it seemed. Oh, he could go to Bidwell and plead his case, but he knew what the result of that would be. Bidwell might arrange shackles for him and put him in a cushioned room where he would be no danger to others or himself. Matthew would fear even mentioning such a theory to the magistrate; even if Woodward were able to hear and respond, he would believe Matthew to be so severely bewitched that the stress might sink him into his grave.

The ratcatcher, it seemed, had done much more than winning a duel. Linch had demonstrated that the war was over and declared himself its absolute and cunning victor.

Matthew drew his knees up to his chin and stared out over the blue water. He had to ask the question that seemed to him the most basic query in existence yet also the most complex: *Why?*

For what reason would Linch put forth such an effort to paint Rachel as a witch? And why, indeed, was a man of his vile nature even *in* Fount Royal? Had he murdered Reverend Grove and Daniel Howarth? If Rachel was only a pawn in this strange game—if, for the sake of conjecture, Bidwell was the real target—then why go to such extremes to destroy Fount Royal? Was it possible Linch had been sent from Charles Town to do these dark deeds?

It seemed to Matthew that the jealous watchdogs in Charles Town might encourage the burning of a few empty houses, but they wouldn't stoop so low as to subsidize murder. Then again, who could say what reigned in a man's heart? It would not be the first time that gold coins were spent on a spill of crimson blood.

Matthew narrowed his eyes slightly, watching the surface of the spring ripple with a passing breeze.

Gold coins. Yes. Gold coins. Gold and silver, that is. Of the Spanish stamp.

Taking shape in Matthew's mind was a theory worth chewing on.

Say that, even though he'd found nothing last night, there was indeed a fortune of pirate coins down at the bottom of the fount. Say that somehow Linch—whoever he really was—had learned of its presence, possibly months or even years before he'd arrived on the scene. When Linch got here, he discovered a town surrounding the treasure vault. What, then, could he do to get the coins for himself and himself alone?

The answer: he could create a witch and cause Fount Royal to wither and die.

Perhaps Linch had gone swimming on more than one occasion, late at night, and discovered . . . *Oh,* Matthew thought, and the realization was like a punch . . . discovered not only gold and silver coins . . . but a sapphire brooch.

What if there was not just coinage in that treasure vault, but also jewelry? Or loose gemstones? If indeed Linch had brought that brooch up from the depths, then the ratcatcher was aware of how necessary it was to clear the town away before a real attempt at salvage could be undertaken.

Yes, Matthew thought. Yes. It was definitely a reason to kill two men and create a witch. But wait . . . Was it not in Linch's best interest that Rachel *not* be burned? With the removal of the "witch," Fount Royal would likely start to grow healthy again. So what was he going to do to make sure the town's decline continued? Create a second witch? That seemed to Matthew to be a task requiring a great deal of risk and months of planning. No, Rachel had been the perfect "witch," and the more reasonable action would be to somehow capitalize on her death.

Perhaps . . . with another murder? And who might find himself throat-slashed by the vengeance of "Satan" in a dimly lit room or hallway some evening hence?

Matthew suspected that this time Linch would go for Fount Royal's jugular. Would it be Dr. Shields lying in a pool of blood? Schoolmaster Johnstone? Edward Winston? No. Those three men, though vital, were replaceable in the future of Fount Royal.

The next victim would be Bidwell himself.

Matthew stood up, his flesh in chillbumps. Near him a woman was dipping two buckets while conversing with a man who was filling a keg. Their faces, though lined by their lives of difficult labor, were free from concern; in them was the statement that all was right with Fount Royal . . . or soon to be right, with the execution of the witch.

Little did they know, Matthew thought. Little did anyone know, except Linch. Especially little did Bidwell know, for as Rachel died writhing in the flames the plan would be set in motion to cut his throat in the same manner as the other victims.

And what could be done about it?

Matthew needed evidence. One sapphire brooch would not do; besides, Matthew was certain Linch would now hide it in a place even a rat couldn't discover. To expose the coins that Goode had found would be beneficial, but would also be a betrayal of Goode's trust. Obviously Linch was the thief who had entered Bidwell's house that night and taken the gold coin from Matthew's room, probably in an effort to ascertain if it was part of the treasure and where it might have come from. That was another question, however: how had an Indian gotten hold of a Spanish coin?

Matthew was feeling more like himself now. He wouldn't return to Linch's house alone for a barrel full of gold coins. But if he could find some piece of evidence that might implicate Linch . . . some hard proof to show Bidwell . . .

"There you are! I was just on my way to see you!" That voice, high-pitched and waspish, struck him with fresh dread.

He turned to face Lucretia Vaughan. She was smiling brightly, her hair contained under a stiff white bonnet, and she wore a lilac-colored dress. In her arms was a small basket. "I hoped to find you in good spirits this day!"

"Uh . . . yes. Good spirits." He was already edging away from her.

"Mr. Corbett, please allow me to present you with a gift! I know . . . well, I know our dinner last night was difficult for you, and I wished to—"

"It's all right," Matthew said. "No gift is necessary."

"Oh, but it is! I realized how much you enjoyed your food—in spite of my daughter's display of willful misbehavior—therefore I wished to bake you a pie. I trust you like sweet yams?" She lifted the golden-crusted pie from the basket to show him. It was held in a pie dish of white clay decorated with small red hearts.

"It . . . truly looks wonderful," Matthew told her. "But I can't accept it."

"Nonsense! Of course you can! And you may return the dish the next time you come to dinner. Say . . . Tuesday evening at six o'clock?"

He looked into her eyes and saw there a rather sad combination of voracity and fear. As gently as possible, he said, "Mrs. Vaughan, I can't accept the pie. And I can't accept your invitation to dinner, either."

She just stared at him, her mouth partway open and the pie dish still offered. "It is not in my power to help your daughter," Matthew continued. "She seems to have her own mind about things, just as you do, and there lies the collision. I regret you have a problem in your household, but I can't solve it for you."

The woman's mouth had opened a little wider.

"Again, thank you for the dinner. I truly did enjoy it, and the company. Now, if you'll excuse—"

"You . . . ungrateful . . . young . . . *bastard!*" she suddenly hissed, her cheeks flaming red and her eyes half-crazed with anger. "'Do you *realize* what *effort* was expended to please you?"

"Uh . . . well . . . I'm sorry, but—"

"You're *sorry,*" she mimicked bitterly. "*Sorry!* Do you know how much money and time I spent on Cherise's gown? Do you know how I worked over that hearth and cleaned that house for your pleasure? Are you sorry about that, too?"

Matthew noticed that several citizens who'd come to the spring for water were watching. If Lucretia noticed, it made no difference to her because she kept firing cannonades at him. "Oh, but you came in our house and ate your fill, didn't you? You sat there like a lord at feast! You even took bread away with you! And now you're *sorry!*" Tears of rage—misguided rage, Matthew thought—wet her eyes. "I thought you were a gentleman! Well, you're a right *sorry* gentleman, aren't you?"

"Mrs. Vaughan," Matthew said firmly, "I cannot save your daughter from what you perceive as—"

"Who asked you to save *anybody,* you self-righteous prig? How dare you speak to me as if I'm a milkmaid! I am a person of esteem in this town! Do you hear me? *Esteem!*"

She was shouting in his face. Matthew said quietly, "Yes, I hear you."

"If I were a man you wouldn't speak to me with such disrespect! Well, damn you! Damn you and Charles Town and damn all you who think you're better than other people!"

"Pardon me," he said, and began walking toward the mansion.

"Yes, go on and *run!*" she hollered. "Run back to Charles Town, where your kind belongs! You city dog!" Something in her voice broke, but she forced it back. "Playing in your ludicrous gardens and dancing at your sinful balls! Go on and run!"

Matthew didn't run, but his walking pace was brisk enough. He saw that the window of Bidwell's upstairs study had opened and there was the master himself, looking out upon this unfortunate scene. Bidwell was grinning, and when he realized Matthew had seen him he put his hand to his mouth to hide it.

"Wait, wait!" the brazen woman shouted. "Here, take your pie!"

Matthew looked back in time to see Lucretia Vaughan hurl the pie—dish and all—into the spring. Then she fired a glare at him that might have scorched iron, turned on her heel, and stalked away, her chin lifted high as if she had put the Charles Town draggletail in his fly-blown place.

Matthew entered the mansion and went directly up the stairs to the magistrate's room. Woodward's shutters were closed, but Matthew thought the woman's enraged vocals must have frightened birds back in the swamp. The magistrate, however, still slept on, though he did shift his position to the side as Matthew stood next to his bed.

"Sir?" Matthew said, touching his shoulder. "Sir?"

Woodward's sleep-swollen eyes opened to slits. He struggled to focus. "Matthew?" he whispered.

"Yes, sir."

"Oh . . . I thought it was you. I had a dream. A crow . . . shrieking. Gone now."

"Can I get you anything?"

"No. Just . . . tired . . . very tired. Dr. Shields was here."

"He was? This morning?"

"Yes. Told me . . . it was Friday. My days and nights . . . they run together."

"I can imagine so. You've been very ill."

Woodward swallowed thickly. "That potion . . . Dr. Shields gives me. It has . . . a very disagreeable taste. I told him I should . . . wish some sugar in it on the next drinking."

Here was a reason for hope, Matthew thought. The magistrate was lucid and his senses were returning. "I think the potion is doing you some good, sir."

"My throat still pains me." He put a hand to it. "But I do feel . . . somewhat lighter. Tell me . . . did I dream this, or . . . did Dr. Shields apply a funnel to my bottom?"

"You had a colonic," Matthew said. He would long remember the aftermath of that particularly repugnant but necessary procedure. So too would the servant who had to wash out the two chamberpots filled with black, tar-like *refusal*.

"Ah. Yes . . . that would explain it. My apologies . . . to all involved."

"No apologies are necessary, sir. You've comported yourself with extreme grace for the . . . uh . . . unpleasantness of your situation." Matthew went to the dresser and got the bowl of fresh water that had been placed there and one of several clean cotton cloths.

"Always . . . the diplomat," Woodward whispered. "This potion . . . does tire me. Matthew . . . what was done . . . to my back?"

"The doctor used blister cups." Matthew dipped the cloth into the water bowl.

"Blister cups," Woodward repeated. "Oh. Yes . . . I do remember now. Quite painful." He managed a grim smile. "I must have been . . . knocking at death's door."

"Not nearly so close as that." Matthew wrang out the wet cloth and then began to gently apply the cool cotton to Woodward's still-pallid face. "Let us just say you were on a precarious street. But you're better now, and you're going to continue improving. Of that I'm positive."

"I trust . . . you are right."

"I am not only right, I am *correct,*" Matthew said. "The worst part of your illness has been vanquished."

"Tell that . . . to my throat . . . and my aching bones. Oh, what a sin it is . . . to be old."

"Your age has nothing to do with your condition, sir." Matthew pressed the cloth to Woodward's forehead. "You have youth in you yet."

"No . . . I have too much past behind me." He stared at nothing, his eyes slightly glazed in appearance, as Matthew continued to dampen his face. "I would . . . give . . . so much . . . to be you, son." Matthew's hand may have been interrupted in its motions for only a few fleeting seconds.

"To be you," Woodward repeated. "And where you are. With the world . . . ahead of you . . . and the luxury of time."

"You have much time ahead of you too, sir."

"My arrow . . . has been shot," he whispered. "And . . . where it fell . . . I do not know. But you . . . you . . . are just now drawing back your bow." He released a long, strengthless sigh. "My advice to you . . . is to aim at a worthy target."

"You will have much further opportunity to help me identify such a target, sir."

Woodward laughed softly, though the act seemed to pain his throat because it ended in a grimace. "I doubt . . . I can help you . . . with much anymore, Matthew. It has come . . . to my attention on this trip . . . that you have a very able mind of your own. You . . . are a man, now . . . with all that manhood entails. The bitter . . . and the sweet. You have made a good start . . . at manhood . . . by standing up for your convictions . . . even against *me*."

"You don't begrudge my opinions?"

"I would feel . . . an utter failure . . . if you had none," he answered.

"Thank you, sir," Matthew said. He finished his application of the cloth and returned it to the water bowl, which he placed atop the dresser again.

"That is *not* to say," Woodward added, in as loud and clear a voice as he could summon, "that . . . we are in agreement. I still say . . . the woman is your nightbird . . . intent on delivering you to the dark. But . . . every man hears a nightbird . . . of some form or fashion. It is the . . . struggle to overcome its call that either . . . creates or destroys a man's soul. You will understand what I mean. Later . . . after the witch is long silenced."

Matthew stood beside the dresser, his head lowered. He said, "Sir? I need to tell you that—" And then he stopped himself. What was the use of it? The magistrate would never understand. Never. He hardly understood it himself, and he'd experienced Linch's power. No, putting these things into words might rob the magistrate of his improving health, and no good could come of it.

"Tell me what?" Woodward asked.

"That Mr. Bidwell is hosting a dinner tonight," was the first thing that entered his mind. "The maskers have arrived early, and evidently there's to be a reception to honor them. I . . . wanted to tell you, in case you heard voices raised in festivity and wished to know why."

"Ah. This Satan-besieged town . . . could benefit . . . from voices raised in festivity." Woodward let his eyes close again. "Oh . . . I am so tired. Come visit me later . . . and we shall talk about . . . our trip home. A journey . . . I sincerely look forward to."

"Yes, sir. Sleep well." Matthew left the room.

In his own bedchamber, Matthew settled down in the chair by the window to continue reading the book on English plays. It was not that he was compelled to do so by the subject matter, but because he wished to give his mind a rest from its constant mazecrawl. It was his belief, also, that one might see a large picture only by stepping back from the frame. He'd been reading perhaps ten minutes when there came a knock at his door.

"Young sir?" It was Mrs. Nettles. "I ha' somethin' sent from Mr. Bidwell."

Matthew opened the door and found that the woman had brought a silver tray on which rested a single, beautifully blown glass goblet filled with amber liquid.

"What's this?"

"Mr. Bidwell asked that I open a verra old bottle of rum. He said ta tell you that you deserved a taste of such, after such a foul taste as ye had just recently." She looked at him questioningly. "Bein' a servant, I did nae ask what he meant."

"He's being kind. Thank you." Matthew took the goblet and smelled its contents. From the heady aroma, the liquor promised to send him to the same peaceful Elysium that the magistrate currently inhabited. Though it was quite early for drinking so numbing a friend, Matthew decided to allow himself at least two good swallows.

"I ha' another direction from Mr. Bidwell," Mrs. Nettles said. "He asks that you take dinner in your room, the kitchen, or at Van Gundy's this eve. He asks me to inform you that your bill at Van Gundy's would be his pleasure."

Matthew realized it was Bidwell's way of telling him he was not invited to the maskers' dinner. Bidwell had no more use for the services of either the magistrate or Matthew, thus out of sight and out of mind. Matthew also suspected that Bidwell was a little wary of allowing him to roam loose at a gathering. "I'll eat at the tavern," he said.

"Yes sir. May I get you anythin' else?"

"No." As soon as he said it, he reversed his course. "Uh . . . yes." The unthinkable thing had entered his mind once more, as if bound to determine how strong was his fortress wall between common sense and insanity. "Would you come in for a moment, please?" She entered and he shut the door.

He drank his first swallow of the rum, which lit a conflagration down his throat. Then he walked to the window and stood looking over the slave quarters in the direction of the tidewater swamp.

"I ha' things ta tend," Mrs. Nettles said.

"Yes. Forgive me for drifting, but . . . what I need to ask you is . . ." He paused again, knowing that in the next few seconds he would be walking a thin and highly dangerous rope. "First of all," he decided to say, "I passed by the field this morning. Where the execution will take place. I saw the stake . . . the firemound . . . everything in preparation."

"Yes sir," she answered, with no emotion whatsoever.

"I know that Rachel Howarth is innocent." Matthew looked directly into Mrs. Nettles's dark, flesh-hooded eyes. "Do you hear me? I *know* it. I also know who is responsible for the two murders and Rachel's predicament . . . but I am absolutely unable to prove any of it."

"Are you free to name this person?"

"No. And please understand that my decision is not because I don't trust you, but because telling you would only compound your agony in this situation, as it has mine. Also, there are . . . circumstances I don't fathom, therefore it's best to speak no names."

"As you wish, sir," she said, but it was spoken with a broad hint of aggravation.

"Rachel will burn on Monday morning. There is no doubt about that. Unless some extraordinary event occurs between now and then to overturn the magistrate's decree, or some revealing proof comes to light. You may be assured I will continue to shake the bushes for such proof."

"That is all well and good, sir, but what does this ha' to do with *me?*"

"For you I have a question," he said. He took his second swallow of rum, and then waited for his eyes to cease watering. Now he had come to the end of the rope, and beyond it lay . . . what?

He took a deep breath and exhaled it. "Do you know anything of the Florida country?"

Mrs. Nettles gave no visible reaction. "The Florida country," she repeated.

"That's right. You may be aware that it's Spanish territory? Perhaps two hundred miles from—"

"I do know your meanin'. And yes, for sure I know them Spaniards are down there. I keep up with my currents."

Matthew gazed out the window again, toward the swamp and the sea. "Do you also then know, or have you heard, that the Spanish offer sanctuary to escaped English criminals and English-owned slaves?"

Mrs. Nettles was a moment in replying. "Yes sir, I've heard. From Mr. Bidwell, talkin' at table one eve with Mr. Winston and Mr. Johnstone. A young slave by the name of Morganthus Crispin took flight last year. He and his woman. Mr. Bidwell believed they was goin' to the Florida country."

"Did Mr. Bidwell try to recapture the slaves?"

"He did. Solomon Stiles and two or three others went."

"Were they successful?"

"Successful," she said, "in findin' the corpses. What was left of 'em. Mr. Bidwell told John Goode somethin' had et 'em, jus' tore 'em up terrible. Likely a *burr,* is what he said."

"Mr. Bidwell told this to John Goode?" Matthew lifted his eyebrows. "Why? To discourage any of the other slaves from running?"

"Yes sir, I 'spect so."

"Were the corpses brought back? Did you see them?"

"No sir, neither one. They left 'em out there, since there wasn't a value to 'em na' more."

"A value." Matthew said, and grunted. "But tell me this, then: was it possible that the slaves were indeed *not* killed? Was it possible they were never found, and Bidwell had to invent such a story?"

"I wouldn't know, sir. Of that Mr. Bidwell would nae confide in me."

Matthew nodded. He took a third drink. "Rachel is going to die for crimes she did not commit, because she fits someone's twisted need. And I can't save her. As much as I wish to . . . as much as I know she is innocent . . . *I can't.*"

Before he could think about it, a fourth swallow of rum had burned down his hatch. "Do you remember saying to me that she needed a champion?"

"I do."

"Well . . . she needs one now more than ever. Tell me this: have any other slaves but Crispin and his wife fled south? Have any tried to reach the Florida country, been caught and returned?"

Her mouth slowly opened. "My Lord," she said softly. "You . . . want to know what the land's like 'tween here and there, don't ye?"

"I said nothing about that. I simply asked if any other—"

"What you asked and what you *meant*," Mrs. Nettles said, "are two different horses. I'm gettin' your drift, sir, and I can't believe what I'm hearin'."

"Exactly what are you hearing, then?"

"You know. That you'd be willin' ta take her out of that gaol and down ta th' Florida country."

"I said nothing of the sort! And please keep your voice lowered!"

"Did you *have* to speak it?" she asked pointedly. "All these questions, like ta run out my ears!" She advanced a step toward him, looking in her severe black dress like a dark-painted wall in motion. "Listen to me, young man, and I trust ye listen *well*. For your further warrant, it is my understandin' that the Florida country lies near a hundred and fifty miles from Fount Royal, nae two hundred . . . but you would nae make *five* miles a'fore you 'n Madam Howarth both were either et by wild animals or scalped by wild Indians!"

"You forget that the magistrate and I arrived here on foot. We walked considerably more than five miles, through mud and in a pouring rain."

"Yes sir," she said, "and look at the magistrate now. Laid low, he is, 'cause of that walk. If you don't believe that had somethin' to do with at least wearin' him out, you're sadly mistook!" Matthew might have become angered, but Mrs. Nettles was only voicing what he already knew to be true.

"The likes of this I've never heard!" She crossed her arms over her massive bosom in a scolding posture, the silver tray gripped in her right hand. "This is a damn dangerous land! I've seen grown men—men with a mite more meat on their bones than *you*—chopped ta their knees by it! What would you do, then? Jus' parade her from the gaol, mount y'selves two horses and ride out th' gate? Ohhhhh, I think nae!"

Matthew finished the glass of rum and hardly felt the fire. "And even if ye *did* fetch her out," the woman continued, "and *did* by some God-awe miracle get her down ta th' Florida country, what then? You think it's a matter of givin' her over ta th' Spanish and then comin' back? No, again you're sadly mistook! There would be *no* comin' back. *Ever.* You'd be livin' the rest of your life out with them *conquista-* . . . them *con-* . . . them squid-eaters!"

"So long as they wouldn't mix it with blood sausage," Matthew muttered.

"What?"

"Nothing. Just . . . thinking aloud." He licked the goblet's rim and then held the glass out. Mrs. Nettles reverted to the role of servant and put the silver tray up to receive the empty goblet.

"Thank you for the information and the candor," Matthew said. Instead of luffing his sails, the rum had stolen his wind. He felt light-headed but heavy at heart. He went to the window and stood beside it with his hand braced against the wall and his head drooping.

"Yes sir. Is there anythin' else?" She walked to the door, where she paused before leaving.

"One thing," Matthew said. "If someone had taken your sister to the Florida country, after she was accused and convicted of witchcraft, she would still be alive today. Wouldn't you have wanted that?"

"Of course, sir. But I wouldn't ask a body to give up his life ta do it."

"Mrs. Nettles, my life will be given up when Rachel is burned on that stake Monday morning. Knowing what I do . . . and unable to save her through the proper legal channels . . . it's going to be more than I can bear. And I fear also that this is a burden that will never disappear, but only grow heavier with the passage of time."

"If that's the case, I regret ever askin' you ta take an interest in her."

"It *is* the case," he replied, with some heat in it. "And you did ask me to take an interest, and I have . . . and here we are."

"Oh, my," Mrs. Nettles said quietly, her eyes widening. "*Oh . . . my.*"

"Is there a meaning behind that? If so, I'd like to hear it."

"You . . . have a *feelin'* for her, do you nae?"

"A feeling? Yes, I care whether she lives or dies!"

"Nae only that," Mrs. Nettles said. "You know of what I'm speakin'. Oh, my. Who'd ha' *thought* such a thing?"

"You may go now." He turned his back to her, directing his attention out the window at some passing figment.

"Does she know? She ought ta. It mi' ease her—"

"Please *go,*" he said, through clenched teeth.

"Yes sir," she answered, rather meekly, and she closed the door behind her.

Matthew eased himself down in the chair again and put his hands to his face. What had he ever done to deserve such torment as this? Of course it was nothing compared to the anguish Rachel would be subjected to in less than seventy-two hours.

He couldn't bear it. He couldn't. For he knew that wherever he ran on Monday morning . . . wherever he hid . . . he would hear Rachel's screams and smell her flesh burning.

He was near drunk from the goblet of fiery rum, but in truth he could have easily swallowed down the bottle. He had come to the end of the road. There was nothing more he could do, say, or discover. Linch had won. When Bidwell was found murdered a week or so hence—after Matthew and the magistrate had left, of course—the tales of Satan's vengeance would spread through Fount Royal and in one month, if that long, the town would be deserted. Linch might even move into the mansion and lord over an estate of ghosts while he plundered the fount.

Matthew's mind was beleaguered. The room's walls had begun to slowly spin, and if he hadn't put down the Sir Richard he might have feared Linch was still trampling through his head.

There were details . . . details that did not fit.

The surveyor, for instance. Who had he been? Perhaps just a surveyor, after all? The gold coin possessed by Shawcombe. From where had the Indian gotten it? The disappearance of Shawcombe and that nasty brood. Where had they gone, leaving their valuables behind?

And the murder of Reverend Grove.

He could understand why Linch had killed Daniel Howarth. But why the reverend? To emphasize that the Devil had no use for a man of God? To remove what the citizens would feel was a source of protection from evil? Or was it another reason altogether, something that Matthew was missing?

He couldn't think anymore. The walls were spinning too fast. He was going to have to stand up and try to reach the bed, if he could. Ready . . . one . . . two . . . three!

He staggered to the bed, barely reaching it before the room's rotation lamed him. Then he lay down on his back, his arms outflung on either side, and with a heaving sigh he gave himself up from this world of tribulations.

Ten

At half-past seven, Van Gundy's tavern was doing a brisk business. On any given Friday night the lamplit, smoky emporium of potables and edibles would have a half-dozen customers, mostly farmers who wished to socialize with their brethren away from the ears of wives and children. On *this* Friday night, with its celebratory air due to the fine weather and the imminent end of Rachel Howarth, fifteen men had assembled to talk, or holler as the case might be, to chew on the tavern's salted beef and drink draught after draught of wine, rum, and apple beer. For the truly adventurous there was available a tavern-brewed corn liquor guaranteed to elevate the earth to the level of one's nose.

Van Gundy—a husky, florid-faced man with a trimmed gray goatee and a few sprouts of peppery hair that stood upright on his scalp—was inspired by this activity to perform. Taking up his gittern, he planted himself amid the revelers and began to howl bawdy songs that involved succulent young wives, chastity belts, duplicate keys, and travelling merchants. This *cattawago* proved so ennobling to the crowd that more orders for strong drink thundered forth and the thin, rather sour-looking woman who tended to the serving was gazed upon by bleary eyes as if she were a veritable Helen of Troy.

"Here is a song!" Van Gundy bellowed, his wind puffing the blue pipe smoke that wafted about him. "I made this up myself, just today!" He struck a chord that would've made a cat swoon and began:

> *"Hi hi ho, here's a tale I know,*
> *'tis a sad sad tale I am sure,*
> *Concerns the witch of Fount Royal,*
> *and her devilish crew,*
> *To call her vile is calling shit mannnnure!"*

Much laughter and tankard-lifting greeted this, of course, but Van Gundy was a fool for music.

> *"Hi hi ho, here's a tale I know,*
> *'tis a sorry sorry tale I know well,*
> *For when the witch of Fount Royal.*
> *has been burnt to cold gray ash,*
> *She'll still be suckin' Satan's cock way down in Hellllll!"*

Matthew thought the roof might be hurled off the tavern by the hurricane of noise generated by this ode. He had chosen his table wisely, sitting at the back of the room as far as possible from the center of activity, but not even the two cups of wine and the cup of apple beer he'd consumed could dull the sickened pain produced by Van Gundy's rape of the ear. These fools were insufferable! Their laughing and gruesome attempts at jokes turned Matthew's stomach. He had the feeling that if he remained much longer in this town he would become an accomplished drunkard and sink to a nadir known only by the worms that thrived in dog dates.

Now Van Gundy turned his talents to tunes concocted on the spot. He pointed at a gent nearby and then walloped a chord:

"Let me sing 'bout old Dick Cushing,
Wore out his wife from his constant pushin'
She called for an ointment to ease her down there,
But all the stuff did was burn off her hair!"

Laughter, hilarity, drinking, and rousting aplenty followed. Another customer was singled out:

"Woe to all who cross Hiram Abercrombie,
For he's got a temper would sting a bee,
He can drink any ten men under a table,
And plow their wives' furrows when they are unable!"

Oh, this was torture! Matthew pushed aside the plate of chicken and beans that had served as a not very appetizing dinner. His appetite had been further killed by that unfortunate filth flung at Rachel, who might have silenced this haven of jesters with a single regal glance.

He finished the last swallow of the apple beer and stood up from his bench. At that moment Van Gundy launched into a new tuneless tune:

"Allow us to welcome fine Solomon Stiles,
Whose talent in life lies in walking for miles,
Through Indian woods and beast-haunted glen,
Searchin' for a squaw to put his prick in!"

Matthew looked toward the door and saw that a man had just entered. As a reply to the laughter and shouts directed at him, this new arrival took off his leather tricorn and gave a mocking bow to the assembled idiots. Then he proceeded to a table and sat down as Van Gundy turned his graceless wit upon the next grinning victim, by name Jethro Sudrucker.

Matthew again seated himself. He'd realized that an interesting opportunity lay before him, if he handled it correctly. Was not this the Solomon Stiles who Bidwell had told him was a hunter, and who had gone out with a party of men in search of the escaped slaves? He watched as Stiles—a lean, rawboned man of perhaps fifty years—summoned the serving-woman over, and then he stood up and went to the table.

Just before Matthew was about to make his introduction, Van Gundy strummed his gittern and bellowed forth:

"We should all feel pity for young Matthew Corbett,
I heard beside the spring he was savagely bit.
By that venomous serpent whose passion is pies,
And whose daughter bakes loaves between her hot thighs!"

Matthew blushed red even before the wave of laughter struck him, and redder yet after it had rolled past. He saw that Solomon Stiles was offering only a bemused smile, the man's square-jawed face weathered and sharp-chiselled as tombstone granite. Stiles had closely trimmed black hair, gray at the temples. From his left eyebrow up across his forehead was the jagged scar of a dagger or rapier slash. His nose was the shape of an Indian tomahawk, his eyes dark brown and meticulous in their inspection of the young man who stood before him. Stiles was dressed simply, in black breeches and a plain white shirt.

"Mr. Stiles?" Matthew said, his face still flushed. Van

Gundy had gone on to skewer another citizen on his gittern spike. "My name is—"

"I'm aware of your name, Mr. Corbett. You are famous."

"Oh. Yes. Well . . . that incident today was regrettable."

"I meant your scuffle with Seth Hazelton. I attended your whipping."

"I see." He paused, but Stiles did not offer him a seat. "May I join you?"

Stiles motioned toward the opposite bench, and Matthew sat down. "How's the magistrate's health?" Stiles asked. "Still poorly?"

"No, actually he's much improved. I have hopes he'll be on his feet soon."

"In time for the execution, possibly?"

"Possibly," Matthew said.

"It seems only fitting he should witness it and have the satisfaction of seeing justice done. You know, *I* selected the tree from which the stake was cut."

"Oh." Matthew busied himself by flicking some imaginary dust from his sleeve. "No, I didn't know that."

"Hannibal Green, I, and two others hauled it and planted it. Have you been out to take a look?"

"I've seen it, yes."

"What do you think? Does it look sufficient for the purpose?"

"I believe it does."

Stiles took a tobacco pouch, a small ebony pipe, and an ivory matchbox from his pocket. He set about filling the pipe. "I inherited the task from Nicholas. That rascal must have gotten down on bended knee to Bidwell."

"Sir?"

"Nicholas Paine. Winston told me that Bidwell sent him to Charles Town this morning. A supply trip, up the coast to

Virginia. What that rascal will do to avoid a little honest labor!" He fired a match with the flame of the table's lantern and then set his tobacco alight.

Matthew assumed Winston had performed trickery upon the morning watchman to advance this fiction of Paine's departure. Obviously an agreement had been reached that would benefit Winston's pockets and status.

Stiles blew out a whorl of smoke. "He's dead."

Matthew's throat clutched. "Sir?"

"Dead," Stiles repeated. "In *my* book, at least. The times I've helped him when he asked me, and then he runs when there's sweating to be done! Well, he's a proper fool to go out on that road alone, I'll tell you. He knows better than that. Bidwell must have some intrigue in the works, as usual." Stiles cocked his head to one side, smoke leaking between his teeth. "*You* don't know what it might be, do you?"

Matthew folded his hands together. He spent a few seconds in thought. "Well," he said. "I might. It *is* interesting what one overhears in that house. Not necessarily meaning to, of course."

"Of course."

"I'm sure both Mr. Bidwell and Mr. Winston would deny it," Matthew said, leaning his head forward in a conspiratorial gesture, "but I might have . . . or might *not* have, you understand . . . overheard the mention of muskets."

"Muskets," Stiles repeated. He took another draw from his pipe.

"Yes sir. Could it be a shipment of muskets? And that might be what Mr. Paine has gone to negotiate?"

Stiles grunted and puffed his pipe. The serving-woman came with a steaming bowl of chicken stew, a spoon, and a rum cup. Matthew asked for another cup of apple beer.

"I was wondering," Matthew said after a space of time

during which Stiles put aside his pipe and began eating the stew, "if Mr. Bidwell might fear an Indian attack."

"No, not that. He would have told me if he feared the redskins were wearing paint."

"There are Indians near Fount Royal, I presume?"

"Near. Far. Somewhere out there. I've seen their signs, but I've never seen a redskin."

"They're not of a warlike nature, then?"

"Hard to say what kind of nature they are." Stiles paused to take a drink of rum. "If you mean, do I think they'd attack us? No. If you mean, would I go in with a band of men and attack *them?* No. Not even if I knew where they were, which I don't."

"But they do know where *we* are?"

Stiles laughed. "Ha! That's a good one, young man! As I said, I've never seen a redskin in these woods, but I *have* seen them before, further north. They walk on leaves as birds fly on air. They disappear into the earth while you're looking in their direction, and come up again at your back. Oh yes. They know everything about us. They watch us with great interest, I'm sure, but we would never see them unless they wanted to be seen. And they definitely do *not.*"

"Then in your opinion a traveller, say, need not fear being scalped by them?"

"I myself don't fear it," Stiles said. He spooned stew into his mouth. "Then again, I always carry a musket and a knife and I always know what direction to run. Neither would I go out there alone. It's not the redskins I would fear most, but the wild beasts."

Matthew's apple beer was delivered. He drank some and waited a time before he made his next move. "If not Indians, then," he said thoughtfully, "there might be another reason for a possible shipment of muskets."

"And what would that be?"

"Well . . . Mrs. Nettles and I were engaged in conversation, and she made mention of a slave who escaped last year. He and his woman. Morganthus Crispin, I think the name was."

"Yes. Crispin. I recall that incident."

"They tried to reach the Florida country, I understand?"

"Yes. And were killed and half-eaten before they got two leagues from town."

"Hm," Matthew said. So it was true, after all. "Well," he went on, "I wonder if possibly . . . just possibly, mind you . . . Mr. Bidwell might be concerned that other slaves could follow Crispin's example, and that he wishes the muskets as a show of . . . shall we say . . . keeping his valuables in their place. Especially when he brings in younger and stronger slaves to drain the swamp." He took a stiff drink and then set the cup down. "I'm curious about this, Mr. Stiles. In your opinion, could anyone . . . a slave, I mean . . . actually reach the Florida country?"

"Two of them almost did," Stiles answered, and Matthew sat very still. "It was during Fount Royal's first year. Two slaves—a brother and sister—escaped, and I was sent after them with three other men. We tracked them to near a half-dozen leagues of the Spanish territory. I suppose the only reason we found them is that they lit a signal fire. The brother had fallen in a gully and broken his ankle."

"And they were brought back here?"

"Yes. Bidwell held them in irons and immediately arranged for them to be shipped north and sold. It wouldn't do for any slave to be able to describe the territory or draw a map." Stiles relit his pipe with a second match from the ivory matchbox. "Tell me this, if you are able," he said as he drew flame into the pipe's bowl. "When Mrs. Nettles mentioned this to you, in what context was it? I mean to ask, have you seen any indication that Bidwell is concerned about the slaves?"

Matthew again took a few seconds to formulate a reply. "Mr. Bidwell did express some concern that I not go down into the quarters. The impression I got was that he felt it might be . . . uh . . . detrimental to my health."

"I wouldn't care to go down there in any case," Stiles said, his eyes narrowing. "But it seems to me he might be in fear of an uprising. Such a thing has happened before, in other towns. Little wonder he'd wish to keep such fears a secret! Coming on the heels of the witch, an uprising would surely destroy Fount Royal!"

"My thoughts exactly," Matthew agreed. "Which is why it's best not spoken to anyone."

"Of course not! I wouldn't care to be blamed for starting a panic."

"And neither would I. My curiosity again, sir . . . and pardon me for not knowing these things an experienced hunter as yourself knows . . . but I would think you might lose your way on such a long journey as from here to the Florida country. How far exactly *is* it?"

"I judge it to be a hundred and forty-seven miles, by the most direct route."

"The most direct route?" Matthew asked. He took another drink. "I am still amazed, though, sir. You must have an uncanny sense of direction."

"I pride myself on my woods craft." Stiles pulled from the pipe, leaned his head slightly back, and blew smoke toward the ceiling. "But I must admit I did have the benefit of a map."

"Oh," Matthew said. "Your map."

"Not *my* map. Bidwell's. He bought it from a dealer in

Charles Town. It's marked in French by the original explorer—that's how old it is—but I've found it to be accurate."

"It so happens I read and speak French. If you have need of a translation, I'd be glad to be of service."

"You might ask Bidwell. He has the map."

"Ah," Matthew said.

"Van Gundy, you old goat!" Stiles shouted toward the tavern-keeper, not without affection. "Let's have some more rum over here! A cup for the young man, too!"

"Oh, not for me, thank you. I think I've had my fill." Matthew stood up. "I must be on my way."

"Nonsense! Stay and enjoy the evening. Van Gundy's going to be playing his gittern again shortly."

"I hate to miss such an experience, but I have some reading to be done."

"That's what's wrong with you legalists!" Stiles said, but he was smiling. "You think too much!"

Matthew returned the smile. "Thank you for the company. I hope to see you again."

"My pleasure, sir. Oh . . . and thank *you* for the information. You can be sure I'll keep it to myself."

"I have no doubt," Matthew said, and he made his way out of the smoke-filled place before that deadly gittern could be again unsheathed.

On his walk back to the mansion, Matthew sifted what he'd learned like a handful of rough diamonds. Indeed, with luck and fortitude, it was possible to reach the Florida country. Planning the trip—taking along enough food, matches, and the like—would be essential, and so too would be finding and studying that map. He doubted it would be in the library. Most likely Bidwell kept the map somewhere in his upstairs study.

But what was he *considering?* Giving up his rights as an

Englishman? Venturing off to live in a foreign land? He might know French and Latin, but Spanish was not a point of strength. Even if he got Rachel out of the gaol—the first problem—and out of the town—the second problem—and down to the Florida country—the third and most mind-boggling problem—then was he truly prepared never to set foot again on English earth?

Or never to see the magistrate again?

Now here was another obstacle. If indeed he surmounted the first two problems and set off with Rachel, then the realization of what Matthew had done could well lay the magistrate in his grave. He might be setting his nightbird free at the cost of killing the man who had opened his own cage from a life of grim despair.

That's what's wrong with you legalists. You think too much.

Candles and lamps were ablaze at the mansion. Obviously the festivity was still under way. Matthew entered the house and heard voices from the parlor. He was intent on unobtrusively walking past the room on his way to the stairs when someone said, "Mr. Corbett! Please join us!"

Alan Johnstone had just emerged on his cane from the dining room, along with the gray-bearded man that Matthew had assumed was the acting troupe's leader. Both men were well dressed—Johnstone certainly more so than the masker—and held goblets of wine. The schoolmaster had adorned his face with a dusting of white powder, just as he'd done the night of Matthew's and the magistrate's arrival. The men appeared fed and satisfied, indicating that dinner had just recently adjourned.

"This young man is Matthew Corbett, the magistrate's clerk," Johnstone explained to his companion. "Mr. Corbett, this is Mr. Phillip Brightman, the founder and principal actor of the Red Bull Players."

"A pleasure!" Brightman boomed, displaying a basso voice powerful enough to wake cemetery sleepers. He shook Matthew's hand with a grip that might have tested the blacksmith's strength, but he was in fact a slim and rather unassuming-looking fellow though he did have that commanding, theatrical air about him.

"Very good to meet you." Matthew withdrew his hand, thinking that Brightman's power had been seasoned by a life of turning a gruelling wheel between the poles of the maskers' art and the necessity of food on the table. "I understand your troupe has arrived somewhat early."

"Early, yes. Our standing engagements in two other communities were . . . um . . . unfortunately cancelled. But now we're glad to be here among such treasured friends!"

"Mr. Corbett!" Winston strolled out of the parlor, wineglass in hand. He was clean, close-shaven, relaxed and smiling, and dressed in a spotless dark blue suit. "Do join us and meet Mr. Smythe!"

Bidwell suddenly appeared behind Winston to toss in his two pence. "I'm sure Mr. Corbett has matters to attend to upstairs. We shouldn't keep him. Isn't that right, Mr. Corbett?"

"Oh, I believe he should at least step in and say hello," Winston insisted. "Perhaps have a glass of wine."

Bidwell glowered at Matthew, but he said with no trace of rancor, "As you please, Edward," and returned to the parlor.

"Come along," Johnstone urged, as he limped on his cane past Matthew. "A glass of wine for your digestion."

"I'm full up with apple beer. But may I ask who Mr. Smythe is?"

"The Red Bull's new stage manager," Brightman supplied. "Newly arrived from England, where he performed excellent service to the Saturn Cross Company and before that to James Prue's Players. I wish to hear firsthand about the witch, too. Come, come!" Before Matthew could make an excuse to leave—since he *did* have a matter to attend to upstairs concerning a certain French-drawn map—Brightman grasped him by the upper arm and guided him into the parlor.

"Mr. David Smythe, Mr. Matthew Corbett," Winston said, with a gesture toward each individual in turn. "The magistrate's clerk, Mr. Smythe. He delivered the guilty decree to the witch."

"Really? Fascinating. And rather fearful too, was it not?" Smythe was the young blond-haired man Matthew had seen sitting beside Brightman on the driver's plank of the lead wagon. He had an open, friendly face, his smile revealing that he'd been blessed with a mouthful of sturdy white teeth. Matthew judged him to be around twenty-five.

"Not so fearful," Matthew replied. "I did have the benefit of iron bars between us. And Mr. Bidwell was at my side."

"Fat lot of good I might have done!" Bidwell said mirthfully, also in an effort to take control of this conversation. "One snap from that damned woman and I would've left my boots standing empty!"

Brightman boomed a laugh. Smythe laughed also, and so did Bidwell at his own wit, but Winston and the schoolmaster merely offered polite smiles.

Matthew was stone-faced. "Gentlemen, I remain unconvinced that—" He felt a tension suddenly rise in the room, and Bidwell's laugh abruptly ended. "—that Mr. Bidwell would have been anything less than courageous," Matthew finished, and the sigh of relief from the master of Fount Royal was almost audible.

"I neither recall meeting the woman nor her husband last year," Brightman said. "Did they not attend our play, I wonder?"

"Likely not." Bidwell crossed the parlor to a decanter of wine and filled his own glass. "He was a rather quiet . . . one might say reclusive . . . sort, and she was surely busy fashioning her own acting skills. Uh . . . *not* to infer that your craft has anything whatsoever to do with the infernal realm."

Brightman laughed again, though not nearly so heartily. "Some would disagree with you, Mr. Bidwell! Particularly a reverend hereabouts. You know we had occasion to oust a certain Bible-thumper from our camp this afternoon."

"Yes, I heard. Reverend Jerusalem possesses a fire that unfortunately sears the righteous as well as the wicked. Not to fear, though: as soon as he applies the rite of sanctimony to the witch's ashes, he'll be booted out of our Garden of Eden."

Oh, the wit overflowed tonight! Matthew thought. "The rite of sanctimony?" He recalled hearing Jerusalem use that phrase when the preacher had first come to the gaol to confront his "enemy mine." "What kind of nonsense is *that*?"

"Nothing you would understand," Bidwell said, with a warning glance.

"I'm sure he would," Johnstone countered. "The preacher plans to administer some kind of ridiculous rite over Madam Howarth's ashes to keep her spirit, phantasm, or whatever from returning to haunt Fount Royal. If you ask me, I think Jerusalem has studied Marlowe and Shakespeare at least as much as he's studied Adam and Moses!"

"Oh, you speak the names of our gods, sir!" Brightman said, with a huge smile. His smile, however, quickly faded as a more serious subject came to mind. "I do heavily regret the passing of *another* reverend, though. Reverend Grove was a man who saw a noble place for theatrical endeavors. I do miss seeing him this trip. David, you would have liked the man. He was of good humor, good faith, and certainly good reason. Mr. Bidwell, I'm sure your community is diminished by his absence."

"It most certainly is. But after the witch is dead—and thank God it will be soon—and our town back on an even keel, we shall endeavor to find a man of similar sterling qualities."

"I doubt you shall find a reverend who was a better player at chess!" Brightman said, smiling again. "Grove trounced me soundly on two occasions!"

"He trounced us all," Johnstone said, with a sip of his wine. "It got to the point I refused to play him."

"He once beat me in a game that took all of five minutes," Winston added. "Of course, with him calling out all his moves in Latin and me being a dunce at that language, I was befuddled from the opening pawn."

"Well," Brightman said, and he lifted his wineglass. "Let me propose a toast to the memory of Reverend Grove. And also the memory of so many others who have departed your town, whether by choice or circumstance."

All but Matthew, who had no glass, participated in the toast. "I do miss seeing others I recall," Brightman continued, sadness in his voice. "A stroll around town told me how much the witch has hurt you. There weren't nearly so many empty houses, were there? Or burned ones?"

"No, there were not," Winston said, with either admirable pluck or stunning gall.

"Demonic doings, I gather?" Brightman asked Bidwell, who nodded. Then the thespian turned his attention to Johnstone. "And the schoolhouse burned too?"

"Yes." The schoolmaster's voice held an angry edge. "Burned to the ground before my eyes. The sorriest sight of my life. If our fire fighters had been at all trained and a great deal less lazy, the schoolhouse might have been saved."

"Let us not delve into that again, Alan." It was obvious to Matthew that Bidwell was trying to soothe a terribly sore point. "We must let it go."

"*I'll* not let it go!" Johnstone snapped, his eyes darting toward Bidwell. "It was a damned crime that those so-called firemen stood there and allowed that schoolhouse—*my schoolhouse*—to burn! After all that work put into it!"

"Yes, Alan, it was a crime," Bidwell agreed. He stared into his glass. "But all the work was done by others, so why should you be so angry? The schoolhouse can be—and shall be—rebuilt." Brightman nervously cleared his throat, because again a tension had entered the room.

"What you mean to say, Robert, is that due to my deformity I simply stood aside while others did the labor?" Johnstone's anger was turning colder. "Is that your meaning?"

"I said . . . and meant . . . nothing of the sort."

"Gentlemen, gentlemen!" Brightman's smile was intended to return warmth to the gathering. "Let us not forget that Fount Royal faces the morning of a wondrous new day! I have no doubt the schoolhouse and all the rest of the structures shall be returned to their former glory, and that those houses vacated by past friends shall be soon inhabited by new ones." Still the chilly air lingered between Bidwell and Johnstone. Brightman looked to Smythe. "David, what was that you were telling me this afternoon? You recall, before that preacher stormed in? Mr. Bidwell, you might find this of interest!"

"Yes?" Bidwell raised his eyebrows, while Johnstone hobbled away to refill his glass.

"Oh . . . about the man," Smythe said. "Yes, this was peculiar. A man came to the camp today. He was looking about. I know it sounds very odd, but . . . I found something familiar about him. His walk . . . his bearing . . . something."

"And you know who it was?" Brightman asked Bidwell. "Of all people, your ratcatcher!" At the mere mention of the man, Matthew's throat seemed to clutch.

"Linch?" Bidwell frowned. "Was he over there bothering you?"

"No, not that," Smythe said. "He seemed to be just . . . inspecting us, I suppose. We'd had several visitors who just strolled around the camp. But this man . . . well, it *does* sound very strange, but . . . I watched him for a moment or two, and then I approached him from behind. He had picked up a blue glass lantern that is used in one of our morality scenes. The way his fingers moved over the glass . . . the way he turned the lantern this way and that . . . I thought I had *seen* such movements before. And I also thought I knew who the man was, yet . . . he was dressed in filthy clothes, and he was so very changed from the last time I'd seen him, when I was perhaps . . . oh . . . sixteen or seventeen years old."

"Pardon me," Matthew said, his throat still tight. "But who did you think Mr. Linch might have been?"

"Well, I spoke the name. I'm sure I sounded incredulous. I said: 'Mr. Lancaster?' and he turned around." Smythe put a finger to his mouth, as if determining whether to continue this tale or not.

"Yes?" Matthew prodded. "What then?"

"I . . . know this is absolutely ridiculous . . . but then again, Mr. Lancaster *did* have an act in the circus that involved trained rats, so when Mr. Brightman explained to me that the man was Fount Royal's ratcatcher, then . . . it's all very puzzling."

"Puzzling?" Johnstone had returned with his fresh glass of wine. "How so?"

"I could swear the man *was* Jonathan Lancaster," Smythe said. "In fact, I *would* swear it. He turned toward me and looked me right in the face . . . and I saw his eyes. Such eyes . . . pale as ice . . . and piercing to the soul. I have seen them before. The man *is* Jonathan Lancaster, but . . ." He shook his head, his blond brows knit. "I . . . had not planned on mentioning this to anyone but Mr. Brightman. I intended first to locate Mr. Lancaster—your ratcatcher, I mean—and find out for myself, in private, why he has . . . um . . . sunken to such a low profession."

"My pardon, please!" Brightman said. "I didn't realize this was a personal matter!"

"Oh, that's all right." He gave Brightman a rather vexed glance. "Once a cat is out of a bag, sir, it is very difficult to put it back in again."

"The same might be said of a fox," Matthew offered. "But tell me: did Linch—or Lancaster—speak to you? Did he seem to recognize you as well?"

"No, I saw no recognition on his part. As soon as I spoke his name, he hurried away. I was going to follow him, but . . . I decided he might be ashamed to be seen dressed in rags. I wished not to intrude on his privacy until I had considered if I was mistaken or not."

"Gwinett Linch has *always* been Gwinett Linch, from what I know," Bidwell contended. "Who *is* this Jonathan Lancaster?"

"Mr. Lancaster was employed at the circus at the same time my father was its manager," Smythe said. "I had the run of the place, and I helped where my father directed me. As I said, Mr. Lancaster had an act that involved trained rats, but he also—"

The door's bell rang with such ferocity that it must have been near pulled off its hinge. Before two seconds had passed, the door burst open and the visitor announced himself with a soul-withering shout: "How *dare* ye! How *dare* ye do me such an injury!"

"Oh my Lord!" Brightman said, his eyes wide. "The storm returns!"

Indeed the black-clad, black-tricorned whirlwind entered the room, his gaunt and wrinkled face florid with rage and the cords standing out in his neck. "I demand to know!" Exodus Jerusalem hollered, aiming his mouth at Bidwell. "Why was I not invited to thy preparations?"

"What preparations?" Bidwell fired back, his own temper in danger of explosion. "And how dare *you* enter my house with such rudeness!"

"If thee wisheth to speak of rudeness, we might speak of the rudeness thou hast not only shown to me, but also shown to thy God Almighty!" The last two words had been brayed so loudly the walls seemed to tremble. "It was not enough for thee to allow such sinful filth as *play-actors* into thy town, but then thou forceth me to abide within nostril's reach of them on the same *street!* God warrant it, I should have given thy town up as lost to Hell's fires that very instant! And I still wouldst, if not for the rite of just layment!"

"The rite of *just layment?*" Bidwell now exhibited a suspicious scowl. "Hold a moment, preacher! I thought you said it was the rite of sanctimony!"

"Oh . . . yes, it *is* also called such!" Jerusalem's voice had faltered, but already it was gathering hot wind again for another bellow. "Wouldst thou believe that so important a rite wouldst only have *one* name? Even God Himself is also called Jehovah! Lord above, deliver thy servant from such blind pride as we vieweth aplenty in this room!"

Matthew was not so blind as to fail to realize that Jerusalem, as was his nature, had taken center stage in the prideful parlor. Brightman and Smythe had retreated for the safety of their ears, Bidwell had backed up several paces, and even the stalwart schoolmaster had staggered back, the knuckles of his cane-gripping hand white with pressure.

Winston, however, had stood his ground. "What's the meaning of bursting in on Mr. Bidwell's private affairs?"

"Sir, in God's great kingdom there are *no* private affairs!" Jerusalem snapped. "It is only Satan who craveth secrecy! That is why I am so amazed and confounded by the fact that thou wouldst hide this meeting with the play-actors from mine eyes!"

"I did *not* hide anything from you!" Bidwell said. "Anyway, how the hell . . . I mean . . . how on earth did you find out the actors were even *here?*"

"I wouldst have remained unenlightened had I not ventured to the play-actors' camp—as a man who loveth peace and brotherhood—to speak with their leader. And *then* I learneth from some fat thespian whose saint must surely be gluttony that Mr. Brightman is here with thee! And I kneweth exactly what must be transpiring!"

"And exactly what *is* transpiring?" Winston asked.

"The planning, as thou well knoweth!" It was spoken with dripping sarcasm. "To cut me out of the execution day!"

"*What?*" Bidwell saw that Mrs. Nettles and two serving-girls had come to peer into the room, perhaps fearing violence from the wall-shaking volume. He waved them away. "Preacher, I fail to understand what you're—"

"I went to see thee, brother Brightman," Jerusalem interrupted, addressing the other man, "for the purpose of creating an agreement. I understand that thou planneth a play after the witch hath been burned. That evening, as I hear. I mineself have intentions that very eve to deliver a message to the citizens upon the burning battleground. As an observer of debased human nature, I fully realize there are more misguided sinners who wouldst attend a pig-and-bear show than hear the word of God Almighty, no matter how compelling the speaker. Therefore I wished—as a peaceful, brotherly man—to offer up mine services to enricheth your performance. Say . . . a message delivered to the crowd between each scene, building to a finale that will hopefully enricheth us *all?*"

A stunned quiet reigned. Brightman broke it, with thunder. "This is *outrageous!* I don't know from where you hear your faulty information, but we're planning no play on the night of the witch's burning! Our plans are to exhibit morality scenes several nights afterward!"

"And from where *do* you get this information, preacher?" Winston challenged.

"From a fine woman of thy town. Madam Lucretia Vaughan came to speak with me earlier this evening. She wisheth to afford the crowd with her breads and pies, a sample of which she was most delighted to give." Matthew had to wonder if that was the only sample the woman had given the lecherous rogue.

"In fact," Jerusalem went on, "Madam Vaughan hath created a special bread to be offered at the burning. She calleth it 'Witch Riddance Loaf.'"

"For God's justice!" Matthew said, unable to hold his silence an instant longer. "Get this fool out of here!"

"Spoken as a true demon in training!" Jerusalem retorted, with a sneering grin. "If thy magistrate knew anything of God's justice, he would have a second stake prepared for *thee!*"

"His magistrate . . . *does* know God's justice, sir," came a weak but determined voice from the parlor's doorway.

Every man turned toward the sound.

And there—miraculously!—stood Isaac Temple Woodward, returned from the land of the near-dead.

"Magistrate!" Matthew exclaimed. "You shouldn't be out of bed!" He rushed to his side to offer him support, but Woodward held out a hand to ward him off while he gripped the wall with his other.

"I am sufficiently able . . . to be out, up, and about. Please . . . allow me room in which to draw a breath."

Not only had Woodward climbed out of bed and negotiated the staircase, he had also dressed in a pair of tan breeches and a fresh white shirt. His thin calves were bare, however, and he wore no shoes. His face was yet very pallid, which made the dark purple hollows beneath his eyes darker still; his scalp was also milk-pale, the age-spots upon his head a deep red in contrast. Gray grizzle covered his cheeks and chin.

"Please! Sit down, sit down!" Bidwell recovered from his shock and motioned to the chair nearest Woodward.

"Yes . . . I think I shall. The stairs have winded me." Woodward, with Matthew's aid, eased to the chair and sank down onto it. Matthew felt no trace of fever from the magistrate, but there was still emanating from him the sweetish-sour odor of the sickbed.

"Well, this is quite amazing!" Johnstone said. "The doctor's potion must have gotten him up!"

"I believe . . . you are correct, sir. A dose of that elixir . . . thrice a day . . . would surely awaken Lazarus."

"Thank God for it!" Matthew pressed his hand to Woodward's shoulder. "I would never have let you get out of bed, if I'd known you were able, but . . . this is wonderful!"

The magistrate put his hand on Matthew's. "My throat still pains me. My chest as well. But . . . any improvement is welcome." He squinted, trying to make out the faces of two men he didn't know. "I'm sorry. Have we met?"

Bidwell made the introductions. Neither Brightman nor Smythe stepped forward to shake hands; in fact, Matthew noted, they stayed well on the other side of the room.

"Some wine, Magistrate?" Bidwell pushed a glass into Woodward's hand, whether he wanted it or not. "We are so very glad you've come out the other side of your ordeal!"

"No one more glad than I," Woodward rasped. He sipped the wine, but couldn't taste a hint of it. Then his gaze went to the preacher, sharpening as it travelled. "In reply to your comment concerning God's justice, sir . . . I must say that I believe God to be the most lenient judge . . . in all of creation . . . and merciful beyond all imaginings. Because if He were not . . . you would have found yourself called to His courtroom on a lightning bolt by now."

Jerusalem braced himself to make some cutting reply, but he seemed to think better of it. He bowed his head. "I humbly apologize for any remark that might have caused thee distress, sir. It is not mine wish to offend the law."

"Why not?" Woodward asked, taking another tasteless drink. "You've offended . . . everyone else hereabouts, it seems."

"Uh . . . pardon, please," Brightman spoke up, a little nervously. "David and I ought to be going. I mean no offense either, Magistrate. We both wish to hear about your experience with the witch, but . . . as you might well understand . . . the ability of a thespian to project lies in the throat. If we should . . . um . . . find difficulty, in that area, then—"

"Oh, I didn't think!" Woodward said. "Please forgive me. Of course . . . you don't wish to risk any health complications!"

"Exactly, sir. David, shall we go? Mr. Bidwell, thank you for a wonderful dinner and a gracious evening." Brightman was obviously in a hurry to leave, fearing that any throat affliction might doom his play-acting. Matthew was eager to know more about Linch or Lancaster or whatever his name was, but now was not the time. He decided that first thing in the morning he would seek out Smythe for the rest of the story.

"I shall join thee!" Jerusalem announced to the two men, and both of them looked further stricken. "It seems we have much to talk over and plan, does it not? Now . . . concerning these morality scenes. How long are they to be? I ask because I wish to keep a certain . . . shall we say . . . rhythm to the pace of my message!"

"Ahhhh, how magnificent it is . . . to be free from that bed!" Woodward said, as Bidwell showed his guests and the pest out. "How goes it, Mr. Winston?"

"Fine, sir. I can't tell you how gratified I am to see you doing so much better."

"Thank you. Dr. Shields should be here soon . . . for my third dose of the day. The stuff has . . . burned my tongue to a cinder, but thank God I can breathe."

"I have to say, you seemed at a dangerous point." Johnstone finished his wine and set the glass aside. "Far *past* a dangerous point, to be more truthful. I'm sure you had no way of knowing this, but there are some—many—who feel Madam Howarth cursed you for handing down the decree."

Bidwell entered again, and had heard the last of what Johnstone had said. "Alan, I don't think it's proper to mention such a thing!"

"No, no, it's all right." Woodward waved a reassuring hand. "I would be surprised if . . . people did *not* say such a thing. If I *was* cursed, it was not by the witch . . . but by the bad weather and my own . . . weak blood. But I'm going to be fine now. In a few days . . . I shall be as fit as I ever was."

"Hear, hear!" Winston said, and raised his glass.

"And fit to travel, too," Woodward added. He lifted his hand and rubbed his eyes, which were still bloodshot and bleary. "This is an . . . incident I wish to put far behind me. What say you, Matthew?"

"The same, sir."

Johnstone cleared his throat. "I should be going myself, now. Robert, thank you for the evening. We shall . . . um . . . have to discuss the future of the schoolhouse at a later date."

"That brings something to mind!" Woodward said. "Alan . . . you should find this of interest. In my delirium . . . I had a dream of Oxford."

"Really, sir?" Johnstone wore a faint smile. "I should say many former students suffer deliriums of Oxford."

"Oh, I was *there!* Right there, on the sward! I was . . . a young man. I had places to go . . . and much to accomplish."

"You heard the tolling of Great Tom, I presume?"

"Certainly I did! One who hears that bell . . . never forgets it!" Woodward looked up at Matthew and gave him a weak smile that nevertheless had the power to rend the clerk's heart. "I shall take you to Oxford one day. I shall show you . . . the halls . . . the great rooms of learning . . . the wonderful *smell* of the place. Do you recall that, Alan?"

"The most singular aroma of my experience was that of the bitter ale at the Chequers Inn, sir. That and the dry aroma of an empty pocket, I fear."

"Yes, that too." Woodward smiled dreamily. "I smelled the *grass.* The chalk. The oaks . . . that stand along the Cherwell. I was there . . . I swear it. I was there as much as . . . any flesh and blood can be. I even found myself at the door of my social fraternity. The old door . . . of the Carleton

Society. And there . . . right there before me . . . was the ram's head bellpull . . . and the brass plaque with its motto. *Ius omni est ius omnibus.* Oh, how I recall that door . . . that bellpull, and the plaque." He closed his eyes for a few seconds, taking in the wondrous memory. Then he opened them again and Matthew saw that Woodward's eyes had grown moist. "Alan . . . your society was . . . what did you say it was?"

"The Ruskins, sir. An education fraternity."

"Ah. Do you recall your motto?"

"Certainly I do. It was . . ." He paused, gathering it from the mist. *"The greatest sin is ignorance."*

"There's a fitting motto for an educator . . . is it not?" Woodward asked. "As a jurist, I might . . . disagree with it . . . but then again, we were all young and yet to be schooled . . . at the university of life, were we not?"

"Oxford was difficult," Johnstone said. "But the university of life is well nigh impossible."

"Yes. It does . . . grade rather harshly." The magistrate gave a long sigh, his newfound strength now almost spent. "Pardon me . . . for my rambling. It seems that when one is ill . . . and so near death . . . the past becomes paramount . . . to ease the dwindling of one's future."

"You need never ask apology of me to reflect on Oxford, Magistrate," Johnstone said with what seemed to Matthew an admirable grace. "I too still walk those halls in my memory. Now . . . if you'll please forgive me . . . my knee also has a memory, and it is calling for liniment. Good night to you all."

"I'll walk with you, Alan," Winston offered, and Johnstone accepted with a nod. "Good night, Mr. Bidwell. Magistrate. Mr. Corbett."

"Yes, good night," Bidwell replied.

Winston followed as Johnstone limped out of the room, leaning even more than usual on his cane. Then Bidwell poured himself the last few swallows of wine from the decanter and went upstairs to avoid any discourse or possible friction with Matthew. As Woodward half-dozed in the chair, Matthew awaited the arrival of Dr. Shields.

The question of Linch/Lancaster was uppermost in Matthew's mind. Here, at last, might be some hope to cling to. If Smythe could positively identify Linch as this other man, it would be a starting point to convince Bidwell that a fiction had been created around Rachel. Was it too much to hope for that all this might be accomplished on the morrow?

ELEVEN

A passing thundershower had wet the earth just before dawn, but Saturday's sun shone through the dissipating clouds, and the blue sky again reappeared before the hour of eight. By then Matthew had finished his breakfast and was on his way to the maskers' camp.

He discovered—by sense of hearing before sense of sight—Phillip Brightman in discourse with two other thespians, all of them sitting in chairs behind a canvas screen, reading over and reciting pages from one of their morality scenes. When Matthew asked where he might find David Smythe, Brightman directed him to a yellow awning set up to protect a number of trunks, lanterns, and sundry other prop items. Beneath it Matthew found Smythe inspecting some brightly hued costumes that one of the troupe's women was adorning with rather used-looking peacock feathers.

"Good morning, Mr. Smythe," Matthew said. "May I have a word with you?"

"Oh . . . good morning, Mr. Corbett. What may I help you with?"

Matthew glanced quickly at the seamstress. "May we speak in private, please?"

"Certainly. Mrs. Prater, these are coming along very well. I'll speak with you again when the work is further advanced. Mr. Corbett, we might go over there if you like." Smythe motioned toward a stand of oak trees about sixty feet behind the encampment.

As they walked, Smythe slid his thumbs into the pockets of his dark brown breeches. "I think an apology is in order for our behavior last night. We left so abruptly . . . and for such an obvious reason. At least we might have tempered it with a more diplomatic excuse."

"No apology is necessary. Everyone understood the reason. And better the truth than a false excuse, no matter how diplomatic."

"Thank you, sir. I appreciate your candor."

"The reason I wished to speak to you," Matthew said as they reached the oak trees' shade, "concerns Gwinett Linch. The man you believe to be Jonathan Lancaster."

"If I may correct you, not *believe* to be. As I said last night, I would swear to it. But he appears . . . so different. So changed. The man I knew would not be . . . well, would not be caught *dead* in such dirty rags. In fact, I recall he had a marked affinity for cleanliness."

"And order?" Matthew asked. "Would you say he had an affinity for that as well?"

"He kept his wagon neat enough. I remember one day he complained to my father about not having a supply of wheel grease on hand to silence a squeak."

"Hm," Matthew said. He leaned against the trunk of an oak and crossed his arms. "Exactly who was . . . I mean, who is . . . Jonathan Lancaster?"

"Well, I mentioned he had an act that involved trained

rats. He had them jump through hoops and run races and such. The children loved it. Our circus travelled through most of England, and we did play London on several occasions but we found ourselves restricted to a very bad part of the city. So we mostly travelled from village to village. My father was the manager, my mother sold tickets, and I did whatever needed doing."

"Lancaster," Matthew said, guiding Smythe back to the subject. "He made his living with this trained rat show?"

"Yes, he did. None of us were exactly wealthy, but . . . we all pulled together." Smythe frowned, and Matthew could tell he was forming his next statement. "Mr. Lancaster . . . was a puzzling man."

"How so? Because he worked with rats?"

"Not only that," Smythe said. "But because of the other act he performed. The one that was done . . . well . . . that was done only behind closed curtains, for a small audience of adults—no children allowed—who wished to pay an extra coin to see it."

"And what was that?"

"His display of animal magnetism."

"Animal magnetism?" Now it was Matthew's turn to frown. "What is *that?*"

"The art of magnetic manipulation. Have you not heard of such a thing?"

"I've heard of the process of magnetism, but never *animal* magnetism. Is this some theatrical whimsy?"

"It's been more popular in Europe than in England, I understand. Particularly in Germany, according to what my father told me. Mr. Lancaster was once a leading light of the cult of magnetism in Germany, though he was English-born. This is also according to my father, who if nothing else has a fortune of friends in the craft of public entertainment.

That was, however, in Mr. Lancaster's younger years. An incident occurred that caused him to flee Germany."

"An incident? Do you know what it was?"

"I know what my father told me, and wished me to keep secret."

"You are no longer in England and no longer under your father's jurisdiction," Matthew said. "It is *vital* that you tell me everything you know about Jonathan Lancaster. *Particularly* the secrets."

Smythe paused and cocked his head to one side. "May I ask why this is so important to you?"

It was a fair question. Matthew said, "I'm going to trust you, as I hope you will trust me. Obviously Lancaster has hidden his true identity from Mr. Bidwell and everyone else in this town. I wish to know why. Also . . . I have reason to believe that Lancaster may be involved with the current situation in which this town finds itself."

"What? You mean the *witch?*" Symthe offered a nervous smile. "You're joking!"

"I am not," Matthew said firmly.

"Oh, that can't be! Mr. Lancaster may have been strange, but he wasn't *demonic.* I'd venture that his closed-curtain talent *appeared* to some to be witchcraft, but it was evidently based on principles of science."

"Ah." Matthew nodded, his heartbeat quickening. "Now we approach the light, Mr. Smythe. What exactly was his closed-curtain talent?"

"Manipulation of the mind," Smythe answered, and Matthew had to struggle to suppress a victorious grin. "By the application of magnetic force, Mr. Lancaster could deliver mental commands to some members of his audience, and cause them to do, believe, and say things that . . . um . . . would probably not suit the eyes and ears of children. I have to admit; I sneaked behind the curtains and watched on more than a few occasions, because it *was* a fascinating show. I recall he would cause some to believe day was night, and that they were getting ready for their beds. One woman he caused to believe was freezing in a snowstorm in the midst of July. A particular scene I remember was a man he caused to believe had stepped into a nest of biting ants, and how that man jumped and hollered was nothing short of ludicrous. The other members of the audience laughed uproariously, but that man never heard a giggle of it until Mr. Lancaster awakened him."

"Awakened him? These people were put to sleep in some way?"

"It was a sleep-like state, yet they were still responsive. Mr. Lancaster used various objects to soothe them into this state, such as a lantern, a candle, or a coin. Anything that served to secure their attention. Then he would further soothe and command them with his voice . . . and once you heard his voice, it was unforgettable. I myself would have fallen under his magnetism, if I hadn't known beforehand what he was doing."

"Yes," Matthew said, staring past Smythe in the direction of Fount Royal. "I can well understand that." He directed his gaze back to the man. "But what is this about *magnetism?*"

"I don't quite fathom it, but it has to do with the fact that all bodies and objects hold iron. Therefore a skilled practitioner can use other objects as tools of manipulation, since the human body, blood, and brain also contain iron. The attraction and manipulation is called magnetism. That, at least, is how my father explained it when I asked him." Symthe shrugged. "Evidently it was a process first discovered by the ancient Egyptians and used by their court magicians."

Matthew was thinking *I have you now, Sir Fox.*

"This must be very important to you indeed," Smythe said, dappled sunlight falling through the oak branches and leaves onto his face.

"It is. As I said, vital."

"Well . . . as you also said, I am no longer in England or under my father's jurisdiction. If it's so vital that you know . . . the secret my father asked me to keep concerns Mr. Lancaster's career before he joined the circus. In his younger years he was known as a healer of sorts. A faith-healer, I suppose, in that he could use magnetism to deliver people from illnesses. Apparently he travelled to Europe to practise this art, and drew the attention of a German nobleman who wished Mr. Lancaster to teach him and his son how to be magnetizers themselves. Now . . . be aware that all this I recall my father telling me, and I might have garbled it in the retelling."

"I shall," Matthew said. "But please continue."

"Mr. Lancaster did not speak German, though his host spoke a little English. There was a translation problem. Whether that had anything to do with the results, I don't know, but my father told me Mr. Lancaster had fled Germany because the nobleman and his son were adversely affected by their studies. The latter killed himself with a poisoned dagger, and the former went half-mad. Which I suppose testifies to the power of magnetism falling into the wrong hands. In any case, a bounty was offered on Mr. Lancaster's head and so he returned to England. But he obviously was a changed man, too, and he sank to the level of trained rats and a few magnetist's tricks behind closed curtains."

"Possibly he wished to keep a low profile," Matthew said, "for fear that someone would seek him out and claim the bounty." He nodded. "Yes, that explains a lot. As, for instance, why Goode told me no Dutchmen or Germans had seen the Devil. It was because Lancaster feared Germans and likely is limited to only the English tongue."

"Goode?" Smythe asked, looking perplexed. "I'm sorry, I'm not following you."

"My apologies. My thoughts became words." Matthew, his nervous energy at high flux, began to pace back and forth. "Tell me this, if you will: what caused Lancaster to leave the circus, and when was this?"

"I don't know. My family and I left before Mr. Lancaster did."

"Oh. Then you haven't seen Lancaster since?"

"No. Certainly we didn't wish to return to that circus."

Matthew caught a hint of bitterness. "Why? Was your father discharged?"

"Not that. It was my father's wish to leave. He didn't care for the way Mr. Cedarholm—the man who owned the circus—had decided to run things. My father is a very decent man, God love him, and he bridled about bringing in the freaks."

Matthew suddenly stopped his pacing. "Freaks?"

"Yes. Three of them, to begin with."

"*Three,*" Matthew repeated. "May I . . . ask what they were?"

"The first was a black-skinned lizard, as big as a ram. The thing had come from some South Sea island, and it near made my mother faint to look upon it."

"The second," Matthew said, his mouth dry. "Might it have been an imp of some kind? A dwarf, possibly, with a childlike face and long white hair?"

"Yes. Exactly that. How did . . ." Now Smythe truly appeared confounded. "How did you *know?*"

"The third," Matthew prompted. "Was it . . . an unspeakable thing?"

"The third one was what made my father pack our bags. It was a hermaphrodite with the breasts of a woman and . . . the tools of a man. My father said even Satan would shrink to look upon such a blasphemy."

"Your father might be interested, Mr. Smythe, to know that all three of those creatures have lately found work in Fount Royal, with Satan's blessing. Oh, I have him now! I have him!" Matthew couldn't restrain himself from smacking his palm with his fist, his eyes bright with the fire of the hunt. He immediately reined in his enthusiasm, as he noted that Smythe took a backward step and appeared concerned that he might be dealing with a lunatic. "I have a request. Again, a very important one. I happen to know where Lancaster lives. It's not very far from here, at the end of this street. Would you go there with me—this moment—and look upon him face-to-face and tell me you positively know he's the man you claim him to be?"

"I've already told you. I saw his eyes, which are as unforgettable as his voice. It *is* him."

"Yes, but nevertheless I require you to identify him in my presence." Matthew also wanted Lancaster to know before another hour had passed that a blade had been thrust into his repugnant, inhuman plans, and twisted for good measure.

"I . . . do have some work to get done. Perhaps later this afternoon?"

"No," Matthew said. "Now." He correctly read the reticence in Smythe's eyes. "As an officer of the court, I must tell you this is official business. Also that I am empowered by Magistrate Woodward to compel you to accompany me." It was an outright falsehood, but Matthew had no time for dawdling.

Smythe, who obviously had well learned the lessons of decency from his esteemed father, said, "No compelling is necessary, sir. If this has to do with a matter of law, I should be glad to go."

Matthew and Smythe proceeded along Industry Street—the former in expectant haste and the latter more understandably moderate in his willingness to advance— toward the house of the formerly known Gwinett Linch. Smythe's pace slowed as they reached the execution field, and he regarded the stake and pyre with dread fascination. An oxcart had been pulled up beside the woodpile, and two men—one of them the giant Mr. Green, Matthew saw—were at work unloading another cargo of witch-burning fuel.

Yes, build it up! Matthew thought. Waste your muscles and your minutes, for when this day is done one less night-bird shall be confined in a cage and one more vulture there in her place!

Further on stood the house. "My God!" Smythe said, aghast. "Mr. Lancaster lives *there?*"

"Lancaster lives within," Matthew replied, his pace yet quickening. "The ratcatcher has groomed the exterior."

He felt a gnaw of disappointment. No smoke rose from the chimney, though indeed the breakfast hour was long past. But all the shutters were closed, indicating that Lancaster was out. Matthew inwardly muttered a curse, for he'd wished to have this identification promptly done and then escort Smythe directly to see Bidwell. It dawned on him that if Lancaster was indeed in there, closed up from the sunlight like a night-faring roach, he might turn violent, and they had no weapon of defense. Perhaps it would be best to go fetch Mr. Green as a precaution. But then another thought hit Matthew, and this one had terrible implications.

What if Lancaster, upon knowing he'd been recognized, had fled Fount Royal? He would have had ample time last night. But what was the procedure for getting out the gate after sunset? Surely such a thing was unheard of. Would the watchman have allowed him to leave without informing Bidwell? But what if Lancaster had saddled a horse and gone yesterday afternoon while it was still light?

"You're near running!" Smythe said, trying to keep up. Without Lancaster, Rachel's fate was still in doubt. Damned right Matthew was nearly running, and he did break into a run the final twenty yards.

He slammed his fist on the door. He had expected no answer, and therefore was immediately prepared to do what he next did: open the door and enter.

Before he could cross the threshold, Matthew was struck in the face.

Not by any physical fist, but rather by the overwhelming smell of blood. He instinctively recoiled, his mouth coming open in a gasp.

These were the things he saw, in a torrent of hideous impressions: light, streaming between the shutter slats and glistening off the dark red blood that had pooled on the floorboards and made large brown blotches on the pallet's sheet; Lancaster's corpse, lying on its right side on the floor, the left hand gripping at the sheet as if to pull itself up, the mouth and icy gray eyes horribly open in a slashed and clawed face, and the throat cut like a red-lipped grin from ear to ear; the formerly meticulous household ravaged as if by a whirlwind, clothes pulled from the trunk and strewn about; desk drawers wrenched out and upturned, cooking implements thrown hither and yon; hearth ashes scooped up and tossed to settle over the corpse like grave dust.

Smythe had also seen. He gave a choked moan and staggered back, and then off he ran along Industry Street in the direction of his companions, his face bone-white and his mouth trailing the shattering cry, "Murder! Murder!"

The shout might have alarmed everyone else who heard it, but it served to steady Matthew's nerves because he knew he had only a short time to inspect this gruesome scene before being intruded upon. He realized as well that the sight of Lancaster lying dead and so brutally disfigured must have been the same sight viewed by Reverend Grove's wife and by Jess Maynard, who had discovered Daniel Howarth's body. Little wonder, then, that Mrs. Grove and the Maynards had fled town.

The cut throat. The face savaged by demonic claws. And, it appeared, the shoulders, arms, and chest also slashed through the bloody ribbons of the man's shirt.

Yes, Matthew thought. A true Satan had been at work here.

He felt sick to his stomach and scared out of his wits, but he had time for neither debility. He looked about the wreckage. The desk's drawers, all the papers and everything else dumped out, the inkwell smashed. He wished to find two items before Mr. Green surely arrived: the sapphire brooch and the book on ancient Egypt. But even as he knelt down to negotiate this mess of blood, ink, and blood-inked papers he knew with a sinking certainty that those two items, above all else, would not be found.

He spent a moment or two in search, but when he suffered the smear of blood on his hands he gave up the quest as both impossible and unreasonable. He was fast weakening in this charnel house, and the desire for fresh air and untainted sunlight was a powerful call. It occurred to him that Smythe had been correct: Lancaster would indeed not be caught dead in his ratcatcher's rags, as he wore what had once been a white shirt and a pair of dark gray breeches.

And now the need to get out was too much to withstand. Matthew stood up and, as he turned to the door—which had not opened to its full extent, but rather just enough to allow his entry—he saw what was scrawled there on its inner surface in the clotted ink of Lancaster's veins.

My Rachel
Is Not
Alone

In the space of a hammered heartbeat Matthew's flesh prickled and the hairs rose at the back of his neck. The first words that came to his mind were *Oh . . . shit.*

He was still staring numbly at that damning declaration a moment later when Hannibal Green came through the door, followed by the other rustic with whom he'd been working. At once Green stopped in his tracks, his red-bearded face twisted with horror. "Christ's Mercy!" he said, stunned to the soles of his fourteen-inch boots. *"Linch?"* He looked at Matthew, who nodded, and then Green saw the clerk's gore-stained hands and hollered, "Randall! Go fetch Mr. Bidwell! *Now!"*

In the time that ensued, Green would have thought Matthew a bloody-handed murderer had not David Smythe, pallid but resolute, returned to the scene and explained they'd both been together when the corpse was discovered. Matthew took the opportunity to wipe his hands on one of the clean shirts that had been so rudely torn from the trunk. Then Green had his own hands full trying to keep people who'd been alerted by Smythe's cry—among them Martin and Constance Adams—out of the house.

"Is that Lancaster?" Matthew asked Smythe, who stood to one side staring down at the corpse.

Smythe swallowed. "His face is . . . so . . . swollen, but . . . I know the eyes. Unforgettable. Yes. This man . . . was Jonathan Lancaster."

"Move back!" Green told the onlookers. "Move back, I said!" Then he had no choice but to close the door in the gawkers' faces, and thereupon he saw the bloody scrawl.

Matthew thought Green might go down, for he staggered as if from a mighty blow. When he turned his head to look at Matthew, his eyes seemed to have shrunken and retreated in his face. He spoke in a very small voice, "I shall . . . I shall guard the door from the *outside.*" So saying, he was gone like a shot.

Smythe had also seen the bloody writing. His mouth opened, but he made not a sound. Then he lowered his head and followed Green out the door with similar haste.

Now the die was well and truly cast. Alone in the house with the deadly departed, Matthew knew this was the funeral bell for Fount Royal. Once word got out about that declaration on the door—and it was probably beginning its circuit of tongues right now, starting with Green—the town wouldn't be worth a cup of cold drool.

He avoided looking at Lancaster's face, which had not only been severely clawed but had become misshapen from such injury. He knelt down and continued his search for the brooch and book, this time using a cloth to move aside blood-spattered wreckage. Presently a wooden box caught his attention, and he lifted its lid to find within the tools of the ratcatcher's trade: the odious long brown seedbag that had served to hold rodent carcasses, the stained deerskin gloves, the cowhide bag, and various wooden jars and vials of—presumably—rat bait. Also in the box was the single blade—wiped clean and shining—that had been secured to the end of the ratcatcher's sticker.

Matthew lifted his gaze from the box and looked around the room. Where was the sticker itself? And—most importantly—where was that fearsome appliance with the five curved blades that Hazelton had fashioned?

Nowhere to be seen.

Matthew opened the cowhide bag, and in doing so noted two drops and a smear of dried blood near its already-loosened drawstring. The bag was empty.

To be such a cleanliness fanatic, why would Lancaster have not wiped the rodent blood from the side of this bag before putting it back into the wooden box? And why was the five-bladed appliance—that "useful device" as Lancaster had called it—not here with the other utensils?

Now Matthew did force himself to look at Lancaster's face, and the claw marks upon it. With a mind detached from his revulsion he studied the vicious slashings on the corpse's shoulders, arms, and chest.

He knew.

In perhaps another fifteen minutes, during which Matthew searched without success for the appliance, the door opened again—tentatively, this time—and the master of Fount Royal peered in with eyes the size of teacup saucers. "What . . . what has happened here?" he gasped.

"Mr. Smythe and I found this scene. Lancaster has left us," Matthew said.

"You mean . . . Linch."

"No. He was never truly Gwinett Linch. His name is—was—Jonathan Lancaster. Please come in."

"Must I?"

"I think you should. And please close the door."

Bidwell entered, wearing his bright blue suit. The look of

sickness contorted his face. He did close the door, but he remained pressed firmly against it.

"You ought to see what you're pressing against," Matthew said.

Bidwell looked at the door, and like Green he staggered and almost fell. His jerking away from it made him step into the bloody mess on the floor and for a dangerous instant he balanced on the precipice of falling alongside the corpse. His fight against gravity was amazing for a man of his size, and with sheer power of determination—and more than a little abject, breeches-wetting terror—he righted himself.

"Oh my Jesus," he said, and he took off both his bright blue tricorn and his gray curled wig and mopped his sandy pate with a handkerchief. "Oh dear God . . . we're doomed now, aren't we?"

"Steady yourself," Matthew instructed. "This was done by a human hand, not a spectral one."

"A human hand? Are you out of your mind? Only Satan himself could have done this!" He pushed the handkerchief to his nose to filter the blood smell. "It's the same as was done to the reverend and Daniel Howarth! Exactly the same!"

"Which should tell you the same man committed all three murders. In this case, though, I think there was a falling out of compatriots."

"What are you running off at the lips about *now?*" Bidwell's sickness had receded and anger was beginning to flood into its mold. "Look at that on the door! That's a message from the damned Devil! Good Christ, my town will be dust and maggots before sunset! *Oh!*" It was a wounded, terrible cry, and his eyes appeared near bursting out. "If the witch is not alone . . . then *who* might the other witches and warlocks be?"

"Shut up that yammering and listen to me!" Matthew advanced upon Bidwell until they stood face to sweating face. "You'll do yourself and Fount Royal no good to fall to pieces! If your town needs anything now, it's a true leader, not a bullier or a weeper!"

"How . . . how *dare* you . . ."

"Put aside your bruised dignity, sir. Just stand there and listen. I am as confounded about this as you, because I thought Linch—Lancaster—was alone in his crimes. Obviously—and stupidly—I was wrong. Lancaster and his killer were working together to paint Rachel as a witch and destroy your town."

"Boy, your love for that witch will put you burning at her side!" Bidwell shouted, his face bright red and the veins pulsing at his temples. He looked to be courting an explosion that would blow off the top of his head. "If you wish to go to Hell with her, I can arrange it!"

"This was written on the door," Matthew said coldly, "by a human hand determined to finish Fount Royal at one fell swoop. The same hand that cut Lancaster's throat and—when he was dead or dying—used the ratcatcher's own five-bladed device to strike him repeatedly, thereby giving the impression of a beast's claws. That device was also used to inflict similar wounds on Reverend Grove and Daniel Howarth."

"Yes, yes, yes! It's all as you say, isn't it? *Everything* is as you say!"

"Most everything," Matthew answered.

"Well, you didn't even see those other bodies, so how can you *know*? And what nonsense is this about some kind of five-bladed device?"

"You've never seen it? Then again, I doubt you would have. Seth Hazelton forged it for the use—he thought—of killing rats. Actually, it was probably planned for its current use all along."

"You're mad! Absolutely roaring mad!"

"I am neither mad," Matthew said, "nor roaring, as you are. To prove my sanity, I will ask Mr. Smythe to go to your house and explain to you Lancaster's true identity as he explained it to me. I think you'll find it worth your while."

"Really?" Bidwell sneered. "If that's the case, you'd best go find him! When my carriage passed their camp, the actors were packing their wagons!"

Now a true spear of terror pierced Matthew's heart. *"What?"*

"That's right! They were in a fever to do it, too, and now I know why! I'm sure there's nothing like finding a Satan-mauled corpse and a bloody message from Hell to put one in mind for a merry play!"

"No! They can't leave yet!" Matthew was out the door faster even than Green's pistol-ball exit. Straightaway his progress was blocked by the seven or eight persons who stood just outside, including Green himself. Then he had to negotiate a half-dozen more citizens who dawdled between the house and Industry Street. He saw Goode sitting in the driver's seat of Bidwell's carriage, but the horses faced west and getting them turned east would take too long. He set off toward the maskers' camp, running so fast he lost his left shoe and had to forfeit precious time putting it back on.

Matthew let loose a breath of relief when he reached the campsite and saw that, though the actors were indeed packing their trunks, costumes, featherboxes, and all the rest of their theatrical belongings, none of the horses had yet been hitched to a wagon. There was activity aplenty, however, and it was obvious to Matthew that Smythe's tale of what was discovered had put the fear of Hell's wrath into these people.

"Mr. Brightman!" Matthew called, seeing the man helping another thespian lift a trunk onto a wagon. He rushed over. "It's urgent I speak with Mr. Smythe!"

"I'm sorry, Mr. Corbett. David is not to be spoken with." Brightman looked past Matthew. "Franklin! Help Charles fold up that tent!"

"I *must*," Matthew insisted.

"That's impossible, sir." Brightman stalked off toward another area of the camp, and Matthew walked at his side. "If you'll pardon me, I have much work to do. We plan on leaving as soon as we're packed."

"You needn't leave. None of your troupe is in danger."

"Mr. Corbett, when we discovered your . . . um . . . situation with the witch from a source in Charles Town, I myself was reluctant—extremely reluctant—to come here. But to be perfectly honest we had nowhere else to go. Mr. Bidwell is a very generous friend, therefore I was talked into making the trip." Brightman stopped walking and turned to face Matthew. "I regret my decision, young man. When David told me what had happened . . . and what he saw in that house . . . I immediately gave the order to break camp. I am not going to risk the lives of my troupe for any amount that Mr. Bidwell might put on our table. End of pronouncement." He began walking once more and boomed, "Thomas! Make sure all the boots are in that box!"

"Mr. Brightman, please!" Matthew caught up with him again. "I understand your decision to leave, but . . . please . . . it is absolutely urgent that I speak to Mr. Smythe. I need for him to tell Mr. Bidwell about—"

"Young man," Brightman said with an exasperated air as he halted abruptly. "I am trying to be as pleasant as possible under the circumstances. We must—I repeat *must*—get on the road within the hour. We'll not reach Charles Town before dark, but I wish to get there before midnight."

"Would it not be better to stay the night here, and leave in the morning?" Matthew asked. "I can assure you that—"

"I think neither you nor Mr. Bidwell can assure us of *anything.* Including the assurance that we'll all be alive in the morning. No. I thought you had only one witch here, and that was bad enough; but to have an unknown number, and the rest of them lurking about ready and eager to commit murder for their master . . . no, I can't risk such a thing."

"All right, then," Matthew said. "But can't I request that Mr. Smythe speak to Mr. Bidwell? It would only take a few minutes, and it would—"

"David cannot speak to anyone, young man," Brightman said firmly. "Did you hear me? I said can *not.*"

"Well, where is he? If I can have a moment with him—"

"You are not listening to me, Mr. Corbett." Brightman took a step toward him and grasped his shoulder with one of those vise-like hands. "David is in one of the wagons. Even if I allowed you to see him, it would do no good. I am being truthful when I say that David cannot speak. After he told me what he'd seen—and particularly about the writing—he broke into a fit of shivering and weeping and thereafter was silent. What you don't know about David is that he is a very sensitive young man. Precariously sensitive, I might say."

Brightman paused, staring intently into Matthew's eyes. "He has had some nervous difficulties in the past. For that reason, he lost his positions with both the Saturn Cross Company and James Prue's Players. His father is an old friend of mine, and so when he asked me to take his son on as a favor—and watch over him—I agreed. I think the sight of that murdered man has sent him to the edge of . . . well, it's best not to say. He has been given a cup of rum and a pair of day-blinders. Therefore I certainly will not let you see him, as he must rest and be quiet for any hope of a prompt recovery."

"Can't I . . . just . . . for one . . ."

"*No,*" Brightman said, his voice like the tolling of a bass-tuned bell. He released his grip on Matthew's shoulder. "I'm sorry, but whatever it is you want with David cannot be granted. Now: it was a pleasure to meet you, and I hope all goes well with this witchcraft situation. I hope you sleep with a Bible in your bed and a candle by your hand tonight. Perhaps also a pistol under your pillow. Good luck to you, and goodbye." He stood with his arms crossed, waiting for Matthew to move away from the camp.

Matthew had to give it one more try. "Sir, I'm begging you. A woman's life lies in the balance."

"What woman?"

He started to speak the name, but he knew it wouldn't help. Brightman regarded him with a stony stare.

"I don't know what intrigues are in progress here," Brightman said, "and neither do I wish to know. It is my experience that the Devil has a long arm." He scanned the vista of Fount Royal, his eyes saddened. "It pains me to say it, but I doubt we shall have need to come this way next summer. Many fine people lived here, and they were very kind to us. But . . . such are the tides of life. Now please pardon me, as I have work to do."

Matthew could say nothing more. He watched as Brightman walked away to join a group of men who were taking down the yellow awning. Horses were being hitched to one of the wagons, and the other horses were being readied. It occurred to him that he might assert his rights and go to each wagon in turn until Smythe was found, but what then? If Smythe was too anguished to speak, what good would it do? But no, he couldn't let Smythe just ride out of here without telling Bidwell who the ratcatcher really was! It was inconceivable!

And it was equally inconceivable to grab an ailing person with a nervous disorder by the scruff of the neck and shake him like a dog until he talked.

Matthew staggered, light-headed, to the other side of Industry Street and sat down at the edge of a cornfield. He watched the camp dwindling as the wagons were further packed. Every few minutes he vowed he would stand, march defiantly over there and find Smythe for himself. But he remained seated, even when a whip cracked and the cry "Get up!" rang out and the first wagon creaked away.

Once the departure of wagons had begun, the others soon followed. Brightman, however, remained with the final wagon and helped the Falstaffian-girthed thespian lift a last trunk and two smaller boxes. Before the work was completed, Bidwell's carriage came into view. Bidwell bade Goode halt, and Matthew watched as the master of Fount Royal climbed down and went to speak with Brightman.

The discussion lasted only three or four minutes. Bidwell did a lot of listening and nodding. It ended with the two men shaking hands, and then Brightman got up onto the driver's plank of his wagon, which the Falstaffian gentleman already occupied. A whip popped, Brightman boomed, "Go on there, go on!" and the horses began their labor.

Matthew felt tears of bitter frustration burn his eyes. He bit his lower lip until it nearly bled. Brightman's wagon trundled away. Matthew stared at the ground until he saw a shadow approaching, and even then he kept his head bowed.

"I have assigned James Reed to guard the house,"

Bidwell said. His voice was wan and listless. "James is a good, dependable man."

Matthew looked up into Bidwell's face. The man had donned both his wig and tricorn again, but they sat at crooked angles. Bidwell's face appeared swollen and the color of yellow chalk, his eyes like those of a shot-stunned animal. "James will keep them out," he said, and then he frowned. "What shall we do for a ratcatcher?"

"I don't know," was all Matthew could say.

"A ratcatcher," Bidwell repeated. "Every town must have one. Every town that wishes to grow, I mean." He looked around sharply as another wagon—this one open-topped and carrying the hurriedly packed belongings of Martin and Constance Adams—passed along Industry Street on its way out. Martin was at the reins, his face set with grim resolve. His wife stared straight ahead also, as if terrified to even glance back at the house they were fleeing. The child, Violet, was pressed between them, all but smothered.

"Essential for a town," Bidwell went on, in a strangely calm tone. "That rats be controlled. I shall . . . I shall put Edward on the problem. He will give me sound advice."

Matthew clasped his fingers to his temples and then released the pressure. "Mr. Bidwell," he said. "We are dealing with a human being, not Satan. *One* human being. A cunning fox of which I have never before seen the like."

"They'll be frightened at first," Bidwell replied. "Yes, of course they will be. They were so looking forward to the maskers."

"Lancaster was murdered because his killer knew he was about to be exposed. Either Lancaster told that man—or a very strong and ruthless woman—about Smythe identifying him . . . or the killer was in your house last night when Smythe related it to me."

"I think . . . some of them will leave. I can't blame them. But they'll come to their senses, especially with the burning so near."

"Please, Mr. Bidwell," Matthew said. "Try to hear what I'm saying." He lowered his head again, his mind almost overwhelmed by what he was thinking. "I don't believe Mr. Winston to be capable of murder. Therefore . . . if indeed the killer was someone in your house last night . . . that narrows the field to Mrs. Nettles and Schoolmaster Johnstone." Bidwell was silent, but Matthew heard his rough breathing.

"Mrs. Nettles . . . could have overheard, from outside the parlor. There may be . . . may be a fact I've missed about her. I recall . . . she said something important to me, concerning Reverend Grove . . . but I can't draw it up. The schoolmaster . . . are you absolutely *certain* his knee is—"

Bidwell began to laugh.

It was possibly the most terrible sound Matthew had ever heard. It was a laugh, yes, but also in the depths of it was something akin to a strangled shriek.

Matthew raised his eyes to Bidwell and received another shock. Bidwell's mouth was laughing, but his eyes were holes of horror and tears had streaked down his cheeks. He began to back away as the laughter spiralled up and up. He lifted his arm and aimed his index finger at Matthew, his hand trembling.

The crazed laughter abruptly stopped. *"You,"* he rasped. And now not only was he weeping, but his nose had begun to run. "You're one of them, aren't you? Sent to ruin my town and drive me mad. But I'll beat you yet! I'll beat all of you! I've never failed and I shall *not* fail! Do you hear me? Never failed! And I shall not . . . shall not . . . shall—"

"Mr. Bidwell, suh?" Goode had stepped beside the man and gently taken hold of his arm. Though it was such an improper gesture between slave and master, Bidwell made no attempt to pull away. "We ought best be goin'."

Bidwell continued to stare at Matthew, his eyes seeing only a prince of destruction. "Suh?" Goode prompted quietly. "Ought be goin'." He gave Bidwell's arm just the slightest tug.

Bidwell shivered, though the sun was bright and warm. He lowered his gaze and wiped the tearstreaks from his face with the back of his free hand. "*Oh,*" he said; it was more the exhalation of breath than speech. "I'm tired. Near . . . worn out."

"Yes suh. You do needs a rest."

"A rest." He nodded. "I'll feel better after a rest. Help me to the carriage, will you?"

"Yes suh, I will." Goode looked at Matthew and put a finger to his lips, warning Matthew to make no further utterances. Then Goode steadied Bidwell, and the slave and master walked together to the carriage.

Matthew remained where he was. He watched Goode help his master into a seat, and then Goode got up behind the horses, flicked the reins, and the horses started off at an ambling pace.

When the carriage had departed from sight, Matthew stared blankly at the empty field where the maskers had been and thought he might weep himself.

His hopes of freeing Rachel were wrecked. He had not a shred of evidence to prove any of the things he knew to be true. Without Lancaster—and without Smythe to lend credence to the tale—the theory of how Fount Royal had been seduced by mental manipulation was a madman's folly. Finding the sapphire brooch and the book on ancient Egypt would have helped, but the killer had already known their value—and must have been well aware of their presence—

and so had stolen them away as efficiently as he had murdered Lancaster. He—or she, God forbid—had even torn up the house so no one would know the ratcatcher's true living habits.

So. What now?

He had come through this maze to find himself at a dead end. Which only meant, he believed, that he must retrace his steps and search for the proper passage. But the time was almost gone.

Almost gone.

He knew he was grasping at straws by accusing either the schoolmaster or Mrs. Nettles. Lancaster might have told his killer yesterday that he'd been recognized, and the cunning fox had waited until long after dark to visit the wretched-looking house. Just because Smythe had revealed his recognition to Matthew in Bidwell's parlor didn't mean the killer had been there to overhear it.

He trusted Mrs. Nettles, and did not *want* to believe she had a hand in this. But what if everything the woman had said was a lie? What if she had been manipulating him all along? It might not have been Lancaster who took the coin, but Mrs. Nettles. She certainly could have laid the magistrate out cold if she'd chosen to.

And the schoolmaster. An Oxford man, yes. A highly educated man. The magistrate had seen Johnstone's deformed knee, it was true, but still . . .

There was the question of the bearded surveyor and his interest in the fount. It was important. Matthew knew it was, but he could not prove it.

Neither could he prove the fount was a pirate's treasure vault, nor indeed that it held a single coin or jewel.

Neither could he prove that any of the witnesses had not actually seen what they believed to see, and that Rachel hadn't made those damning poppets and hidden them in her house.

Neither could he prove that Rachel had been chosen as the perfect candidate to paint as a witch by two persons—possibly more?—who both were masters of disguise.

Certainly he couldn't prove that Linch was Lancaster and Lancaster had been murdered by his accomplice, and that Satan himself didn't scrawl that message on the door.

Now Matthew truly felt close to weeping. He knew everything—or almost everything—of how it had been done, and he felt sure he knew why it had been done, and he knew the name of one of the persons who'd done it . . .

But without proof he was a beggar in the house of justice, and could expect not a single scrap.

Another wagon passed along Industry Street, carrying a family and their meager belongings away from this accursed town. The last days of Fount Royal had come.

And Matthew was keenly aware that Rachel's last hours were passing away, and that on Monday morning she would surely burn and for the rest of his life—the rest of his miserable, frost-souled life—only he would know the truth.

No, that was wrong. There would be one other, who would grin as the flames roared and the ashes flew, as the houses emptied and the dream perished. Who would grin as the thought came clear: *All the silver, gold, and jewels . . . all mine now . . . and those fools never even knew.*

Only one fool knew. And he was powerless to stop either the flow of time or the flow of citizens fleeing Fount Royal.

TWELVE

And now the whole world was silent.

Or at least it seemed so, to Matthew's ears. In fact, the world was so silent that the sound of his feet creeping on the hallway's floorboards sounded to him like barely muffled cannonades, and the errant squeak of a loose timber like a high-pitched human shriek.

He had a lantern in hand. He was dressed in his bedclothes, as he had retired to sleep several hours ago. In reality, though, he had retired to ponder and wait. The time had arrived, and he was on a journey to Bidwell's upstairs study.

It was now the Sabbath morning. He reasoned it was sometime between midnight and two o'clock. The previous day had truly been nightmarish, and this current day promised to be no less an ordeal.

Matthew had himself seen eight more wagons departing Fount Royal. The gate had been opened and closed with a regularity that would have been comical had it not been so tragic. Bidwell had remained in his bedchamber all day. Winston had gone in to see him, as had Dr. Shields, and once Matthew had heard Bidwell's voice raving and raging with a frightful intensity that made one believe all the demons of Hell had ringed his bed to pay their ghastly respects. Perhaps in Bidwell's tortured mind they had.

During the course of the day Matthew had sat at the magistrate's bedside for several hours, reading the book on English plays and attempting to keep his mind from wandering to the Florida country. He was also there to guard against the magistrate finding out what had occurred this morning, as it might cause Woodward deep grief that would sink him again into sickness. The magistrate, though certainly able to communicate more clearly and feeling positive about his chances of improvement, was yet weak and in need of further rest. Dr. Shields had administered three more doses of the powerful medicine, but had been wise enough during his visits not to mention anything that could harm his patient's outlook. The medicine did what it was meant to do: it sent Woodward to the dreamer's land, where he could not know what tumult was taking place in reality.

Fortunately, the magistrate had been asleep—or, rather, drugged—when Bidwell had carried out his raging. In the evening, as darkness called upon Fount Royal and many fewer lamps answered than the night before, Matthew had asked Mrs. Nettles for a deck of cards and played a dozen or so games of five and forty with the magistrate, who was delighted at the chance to challenge his sluggish mind. As they played, Matthew made mention of Woodward's dream of Oxford, and how Johnstone had also seemed to enjoy the recollections.

"Yes," Woodward had said, studying his cards. "Once an Oxford man . . . always so."

"Hm." Matthew had decided to let another hand go by before he mentioned the schoolmaster again. "It *is* a shame about Mr. Johnstone's knee. Being so deformed. But he does get around well, doesn't he?"

A slight smile had crept across the magistrate's mouth. "Matthew, Matthew," he'd said. "Do you never quit?"

"I'm sorry, sir?"

"Please. I am not . . . so ill and . . . weak-minded that I can't see through you. What is this now . . . about his knee?"

"Nothing, sir. I was just making mention of it, in passing. You *did* say you saw it, did you not?"

"I did."

"At close quarters?"

"Close enough. I could smell nothing . . . because of my condition . . . but I recall that Mr. Winston was . . . quite repelled . . . by the odor of Mr. Johnstone's hogsfat liniment."

"But you did clearly view the deformity?"

"Yes," Woodward had said. "Clearly, and . . . it was a viewing . . . I would not care to repeat. Now . . . may we return to our game?"

Not long after that, Dr. Shields had arrived with the magistrate's third dose of the day, and Woodward had been sleeping calmly ever since.

Matthew had, in the afternoon, taken the opportunity for a quick look into Bidwell's study, so now in the middle of the night he had no problem getting inside. He closed the door behind him and crossed the gold-and-red Persian rug to the large mahogany desk that commanded the room. He sat down in the desk's chair and quietly pulled open the topmost drawer. He found no map there, so he went on to the next drawer. A careful search through papers, wax seals with the scrolled letter *B,* official-looking documents and the like revealed no map. Neither did the third drawer, nor the fourth and final one.

Matthew stood up, taking his lantern to the study's bookshelves. On the way, the squeal of a loose pinewood floorboard made his flesh crawl. Then he began to methodically move all the leatherbound books one from another, thinking that perhaps the map might be folded up and stored between two of them. Of course, the map might also be folded up *inside* one of the books, which was going to necessitate a longer search than he'd anticipated.

He was perhaps near midway in his route through the bookshelves when he heard the sound of footsteps on the stairs. He hesitated, listening more intently. The footsteps reached the top of the stairs and also hesitated. There was a space of time in which neither Matthew nor the person in the hallway moved. Then he heard the footsteps approaching and he saw lantern light in the space between door and floorboards.

Quickly he opened the glass of his own lamp and blew out the flame. He retreated to the protection of the desk and crouched down on the floor.

The door opened. Someone entered, paused for a few seconds, and then the door was closed again. Matthew could see the ruddy glow of the person's lantern upon the walls as it moved from side to side. And then the voice came, but cast low so as not to leave the room: "Mr. Corbett, I know ye just blew out a candle. I can smell it. If you'd show y'self, please?"

He stood up and Mrs. Nettles centered her lamplight on him. "Ye mi' care to know that my own quarters are 'neath this room," she said. "I heard someone walkin' and 'sumed it must be Mr. Bidwell, as this is his private study."

"Pardon me, I didn't mean to wake you."

"I'm sure you didn't, but I was already waked. I was plannin' on comin' up and lookin' in on 'im, since he was in such an awful bad way." She approached him and set the lantern down on the desktop. She wore a somber gray nightcap and a nightgown of similar hue, and on her face was a smoothing of ghastly green-tinted skin cream. Matthew had to believe that if Bidwell saw Mrs. Nettles in this state, he might think a froggish phantasm had crawled from its Hellish swamp. "Your intrusion in this room," she said sternly, "canna' be excused. What're you *doin'* in here?"

There was nothing to be done but tell the truth. "I understand from Solomon Stiles that Bidwell has a map of the Florida country, drawn by a French explorer. I thought it might be hidden in this room, either in his desk or on the bookshelves."

Mrs. Nettles made no reply, but simply stared holes through him. "I am not saying I've decided," Matthew continued. "I'm only saying I wish to see the map, to gain some idea of what the terrain is like."

"It would kill you," she said. "And the lady too. Does she know what you're wantin'?"

"No."

"Don't ye think askin' her oughta be the first thing, a'fore ye start the plannin'?"

"I'm not planning. I'm only looking."

"Plannin', lookin' . . . whate'er. Mi' be she doesn't care ta perish in the jaws of a wild beast."

"What, then? She'd rather perish by burning? I think not!"

"Keep your voice reined," she warned. "Mr. Bidwell mi' be mind-sick, but he's nae ear-deef."

"All right. But . . . if I were to continue my search for this map . . . would you leave the room and forget you saw me here? This is my business and my business alone."

"Nae, you're wrong. It's *my* business too, for it was my

urgin' brought you into this. If I'd kept my tongue still, then—"

"Pardon," Matthew interrupted, "but I must disagree. Your urging, as you put it, simply alerted me to consider that not all was as it seemed in this town. Which, whether you realize it or not, was a grand understatement. I would have had serious doubts as to Rachel's being a witch even if you had been one of the witnesses against her."

"Well then, if her innocence is all so clear to you, why canna' the magistrate see it?"

"A complicated question," he said. "The answer involves age and life experience . . . both of which, in this case, seem to be liabilities to clear thinking. Or rather, I should say, liabilities to thinking beyond the straight furrow in a crooked field, which you so elegantly pointed out on our first meeting. Now: Will you allow me to search for the map?"

"Nae," she answered. "If you're so all-fired to find it, I'll point it out." She picked up the lantern and directed its glow to the wall behind the desk. "There it hangs."

Matthew looked. Indeed on the wall hung a brown parchment map, stretched by a wooden frame. It was about fifteen inches or so across and ten inches deep, and it was positioned between an oil portrait of a sailing ship and a charcoal drawing of what appeared to be the London dockside. "Oh," he said sheepishly. "Well . . . my thanks."

"Best make sure it's what you're needin'. I know it's French, but I've never paid much mind to it." She offered him the lantern.

Matthew found in another moment that it was indeed what he was needing. It actually appeared to be part of a larger map, and displayed the country from perhaps thirty miles north of Fount Royal to the area identified, in faded quill pen, as *Le Terre Florida*. Between Fount Royal and the

Spanish territory the ancient quill had drawn a representation of vast forest, broken here and there by clearings, the meandering of rivers, and a number of lakes. It was a fanciful map, however, as one lake displayed a kraken-like creature and was named by the mapmaker *Le Lac de Poisson Monstre.* The swamp—identified with symbols of grass and water instead of tree symbols—that stretched along the coastline all the way from Fount Royal to the Florida country was titled *Marais Perfide.* And there was an area of swamp in the midst of the forest, some fifty or sixty miles southwest of Fount Royal, that was named *Le Terre de Brutalitie.*

"Is it he'pful to ye?" Mrs. Nettles asked.

"More daunting than helpful," Matthew said. "But yes, it does do *some* good." He had seen what looked to be a clearing in the wilderness ten or twelve miles southwest of Fount Royal that stretched for what might have been—by the strange and skewed dimensions of this map—four miles in length. Another clearing of several miles lay to the south of the first, and in this one was a lake. A third, the largest of the three, was reachable to the southwest. They were like the footprints of some primordial giant, and Matthew thought that if indeed those cleared areas—or at least areas where the wilderness was not so *perfide*—existed, then they constituted the route of least resistance to the Florida country. Perhaps this was also the "most direct route" Solomon Stiles had mentioned. In any case, it appeared somewhat less tasking than day after day of negotiating unbroken woodland. Matthew also noted the small scratchings of *Indien?* at three widely separate locations, the nearest being twenty miles or so southwest of Fount Royal. He assumed the question mark indicated a possible sighting of either a live Indian, the discovery of an artifact, or even the sound of tribal drums.

It was not going to be easy. In fact, it would be woefully hard.

Could the Florida country be reached? Yes, it could. By the directions of southwest, south, southwest and the linking together of those less-wooded giant's footprints. But, as he had previously considered, he was certainly no leather-stocking and the merest miscalculation of the sun's angle might lead him and Rachel into the *Terre Brutalitie.*

Then again, all of it was *terre brutalitie,* was it not?

It was insane! he thought as the frustration of reality hit him. Absolutely insane! How could he have ever imagined doing such a thing? To be lost in those terrible forests would be death a thousand times over!

He handed the lantern back to Mrs. Nettles. "Thank you," he said, and he heard the defeated resignation in his voice.

"Aye," she said as she took the lamp, "it does seem a beast."

"More than a beast. It seems impossible."

"You're puttin' it out of mind, then?"

He ran a hand across his brow. "What am I to do, Mrs. Nettles? Can you possibly tell me?"

She shook her head, looking at him with saddened compassion. "I'm sorry, but I canna'."

"No one can," he said wearily. "No one, except myself. The saying may be that no man is an island . . . but I feel very much like at least a solitary dominion. Rachel will be led to the stake within thirty hours. I know she is innocent, yet I can do nothing to free her. Therefore . . . what *am* I to do, except devise outlandish schemes to reach the Florida country?"

"You are ta forget her," Mrs. Nettles said. "You are ta go on about your own life, and let the dead be dead."

"That is the sensible response. But part of me will die on Monday morning too. The part that believes in justice. When that dies, Mrs. Nettles, I shall never be worth a damn again."

"You'll recover. Ever'one goes on, as they must."

"Everyone goes on," he repeated, with a taint of bitter mockery. "Oh, yes. They go on. With crippled spirits and broken ideals, they do go on. And with the passage of years they forget what crippled and broke them. They accept it grandly as they grow older, as if crippling and breaking were gifts from a king. Then those same hopeful spirits and large ideals in younger souls are viewed as stupid, and petty . . . and things to be crippled and broken, because everyone does go on." He looked into the woman's eyes. "Tell me. What is the point of life, if truth is not worth standing up for? If justice is a hollow shell? If beauty and grace are burnt to ashes, and evil rejoices in the flames? Shall I weep on that day, and lose my mind, or join the rejoicing and lose my soul? Shall I sit in my room? Should I go for a long walk, but where might I go so as not to smell the smoke? Should I just go on, Mrs. Nettles, like everyone else?"

"I think," she said grimly, "that you do nae have a choice." He had no response for this, which by its iron truth crushed him.

Mrs. Nettles sighed, her face downcast and her shadow thrown huge by the lamplight. "Go ta bed, sir," she said. "There's nae any more can be done."

He nodded, retrieved his dark lantern, and took the first two steps to the door, then hesitated. "You know . . . I really thought, for a brief while at least, that I might be able to do it. That I might be able, if I dared hard enough."

"Ta do what, sir?"

"To be Rachel's champion," he said wistfully. "And when Solomon Stiles told me about the two slaves who'd escaped—

the brother and sister—and that they'd nearly reached the Florida country . . . I thought . . . it *is* possible. But it's not, is it? And it never was. Well. I do need to get to bed, don't I?" He felt as if he could sleep for a year, and awaken bearded and forgetful of time. "Good night. Or rather . . . good morning."

"The brother and sister?" Mrs. Nettles said, with a perplexed expression. "You mean . . . the two slaves who ran away . . . oh, I s'pose it must'a been the verra first year."

"That's right. Stiles told me it was the first year."

"Those two got near ta the Florida country? Mr. Corbett, they were but *children!*"

"Children?"

"Yes sir. Oakley Reeves and his sister, Dulcine. I recall they ran away after their mother died. She was a cook. The boy was all of thirteen, sir, and the girl no older'n twelve."

"What? But . . . Stiles told me they were put in irons. I assumed they were adults!"

"Oh, they *were* held in irons, even though the boy was lamed. They were both put on a wagon and taken away. I knew they'd run a piece, but I had nae an idea they'd gotten so *far.*"

"Children," Matthew repeated. He blinked, stunned by this revelation. "My God. If two children could make it that distance . . ." He took the lantern from her hand and again studied the French explorer's map, this time with a silent intensity that spoke volumes.

"They were desperate," Mrs. Nettles said.

"No more so than I."

"They cared nae if they lived or died."

"I care that Rachel lives. And myself as well."

"I'm sure they had someone helpin' 'em. An older slave, gatherin' what they needed."

"Yes," Matthew said. "They probably did." He turned

toward her, his eyes glittering with fierce resolve. "Would you perform such a function for *me,* Mrs. Nettles?"

"Nae, I wouldn't!" she answered. "I'm dead set against it!"

"All right, then. Would you betray me if I myself gathered the necessary items? Some of them would be matches and a flint, a knife, clothing and shoes both for myself and Rachel, and a supply of food. I would have to take those items from the household."

Mrs. Nettles did not reply. She scowled, her froggishly green face nothing short of fearsome.

"I ask only of you what you once asked of me," he said.

"The Lord my witness, I canna' bear ta see ye go on such a folly and lose your young life. And what of the magistrate? Would you abandon him?"

"I thank the same Lord who is your witness that Magistrate Woodward is on the path to recovery. There is nothing I can do to speed his progress."

"But leavin' him like this can ruin it. Have you thought on that?"

"I have. It is a bitter choice to have to make, between the magistrate and Rachel. But that's where I find myself. I intend on writing a letter to him, explaining everything. I must hope that he reads that letter and fully understands my reasoning. If not . . . then not. But I hope—I believe—the magistrate will."

"Your time. It's awful wee."

"Everything would have to be gathered and readied within twenty-four hours. I want to get her out of there and be gone long before sunrise."

"This is daft!" she said. "How do ye plan on gettin' that key from Green? He won't likely open up the door and let you march in and out!"

"I'll have to give that some thought."

"And how will you go, then? Right through the front gate?"

"No," Matthew said. "Through the swamp, the same as the slaves."

"Ha! If ye make five miles, you'll have the luck of Angus McCoody!"

"I have no idea who that might be, but I presume it's some personage of fortune in your native land. If it's a blessing, I accept it." He had put his own darkened lantern on the desk and was measuring with the fingers of his free hand the distances involved. "I must have a compass," he decided. "I'll never find the way without one." A thought came to him. "I would wager Paine owned a compass. I don't think he would mind if I searched his house. Alas, Mrs. Nettles, I shall also have to free this map from its prison."

"Don't tell me such a thing. I don't care ta know."

"Well, I'll leave it alone for the time being. There's no point in advertising my intentions."

"They'll be after you," she said. "Most likely Mr. Stiles, leadin' the way. They'll hunt ye down quick enough."

"Why should they? Rachel and I have no value to Bidwell. In fact, he may be more pleased to see the last of me than of her. I think he'll send Stiles out to make a quick search, but it will be only rudimentary."

"I say you're mistaken. Mr. Bidwell wants ever'one here ta see her burn."

"I doubt there will be many remaining to watch the display." Matthew removed the candle from his lantern and lit it with hers. Then he returned the lamp to her hand. "After I get Rachel there—to a place of safety, a town or fort or some such—and come back, I'll explain everything to him."

"Hold." Mrs. Nettles regarded him now as if his bell was severely cracked. "What're you *sayin'*? Come *back*?"

"That's correct. I'm taking Rachel to the Florida country, but I don't intend to stay. If I can follow the map and compass there, I can follow them back."

"You young fool! They won't *let* you come back! No, sirrah! Once those Spaniards get their claws on you—an English citizen—they'll ship you right quick ta their own damned land! Oh, they'll treat Rachel fair enough, her bein' a Portuguese, but you they'll parade through their streets like a dancin' monkey!"

"Not if they don't *get* their claws—as you put it—on me. I said I would take Rachel to some town or fort, but I didn't say I myself would enter it. Oh . . . one more thing I need to find: a stick, line, and hook I might use for fishing."

"You're a city boy," she said, shaking her head. "What do ye know of *fishin'?* Well, that wilderness will cure your insanity soon enough. God help you and that poor woman, and bless your bones when they're a-layin' in a beast's lair chewed ta the marra!"

"A delightful image to sleep upon, Mrs. Nettles. And now I must leave your company, as my day will surely be full." He took his lantern and went to the door, treading lightly.

"A moment," she said. She stared at the floor, a muscle working in her jaw. "If ye haven't yet considered this . . . you mi' think to fetch some clothes and the like from her house. All her belongin's are still in there, I believe. If you're wantin' an extra pair a' boots . . . I mi' can he'p you with that."

"Any help would be greatly appreciated."

She looked up sharply at him. "Sleep on this, and think on it again with a clear mind. Hear me?"

"I do. And thank you."

"You ought ta curse me, and thank me only if I put a pan ta the side of your head!"

"That makes me think of breakfast. Would you awaken me promptly at six o'clock? And grant me an extra helping of bacon?"

"Yes," she said glumly. "Sir."

Matthew left the room and went to his own. He got into bed, extinguished the lantern, and lay on his back in the dark. He heard Mrs. Nettles go along the hallway to Bidwell's room and quietly open the door. There was a period of quiet, during which Matthew could envision the woman lifting her light to check on her sleeping—and near-mad—master. Then he heard her walk back along the hall and descend the stairs, after which all was silent again.

He had less than four hours to sleep, so he ought to get to it. There was indeed much to do on the morrow, most of it not only duplicitous but highly dangerous.

How was that key to be gotten from Green? Possibly something would come to him. He hoped. It was vital to find a compass. And clothes and proper shoes for Rachel, as well. Then food must be procured; preferably dried beef, though if it was heavily salted the need for water would increase. He had to write a letter to the magistrate, and that might be the most difficult task of all.

"My God," he whispered. "What am I about to do?"

At *least* a hundred and forty miles. On foot. Through a land cruel and treacherous, following a path of least resistance mapped out by a long-dead hand. Down to the Florida country, where he would set his nightbird free. And then *back* again, alone?

Mrs. Nettles was right. He didn't know a damn thing about fishing.

But he had once survived by his wits for four months at the harbor of Manhattan. He had fought for crumbs, stolen, and scavenged in that urban wilderness. He had endured all manner of hardships, because he had to. The same was true of his trek with the magistrate through the wet woods and across the sodden earth from Shawcombe's tavern. He had kept the magistrate going, when Woodward had wanted to quit and sit down in the muck. And Matthew had done that because he had to.

Two children had nearly made the Florida country. And might have, had not the eldest broken his ankle.

It was possible. It *had* to be possible. There was no other answer.

But the question remained in his mind, and it disturbed him so much that sleep became more elusive: *What am I about to do?*

He turned over on his side, curling up like an infant about to be expelled from a womb into the hard reality of life. He was afraid to the very marrow of those bones that Mrs. Nettles predicted would be chewed in a beast's lair. He was afraid, and hot tears born of that fear burned his eyes but he wiped them away before they spilled. He was no champion, no leatherstocking, and no fisherman.

But, by God, he was a survivor, and he intended for Rachel to survive as well.

It was possible. It was.

It was. It was. It was.

He would say that to himself a hundred times, but at the rising of the sun and the first cock's crow he would be no less afraid than he was in this merciless dark.

THIRTEEN

"Are you well? Truthfully, now."

Matthew had been staring out the open window in the magistrate's room, out over the sun-washed roofs and the fount's sparkling blue water. It was mid-afternoon, and he was watching yet another wagon pass through the distant gate. This morning he'd been aware of an almost-continual departure of wagons and oxcarts, their rumbling wheels and thudding animal hooves kicking up a haze of yellow dust that blotted the air around the gate like a perpetual stain. A sad sight had been that of Robert Bidwell, his wig dusty and his shirttail hanging out, as he stood on Harmony Street pleading with his citizens to remain in their homes. At last Winston and Johnstone had led him away to Van Gundy's tavern, even though it was the Sabbath. Van Gundy himself had loaded his belongings—included that wretched gittern—and quit Fount Royal. Matthew assumed that a few bottles still stocked the tavern, and in them Bidwell was seeking to lessen the agony of his perceived failure.

Matthew would have been surprised if any less than sixty persons had departed Fount Royal since dawn. Of course the threat of meeting nightfall between here and Charles Town had choked off the flow as the day progressed, but obviously there were those who preferred to risk the night journey rather than spend another eve in a witch-haunted town. Matthew predicted a similar flight at tomorrow's sunrise, notwithstanding the fact that it was Rachel's execution morn, since by the declaration so cleverly written in Lancaster's house, every neighbor might be a servant of Satan.

Today the church had been empty, but Exodus Jerusalem's camp had been full of terrified citizens. Matthew mused that Jerusalem must have thought he'd truly found himself a goldpot. The preacher's braying voice had risen and fallen like the waves of a storm-whipped sea, and also rising and falling in accord had been the frenzied cries and shrieks of his fear-drowned audience.

"Matthew? Are you well?" Woodward asked again, from his bed.

"I was just thinking," Matthew said. "That . . . even though the sun shines brightly, and the sky is clear and blue . . . it is a very ugly day." So saying, he closed the shutters, which he had only opened a minute or two before. Then he returned to his chair at the magistrate's bedside and sat down.

"Has something . . ." Woodward paused, as his voice was still frail. His throat was again in considerable pain and his bones ached, but he wished not to mention such worrisome things to Matthew on the eve of the witch's death. "Has something happened? My ears seem stopped up, but . . . I think I have heard wagon wheels . . . and much commotion."

"A few citizens have decided to leave town," Matthew explained, deliberately keeping his tone casual. "I suspect it has something to do with the burning. There was an unfortunate scene in the street, when Mr. Bidwell stationed himself to try to dissuade their departure."

"Was he successful?"

"No, sir."

"Ah. That poor soul. I feel for him, Matthew." Woodward leaned his head back on his pillow. "He has done his best . . . and the Devil has done his worst."

"Yes, sir, I agree."

Woodward turned his face so he had a good view of his clerk. "I know we have not been in agreement . . . on very much of late. I regret that any harsh words were spoken."

"As do I."

"I know also . . . how you must be feeling. The despondence and despair. Because you still believe her to be innocent. Am I correct?"

"You are, sir."

"Is there nothing . . . I can say or do to change your mind?"

Matthew offered him a slight smile. "Is there nothing I can say or do to change *yours?*"

"No," Woodward said firmly. "And I suspect that . . . we might never come to common ground on this." He sighed, his expression pained. "You will disagree, of course . . . but I appeal to you . . . to lay aside your obvious emotion and consider the facts as I did. I made my decree . . . based on those facts, and those facts alone. *Not* based on the accused's physical beauty . . . or her prowess at twisting words . . . or her misused intelligence. The facts, Matthew. I had no choice . . . but to pronounce her guilty, and to sentence her to such a death. Can you not understand?"

Matthew didn't reply, but instead stared at his folded hands.

"No one ever told me," Woodward said softly, "that . . . being a judge would be *easy*. In fact . . . I was promised . . . by my own mentor that it would be an iron cloak . . . once put on, impossible to remove. I have found it doubly true. But . . . I have tried to be fair, and I have tried to be correct. What more can I do?"

"Nothing more," Matthew said.

"Ah. Then perhaps . . . we might return to common ground after all. You will understand these things so much better . . . after *you* wear the iron cloak yourself."

"I don't believe I ever shall," came Matthew's answer, before he could guard his speech.

"You say that now . . . but it is your youth and despair speaking. Your affronted sense of . . . what is right and wrong. You are looking at the dark side of the moon, Matthew. The execution of a prisoner . . . is never a happy occasion, no matter the crime." He closed his eyes, his strength draining away. "But what joy . . . what relief . . . when you are able to discover the truth . . . and set an innocent person free. That alone . . . justifies the iron cloak. You will see . . . all in God's time."

A tap at the door announced a visitor. Matthew said, "Who is it?"

The door opened. Dr. Shields stood on the threshold, holding his medical bag. Matthew had noted that since the murder of Nicholas Paine, the doctor's countenance had remained gaunt and hollow-eyed, much as Matthew had found him at the infirmary. In truth, the doctor appeared to Matthew to be laboring under an iron cloak of his own, as Shields's moist face was milk-pale, his eyes watery and red-rimmed beneath the magnifying lenses of his spectacles. "Pardon my intrusion," he said. "I've brought the magistrate's afternoon dose."

"Come in, doctor, come in!" Woodward pulled himself up to a sitting position, eager for a taste of that healing tonic.

Matthew got up from his chair and moved away so Dr. Shields might administer the dose. The doctor had already this morning been cautioned again—as yesterday—not to mention the events transpiring in Fount Royal, which he had the good sense not to do even if he hadn't been cautioned. He agreed with Matthew that, though the magistrate appeared to be gaining strength, it was yet wise not to pressure his health with the disastrous news.

When the dose had been swallowed and Woodward settled again to await the oncoming of precious sleep, Matthew followed Dr. Shields out into the hallway and closed the magistrate's door.

"Tell me," Matthew said in a guarded tone. "Your best and honest opinion: When will the magistrate be able to travel?"

"He does improve daily." Shields's spectacles had slipped down his beak, and he pushed them up again. "I am very pleased with his response to the tonic. If all goes well . . . I would say two weeks."

"What do you mean, 'if all goes well'? He's out of danger, isn't he?"

"His condition was very serious. Life-threatening, as you well know. To say he's out of danger is an oversimplification."

"I thought you were so pleased with his response to the tonic."

"I am," Shields said forcefully. "But I must tell you something about that tonic. I created it myself from what I had at hand. I purposefully strengthened it as much as I dared, to encourage the body to increase its blood flow and thereby—"

"Yes, yes," Matthew interrupted. "I know all that about the stagnant blood. What of the tonic?"

"It is . . . how shall I say this . . . an extreme experiment. I've never before administered that exact mixture, in so powerful a dosage."

Matthew had an inkling now of what the doctor was getting at. He said, "Go on."

"The tonic was mixed strong enough to make him feel better. To lessen his pain. To . . . reawaken his natural healing processes."

"In other words," Matthew said, "it's a powerful narcotic that gives him the *illusion* of well-being?"

"The word *powerful* is . . . uh . . . an understatement, I fear. The correct term might be *Herculean*."

"Then without this tonic he would regress to the state he was in before?"

"I can't say. I do know for certain that his fever is much reduced and his breathing greatly freed. The condition of his throat has also improved. So: I have done what you required of me, young man. I have brought the magistrate back from death's door . . . at the penalty of his being dependent on the tonic."

"Which means," Matthew said grimly, "that the magistrate is also dependent on the tonic's *maker*. Just in case I might wish to pursue you in the future for the murder of Nicholas Paine."

Shields flinched at this, and pressed a finger to his mouth to request that Matthew regulate his volume. "No, you're wrong," he said. "I swear it. That had nothing to do with my mixing the tonic. As I said, I used what was at hand, in a strength I judged sufficient for the task. And as for Paine . . . if you'd please not mention him again to me? In fact, I demand you do not."

Matthew had seen what might have been a blade-twist of agony in the doctor's eyes, a fleeting thing that had been pushed down as quickly as it had appeared. "All right, then," he said. "What's to be done?"

"I am planning, after the execution, to begin watering the dosage. There will still be three cups a day, but one of them will be half strength. Then, if all goes well, we shall cut a second cup to half strength. Isaac is a strong man, with a strong constitution. I am hopeful his body will continue to improve by its own processes."

"You're not going back to the lancet and blister cups, are you?"

"No, we have crossed those bridges."

"What about taking him to Charles Town? Could he stand the trip?"

"Possibly. Possibly not. I can't say."

"Nothing more can be done for him?"

"Nothing," Shields said. "It is up to him . . . and to God. But he does feel better and he does breathe easier. He can communicate, and he is comfortable. These days . . . with the medicines I have on hand . . . I would say that is a miracle of sorts."

"Yes," Matthew said. "I agree, of course. I . . . didn't wish to sound ungrateful for what you've done. I believe that under the circumstances you've performed with admirable skill."

"Thank you, sir. Perhaps in this case there was more luck involved than skill . . . but I have done my best."

Matthew nodded. "Oh . . . have you finished your examination of Linch's body?"

"I have. I calculate from the thickness of blood that he had been dead some five to seven hours before discovery. His throat wound was the most glaring, but he was also stabbed twice in the back. It was a downward thrust, both stabs piercing his lung on the right side."

"So he was stabbed by someone standing behind and over him?"

"It would appear so. Then I believe his head was pulled backward and the throat wound administered."

"He must have been sitting at his desk, " Matthew said. "Talking to whoever killed him. Then, when he lay dying on the floor, the slash marks were applied."

"Yes, by Satan's claws. Or by the claws of some unknown demon."

Matthew was not going to argue the matter with Dr. Shields. Instead, he changed the subject. "And what of Mr. Bidwell? Has he recovered?"

"Sadly, no. He sits at the tavern with Winston as we speak, getting drunker than I've ever seen him. I can't blame him. Everything is crumbling around him, and with more witches yet to be identified . . . the town will soon be empty. I slept last night—the little I *did* sleep—with a Bible at both ends of my bed and a dagger in my hand."

Matthew's thought was that Shields could use a lancet with far deadlier effect than a dagger. "You needn't fear. The damage has been done, and there's no need for the fox now to do anything but wait."

"The fox? Satan, you mean?"

"I mean what I said. Pardon me, doctor. I have some things to tend to."

"Certainly. I shall see you later this evening."

Matthew retired to his room. He drank a cup of water and picked up the ebony-wood compass he'd found in Paine's house early this morning. It was a splendid instrument, the size of his palm, with a blued steel needle on a printed paper card indicating the degrees of direction. He'd realized the compass was a prime example of the process of magnetism, the needle having been magnetized—by a method he didn't fully understand—so as to point north.

Matthew had made other discoveries in Paine's bloodless house, not including the body-sized area of floorboards that had been pulled up and then hastily laid down again underneath the pallet. A brown cotton bag with a shoulder strap served to hold his other finds: a knife with a seven-inch-long blade and an ivory handle; a buckskin bladesheath and waistbelt; and a pair of knee-high boots that could be made useable by an inch of padding at the toes. He also found Paine's pistol and the wheel-lock spanner, but as he knew absolutely nothing about loading, preparing, and firing the temperamental weapon, its use would probably result in his shooting himself in the head.

Matthew had much to do, now that he'd decided.

Near midday, his decision—which up until that point had been wavering—was made solid. He had walked to the execution field and actually gone right up to the pyre and the stake. He'd stood there imagining the horror of it, yet his imagination was not so deranged as to permit him a full and complete picture. He could not save Fount Royal, but at least he might cheat the fox of Rachel's life.

It was possible, and he was going to do it.

He had been on his way to the gaol, to inform Rachel, when his steps had slowed. Of course she needed to know beforehand . . . or did she? If his resolve failed tonight, should she be waiting in the dark for a champion who never arrived? If he tried with all his intelligence and might and could not get the key from Green, should Rachel be waiting, hopeful of freedom?

No. He would spare her that torment. He had turned away from the gaol, long before he'd reached its door.

Now, in his room, Matthew sat down in his chair with the document box. He opened it and arranged before him three clean sheets of paper, a quill, and the inkpot.

He spent a moment arranging his thoughts as well. Then he began writing.

Dear Isaac:

By now you have discovered that I have taken Rachel from the gaol. I regret any distress this action may cause you, but I have done such because I know her to be innocent yet I cannot offer proof.

It is my knowledge that Rachel has been the pawn in a scheme designed to destroy Fount Royal. This was done by a manipulation of the mind called "animal magnetism" which I understand will be as much of a puzzle to you as it was to me. Fount Royal's ratcatcher was not who he appeared to be, but indeed was a master at this process of manipulation. He had the ability to paint pictures in the air, as it were. Pictures that would seem to be true to life, except for the lack of several important details such as I have pointed out in our conversations. Alas, I have no proof of this. I learned Linch's true identity from Mr. David Smythe, of the Red Bull Players, who knew him from a—

Matthew stopped. This sounded like utter madness! What was the magistrate going to think when he read these ramblings!

Go on he told himself. Just go on.

—circus in England several years ago; I do not wish to ramble any further and alarm you. Suffice it to say I was devastated when Mr. Smythe and the players left town, as he was my last hope at proving Rachel guiltless.

I have a great concern for the safety of Mr. Bidwell. The person who murdered Linch did so before that true identity could be revealed. That same person has been behind the scheme to destroy Fount Royal all along. I believe I know the reason, but as I have no proof it matters not. Now about Mr. Bidwell's safety: if Fount Royal is not soon totally abandoned, Mr. Bidwell's life may be in jeopardy. To save himself, he may have to leave his creation. I am sorry to pass this news on, but it is vital that Mr. Winston remain at Mr. Bidwell's side day and night. I do trust Mr. Winston.

Please believe me, sir, when I tell you I am neither out of my mind nor bewitched. However, I cannot and will not bear to see justice so brutally raped. I am taking Rachel to the Florida country, where she might proclaim herself a runaway slave or English captive and thereby receive sanctuary by the Spanish.

Yes, I can hear your bellow, sir. Please calm yourself and let me explain. I plan on returning. When, I do not know. What will happen to me when I do return, I do not know either. It will be your judgment, and I bow before your mercy. At the same time, I would hope that Mr. Smythe might be found and encouraged to speak, as he will make everything clear to you. And, sir, this is very important: make certain *you ask Mr. Smythe to explain why his family left the circus. You will understand much.*

As I said, I do plan on returning. I am an English subject, and I do not wish to give up that privilege.

Matthew paused. He had to think about the next part.

Sir, if by some chance or the decision of God that I should not return, I wish to here and now thank you for your intercession in my life. I wish to thank you for your lessons, your labors, and—

Go on, he told himself.

—your love. Perhaps you did not come to the almshouse that day in search of a son. Nevertheless, you found one.

Or, more accurately, sir, you crafted one. I would like to think that I made as good a son as Thomas might have been. You see, sir, you have been a magnificent success at crafting a human being, if I may speak so grandly of myself. You have given me what I consider to be the greatest gifts: that of self-worth and a knowledge of the worth of others.

It is because I understand such worth that I choose to free Rachel from her prison and her unjust fate. No one has made this decision but myself. When I go to the gaol tonight to free her, she will be unaware of my intentions.

There is no way you could have known that Rachel was not guilty. You have steadfastly followed the rules and tenets of law as outlined for cases of this nature. Therefore you came to the only conclusion available to you, and performed the necessary action. In doing what I have done this night, I have put on my own iron cloak and performed the only action available to me.

I suppose that is everything I need to say. I will close by saying that I wish you good health, a long life, and excellent fortunes, sir. I intend to see you again, at some future date. Again, please attend to Mr. Bidwell's safety.

I remain Sincerely Your Servant, Matthew—

He was about to sign his last name, but instead he made one final dot.

Matthew.

Folding the pages carefully, he slid them into an envelope he'd taken from the desk in Bidwell's study. He wrote on the front of the envelope *To Magistrate Woodward,* then he lit a candle and sealed the letter with a few drops of white wax.

It was done.

The evening crept up, as evenings will. In the fading purple twilight, with the last bold artist's stroke of red sun painting the bellies of clouds across the western horizon, Matthew took a lantern and went walking.

Though his pace was leisurely, he had a purpose other than taking in a sunset view of the dying town. He had at dinner inquired of Mrs. Nettles where Hannibal Green lived, and had been directed to it by a single clipped and disapproving sentence. The small whitewashed house stood on Industry Street, very near the intersection and the fount. Thankfully it wasn't as far down the street as Jerusalem's firelit camp, from which hollering and shrill lamentations issued forth to hold back the devils of night. To the right of Green's house was a neatly arranged garden of flowers and herbs, indicating either that the giant gaol-keeper was a man of varied interests or he was graced with a wife who had—yes, it was true—a green thumb.

The shutters were cracked open only a few inches. Yellow lamplight could be seen within. Matthew had noticed that the shutters of most of the still-occupied houses were closed, presumably on this warm evening to guard against the invasion of those same demons Reverend Jerusalem currently flailed. The streets were all but deserted, save for a few wandering dogs and the occasional figure hurrying from here to there. Matthew also couldn't fail to note the alarming number of wagons that were packed with furniture, household goods, baskets, and the like, in preparation for a sunrise departure. He wondered how many families would lie on bare floors tonight, restless until the dawn.

Matthew stood in the middle of Industry Street and looked from Green's house toward Bidwell's mansion, studying the windows that could be seen from this perspective. Then, satisfied with his findings, he walked back the way he'd come.

Winston and Bidwell were in the parlor when he arrived, the former reading over figures in a ledgerbook while the latter slumped gray-faced in a chair, his eyes closed and an empty bottle on the floor beside him. Matthew approached with the intention to ask how Bidwell was feeling but Winston lifted a hand in warning, his expression telling Matthew that the master of Fount Royal would not be pleased to awaken and set eyes upon him. Matthew retreated and quietly climbed the stairs.

When he entered his room, he found on his dresser a package wrapped in white waxed paper. Opening it he discovered a loaf of dense dark bread, a fist-sized chunk of dried beef, a dozen slices of salted ham, and four sausages. Matthew saw also that on his bed lay three candles, a package of matches and a flint, a corked glass bottle filled with water, and—lo and behold—a coil of cat-gut line with a small lead ballweight and a hook already tied, a small bit of cork pressed onto the sharp point. Mrs. Nettles had done all she could; it was up to him to find the stick.

Later that night, Dr. Shields arrived to give the magistrate his third dose. Matthew remained in his room, lying on the bed with his gaze directed to the ceiling. Perhaps an hour after that, the sound of Bidwell's intoxicated raging came up the stairs along with the sound of his footsteps and those of the person—two persons, it sounded to be—assisting him. Matthew heard Rachel's name hurled like a curse, and God's name taken in vain. Bidwell's voice gradually quieted, until at last it faded to nothing.

The house slept, fitfully, on this execution eve.

Matthew waited. Finally, when there were no more noises for a long while and his inner clock sensed the midnight hour had been passed, Matthew drew a breath, exhaled it, and stood up.

He was terrified, but he was ready.

He struck a match, lit his lantern, and put it on the dresser, then he soaped his face and shaved. It had occurred to him that his next opportunity to do so would be several weeks in the future. He used the chamberpot, and then he washed his hands and put on a clean pair of brown stockings, sand-colored breeches, and a fresh white shirt. He tore up another pair of stockings and padded the boot toes. He worked his feet into the boots and pulled them up snugly around his calves. In his bag, grown necessarily heavy with the food and other items, he packed the soapcake and a change of clothes. He placed the explanatory letter on his bed, where it would be seen. Then he slipped the bag's strap over his shoulder, picked up the lantern, and quietly opened the door.

A feeling of panic struck him. *I can yet change my mind,*

he thought. I can step back two paces, shut the door and—
Forget?

No.

Matthew shut the door behind him when he entered the hallway. He went into the magistrate's room and lit the double-candled lantern he had earlier brought there from downstairs. Opening the shutters, he set the lantern on the windowsill.

The magistrate made a muffled noise. Not of pain, simply some statement in the justice hall of sleep. Matthew stood beside the bed, looking down at Woodward's face and seeing not the magistrate but the man who had come to that almshouse and delivered him to a life he never would have imagined.

He almost touched Woodward's shoulder with a fond embrace, but he stayed his hand. Woodward was breathing well, if rather harshly, his mouth partway open. Matthew gave a quick and silent prayer that God would protect the good man's health and fortunes, and then there was no more time for lingering.

In Bidwell's study, that damned floorboard squealed again and almost sent Matthew out of his stolen boots. He lifted the map from its nail on the wall, carefully removed it from its frame and then folded it and put it down into his bag.

Downstairs—after an agonizingly slow descent meant to avoid any telltale thumps and squeaks that might bring Bidwell staggering out into the hallway—Matthew paused in the parlor to shine his lantern on the face of the mantel clock. It was near quarter to one.

He left the mansion, closed the door, and without a backward glance set off under a million stars. He kept the lantern low at his side, and shielded by his body in case the gate watchman—if indeed there remained in town anyone brave or foolish enough to sit up there all night—might happen to spy the moving flame and set off a bell-ringing alarm.

At the intersection he turned onto Truth Street and proceeded directly to the Howarth house. It was wretched in its abandonment, and made even more fearsome by the fact that Daniel Howarth had been found brutally murdered nearby. As Matthew opened the door and crossed the threshold, shining the lantern before him, he couldn't help but wonder that a ghost with a torn throat should be wandering within, forever searching for Rachel.

Ghosts there were none, but the rats had moved in. The gleam of red eyes and rodent teeth glittering under twitching whiskers greeted him, though he was certainly not a welcome guest. The rats scurried for their holes, and though Matthew had seen only five or six it sounded as if a duke's army of them festered the walls. He searched for and found the floorboard that had been lifted up to display the hidden poppets, and then he followed the lantern's glow into another room that held a bed. Its sheets and blanket were still crumpled and lying half on the floor from the March morning when Rachel was taken away.

Matthew found a pair of trunks, one containing Daniel's clothing and the other for Rachel's. He chose two dresses for her, both with long hems and full sleeves, as that was both the fashion and her favor. One dress was of a cream-colored, light material that he thought would be suitable for travelling in warm weather, and the other a stiffer dark blue printed material that impressed him as being of sturdy all-purpose use. At the bottom of the trunk were two pairs of Rachel's no-nonsense black shoes. Matthew put a pair of the shoes into his bag, the garments over his arm, and gladly left the sad, broken house to its current inhabitants.

His next destination was the gaol. He didn't go inside yet, however. There was still a major obstacle to deal with, and its name was Hannibal Green. Pinpricks of sweat had formed on his cheeks and forehead, and his insides had jellied at the thought of what could go wrong with his plan.

He left the garments and the shoulderbag in the knee-high grass beside the gaol. If all went as he hoped, he wouldn't be gone long enough for any rodent to find and investigate the package of food. Then he set his mind to the task ahead and began walking to Green's house.

As he went west on Truth Street he glanced quickly around and behind, just as a matter of reassurance—and suddenly he stopped in his tracks, his heart giving a vicious kick. He stood staring behind him, toward the gaol.

A light. Not there now, but he thought he'd seen a very brief glow there on the right side of the street, perhaps seventy or eighty feet away.

He paused, waiting, his heart slamming so hard he feared Bidwell might hear it and think a night-travelling drum corps had come to town.

If a light had indeed been displayed, it was gone. Or hidden when someone carrying it had dodged behind the protection of a hedge or wall, he thought grimly.

And another thought came to him, this one with dark consequences: had a citizen seen the flame of his lantern and emerged from a house to follow him? He realized someone might think he was either Satan incarnate or a lesser demon, prowling Fount Royal for another victim here in the dead of night. A single pistol shot would end his plans and possibly his life, but a single shout would have the same effect.

He waited. The urge to blow out his lamp was upon him, but that might truly be an admittance of foul deeds in progress. He scanned the dark. No further light appeared, if it had been there at all.

Time was passing. He had to continue his task. Matthew went on, from time to time casting a backward glance but seeing no evidence that he was being tracked. Presently he found himself in front of Green's house.

Now was the moment of truth. If he failed in the next few moments, everything would be ended.

He swallowed down a lump of fear and approached the door. Then, before he could lose his nerve, he balled up his fist and knocked.

FOURTEEN

"W ho . . . who's *there?*"

Matthew was taken aback. Green actually sounded frightened. Such was the double power of murder and fear, to imprison persons inside their own homes.

"It's Matthew Corbett, sir," he said, emboldened by the tremor in Green's voice. "I have to speak with you."

"*Corbett?* My Lord, boy! Do you know the hour?"

"Yes, sir, I do." And here was the beginning of the necessary lie. "I've been sent by Magistrate Woodward." Amazing, how such a falsehood could roll off a desperate tongue!

A woman's voice spoke within, the sound muffled, and Green answered her with, "It's that magistrate's clerk! I'll have to open it!" A latch was thrown and the door cracked. Green looked out, his red mane wild and his beard a fright. When he saw that it was only Matthew standing there and not an eight-foot-tall demon he opened the door wider. "What's the need, boy?"

Matthew saw a rotund but not unpleasant-looking woman standing in the room behind him. She was holding a lantern in one hand and the other arm cradled a wide-eyed, red-haired child two or three years of age. "The magistrate wishes to have Madam Howarth brought before him."

"What? Now?"

"Yes, now." Matthew glanced around; no other lights had appeared in the houses surrounding Green's, which was either a testament to fear or the fact that they had been abandoned.

"She'll be led to the stake in three or four hours!"

"That's why he wishes to see her now, to offer her a last chance for confession. It's a necessary part of the law." Again, an able-tongued lie. "He's waiting for her." Matthew motioned toward Bidwell's mansion.

Green scowled, but he took the bait. He emerged from his house, wearing a long gray nightshirt. He looked in the direction of the mansion and saw the light in the upstairs window.

"He would have preferred to go to the gaol, but he's too ill," Matthew explained. "Therefore I'm to accompany you to the gaol to remove the prisoner, and from there we shall escort her to the magistrate."

Green was obviously dismayed at this request, but since he was the gaol-keeper and this was official business he could not refuse. "All right, then," he said. "Give me a minute to dress."

"A question for you, please," Matthew said before Green could enter the house again. "Can you tell me if the watch-towers are manned tonight?"

Green snorted. "Would you sit up there tonight, alone, so somethin' might swoop in and get you like Linch was got?

Every man, woman and child in Fount Royal—*left* in Fount Royal, I mean to say—are huddled in their houses behind latched doors and closed shutters!"

"I thought as much," Matthew said. "It's a shame, then, that you should have to leave your wife and child alone. Undefended, I mean. But then again, it *is* an official request."

Green looked stricken. He rumbled, "Yes, it is. So there's no use jawin' about it."

"Well . . . I might make a suggestion," Matthew offered. "This is a very precarious time, I know. Therefore you might give me the key, and I'll take Madam Howarth to the magistrate. She'll probably not need to be returned to her cell before the execution hour. Of course, I wouldn't care to face her without a pistol or sword. Do you have either?"

Green stared him in the face. "Hold a minute," he said. "I've heard talk you were sweet on the witch."

"You have? Well . . . yes, it was true. *Was* true. She blinded me to her true nature while I was imprisoned with her. But I've since realized—with the magistrate's help—the depth of her powers."

"There are some who say *you* might be turned to a demon," Green said. "Lucretia Vaughan spoke such at the reverend's camp on the Sabbath."

"Oh . . . did she?" That damned woman!

"Yes, and that you might be in league with the witch. And Reverend Jerusalem said he knew you to be desirous of her body."

It was very difficult for Matthew to maintain a calm expression, when inside he was raging. "Mr. Green," he said, "it was I who delivered the execution decree to the witch. If I were truly a demon, I would have entranced the magistrate to prevent him from finding her guilty. I had every opportunity to do so."

"The reverend said it could'a been you made Woodward sick, hopin' he'd die 'fore he could speak the decree."

"Was I the central subject of the reverend's rantings? If so, I should at least ask for a percentage of the coin he made off my name!"

"The central subject was the Devil," Green said. "And how we're to get out of this town still wearin' our skins."

"After the reverend is done, you'll still have your skins, but your wallets will be missing." He was wandering from the point of his mission, and doing himself no good. "But please . . . there is the magistrate's request to consider. As I said, if you'll give me the key, I might—"

"No," Green interrupted. "Much as I despise to leave my home, the prisoner's my charge, and no hand shall unlock her cage but my own. Then I'll escort the both of you to the magistrate."

"Well . . . Mr. Green . . . I think that, in light of the reason to stay and defend your—" But Matthew was left talking to the air, as the giant gaol-keeper turned and entered his house.

His plan, tenuous at best, had already begun unravelling. Obviously Green was wary of Matthew's intentions. Also, the red-bearded monolith was faithful to duty even to the point of leaving his wife and child on this Satan-haunted eve. The man was to be commended, if Matthew wasn't so busy cursing him.

In a few moments Green emerged again, wearing his nightshirt over his breeches and heavy-soled boots on his feet. Around his neck was the leather cord and two keys. He carried a lantern in his left hand and his right paw brandished, to Matthew's great discomfort, a sword that might be used to behead an ox. "Remember," he said to his wife, "keep this door latched! And if anyone even tries to get in, let out the loudest holler your lungs ever birthed!" He closed the door, she latched it, and he said to Matthew, "All right, off with you! You walk ahead!"

It was time, Matthew thought, for his second plan.

The only problem was that there was no second plan. He led Green toward the gaol. He didn't look but, from the way the flesh on the back of his neck crawled, he assumed Green kept the sword's point aimed at it. The barking of a dog further up on Harmony Street caused a second canine to reply from Industry, which Matthew knew would be no soothing melody to Green's nerves.

"Why wasn't I told about this?" Green asked, as they approached the gaol. "If it is such a necessary part of the law. Couldn't it have been done in daylight?"

"The law states the accused in a witchcraft trial shall be afforded the opportunity for confession no more than six hours and no less than two hours before execution. It is called the law of . . . um . . . *confessiato.*" If Jerusalem could get away with his rite of sanctimony, Matthew figured he might employ a similar stratagem. "Usually the magistrate would visit the accused's cell in the company of a clergyman, but in this case it is impossible."

"Yes, that makes sense," Green admitted. "But still . . . why wasn't I told to expect it?"

"Mr. Bidwell was supposed to inform you. Didn't he?"

"No. He's been ill."

"Well," Matthew said with a shrug, "there you have it."

They entered the gaol, Matthew still leading. Rachel spoke to the lights instead of the persons carrying them, her voice wan and resigned to her fate. "Is it time?"

"Almost, madam," Matthew said stiffly. "The magistrate wishes to see you, to allow you opportunity for confession."

"For *confession?*" She stood up. "Matthew, what's this about?"

"I suggest you be silent, witch, for your own good. **Mr. Green, open the cell.**" He stepped aside, feverishly trying to think of what he was going to do when the key had turned.

"You step over there, away from me," Green instructed, and Matthew did.

Rachel came to the bars, her face and hair dirty, her amber eyes piercing him. "I asked you a question. What is this about?"

"It is about your life *after* you leave this place, witch. Your afterlife, in a faraway realm. Now please hold your tongue."

Green slid the key into its lock, turned it, and opened the cage's door. "All right. Come out." Rachel hesitated, gripping the bars. "It's the law of *confessiassho!* Come on, the magistrate's waitin'!"

Matthew's mind was racing. He saw the two buckets in Rachel's cell, one for drinking water and the other for bodily functions. Well, it wasn't much but it was all he could think of. "By God!" he said, "I think the witch wants to *defy* us, Mr. Green! I think she refuses to come out!" He stabbed an urgent finger at her, motioning toward the rear of the cell. "Will you come out, witch, or shall we drag you?"

"I don't . . ."

"By *God*, Mr. Green! She's defying the magistrate, even at this final hour! Will you come out, or will you *make things difficult?*" He added the emphasis on the last three words, and he saw that Rachel was still puzzled but she'd realized what he wanted her to do. She retreated from the bars, stopping only when her back met the wall.

"Matthew?" she said. "What game is this?"

"A game you will regret, madam! And don't think speaking so familiarly to me shall prevent Mr. Green from going in there and dragging you out! Mr. Green, have at it!"

Green didn't budge. He leaned on his sword. "I ain't goin' in there and risk gettin' my eyeballs scratched out. Or worse. You want her so bloody bad, *you* go get her."

Matthew felt the wind leave his sails. This was becoming a farce worthy of a drunken playwright's most fevered scribblings. "Very well then, sir." He clenched his teeth and held out his hand. "Your sword, please?"

Green's eyes narrowed. "I'll go in and drag her out," Matthew pressed on, "but you don't expect me to enter a tiger's den without a weapon, do you? Where's your Christian mercy?"

Green said nothing, and did not move. "Matthew?" Rachel said. "What's this—"

"Hush, witch!" Matthew answered, his gaze locked with the giant's.

"Ohhhhh, no." A half-smile slipped across Green's mouth. "No, sirrah. I ain't givin' up my sword. You must think me a proper fool, if you'd believe I'd let it out of my hand."

"Well, *someone* has got to go in there and pull her out! It seems to me it should be the man with the *sword!*" By now Matthew was a human sweatpond. Still Green hesitated. Matthew said, with an exasperated air, "Shall I go to the magistrate and tell him the execution will be postponed because the law of confessiato cannot be applied?"

"She doesn't care to confess!" Green said. "The magistrate can't force her to!"

"That's not the point. The law says . . ." Think, think! ". . . the accused must be afforded an opportunity, in the *pres-*

ence of a magistrate, whether they want to confess or not. Go on, please! We're wasting time!"

"That's a damn ridiculous law," Green muttered. "Sounds just like somethin' from a bunch of highwigs." He aimed his sword at Rachel. "All right, witch! If you won't move on your own will, you'll move at a prick on your arse!" Sweat glistening on his face, he entered the cell.

"Look how she steps back!" Quickly, Matthew set his lantern on the floor and entered directly behind him. "Look how she hugs the wall! Defiant to a fault!"

"Come on!" Green stopped, motioning with the sword. "Out with you, damn it!"

"Don't let her make a fool of you!" Matthew insisted. He looked down at the buckets and made the choice of the one that was about half-full of water. "Go on!"

"Don't rush me, boy!" Green snapped. Rachel had slid away from him along the wall toward the bars of the cell Matthew had occupied during his incarceration. Green went after her, but cautiously, the lantern in his left hand and the sword in his right.

Matthew picked up the water bucket. *Oh God,* he thought. Now or never!

"I don't want to draw blood," Green warned Rachel as he neared her, "but if I have to I'll—"

Matthew said sharply, "Look here, Mr. Green!"

The giant gaol-keeper whipped his head around. Matthew was already moving. He took two steps and flung the water into Green's face.

It hit the behemoth directly, blinding him for an instant but an instant of blindness was all Matthew had wanted. He followed the water by swinging the empty bucket at Green's head. *Wham!* went the sound of the blow, wood against skull, and skull won. The sturdy bucket fairly burst to pieces on impact, leaving Matthew gripping the length of rope that had served as its handle.

Green staggered backward, past Rachel as she scrambled aside. He dropped the lantern and collided with the bars with a force that made the breath whoosh from his lungs. His eyes had rolled back in his head. The sword slipped from his fingers. Then Green toppled to his knees in the straw, the floor trembling as he hit.

"Have you . . . have you gone *mad?*" was all Rachel could think to say.

"I'm getting you out of here." Matthew bent, picked up the sword—a heavy beast—and pushed it between the bars into the next cell.

"Getting me . . . out? What're you—?"

"I'm not going to let you burn," he said, turning to face her. "I have clothes for you, and supplies. I'm taking you to the Florida country."

"The . . . Florida . . ." She stepped back, and Matthew thought she might fall as Green had. "You . . . *must* be mad!"

"The Spanish will give you sanctuary there, if you pass yourself as a runaway slave or English captive. Now, I really don't think we have time to debate this, as I have crossed my own personal point of no return."

"But . . . why are you—"

She was interrupted by a groan from the awakening gaol-keeper, who was still on his knees. Matthew looked at Green in alarm and saw his eyes fluttering. Then, suddenly, Green's bloodshot eyes opened wide. They darted from Matthew to Rachel and back again—and then Green's mouth opened to deliver a yell that would awaken not only Fount Royal but the sleepers in Charles Town.

In a heartbeat, Matthew grabbed up a double-handful of

straw and jammed it deeply into Green's mouth even as the yell began its exit. Perhaps a syllable escaped before the straw did its work. Green began to gag and choke, and Matthew followed the act with a blow to the gaol-keeper's face that seemed to do not a whit of damage except to Matthew's knuckles. Then, still dazed and his voice unavailable, Green grasped the front of Matthew's shirt and his left forearm, lifted him off the floor like one of the demonic poppets, and flung him against the wall.

Now it was Matthew's turn to lose his breath as he crashed against the timbers. He slid down to the floor, his ribs near caved in, and saw through a haze of pain that Green was reaching through the bars to grasp the sword's handle, bits of straw flying around his face as he tried to cough the stuff out. Green's fingers closed on the weapon, and he began drawing it toward himself.

Matthew looked at Rachel, who was still too stunned at this turn of events to react. Then he saw the wooden bench beside her, and he hauled himself up.

Green almost had the sword pulled through. His large hand, clasping the sword's grip, had lodged between the bars. He gave a mighty heave, near tearing the flesh from his paw, and suddenly the sword was again his protector.

But not for long, if Matthew had his way. Matthew had picked up the bench, and now he slammed it down across Green's head and shoulders with all his strength. The bench went the way of the bucket, exploding upon impact. Green shuddered and made a muffled groan, his throat still clogged, and again the sword fell from his spasming fingers.

Matthew reached down to get that damned blade and do away with it once more—and Green's hands, the right one bruised and blackening from its contest with the bars, seized his throat.

Green's face was mottled crimson, the eyes wild with rage and terror, a stream of blood running from the top of his head down to his eyebrows and straw clenched between his teeth. He stood up to his full height, lifting Matthew by the throat, and began to strangle him as surely as if Matthew had been dangling from a gallows-tree. Matthew's legs kicked and he pushed against Green's bearded chin with both hands, but the giant's grasp was killing him.

Rachel now saw that she must act or Matthew would die. She saw the sword, but her wish was not to kill to save. Instead she launched herself at Green's back like a wildcat, scratching and pummelling at his face. He turned and with a motion that was almost casual flung her off, after which he continued his single-minded execution as Matthew thrashed ineffectually.

A shimmering red haze was starting to envelope Matthew's head. He cocked back his right fist, judging where he should strike to inflict the most pain. It hardly mattered. Green gave the threatening fist a quick glance and a straw-lipped sneer and his crushing hands tightened even more.

The blow was delivered, with a sound like an axe striking hardwood. Green's head snapped back, his mouth opened, and a tooth flew out, followed by a spatter of blood.

Instantly the giant's hands loosened. Matthew dropped to the floor. He clutched at his throat, his lungs heaving.

Green turned in a dazed circle, as if he were dancing a reel with an invisible partner. He coughed once, then again, and straw burst from his throat. His eyes showing only red-tinged whites, he fell like a hammer-knocked steer and lay stretched out on the floor.

It had been one hell of a blow.

However, it had been delivered before Matthew's own puny offering. Mrs. Nettles spat on her knuckles and wrung her hand. "Ow," she said. "I've nae hit a harder head!"

Matthew croaked, *"You?"*

"Me," she answered. "I heard you up 'n' about in Mr. Bidwell's study. I thought I'd tag along, keep a watch o'er ye. Near saw my lantern, 'fore I dowsed it." She looked at Rachel, and then cast a disapproving eye around the cell. "Lord, what a filthpot!"

Rachel was so amazed at all this, when she'd been preparing herself for the final morn, that she felt she must be in some strange dream even though she'd not slept since early afternoon.

"Here, c'mon." Mrs. Nettles reached down, grasped Matthew's hand, and hauled him up. "You'd best be off. I'll make sure Mr. Green keeps his silence."

"You're not going to hurt him, are you? I mean . . . any more than you already have?"

"No, but I'm gonna strip him naked and bind his wrists and ankles. His mouth, too. That nightshirt ought ta give up some ropes. But it wouldn't do for him ta ever know I was here. Go on now, the both of you!"

Rachel shook her head, still unbelieving. "I thought . . . I was to burn today."

"You shall *yet* burn, and the young man too, if you do'nae go." Mrs. Nettles was already pulling the nightshirt off Green's slumbering body.

"We have to hurry." Still rubbing his bruised throat, Matthew took Rachel's hand and guided her toward the threshold. "I have clothes and shoes for you outside."

"Why are *you* doing this?" Rachel asked Mrs. Nettles. "You're Bidwell's woman!"

"Nae, lass," came the reply. "I am employed by Mr. Bidwell, but I am my *own* woman. And I am doin' this 'cause I never thought you guilty, no matter what was claimed. Also . . . I am rightin' an old wrong. Off with ye!"

Matthew picked up his lantern. "Thank you, Mrs. Nettles!" he said. "You saved my life!"

"No, sir." She continued her methodical stripping of Green, her back turned to Matthew. "I just sentenced you both ta . . . whatever's out there."

Outside, Rachel staggered and held out her arms as if to embrace the night and the stars, her face streaked with tears. Matthew grasped hold of her hand again, and hurried her to where he'd left the shoulderbag, garments, and shoes. "You can change clothes after we get out," he said, slipping the bag's strap over his shoulder. "Will you carry these?" He gave her the garments. "I thought the light one would be best for travelling."

She gave a soft gasp as she took the dresses, and she caressed the cream-colored garment as if it were the returning to her of a wonderful treasure. Which it was. "Matthew . . . you've brought my wedding dress!"

If he'd had the time to spare, he might have laughed or he might have cried, but which one he was never to know. "Your shoes," he said, giving them to her. "Put them on, we're going through rough country."

They started off, Matthew leading the way toward Bidwell's house and the slave quarters. He had considered going out the front gate, as there was no watchman, but the gate's locking timber was too heavy for one man, and certainly for one man who had nearly been rib-busted and choked to death.

He looked up at the lantern in Isaac's window and wished the man might truly know what he meant to

Matthew. Alas, a note was a poor goodbye but the only one available to him.

Through the slave quarters, Matthew and Rachel moved as if they were dark, flying shadows. Perhaps the door of John Goode's house cracked open a few inches, or perhaps not.

Freedom awaited, but first there was the swamp.

FIFTEEN

The land was God and Devil both.

Matthew had this thought during the third hour of daylight, as he and Rachel paused at a stream to refill the water bottle. Rachel dipped the hem of her bride's dress into the water and pressed the cool cloth—once white on her wedding day, but faded by the Carolina humidity to its current cream hue—against her face. She scooped up a handful of water, which gurgled over flat stones and moved quietly through reeds and high grasses, and wet her thick ebony hair back from her forehead. Matthew glanced at her as he went about uncorking and filling the bottle, thinking of Lucretia Vaughan's repugnant idea concerning Rachel's locks.

Rachel took off her shoes and slid her sore feet into the sun-warmed stream. "Ahhhhh," she said, her eyes closed. "Ahhhhhh, that feels better."

"We can't tarry here very long." Matthew was already looking back through the woods in the direction they'd come. His face was red-streaked from an unfortunate encounter with a thorn thicket before the sun had appeared, and patches of sweat blotched his shirt. This certainly wasn't horse country, though, and therefore Solomon Stiles and whoever else might be with him would also be travelling on foot. It was rough going, no matter how experienced the leatherstocking. Still, he knew better than to underestimate Stiles's tracking skills, if indeed Bidwell had sent men in pursuit.

"I'm tired." Rachel lowered her head. "So tired. I could lie in the grass and sleep."

"I could, as well. That's why we have to keep moving."

She opened her eyes and looked at him, a pattern of leaf-shadow and morning sun on her face. "Don't you know you've given up everything?"

Matthew didn't respond. She'd asked him this question earlier, at the violet-blushed dawn, and neither had he answered then.

"You have," she said. "For what? Me?"

"For the truth." He removed the bottle from the stream and pushed its cork back in.

"The truth was worth so much?"

"Yes." He returned the bottle to his shoulderbag, and then he sat down in the wiry grass because—though his spirit was willing—his aching legs were not yet ready to travel again. "I believe I know who killed Reverend Grove and your husband. Also this person was responsible for the ratcatcher's murder."

"*Linch* was murdered?"

"Yes, but don't trouble yourself over him. He was as vile as his killer. Almost. But I believe I know the motive, and how these so-called witnesses were turned against you. They really did think they saw you . . . um . . . in unholy relations, so they were not lying." He cupped some water from the stream and wet his face. "Or, at least, they didn't realize they were."

"You *know* who killed Daniel?" Her eyes had taken on a hint of fury. "Who was it?"

"If I spoke the name, your response would be incredulity. Then, after I'd explained the reasoning, it would be anger. Armed with what you know, you would wish to go back to Fount Royal and bring the killer to justice . . . but I fear that is impossible."

"Why? If you *know* the name?"

"Because the cunning fox has erased all evidence," Matthew said. "Murdered it, so to speak. There is no proof whatsoever. So I would say a name to you, and you would be forever anguished that nothing can be done, just as I shall be." He shook his head. "It's best that only one of us drinks from that poisoned cup."

She pondered this for a moment, watching the flowing stream, and then she said, "Yes. I *would* want to go back."

"You may as well forget Fount Royal. I think the final hand has been dealt to Bidwell's folly, anyway." He roused himself and, considering that he wanted to put at least ten more miles at their backs before sundown, he stood up. He took a moment to study the map and align himself with the compass, during which Rachel put her shoes back on. Then Rachel pulled herself up too, wincing at the stiffness of her legs.

She looked around at the green-leafed trees, then up at the azure sky. After so long being confined, she was still half-dazed with the pine-perfumed breeze of freedom. "I feel so small," she said. "Hardly worth the sacrifice of a young man's life."

"If the young man has anything to do with it," he said, "it will not be a sacrifice. Are you ready?"

"I am."

They set off again, crossing the stream and heading once more into the dense forest. Matthew might not be a leatherstocking, but he was doing all right. Even very well, he thought. He had gone so far as to cinch the buckskin knife in its sheath around his waist in the best Indian-scout tradition, so the blade's handle was within easy reach.

Of Indians they'd seen not a footprint nor a feather. The wild beasts they'd encountered, not counting the chirping birds in the trees, consisted of a profusion of squirrels and a black snake coiled on a sun-splashed rock. The most difficult part of the journey so far had been the two miles of tidewater swamp they'd negotiated upon leaving Fount Royal.

But the land was God and Devil both, Matthew mused, because it was so beautiful and frighteningly vast in the sunny hours—but in the night, he knew, the demons of the unknown would creep to their pinestick fire and whisper of terrors beyond the circle of light. He had never ventured into a territory where there were no paths at all, just massive oaks, elms, and huge pines with cones the size of cannonballs, a carpet of leaf decay and pine needles in some places ankle deep, and the feeling that one would survive or perish here almost at the whim of Fate. Thank God for the map and the compass, or he would have already misplaced his sense of direction.

The land rose, forcing them up a slight but rugged incline. At its top, a crust of red rocks afforded a view of more unbroken wilderness stretching beyond the power of the eye. God spoke to Matthew and told him of a country almost too grand to imagine; the Devil spoke in his other ear, and told him such tremendous, fearful expanse and space would be seeded by the bones of some future generation.

They descended, Rachel walking a few paces behind Matthew as he cleaved a path through waist-high grass. Her wedding dress made a rustling sound, and small thorny pods stung her legs and clung to her hem.

As the sun continued its climb, the day warmed. Matthew and Rachel walked through a forest of gigantic, primeval trees where the hot sun was bright one second, streaming between the limbs seventy feet above, and the next second the shadows were dark green and as cool as caverns. Here they saw their first true wilderness creatures: four grazing does and a huge, watchful buck with a spread of antlers easily five feet across. The does lifted their heads to stare at the two humans, the buck gave a snort and bounded between his charges and the intruders, and then suddenly all the animals turned and vanished into the green curtains.

Not very further on, Matthew and Rachel again stopped at the edge of light and shadows. "What are those?" Rachel asked, her voice tensing.

Matthew approached the nearest oak. It was a Goliath of a tree that must've stood a hundred feet tall and had a trunk thirty feet around, but it was by no means the largest in these ancient woods. Lichens and moss had been pulled away from the trunk. Carved into the bark were man-shaped pictograms, swirling symbols, and sharp-edged things that might have been the representations of arrowheads. Matthew saw that it was indeed not the only trunk so adorned; a dozen more trees had been carved upon, displaying the figures of more humans, deer, what might have been the sun or moon, and waved lines that possibly stood for wind or water, among a variety of other symbols.

"They're Indian signs," Rachel said, answering her own question, as Matthew ran his fingers over a head-high symbol that seemed to either be a frightfully large man or a bear. "We must be in their territory."

"Yes, we must." Ahead of them, in that vast shadowy forest, were a few more carved trunks beyond the main line of decorated trees, and then beyond those the oaks were unadorned. Matthew consulted his map and compass once again.

"Perhaps we should change our route," Rachel suggested.

"I don't think changing our route would suffice. According to the compass, we're moving in the proper direction. I also think it would be difficult to say what was Indian territory and what was not." Uneasily, he looked around. A breeze stirred the leaves far overhead, making the shadows and sunlight shift. "The sooner we get through here, the better," he said, and he started walking again.

In an hour of rigorous travel, during which they saw thirty or forty more grazing deer, they emerged from the green forest into a wide clearing and in so doing were greeted with an amazing sight. Nearby a hundred wild turkeys the size of sheep were pecking in the grass and brush, and the intrusion of humans startled them to ungainly flight. The wind of their wings fanned the clearing and made a sound like the onrush of a hurricane.

"Oh!" Rachel cried out. "Look there!" She pointed, and Matthew's sight followed the line of her finger to a small lake whose still water reflected blue sky and golden Sol. "I'm going to rest here," she told him, her eyes weary. "I'm going to take a bath and wash the gaol smell off me."

"We should keep moving."

"Can we not make our camp here for the night?"

"We could," Matthew said, judging the sun's progress, "but there's still plenty of light. I didn't intend to camp until nightfall."

"I'm sorry, but I *must* rest," she insisted. "I can hardly feel my legs anymore. And I must bathe, too."

Matthew scratched his forehead. He, as well, was just about worn to a nubbin. "All right. I think we might stay here for an hour or so." He slipped the bag's strap off his chafed shoulder and retrieved the soapcake, offering it to her further amazement. "Never let it be said I did not bring civilization to the wilderness."

At this point in their relationship, which seemed more intimate than the wedded state, it was nonsense for Matthew to walk into the dark line of woods and afford Rachel privacy. Neither did she expect it. On the edge of the lake, as Matthew reclined on his back and stared up at the sky, Rachel took off her shoes and the faded bridal dress and waded naked into the water to her waist. She turned her back to the shore and soaped her private area, then her stomach and breasts. Matthew glanced once . . . then again . . . a third time, more than a glance . . . at her brown body, made lean by gaolhouse soup. He might have counted her ribs, if he'd chosen. Her body was womanly, yes, but there was a hardness of purpose to it as well, a purity of the will to survive. He watched as she walked deeper into the water, chillbumps rippling across her taut skin even as the sun soothed her. She leaned over and wet her hair, then soaped a lather into it.

Matthew sat up and pulled his knees to his chin. His thorn-cut face had blushed at the image in his mind: that of his own hands, moving over the curves and hollows of Rachel's body as if they too were explorers in a new territory. A winged insect of some kind buzzed his head, which helped to distract him from that line of thought.

After her hair was washed and she was feeling clean, Rachel's attention returned again to Matthew. Also returned was her sense of modesty, as if the gaol's grime had clothed her from view and now she was truly naked. She knelt down in the water, up to her neck, and approached the shore.

Matthew was eating half of a slice of ham from the food package, and had set aside the other half for Rachel. He saw she intended to emerge from the water, so he turned his back. She came out of the lake, dripping, and stood for a moment to dry herself, her face offered to the sun.

"I fear you'll have to invent a falsehood when you enter a Spanish town or stockade," Matthew said, painfully aware of how near she stood. "I doubt even the Spanish would care to grant sanctuary to an accused witch." He finished the ham and licked his fingers, watching her shadow on the ground. "You should claim yourself to be an escaped household servant, or simply a wife who sickened of British rule. Once they know your country of birth, you should have no troubles." Again that insect—no, two of them—buzzed around him, and he waved them away.

"Wait," she said, picking up her wedding dress. "You're speaking only of me. What about *you?*"

"I am helping you reach the Florida country . . . but I'm not going to stay there with you." Rachel let this revelation sink in as she put her dress back on.

He had seen her shadow don the garment, so he turned toward her again. Her beauty—the thick, wet black hair, the lovely proud face and intense amber eyes—was enough to quicken his heart. The nightbird was even more compelling by day. He sighed and chose to stare at the ground once more. "I'm an Englishman," he said. "Bound by the conventions and laws of English life, whether I like them or not. I couldn't survive in a foreign land." Matthew managed a brief, halfhearted smile. "I should be too longing for boiled potatoes and roast beef. Besides . . . Spanish is not my tongue."

"I don't understand you," she said. "What kind of man are you, who does what you've done and expects nothing in return?"

"Oh, I do expect something, make no mistake. I expect to be able to go on living with myself. I expect you will return to Portugal, or Spain, and rebuild your life. I expect to see Magistrate Woodward again and plead my case before him."

"I expect you'll find yourself behind stronger bars than held me," Rachel said.

"A possibility," he admitted. "A *likelihood*. But I won't stay there long. Here, do you want this?" He held up the portion of ham for her.

She accepted it. "How can I tell you how much this means to me, Matthew?"

"What? One half slice of ham? If it means so much, you can have a whole—"

"You know what I'm saying," she interrupted. "What you've done. The incredible risk." Her face was grim and set, but tears glistened in her eyes. "My God, Matthew. I was ready to die. I had given up my spirit. How can I ever repay such a debt?"

"It is I who owe the debt. I came to Fount Royal a boy. I left it as something more," Matthew said. "You should sit down and rest."

She did sit down, and pressed her body against his as if they sat crushed by a crowd of a thousand people, instead of just alone in this God-made, Devil-touched land. He started to move away, discomforted by his own reaction to her closeness, but she gently grasped his chin with her left hand.

"Listen to me," Rachel said, in what was nearly a whisper. Her eyes stared into his own, their faces only parted by a few inches of inconsequential air. "I loved my husband very much," she said. "I gave him my heart and my soul. Even so, I think . . . I could love you the same . . . if you would allow it."

The few inches of air shrank. Matthew did not know who had first leaned toward the other, but did it really matter? One leaned and one met, and that was both the geometry and poetry of their kiss.

Though Matthew had never before done this, it seemed a natural act. What was most alarming was the speed of his heart, which if it had been a horse might have reached Boston by first star. Something inside him seemed molten, like blue-flamed glass being changed and reshaped by the power of a breath. It was both strengthening and weakening, thrilling and frightening—again that conjunction of God and Devil that seemed to be at the essence of all things.

It was a moment he would remember the rest of his life.

Their lips remained sealed together, melded by bloodheat and heartbeat. Who drew away first was also unknown to Matthew, as time had slipped its boundaries like rain and river.

Matthew looked into Rachel's eyes. The need to speak was as strong as a force of nature. He knew what he would say. He opened his mouth. "I—"

A winged insect suddenly landed on the shoulder of Rachel's wedding dress. His attention was drawn to it, and away from the moment. He saw it was a honeybee. The insect hummed its wings and took flight, and then Matthew was aware of several more of them circling round and round.

"I—" Matthew said again, and suddenly he was not sure at all what he was going to say. She waited for him to speak, but he was speechless.

He stared into her eyes once more. Was it the desire to

love him he saw there, or the desire to thank him for the gift of her life? Did she even know which emotion reigned in her heart? Matthew didn't think so.

Even as they travelled together, they were moving in opposite directions. It was a bitter realization, but a true one. Rachel was bound for a place he could not live, and he must live in a place where she could not be bound.

He dropped his gaze from her. She, too, had realized that there could be no future for two such as them, and that Daniel was still as close to her as the dress she had worn on the day of their joining. She drew away from Matthew, and then noticed the circling insects.

"Honeybees." Matthew scanned the clearing, his eyes searching. And there it was!

A stand of two dead oaks—probably lightning-struck, he thought—stood apart from the main line of forest, fifty yards from the lake's edge. Near the top of one of them was a large knothole. Around it the air was alive with a dark, shifting mass. Sunlight made a stream of liquid down the tree's trunk shine gold.

"Where there are honeybees," Matthew said, "there is honey." He took the bottle from the bag, emptied its water—since fresh water was an abundant resource at this distance from the seacoast and swamp—and stood up. "I'll see if I can obtain us some."

"I'll help." She started to stand, but Matthew put his hand on her shoulder.

"Rest while you can," he advised. "We're going to have to move on very soon."

Rachel nodded and relaxed again. In truth, she would have to summon the energy for their continued journey, and a walk to a dead tree fifty yards there and back—even for the sweet delicacy of honey—strained her imagination.

Matthew, however, was intent on it, particularly after their kiss and the jarring return to reality that had followed. As Matthew started toward the tree, Rachel warned, "Take care you're not stung! The honey wouldn't be worth it!"

"Agreed." But he'd seen the spill of golden nectar down the trunk from what appeared a very copious comb, and he felt sure he might at least get a bottleful without incurring rage.

The bees had been highly productive. The honey had streamed down from forty feet above all the way to the ground, where a sticky puddle had accumulated. Matthew drew the knife from its sheath, uncorked the bottle, and held it into the flow, at the same time pushing the thick elixir—a natural medicine good for all ills, Dr. Shields would have said—in with his blade. A few bees hummed around, but they did not strike and seemed mostly curious. He could hear the steady, more ominous tone of the large dark mass of them as they went about their business tending the comb.

As he worked, Matthew's mind went to the magistrate. The letter would have been long read by now. Whether it had been digested or not was more difficult to say. Matthew listened to the singing of birds in the forest beyond, and wondered whether the magistrate might be able to hear such song at this very moment, or be able to see the sun on this cloudless day. What must Isaac be thinking? Matthew fervently hoped that he'd written the missive coherently—and eloquently—enough so that Isaac would know he was in his right mind, and adamant about Smythe being located. If that man would agree to talk, then much could be—

Matthew paused in his work, the bottle near halfway filled. Something had changed, he thought.

Something.

He listened. He could still hear the drone of the working bees. But . . . the birdsong. Where was the birdsong? Matthew looked toward the shadowed line of forest.

The birds had ceased their singing.

A movement to the left caught his eye. Three crows burst from the foliage, cawing loudly as they shot across the clearing.

Beside the lake, Rachel lay on her back, drowsing. The voices of the crows came to her, and she opened her eyes in time to watch the birds pass overhead.

Matthew stood motionless, staring at the impenetrable area from which the crows had come.

Another movement seized his attention. Far up in the sky, a single vulture was slowly wheeling around and around.

All the saliva had left his mouth and become cold sweat on his face. The sensation of danger stabbed him like a knife in the neck.

He felt certain something in the woods was watching him.

Moving with careful deliberation though his nerves shrieked to turn and run, Matthew pushed the cork back into the bottle. His right fist tightened around the knife's handle. He began to retreat from the honey-flowing tree, one step at the time, his eyes darting back and forth across the treacherous woods.

"Rachel?" he called. His voice cracked. He tried again. "Rachel?!" This time he looked over his shoulder to see if she'd heard.

A heavy form suddenly exploded from its place of concealment at the forest's edge. Rachel was the first to see it, by only a second, and she let go a scream that savaged her throat.

Then Matthew faced it too. His feet seemed rooted to the earth, his eyes wide and his mouth open in a soundless cry of terror.

The monstrous bear that was racing toward him was an old warrior and fully gray. Patches of ashy malignant mange infected its shoulders and legs. Its jaws were stretched to receive human flesh, streams of drool flying back past its head. Matthew had just an instant to register that the bear's left eye socket was puckered and empty, and he knew.

He was about to be embraced by Jack One Eye.

Maude . . . at Shawcombe's tavern . . . *Jack One Eye hain't jus' a burr. Ever'thin' dark 'bout this land . . . ever'thin' cruel, and wicked.*

"Rachel!" he screamed, twisting toward her and running for his life. "Get in the water!"

There was nothing she could do to help him except pray to God he made the lake. She ran toward the water and leaped into it, swimming in her bridal dress toward deep water.

Matthew dared not look behind. His legs were pumping furiously, his face distorted by fear, his heart on the verge of bursting. He heard the thunderous impact of paws behind him, gaining ground, and he knew with awful certainty that he would never reach the lake.

He clenched his teeth and threw himself to the left—the bear's blind side—at the same time letting out a shriek that he hoped might startle the beast enough to give him extra time. Jack One Eye hurtled past him, its rear claws digging up furrows of earth. A front claw swung and made the air between them shimmer.

Then Matthew was running for the lake again, dodging and swerving with every step. Again the earth trembled at his heels. The bear was bigger than the biggest horse he'd

ever seen, and it could crush every bone in his body just with
its forward progress alone.

Matthew leaped to the left in a maneuver that nearly
snapped his knees. He almost lost his balance as the bear
went past, its massive mange-riddled head thrusting in
search of him. The jaws came together with a noise like a
musket shot. He smelled the reeking bestial stink of the
thing, and was close enough to see the broken shafts of four
arrows in its side. Then he was running again, and he prayed
that God grant him the speed of a crow.

Again Jack One Eye was almost upon him. Again
Matthew lunged to the left—but this time he had mis-
judged both the geometry and the flexibility of his knees.
The angle was too sharp and his feet skidded out from
beneath him. He went down on his right side in the grass.
He was only vaguely aware of Rachel's screams through the
thunder in his head. The gray wall of Jack One Eye rose
before him. He staggered up, fighting for balance.

Something hit him.

He had the impression of the world turned upside
down. A searing pain filled his left shoulder. He knew he
was tumbling head over heels, but could do nothing about
it. Then he landed hard on his back, the breath bursting
from his lungs. He tried to scramble away, as again that
gray wall came upon him. Something was wrong with his
left arm.

Matthew was struck in the ribs on the left side by a red-
hot cannonball that picked him up and flung him like a
grainsack. Something grazed by his forehead while he was
tumbling—a musket ball, he thought it must be, here on
this field of battle—and a red film descended over his eyes.
Blood, he thought. Blood. He hit the ground, was dragged
and tossed again. His teeth snapped together. I'm going to

die, he thought. Right here. This sunny, clear day. I am going to die.

His left arm was already dead. His lungs hitched and gurgled. The mangy gray wall was there in his face again, there with an arrow shaft stuck in it.

He decided, almost calmly, that he would do his own sticking.

"Hey!" he hollered, in a voice that surprised him with its desperate power. "Hey!" He brought the knife up and stabbed and twisted and wrenched and stabbed and twisted and wrenched, and the beast grunted roared roared breath hot as Hades smelling of decayed meat and rotten teeth *stabbed and twisted and wrenched* blood red on the gray streaming down a glorious sight *die you bastard you bastard you!*

Jack One Eye might be huge, but it had not grown to such a ripe old age by being stupid. The stickings had an effect, and the bear backed away from the mosquito.

Matthew was on his knees. In his right hand, the blade was covered with blood. He heard a dripping, pattering sound, and he looked down at the gore falling into the red-stained grass from the twitching fingers of his left hand. He seemed to be burning up from within, yet the fiery pain of shoulder and ribs and forehead was not what made him sob. He had peed in his breeches, and he had brought no other pair.

Jack One Eye circled him to the left. Matthew turned with the beast, dark waves beginning to fill his head. He heard, as if from another world, the sound of a woman— Rachel was her name, Rachel yes Rachel—screaming his name and crying. He saw blood bubbling around the bear's nostrils, and crimson matted the gray fur at its throat. Matthew was near fainting, and he knew when that happened he was dead.

The bear suddenly stood up on its hind legs, to a height of eight feet or more. It opened its broken-toothed mouth. What emerged was a hoarse, thunderous, and soul-shaking roar that brimmed with agony and perhaps the realization of its own mortality. Two snapped arrow shafts were buried in festered flesh at the beast's belly, near a bloody-edged claw wound that must have been delivered by one of its own breed. Matthew also saw that a sizeable bite had been ripped from Jack One Eye's right shoulder, and this ugly wound was green with infection.

It occurred to him, in his haze of pain and the knowledge of his impending departure from this earth, that Jack One Eye was dying too.

The bear fell back down onto its haunches. And now Matthew pulled himself up, staggered and fell, pulled himself up again, and shouted, "Haaaaaaaaaaa!" in the maw of the beast.

After which he fell to the ground once more, into his own blood. Jack One Eye, its nostrils dripping gore, shambled toward him with its jaws open.

Matthew wasn't ready to die yet. Come all this way, to die in a clearing under the sun and God's blue sky? No, not yet.

He came up with the sheer power of desperation and drove the blade under the bear's jaw, giving the knife a violent ripping twist. Jack One Eye gave a single grunt, snorted blood into Matthew's face, and pulled back, taking the imbedded blade with it. Matthew fell on his belly, the pain in his ribs making him curl up like a stomped worm.

Again the bear circled him to the left, shaking its head back and forth in an effort to rid itself of the stinger that had pierced its throat. Banners of blood flew in the air from its nostrils. Even on his belly, Matthew crawled to keep the beast from getting behind him. Suddenly Jack One Eye came in again, and Matthew pulled himself up, throwing his right arm up over his face to protect what was left of his skull.

The movement made the bear turn aside. Jack One Eye backed away, its single orb blinking and glazed. The bear lost its equilibrium for a second and staggered on the edge of falling. It caught itself, then stood less than fifteen feet from Matthew, staring at him with its head lowered and its arrow-stubbled sides heaving. Its gray tongue emerged, licking at the bleeding nostrils.

Matthew pulled himself up to his knees, his right hand clutching his ribs on the left side. It seemed the most important thing in the world to him, to keep his hand pressed there so that his entrails would not stream out.

The world, red-tainted and savage, had dwindled to the single space of distance between man and animal. They stared at each other, measuring pain, blood, life, and death each by their own calculations.

Jack One Eye made no sound. But the ancient, wounded warrior had reached a decision.

It abruptly turned away from Matthew. It began half-loping, half-staggering across the clearing the way it had come, shaking its head back and forth in a vain effort to dislodge the blade. In another moment the beast entered its wilderness again.

And Jack One Eye was gone.

Matthew fell forward onto the bloody battleground, his eyes closed. In his realm of drifting, he thought he heard a high-pitched and piercing cry: *Hiyiiiiiii! Hiyiiiiiii! Hiyiiiiiii!* The vulture's voice, he thought. The vulture, swooping down upon him.

Tired. So . . . very . . . very . . . tired. Rachel. What . . . is to . . . become . . . of . . .

The vulture, swooping down.

Screaming *Hiyiiiiiii! Hiyiiiiiii! Hiyeeeeee!*

Matthew felt himself fall away from the earth, toward that distant territory so many explorers had gone to journey through, and from which return was impossible.

SIXTEEN

Matthew's first realization of his descent to Hell was the odor.

It was as strong as demon's sweat and twice as nasty. It entered his nostrils like burning irons, penetrated to the back of his throat, and he was suddenly aware that he was being wracked by a fit of coughing though he had not heard it begin.

When the smell went away and his coughing ended, he tried to open his eyes. The lids were heavy, as if weighted by the coins due Charon for his ferry trip across the Styx. He couldn't open them. He heard now a rising and falling voice that must surely be the first of untold many souls lamenting their scorched fate. The language sounded near Latin, but Latin was God's language. This must be Greek, which was more suitably earthy.

A few more breaths, and Matthew became knowledge-able of the torment of Hell as well as its odor. A fierce, stabbing, white-hot pain had begun to throb at his left shoulder and down the arm. The ribs on that side also began an agonizing complaint. There was a pain at his forehead too, but that was mild compared to the others. Again he tried to open his eyes and again he failed.

Neither could he move, in this state of eternal damnation. He thought he was attempting to move, but he couldn't be sure. There was so much pain, growing worse by the second, that he decided it was more reasonable to give up and conserve his energy, as surely he would need it when he walked through the brimstone valley. He heard the crackling of a fire—of course, a fire!—and felt an oppressive, terrible heat as if he were being roasted over an inferno.

But now a new feeling began to come over him: anger. It threatened to burst into full-flamed rage, which would put him right at home here.

He had considered himself a Christian and had tried his very best to follow the Godly path. To find himself cast into Hell like this, with no court to hear his case, was a damned and unreasonable sin. He wondered in his increasing fury what it was he'd done that had doomed him. Run with the orphans and young thugs on the Manhattan harbor? Flung a horse-apple at the back of a merchant's head, and stolen a few coins from the dirty pocket of a capsized drunk? Or had it been more recent wrongdoing, such as creeping into Seth Hazelton's barn and later cutting the man's face with a tin lantern. Yes, that might be it. Well, he would be here to greet that lover of mares when Hazelton arrived, and by that time Matthew hoped to have built up some seniority in this den of lawyers.

The pain was now excruciating, and Matthew clenched his teeth but he felt the cry rising up from his parched throat. He couldn't restrain it. He was going to have to scream, and what would the company of *diaboliques* then think of his fortitude?

His mouth opened, and he let loose not a scream but a dry, rattling whisper. Even so, it was enough to further drain him. He was aware that the murmuring had ceased.

A hand—so rough-fleshed it might have been covered with treebark—touched his face, the fingers starting at his chin and sliding up his right cheek. The singsong murmuring began once more, still in that undecipherable language. What felt like a thumb and finger went to his right eye, and endeavored to push the lid up.

Matthew had had enough of this blindness. He gave a soft gasp at the effort it involved, but he forced his eyes open of his own accord.

Immediately he wished he had not. In the red, leaping light and drifting smoke of Hades, the visage of a true demon greeted him.

This creature had a narrow, long-chinned brown face with small black eyes, its flesh wrinkled and weathered like ancient wood. Blue whorls decorated the gaunt cheeks, and a third eye—daubed bright yellow as the sun—was painted in the center of the forehead. The earlobes were pierced with hooks from which dangled acorns and snail shells. The head was bald save for a topknot of long gray hair that grew from the back of the scalp and was adorned with green leaves and the bones of small animals.

To make Matthew's induction to Hell even worse, the demon opened its mouth and displayed a set of teeth that might have served as a sawblade. "Ayo pokapa," the creature said, nodding. Or at least that was the sound Matthew heard. "Ayo pokapa," the demon spoke again, and lifted to its lips half of a broken clay dish in which something was densely smoking. With a quick inhalation, the creature pulled smoke into its mouth and then blew the noxious fumes—that nasty demon's-sweat odor—into Matthew's nostrils.

Matthew attempted to turn his head aside, and that was when he realized his skull was bound in some way to whatever hard pallet he lay upon. Avoiding the smoke was impossible.

"Yante te napha te," the creature began to murmur. "Saba yante napha te." It slowly rocked back and forth, eyes half-closed. The light from one or more hellfires glowed red through the dense pall of smoke that drifted above Matthew. What sounded like a pineknot burst, and then there came a hissing noise like a roomful of rattlesnakes from beyond the murmuring, rocking diabolist. The acrid woodsmoke seemed to thicken, and Matthew feared that the little breath he could grasp would soon be poisoned. "Yante te napha te, saba yante napha te," went the repeated, rising and falling voice. Again the ritual with the broken dish and the inhalation was repeated, and again the smoke—damn Hell, if there was such a powerful stink to be smelled for eternity!—was blown up Matthew's nostrils.

He couldn't move, and assumed that not only his head was bound down but also both wrists and ankles. He wished to be a man about this, but tears sprang to his eyes.

"Ai!" the demon said, and patted his cheek. "Mouk takani soba se ha ha." Then it was back to the steady murmuring and rocking, and another blast of smoke up the nose.

After a half-dozen draughts, Matthew was feeling no pain. The cogwheels that usually regulated the order of his mind had lost their timing, and one rocking motion by the demon stretched to the speed of the snails whose shells hung from the earlobe hooks, while the next was gone past in an eyeblink. Matthew felt as if he were floating in a red-flamed, smoky void, though he could of course sense the hard pallet at his back.

And then Matthew knew he must be truly insane, for he suddenly realized something very strange about the piece of broken dish from which the murmuring, smoke-blowing creature was inhaling.

It was white. And on it was a decoration of small red hearts.

Yes, he was insane now. Absolutely insane, and ready for Hell's Bedlam. For that was the same dish Lucretia Vaughan had thrown into the fount, only then it had been whole and contained a sweet yam pie.

"Yante te napha te," the demon crooned, "saba yante napha te."

Matthew was fading again. Losing himself to the swelling dark. Reality—such as it was in the Land of Chaos—disappeared in bits and pieces, as if the darkness were a living thing that hungered first for sound, then light, and then smell.

If it was possible to die a death in the country of the dead, then that was Matthew's accomplishment.

But he found that such a death was fleeting, and there was very little peace in it. The pain grew again, and again ebbed. He opened his eyes, saw moving, blurred figures or shadows, and closed them for fear of what had arrived to visit him. He thought he slept, or died, or suffered nightmares of Jack One Eye running him down in a bloody clearing while the ratcatcher rode the bear's back and thrust at him with the five-bladed sticker. He awakened sweating summer floods, and fell to sleep again dry as a winter leaf.

The smoke-breathing demon returned, to continue its tortures. Matthew once more saw that the broken dish was white, with small red hearts. He dared to speak to the creature, in a feeble and fearful voice, "Who are you?" The murmured chant went on.

"What are you?" Matthew asked. But no answer was given.

He slept and waked, slept and waked. Time had no meaning. He was tended to by two more demons, these more in the female shape with long black hair similarly adorned by leaves and bones. They lifted the mat of woven grasses, moss, feathers, and such that covered his nakedness, cleaned him when he needed to be cleaned, fed him a gray paste-like food that tasted strongly of fish, and put a wooden ladle of water to his lips.

Fire and smoke. Shifting shadows in the gloom. That murmured, singsong chanting. Yes, this was surely Hell, Matthew thought.

And then came the moment when he opened his eyes and found Rachel standing beside him in this realm of flames and fumes. "Rachel!" he whispered. "You too? Oh . . . my God . . . the bear . . ."

She said nothing, but pressed a finger to her lips. Though dead, her eyes were as bright as gold coins. Her hair cascaded in ebony waves about her shoulders, and Matthew would have been lying if he'd said the infernal light didn't make her heart-achingly beautiful. She was wearing a dark green shift decorated around the neck with intricate blue beadwork. He stared at the pulse that beat in the hollow of her throat, and saw moisture glisten on her cheeks and forehead.

It must be said, these demons did excellent work at the illusion of life.

He tried to angle his face toward her, but still his head was confined as were his arms and legs. "Rachel . . . I'm sorry," he whispered. "You shouldn't be here. Your time in Hell . . . was already served on earth."

Her finger went to his lips, to bid him be silent.

"Can you ever . . . ever forgive me?" he asked. "For bringing you to . . . such a bad end?" Smoke drifted between them, and somewhere beyond Rachel the fires crackled and seethed.

She gave him an eloquent answer. Leaning down, she pressed her lips to his own. The kiss lingered, and became needful.

His body—the illusion of a body, after all—reacted to this kiss as it would have done in the earthly sphere. Which didn't surprise Matthew, for it was a well-known fact Heaven would be full of angelic lutes and Hell full of flesh flutes. In that particular regard, perhaps it was not such a disagreeable place.

Rachel pulled back. Her face remained within his field of vision, her lips damp. Her eyes were shining, and the fire shadows licked her cheek.

She reached back and undid something. Suddenly the blue-beaded garment slipped off her and fell to the ground.

Her hands returned, lifting the woven mat from Matthew's body. Then she stepped up onto what must be a platform of some kind and slowly, gently eased her naked body down against his own, after which she pulled the grass mat over them again and kissed his mouth with longing.

He wanted to ask her if she knew what she was doing. He wanted to ask her if this was love, or passion, or if she looked at him and saw Daniel's face.

But he didn't. Instead, he surrendered to the moment; to be more accurate, the moment demanded him. He returned her kiss with a soul-deep longing of his own, and her body pressed against his with undeniable urgency.

As they kissed, Rachel's hand found the scrivener's readied instrument. Her fingers closed about him. With a slow shifting of her thighs, she eased him into her, into the moist and heated opening that relaxed to allow entry and then more firmly grasped once he was sheathed deep.

Matthew was unable to move, but Rachel was unrestricted. Her hips began a leisurely, circular motion punctuated by stronger thrusts. A groan left Matthew's mouth at the incredible, otherworldly sensation, and Rachel echoed it with her own. They kissed as if eager to merge one into the other. As the woodsmoke swirled about them and the fires burned, as their lips sought and held and Rachel's hips moved up and then down to push him still deeper, Matthew cried out with a pleasure that was verging on pain. Even this central act, he thought in his state of sweating rapture, was a cooperation of God and Devil.

Then he just stopped thinking and allowed nature to rule.

Rachel's movements were steadily strengthening. Her mouth was against his ear, her pine-scented hair in his face. She was breathing quickly and harshly. His heartbeat slammed, and hers pounded against his damp chest. She gave two more thrusts and her back arched, her head coming up and her eyes squeezed tightly shut. She shivered and her mouth opened to release a long, soft moan. An instant later, the feeling of pleasure did translate into a white flashing pain for Matthew, a fierce jolt that rippled from the top of his head down his spine. In the midst of this riot of sensations, he was aware of his burst into Rachel's clinging humidity, an explosion that brought a grimace to his face and a cry from his lips. Rachel kissed him again, so ardently as if she wished to capture that cry and keep it forever like a golden locket in the secret center of her soul.

With a strengthless sigh, Rachel settled against him yet supported herself on her elbows and knees so as not to rest all her weight. He was still inside her, and still firm. His virginity was a thing of the past and its passage left him with a delicious aching, but his flame had not yet been extinguished. And obviously neither had Rachel's, for she looked him in the face, her wondrous eyes sparkling in the firelight and her hair damp from the heat of exertion, and began to move upon him once again.

If this was indeed Hell, Matthew thought, no wonder everyone was in such a fever to make their reservations.

The second time was slower-paced, though even more intense than the first. Matthew could only lie and vainly attempt to match Rachel's motions. Even if his movements had been totally free, a weakness that affected every muscle save one had claimed his strength.

Finally, she pressed down on him and—though he'd tried to restrain it for as long as he might—he again experienced the almost-blinding combination of pleasure and pain that signalled the imminent nearing of a destination two lovers so vigorously sought to reach.

Then, in the warm wet aftermath, as they breathed and kissed and played a game of tongues, Matthew knew the coach must by necessity be retired to its barn, as the horses had gone their distance.

Presently, he closed his eyes and slumbered again. When he opened them—who knew how much later—the demon with a yellow third eye was at his side, using a white stone to crush up a foul-looking brown mixture of seeds, berries, and fetid whatnot—and the whatnot was the worst of it—in a small wooden bowl. Then the demon gave a combination grunt-and-whistle and pushed some of the stuff toward Matthew's mouth between thumb and forefinger.

Ah ha! Matthew thought. Now the true torments were to begin! The mixture being forced upon him looked like dog excrement and smelled like vomit. Matthew clamped his lips shut. The demon pushed at his mouth, grunting and whistling in obvious irritation, but Matthew steadfastly refused to accept it.

Another figure emerged from the smoke and stood beside Matthew's pallet. He looked into her face. Without speaking, she took up a pinch of the exquisite garbage and put it into her own mouth, chewing it as a display of its worth.

Matthew couldn't believe his eyes. Not because she'd voluntarily eaten it, but because she was the dark-haired, thin mute girl he'd last seen at Shawcombe's tavern. Only she was much changed, both in demeanor and dress. Her hair was clean and shining, more chestnut colored than truly dark brown, and on her head was a tiara-like toque formed of densely woven, red-dyed grass. Smudges of ruddy paint had been applied to her cheekbones. Her eyes were no longer glazed and weak but held determined purpose. Also, she wore a deerskin garment adorned with a pattern of red and purple beads down the front.

"You!" Matthew said. "What are *you* doing h—" The thumb and forefinger struck, getting some of that gutter porridge past his lips. Matthew's first impulse was to spit, but the demon had already clamped one hand to his mouth and was massaging his throat with the other.

Matthew had no choice but to swallow it. The stuff had a strange, oily texture, but he'd tasted cheese that was worse. In fact, it had a complexity of tastes, some sour and some sweet, that actually . . . well, that actually called for a second helping.

The girl—*Girl,* he recalled Abner saying with a laugh when Matthew had asked her name—moved away into the fire-thrown shadows before he could ask her anything else. The demon continued to feed him until the bowl was empty.

"What is this place?" Matthew asked, his tongue picking at seeds in his teeth. There was no answer. The demon took his bowl and began to also move away. "This *is* Hell, isn't it?" Matthew asked.

"Se hapna ta ami," the demon said, and then made a clucking noise.

In another moment Matthew sensed he was alone. Up above, he now could make out through the smoke haze what looked to be wooden rafters—or rather, small pine-trees with the bark still on them.

It wasn't long before his eyelids grew heavy. There was no resisting this sleep; it crashed over him like a green sea wave and took him down to depths unknown.

Dreamless. Drifting. A sleep for the ages, absolute in its peace and silence. And then, a voice.

"Matthew?"

Her voice.

"Can you hear me?"

"Ahhhhh," he answered: a sustained, relaxed exhalation of breath.

"Can you open your eyes?"

With only a little difficulty—and regret, really, for his rest had been so deeply satisfying—he did. There was Rachel, her face close to his. He could see her clearly by the flickering firelight. The dense smoke had gone away.

"They want you to try to stand up," she said.

"They?" He had a burned, ashy taste in his mouth. "Who?"

The demon, who no longer wore the third eye, came up and stood beside her. With an uplifting motion of the hands and a guttural grunting, the meaning was made plain.

Two of the females who'd attended Matthew appeared, and began to work around his head. He heard something being cut—a leather strap, he thought it might be—and suddenly his head was free to move, which immediately put a cramping pain in his neck muscles.

"I want you to know," Rachel said as the two females continued to cut Matthew free from his pinewood pallet, "that you've been terribly injured. The bear——"

"Yes, the bear," Matthew interrupted. "Killed me, and you as well."

She frowned. "What?"

"The bear. It killed——" He felt the straps give way around his left wrist, then around the right. He'd stopped speaking because he realized Rachel wore her wedding dress. On it were grass stains. He swallowed thickly. "Are we . . . not dead?"

"No, we're very much alive. *You* nearly died, though. If they hadn't come when they did, you would have bled to death. One of them bound your arm to stop the flow."

"My arm." Matthew remembered now the terrible pain in his shoulder and the blood dripping from his fingers. He couldn't move—or even feel—the fingers of his left hand. He had a sickened sensation in the pit of his stomach. Dreading to even glance at the limb, he asked, "Do I still have it?"

"You do," Rachel answered grimly, "but . . . the wound was very bad. As deep as the bone, and the bone broken."

"And what else?"

"Your left side. You took an awful blow. Two, three ribs . . . how many were broken I don't know."

Matthew lifted his right arm, unscathed save for a scabbed wound on his elbow, and gingerly touched his side. He found a large patch of clay covering the area, adhered by some sort of sticky brown substance, with a bulge underneath that to indicate something else pressed directly to the wound.

"The doctor made a poultice," Rachel said. "Herbs, and tobacco leaves, and . . . I don't know what all."

"What doctor?"

"Um." Rachel glanced toward the watchful demon. "This is their physician."

"My God!" Matthew said, dumbstruck. "I *must* be in Hell! If not, then where?"

"We have been brought," Rachel answered calmly, "to an Indian village. How far it is from Fount Royal, I can't say. We travelled over an hour from where the bear attacked you."

"An Indian village? You mean . . . I've been doctored by an *Indian?*" This was absolutely unthinkable! He would have preferred a demonic doctor to a savage one!

"Yes. And well doctored, too. They have been very kind to me, Matthew. I've had no reason to fear them."

"Pok!" the doctor said, motioning for Matthew to stand. The two women had cut the leather thongs that had secured his ankles, then had withdrawn. "Hapape pok pokati!" He reached out, picked up the woven mat that covered Matthew's torso, and threw it aside, leaving Matthew naked to the world. "Puh! Puh!" the doctor insisted, slapping his patient's legs.

Reflexively, Matthew started to cover his private area with both hands. His right hand went quickly enough, but a searing pain shot through his shoulder at the mere nerve impulse of moving the left. He gritted his teeth, fresh sweat on his face, and made himself look at the injury.

His shoulder all the way past his elbow was wrapped in clay, and presumably other so-called medicines were pressed to the wound beneath the earthen bandage. The clay also was smoothed over a wooden splint, and his elbow was immobilized in a slightly bent position. From the edge of the clay to the fingertips, the flesh was mottled with ugly black and purple bruises. It was a ghastly sight, but at least he still had the arm. He lifted his free hand to touch his forehead. He found another clay dressing, secured with the sticky paste-like material.

"Your head was gashed," Rachel said. "Do you think you can stand?"

"I might, if I don't fall to pieces." He looked at the doctor. "Clothes! Do you understand me? I need clothes!"

"Puh! Puh!" the doctor said, again slapping Matthew's legs.

Matthew directed his appeal at Rachel. "Might you please get me some clothes?"

"You have none," she told him. "Everything you wore was covered with blood. They performed some kind of ritual over them, the first night, and burned them."

What she'd said sent a spear through him. "The first night? How long have we been here?"

"This is the fifth morning."

Four whole days in the grasp of the Indians! Matthew couldn't believe it. Four whole days, and they still had their scalps! Were they waiting for him to get well enough to slaughter both him and Rachel together?

"I think we've been summoned by their mayor, or chief, or whatever he is. I've not seen him yet, but there's some special activity going on."

"Puh! Puh!" the doctor insisted. "Se hapape ta mook!"

"All right," Matthew said, choosing to face the inevitable. "I'll try to stand."

With Rachel's help, he eased down off the pallet onto a dirt floor. Modesty called him but he couldn't answer. His legs held him though they were fairly stiff. The clay dressing on his broken arm was heavy, but the way the splint crooked his elbow made it bearable. At his left side his ribs thundered with dull pain under the clay and poultice, but that too could be borne if he didn't try to breathe too deeply.

He knew he would have been instantly killed if Jack One Eye himself hadn't been so old and infirm. To meet that beast in its younger years would have meant a quick decapitation, or a long suffering death by disembowelment such as Maude's husband had endured.

The Indian doctor—who would have been naked himself but for a small buckskin garment and strap covering his groin—walked ahead, to the far side of the rectangular wooden structure that housed a number of pallets. Matthew realized it was their version of an infirmary. A small fire crackled in a pit ringed with stones, but from the huge pile of ashes nearby it was evident a smoky inferno had raged in here.

He leaned on Rachel for support, if just until his legs grew used to holding him up again. His mind was still hazed. It wasn't clear to him now if his amorous encounter with Rachel had been real or a fevered dream brought on by his injuries. Surely she wouldn't have crawled up on that pallet to make love to a dying man! From her there was no indication that anything had occurred between them.

Yet still . . . *might* it have happened?

But here was something real that he'd imagined to be a figment of his dreams: on the floor, along with other clay cups and wooden bowls and carved bone pipes around the fire, was the broken half of Lucretia Vaughan's heart-decorated pie dish.

The healing savage—who would have made his compatriot Dr. Shields blanch with terror—drew aside a heavy black-furred bearskin from the infirmary's entryway.

Blinding white sunlight flooded across the floor, making

Matthew squeeze his eyes shut and stagger. "I have you," Rachel said, leaning into him so he might not fall.

There was a great excited clamor from outside, complete with squeals, whoops, and giggling. Matthew was aware of a brown mass of grinning faces pressing forward. The Indian doctor began to shout in a voice whose irritated tone was universal: *Stand back, and give us space to breathe!*

Rachel led Matthew, naked and dazed, into the light.

SEVENTEEN

The assembled multitude, which numbered eighty to a hundred or thereabouts, went silent as Matthew emerged. The foremost group of them backed away, heeding the doctor's continued shouts. As Matthew and Rachel followed the loinclothed healer, the Indians trailed in their wake and the shouting, giggling, and excited vocals began to surge loudly again.

Matthew would have never dreamed in a barrel of rum that he might have found himself naked before the world, clinging to Rachel and walking through a horde of grinning, hollering Indians. His vision was returning, though he was still overwhelmed by all this light. He saw a score of round wooden huts, some covered with dried mud and others moss-grown, with roofs upon which grass grew as thickly as from the earth. He caught sight of a lush plot of cornstalks that would have dropped the farmers of Fount Royal to their knees. Two dogs—one gray and the other dark brown—came to sniff around Matthew's legs, but a shout from the doctor sent them running. The same happened when a giggling pack of four naked brown children neared the pallid patient, and they ran away squealing and jumping.

Matthew saw that most of the men—who shared the doctor's narrow facial structure, lean body, and topknot of hair growing from an otherwise shaved head—were nearly nude, but the women were clothed in either deerskin garments or brightly dyed shifts that appeared to be woven from cotton. Some of the females, however, had chosen to let their breasts be bared, a sight that would have made the citizens of Fount Royal swoon. Their feet were either bare or clad in deerskin slippers. Many of the men were adorned with intricate blue-dye tattoos, and also a few of the older women. These tattoos appeared not only on the face but also on the chest, arms, thighs, and presumably just about everywhere else.

The mood was festive. Men and women were childlike in their glee, and the children—of which there were many—like little scampering squirrels. Of real creatures, there were aplenty as well: pigs, chickens, and a barking battery of dogs. Then the doctor led Matthew and Rachel to a hut that seemed to be centrally located within the village, drew back a buckskin decorated with blade carvings to gain admittance, and escorted the visitors into the cool, dimly lit interior.

The light came from small flames burning in clay bowls that held pools of oil, set in a circle. Facing this circle, a man sat crosslegged on a dais supported by wooden poles about three feet off the ground, and cushioned by various animal skins.

It was the sight of this man that made Matthew stop in his tracks. His mouth opened and his teeth might have fallen out, so great was his shock.

The man—who obviously was the village's chief, governor, lord, or however the savages termed him—wore a buckskin loincloth that barely covered his genitalia. That, however, was by now a commonplace. What so shocked Matthew was that the chief had a long, white, tightly curled judicial wig on his head, and his chest was covered by . . .

I'm dreaming! Matthew thought. I *have* to be insensible to imagine *this!*

. . . Magistrate Woodward's gold-striped waistcoat.

"Pata ne." The doctor motioned Matthew and Rachel into the circle, and then made gestures for them to sit. "Oha! Oha!"

Rachel obeyed. When Matthew started to lower himself, pain stabbed his ribs and he clutched at the clay bandage, his face tightening.

"Uh!" the chief spoke. He had the long-jawed, narrow face and wore circular blue tattoos on both cheeks, more tattoos trailing down his arms, like blue vines, and covering his hands. The tips of his fingers were dyed red. "Se na oha! Pah ke ne su na oha sau-papa!" His commanding voice instantly stirred the doctor to action, namely that of grasping Matthew's right arm and pulling him up straight. When Rachel saw, she thought the chief wanted her to rise as well, but as she began to stand she was pushed down again— rather firmly—by the doctor.

The chief stood up on his dais. His legs were tattooed from the knees to the bare feet. He put his hands on his hips, his deep-set black eyes fixed on Matthew, and his expression serious as demanded his position of authority. "Te te weya," he said. The doctor retreated, walking backward, and left the hut. The next words were directed at Matthew: "Urn ta ka pa pe ne?"

Matthew simply shook his head. He saw that the chief wore Woodward's prized waistcoat unbuttoned, and more

tattoos adorned his chest. Though age was difficult to esti-
mate among these foreign people, Matthew thought the
chief was a young man, possibly only five or six years older
than himself.

"Oum?" the chief asked, frowning. "Ka taynay calmet?"

Again, Matthew could only shake his head.

The chief looked down at the ground for a moment, and
crossed his arms over his chest. He sighed and seemed lost in
thought; deliberating, Matthew feared, how best to murder
his captives.

Then the chief lifted his gaze again and said, *"Quel chapeau portez-vous?"*

Matthew now almost fell down. The Indian had spoken
French. A bizarre question, yes, but French all the same.
The question had been: "What hat do you wear?"

Matthew had to steady himself. That this tattooed savage
could speak a classic European language boggled the mind.
It was such a jolt that Matthew even forgot for a few seconds
that he was standing there totally naked. He replied, *"Je ne
porte pas de chapeau."* Meaning "I don't wear a hat."

"Ah ah!" The chief offered a genuine smile that served to
further light and warm the chamber. He clapped his hands
together, as if equally amazed and delighted at Matthew's
understanding of the language. *"Tous les hommes portent des
chapeaux. Mon chapeau est Nawpawpay. Quel chapeau portez-
vous?"*

Matthew now understood. The chief had said, "All men
wear hats. My hat is Nawpawpay. What hat do you wear?"

"Oh," Matthew said, nodding. *"Mon chapeau est Mathieu."*

"Mathieu," Nawpawpay repeated, as if testing its weight
on his tongue. *"Mathieu . . . Matthew,"* he said, still speaking
French. "That is a strange hat."

"Possibly it is, but it's the hat I was given at birth."

"Ah! But you've been reborn now, and so you must be given a new hat. I myself will give it to you: Demon Slayer."

"Demon Slayer? I don't understand." He glanced down at Rachel, who—not having a grasp of French—was totally confounded at what they were saying.

"Did you not slay the demon that almost took your life? The demon that has roamed this land for . . . oh . . . only the dead souls know, my father among them. I can't say how many brothers and sisters have passed away by those claws and fangs. But we tried to slay that beast. Yes, we tried." He nodded, his expression grave again. "And when we tried, the demon worked its evil on us. For every arrow that was shot into its body, it delivered ten curses. Our male infants died, our crops withered, the fishing was poor, and our seers had dreams of the end of time. So we stopped trying, for our own lives. Then everything got better, but the beast was always hungry. You see? None of us could slay it. The forest demons look after their own kind."

"But the beast still lives," Matthew said.

"No! I was told how the hunters saw you travelling, and followed you. Then the beast struck! I was told how it attacked you, and how you stood before it and gave a mighty war cry. That must have been a sight to see! They said it was hurt. I sent some men. They found it, dead in its den."

"Oh, I see. But . . . it was old and tired. I think it was already dying."

Nawpawpay shrugged. "That may be so, Matthew, but who struck the last blow? They found your knife, still under here." He pressed beneath his own chin with a forefinger. "Ah, if it's the forest demons that concern you, you may rest knowing they only haunt our kind. Your kind frightens them."

"Of that I have no doubt," Matthew said.

Rachel could stand it no longer. "Matthew! What's he saying?"

"They found the bear dead and they believe I killed it. He's given me a new name: Demon Slayer."

"Is it French you're speaking?"

"Yes, it is. I have no idea how—"

"An interruption, my pardon," Nawpawpay said. "How is it you come to know King LaPierre's tongue?"

Matthew shifted his thinking from English back to French once more. "King LaPierre?"

"Yes, from the kingdom of Franz Europay. Are you a member of his tribe?"

"No, I'm not."

"But you've had some word from him?" It was said with eagerness. "When will he return to this land?"

"Um . . . well . . . I'm not certain," Matthew said. "When was he last here?"

"Oh, during my grandfather's father's time. He left his tongue with my family, as he said it was the tongue of kings. Do I speak it well?"

"Yes, very well."

"Ah!" Nawpawpay beamed like a little boy. "I do recite it, so as not to lose its taste. King LaPierre showed us sticks that shot fire, and he caught our faces in a pouch pond. *And* . . . he had a little moon that sang. All these are carved down on the tablet." He frowned, perplexed. "I do wish he would return, so I might see those wonders as my grandfather's father did. I feel I'm missing something. You're not of his family? Then how do you speak the king's tongue?"

"I learned it from a member of King LaPierre's tribe," Matthew decided to say.

"I see now! Someday . . . someday . . ." He lifted a finger for emphasis. "I shall go over the water in a cloudboat to Franz Europay. I shall walk in that village and see for myself the hut of King LaPierre. It must be a grand place, with a hundred pigs!"

"Matthew!" Rachel said, about to go mad from this conversation of which she could not partake. "What is he *saying?*"

"Your woman, sad to say, is not civilized like you and I," Nawpawpay ventured. "She speaks mud words like that white fish we caught."

"White fish?" Matthew asked. He motioned for Rachel to remain quiet. "What white fish?"

"Oh, he's nothing. Less than nothing, for he's a murderer and thief. The least civilized beast I have ever had the misfortune to look upon. Now: can you tell me anything more of the village of Franz Europay?"

"I'll tell you everything I know of that place," Matthew answered, "if you'll tell me about the white fish. Did you . . . find your present clothing . . . and your headdress, at his hut?"

"These? Yes. Are they not wonderful?" He spread his arms wide, grinning, so as to better display the gold-striped waistcoat.

"May I ask what else you found there?"

"Other things. They must have some use, but I just like to look at them. And . . . of course . . . I found my woman."

"Your woman?"

"Yes, my bride. My princess." His grin now threatened to slice his face in two. "The silent and lovely one. Oh, she shall share all my treasures and give me a hut full of sons! First, though, I'll have to make her fat."

"And what of the white fish? Where is he?"

"Not far. There were two other fish—old ones—but they have gone."

"Gone? To where?"

"Everywhere," Nawpawpay said, spreading his arms wide again. "The wind, the earth, the trees, the sky. You know."

Matthew feared that he did know. "But you say the white fish is still here?"

"Yes, still here." Nawpawpay scratched his chin. "You have a nature full of questions, don't you?"

"It's just that . . . I might know him."

"Only uncivilized beasts and dung buzzards know him. He is unclean."

"Yes, I agree, but . . . why do you say he's a murderer and thief?"

"Because he is what he is!" Like a child, Nawpawpay put his hands behind himself and began to bounce up and down on his toes. "He murdered one of my people and stole a courage sun. Another of my people saw it happen. We took him. Took them all. They were all guilty. All except my princess. She is innocent. Do you know how I know that? Because she was the only one who came willingly."

"A courage sun?" Matthew realized he must mean the gold coin. "What is that?"

"That which the water spirit gives." His bouncing ceased. "Go visit the white fish, if you like. See if you know him, and ask him to tell you what crimes he's committed."

"Where can I find him?"

"This direction." Nawpawpay pointed to Matthew's left. "The hut that stands nearest the woodpile. You will know it."

"What's he pointing to, Matthew?" Rachel asked. "Does he want us to go somewhere?" She started to stand.

"Ah, no no!" Nawpawpay said quickly. "A woman doesn't stand before me in this place."

"Rachel, please stay where you are." Matthew rested his hand on her shoulder. "Evidently it's the chief's rule." Then, to Nawpawpay, "Might she go with me to see the white fish?"

"No. That hut is not a woman's territory. You go and come back."

"I'm going to go somewhere for a short time," he told her. "You'll need to stay here. All right?"

"Where are you going?" She grasped his hand.

"There's another white captive here, and I want to see him. It won't take long."

He squeezed her hand and gave her a tight but reassuring smile. Rachel nodded and reluctantly let go.

"Oh . . . one other thing," Matthew said to Nawpawpay. "Might I have some clothing?"

"Why? Are you cold on such a hot day as this?"

"Not cold. But there is a little too much air here for my comfort." He gestured toward his exposed penis and testicles.

"Ah, I see! Very well, I shall give you a gift." Nawpawpay stepped out of his own loincloth and offered it.

Matthew got the thing on with a delicate balancing act, since he was able only to use one arm. "I'll return presently," he told Rachel. Then he retreated from the hut, out into the bright sun.

The hut and the woodpile were not fifty paces from the chief's abode. A small band of chattering, giggling children clung to his shadow as he walked, and two of them ran round and round him as if to mock his slow, pained progress. When he neared the hut, however, they saw his destination, fell back, and ran away.

Nawpawpay had been correct, in saying that Matthew would know the place.

Blood had been painted on the outside walls, in strange patterns that a Christian would say was evidence of the Indians' satanic nature. Flies feasted on the gore paintings and buzzed about the entrance, which was covered with a black bearskin.

Matthew stood outside for a moment, steeling himself. This looked very bad indeed. With a trembling hand, he pulled aside the bearskin. Bitter blue smoke drifted into his face. There was only a weak red illumination within, perhaps the red embers of a past fire still glowing.

"Shawcombe?" Matthew called. There was no answer. "Shawcombe, can you hear me?"

Nothing.

Matthew could make out only vague shapes through the smoke. "Shawcombe?" he tried again, but in the silence that followed he knew he was going to have to cross the dreadful threshold.

He took a breath of the sulphuric air and entered. The bearskin closed behind him. He stood where he was for a moment, waiting for his eyes to grow used to such darkness again. The awful, suffocating heat coaxed beads of sweat from his pores. To his right he could make out a large clay pot full of seething coals from which the light and smoke emitted.

Something moved—a slow, slow shifting—there on his left.

"Shawcombe?" Matthew said, his eyes burning. He moved toward the left, as currents of smoke undulated before him.

Presently, with some straining of the vision, he could

make out an object. It looked like a raw and bloody side of beef that had been strung up to dry, and in fact was hanging from cords that were supported further up in the rafters.

Matthew neared it, his heart slamming.

Whatever hung there, it was just a slab of flayed meat with neither arms nor legs. Matthew stopped, tendrils of smoke drifting past his face. He couldn't bear to go any further, because he knew.

Perhaps he made a sound. A moan, a gasp . . . something. But—as slowly as the tortures of the inner circle of Hell— the scalped and blood-caked head on that slab of meat moved. It lolled to one side, and then the chin lifted.

His eyes were there, bulging from their sockets in that hideously swollen, black-bruised, and black-bloodied face. He had no eyelids. His nose had been cleaved off, as had been his lips and ears. A thousand tiny cuts had been administered to the battered torso, the genitals had been burned away and the wound cauterized to leave a glistening ebony crust. Likewise sealed with terrible fire were the hacked-off stumps of arms and legs. The cords had been tied and knotted around those gruesomely axed ruins.

If there was a description for the utter horror that wracked Matthew, it was known only by the most profane demon and the most sacred angel.

The motion of that lifted chin was enough to cause the torso to swing slightly on its cords. Matthew heard the ropes squeak up in the rafters, like the rats that had plagued Shawcombe's tavern.

Back and forth, and back and forth.

The lipless mouth stretched open. They had spared his tongue, so that he might cry for mercy with every knife slash, hatchet blow, and kiss of flame.

He spoke, in a dry rattling whisper that was almost

beyond all endurance to hear. "Papa?" The word was as mangled as his mouth. "Wasn't me killed the kitten, was Jamey done it." His chest shuddered and a wrenching sob came out. The bulging eyes stared at nothing. His was the small, crushed whine of a terrified child: "Papa please . . . don't hurt me no more . . ."

The brutalized bully began to weep.

Matthew turned—his eyes seared by smoke and sight—and fled lest his own mind be broken like Lucretia Vaughan's pie dish.

He got outside, was further blinded and disoriented by the glare. He staggered, was aware of more naked children ringing him, jumping and chattering, their grins joyful even as they danced in the shadow of the torture hut. Matthew nearly fell in his attempts to get away, and his herky-jerky flailing to retain his balance made the children scream with laughter, as if they thought he was joining in their dance. Cold sweat clung to his face, his insides heaved, and he had to bend over and throw up on the ground, which made the children laugh and leap with new energy.

He staggered on, the pack of little revelers now joined by a brown dog with one ear. A fog had descended over him, and he knew not if he was going in the right direction amid the huts. His progress attracted some older residents who put aside their seed-gathering and basket-weaving to accompany the merry throng, as if he were some potentate or nobleman whose fame rivalled the very sun. The laughter and hollering swelled as did the numbers of his followers, which only served to heighten Matthew's terror. Dogs barked at his heels and children darted underfoot. His ribs were killing him, but what was pain? In his dazed stupor he realized he had never known pain, not an ounce of it, compared to what Shawcombe had suffered. Beyond the grinning brown faces he saw sunlight glitter, and suddenly there was water before him and he fell to his knees to plunge his face into it, mindless of the agony that seized his bones.

He drank like an animal and trembled like an animal. A fit of strangulation struck him and he coughed violently, water bursting from his nostrils. Then he sat back on his haunches, his face dripping, as behind him the throng continued its jubilations.

He sat on the bank of a pond. It was half the size of Fount Royal's spring, but its water was equally blue. Matthew saw two women nearby, both filling animal-skin bags. The sunlight glittered golden off the pond's surface, putting him in mind of the day he'd seen the sun shine with equal color on Bidwell's fount.

He cupped his hand into the water and pressed it to his face, letting it stream down over his throat and chest. His mind's fever was cooling and his vision had cleared.

The Indian village, he'd realized, was a mirror image of Fount Royal. Just like Bidwell's creation, the village had probably settled here—who could say how long ago—to be so near a water supply.

Matthew was aware that the crowd's noise had quietened. A shadow fell over him, and spoke. "Na unhuh pah ke ne!"

Two men grasped Matthew, careful to avoid his injuries, and helped him to his feet. Then Matthew turned toward the speaker, but he knew already who'd given that command.

Nawpawpay stood four inches shorter than Matthew, but the height of the judicial wig gave the chief the advantage. The waistcoat's gold stripes glowed in this strong sunlight. Add to that the intricate tattoos, and Nawpawpay was an absorbing sight as well as a commanding presence. Rachel stood a few feet behind him, her eyes also the color of Spanish coins.

"Forgive my people," Nawpawpay said in the tongue of kings. He gave a shrug and a smile. "We don't often entertain visitors."

Matthew still felt faint. He blinked slowly and lifted his hand to his face. "Is . . . what you've done to . . . Shawcombe . . . the white fish . . . part of your entertainment?"

Nawpawpay looked shocked. "Oh, no! Surely not! You misunderstand, Demon Slayer! You and your woman are honored guests here, for what you've done for my people! The white fish was an unclean criminal!"

"You did such to him for murder and thievery? Couldn't you finish the task and display some mercy?"

Nawpawpay paused, thinking this over. "Mercy?" he asked. He frowned. "What is this *mercy?*"

Evidently it was a concept the French explorer who'd passed himself off as a king had failed to explain. "Mercy," Matthew said, "is knowing when . . ." He hesitated, formulating the rest of it. "When it is time to put the sufferer out of his misery."

Nawpawpay's frown deepened. "Misery? What is that?"

"How you felt when your father died," Matthew answered.

"Ah! That! You're saying then the white fish should be slit open and his innards dug out and fed to the dogs?"

"Well . . . perhaps a knife to the heart would be faster."

"Faster is not the point, Demon Slayer. The point is to punish, and let all who see know how such crimes are dealt with. Also, the children and old people so enjoyed hearing him sing at night." Nawpawpay stared at the pond, still deliberating. "This mercy. This is how things are done in Franz Europay?"

"Yes."

"Ah, then. This is something we should seek to emulate. Still . . . we'll miss him." He turned to a man standing next to him. "Se oka pa neha! Nu se caido na kay ichisi!" At the last hissed sound he made a stabbing motion . . . and, then, to Matthew's chagrin, a twist and a brutal crosscutting of the invisible blade. The man, who had a face covered with tattoos, ran off hollering and whooping, and most of the onlookers—men, women, and children alike—ran after him making similar noises.

Matthew should have felt better but he did not. He turned his mind to another and more important subject. "A courage sun," he said. "What is that?"

"What the water spirit gives," Nawpawpay answered. "Also moons and stars from the great gods."

"The water spirit?"

"Yes." Nawpawpay pointed at the pond. "The water spirit lives there."

"Matthew?" Rachel asked, coming to his side. "What's he saying?"

"I'm not sure," he told her. "I'm trying to—"

"Ah ah!" Nawpawpay wagged a finger at him. "The water spirit might be offended to hear mud words."

"My apologies. Let me ask this, if I may: how does the water spirit give you these courage suns?"

In answer, Nawpawpay walked into the water. He set off from shore, continuing as the water rose to his thighs. Then Nawpawpay stopped and, steadying the wig on his head with one hand, leaned over and searched the bottom with the other. Every so often he would bring up a handful of mud and sift through it.

"What's he looking for?" Rachel asked quietly. "Clams?"

"No, I don't think so." He was tempted to tell her about Shawcombe, if just to relieve himself of what he'd seen, but

there was no point in sharing such horror. He watched as
Nawpawpay waded to a new location, a little deeper, bent
over, and searched again. The front of Woodward's waistcoat was drenched.

After another moment, the chief moved to a third location. Rachel slipped her hand into Matthew's. "I've never
seen the like of this place. There's a wall of trees around the
whole village."

Matthew grunted, watching Nawpawpay at work. The
protective wall of trees, he thought, was a further link
between the village and Fount Royal. He had a feeling that
the two towns, untold miles apart, were also linked in a way
that no one would ever have suspected.

The nearness of her and the warmth of her hand put their
lovemaking in mind. As if it were ever really a stone's toss
from the center of his memory. But it had all been an illusion. Hadn't it? Of course it had been. Rachel would not
have climbed up on a pallet to give herself to a dying man.
Not even if he *had* saved her life. Not even if she *had*
thought he was not much longer for this earth.

But . . . just a speculation . . . what if by then it was
known he was on the road to recovery? And what if . . . the
doctor had actually *encouraged* such physical and emotional
contact, as an Indian method of healing akin to . . . well . . .
akin to bloodletting?

If that were so, Dr. Shields had a lot to learn.

"Rachel?" Matthew said, his fingers gently caressing her
hand. "Did you . . ." He stopped, not knowing how to
approach this. He decided on a roundabout method. "Have
you been given any other clothes to wear? Any . . . uh . . .
native clothing?"

She met his gaze. "Yes," she said. "That silent girl

brought me a garment, in exchange for the blue dress that was in your bag."

Matthew paused, trying to read her eyes. If he and Rachel had actually made love, her admittance of it was not forthcoming. Neither was it readable in her countenance. And here, he thought, was the crux of the matter: she might have given her body to him, as a gesture of feeling or as some healing method devised by the doctor, who sounded to Matthew to be cut from Exodus Jerusalem's cloth; or it might have been a wishful fantasy induced by fever and drugged smoke.

Which was the truth? The truth, he thought, was that Rachel still loved her husband. Or, at least, the memory of him. He could see that, by what she would not say. If indeed there was something to be said. She might hold a feeling for him, Matthew thought, like a bouquet of pink carnations. But they were not red roses, and that made all the difference.

He might ask what color the garment was. He might describe it for her exactly. Or he might start to describe it, and she tell him he could not be more wrong.

Perhaps he didn't need to know. Or wish to know, really. Perhaps things were best left unspoken, and the boundary between reality and fantasy left to run its straight and undisturbed course.

He cleared his throat and looked toward the pond again. "I recall you told me we'd travelled an hour after the Indians came. Do you know in which direction?"

"The sun was on our left for a while. Then at our backs."

He nodded. They must have travelled an hour's distance back toward Fount Royal. Nawpawpay moved to a fourth location, and called out, "The water spirit is a trickster!

Sometimes he gives them freely, other times we must search and search to find one!" Then, with a child's grin, he returned to his work.

"It's amazing!" Rachel said, shaking her head. "Absolutely amazing!"

"What is?"

"That he should speak French, and you can understand him! I wouldn't be more surprised if he should know Latin!"

"Yes, he *is* a remarkable—" He stopped abruptly, as if a wall of rough stones had crashed down upon him. "My God," he whispered. "That's it!"

"What?"

"No Latin." Matthew's face had flushed with excitement. "What Reverend Grove said to Mrs. Nettles, in Bidwell's parlor. 'No Latin.' That's the key!"

"The key? To what?"

He looked at her, and now his grin was childlike too. "The key to proving you innocent! It's the proof I've been needing, Rachel! It was right there, as close as . . ." He struggled for an analogy, and touched his grizzled chin. "Whiskers! The cunning fox can't—"

"Ah!" Nawpawpay's hand lifted, muddy to the wrist. "Here is a find!" Matthew waded into the water to meet him. The chief opened his hand and displayed a single silver pearl. It wasn't much but, coupled with the fragment of pie dish, was enough. Matthew was curious about something, and he waded on past the chief until the water neared his waist.

And there! His suspicion was confirmed; he felt a definite current swirling around his knees. "The water moves," he said.

"Ah, yes," Nawpawpay agreed. "It is the breathing of the

spirit. Sometimes more, sometimes less. But always, it breathes. You find interest in the water spirit?"

"Yes, very much."

"Hm." He nodded. "I didn't know your kind was religious. I shall take you to the house of the spirits, as an honored guest."

Nawpawpay led Matthew and Rachel to another hut near the pond. This one had walls daubed with blue dye, its entrance cloaked by a fantastically woven curtain of turkey and pigeon feathers, rabbit fur, fox skins with the heads still attached, and various other animal hides. "Alas," Nawpawpay said, "your woman can't have entrance here. The spirits deign only to speak to men, and to women through men. Unless, of course, the woman was born with the spirit marks and becomes a seer."

Matthew nodded. It had occurred to him that one culture's "spirit marks" were another culture's "marks of the devil." He told Rachel that the chief's custom required her to wait while they went inside. Then he followed Nawpawpay.

The interior was very dim, only one flame burning in a small clay pot full of oil. Thankfully, though, there was no eye-searing smoke. The house of the spirits appeared empty, as far as Matthew could tell.

"We speak respectfully here," Nawpawpay said. "My father built this, many passings of seasons ago. I often come here, to ask his advice."

"And he answers?"

"Well . . . no. But then again, he does. He listens to my problem, and then his answer is always: Son, decide for yourself." Nawpawpay picked up the clay pot. "Here are the gifts the water spirit gives." He followed the flickering

flame deeper into the hut, with Matthew a few paces
behind.

Still, there was nothing. Except one thing. On the floor
was a larger bowl full of muddy water. Nawpawpay reached
into it with the same hand that held the pearl, and then his
hand reappeared muddy and dripping. "We honor the water
spirit in this way," he said. As Matthew watched,
Nawpawpay approached a wall. It was not pinewood, as the
others were, but was thickly plastered with dried brown
mud from the pond.

Nawpawpay pressed his handful of mud and the pearl
into the wall and smoothed it down. "I must speak to the
spirit now," he said. And then, in a soft singsong chant,
"Pa ne sa nehra cai ke panu. Ke na pe pe kairu." As he
chanted, he moved the flame back and forth along the
mud-caked wall.

There was a red glint, first. Then a blue one.

Then . . . red . . . gold . . . more gold, a dozen gold . . .
and silver . . . and purple and . . .

. . . a silent explosion of colors as the light moved back
and forth along the wall: emerald green, ruby crimson, sapphire blue . . . and gold, gold, a thousand times gold . . .

"*Oh,*" Matthew gasped, as the hairs stood up on the back
of his neck.

Held in that wall was the treasure.

A pirate's fortune. Jewels by the hundreds—sky blue,
deep green, pale amber, dazzling white—and the coins,
gold and silver enough to make the king of Franz Europay
gibber and drool. And the most stunning thing was that
Matthew realized he was seeing only the outermost layer.
The plastering of dried mud had to be at least four inches
thick, six feet tall, and four feet wide.

Here it was. In this dirt wall, in this hut, in this village, in this wilderness. Matthew wasn't sure, but he thought he could hear God and the Devil joined together in common laughter.

He knew. What was put into the spring at Fount Royal was carried out by the current of an underground river. It might take time, of course. Everything took time. The entrance to that river, there somewhere in the depths of Bidwell's spring, might only be the diameter of Lucretia Vaughan's pie plate. If a pirate had taken a sounding of the fount before lowering bags of jewels and coins, he would have found a bottom at forty feet—but he would not have found the hole that eventually pulled everything into the subterranean flow. Perhaps the current drew more power-fully in a particular season, or was affected by the moon just as were the ocean's tides. In any case, the pirate—most probably a man who was only smart enough to loot vessels, but not to vessel his loot in a sturdy container—had chosen a vault that suffered the flaw of a funnel at its bottom.

Spellbound, Matthew approached the wall. "Se na caira pa pa kairu," chanted Nawpawpay, as he slowly moved the flame back and forth and the small sharp glints and explo-sions of reflected light continued.

Matthew saw in another moment that the dried mud also held bits of pottery, gold chains, silver spoons, and so forth. Here the gold-encrusted hilt of a knife protruded, and there was the cracked face of a pocket watch.

It made sense that Lucretia Vaughan's pie dish would go to the doctor, as some sort of enchanted implement sent from the water spirit. After all, it was decorated with a pat-tern that they most likely had figured out was a human organ.

"Na pe huida na pe caida," Nawpawpay said, and that seemed to finish it, as he held the flame toward Matthew.

"The courage—" Matthew's voice cracked. He tried again. "The courage suns. You say the white fish stole one?"

"Yes, and murdered the man to whom it was given."

"May I ask why it was given to this man?"

"As a reward," Nawpawpay said, "for courage. This man saved another who was gored by a wild tusked pig, and afterward killed the pig. It's a tradition my father began. But that white fish has been luring my people with his bad ways, making them sick in the mind with strong drink, and then making them work for him like common dogs. It was time for him to go."

"I see." Matthew recalled that Shawcombe had said his tavern had been built with Indian labor. And now he really did see. He saw the whole picture, and how it fit together in an intricate pattern.

"Nawpawpay," Matthew said, "my . . . uh . . . woman and I must leave this place. Today. We have to go back from where we came. Do you know the village near the sea?"

"Of course I do. We watch it all the time." Nawpawpay wore an expression of concern. "But Demon Slayer, you can't leave *today!* You're still too weak to travel that distance. You must tell me what you know of Franz Europay, and I also have a celebration planned for you tonight. Dancing and feasting. And we have the demon's head, carved out for you to wear."

"Um . . . well . . . I—"

"In the morning you may leave, if you still desire to. Tonight we celebrate, to honor your courage and the death of that beast." He directed the light to the treasure wall again. "Here, Demon Slayer! A gift for you, as is proper. Take one thing you see that shines strong enough to guide your hand."

It was astounding, Matthew thought. Nawpawpay

didn't realize—and God protect him from ever finding out—that there were those in the outside world, the civilized world, who would come through the forest to this place and raze it to the ground to obtain one square foot of dirt from that wall.

But a gift of fantastic worth had been offered, and Matthew's hand was so guided.

EiGHTEEN

As the sun settled and the blue shadows of evening advanced, Fount Royal slumbered in a dream of what might have been.

It was a slumbering that prefigured death. Stood the empty houses, stood the empty barns. A scarecrow drooped on its frame in a fallow field, two blackbirds perched upon its shoulders. A straw hat lay discarded on Harmony Street, and had been further destroyed by the crush of wagon wheels. The front gate was ajar, its locking timber thrown aside and left in the dirt by the last family who'd departed. Of the thirty or so persons who remained in the dying dream of Fount Royal, not one could summon the energy of spirit to put the gate in order. It seemed madness, of course, to leave the gate unlocked, for who knew what savages might burst through to scalp, maim, and pillage?

But in truth, the evil *within* Fount Royal seemed much worse, and to secure the gate was like locking oneself in a dark room with a beast whose breath stroked the back of the neck.

It was all clear now. All of it, very clear to the citizens.

The witch had escaped with the help of her demon-possessed lover. *That boy! You know the one! That clerk had fallen in with her—had fallen into the pit of Hell, I say—and he overcame Mr. Green and got her out. Then they fled. Out into the wilderness, out where Satan has his own village. Yes, he does, and I've heard tell Solomon Stiles saw it himself! You might ask him, but he's left town for good. This is the story, though, and guard your souls at the listening: Satan's built a village in the wilderness and all the houses are made of thornwood. They have fields that seethe of hellfire, and they grow crops of the most treacherous poison. You know the magistrate's fallen sick again, don't you? Yes, he has. Sick unto death. He's near given out. Now this is what I hear: someone in that mansion house is a witch or warlock themselves, and has fed that poor magistrate Satan's poisoned tea! So guard what you drink! Oh my . . . I was just thinking . . . what a horror to think on . . . mayhaps it wasn't the tea that was poisonous, but the very water. Oh my . . . if Satan had it in mind . . . to curse and poison the fount itself . . . we would all die writhing in our beds, wouldn't we?*

Oh my . . . oh my . . .

A breeze moved across Fount Royal on this warm and darkening eve. It rippled the waters of the fount, and kissed the roofs of lightless houses. It moved along Industry Street, where it had been sworn that the phantasm of Gwinett Linch had been seen, hurrying along with its rat sticker and its torn throat, warning in a ghastly cry that the witches of Fount Royal were hungry for more souls . . . more souls . . .

The breeze stirred dust from Harmony Street, and whirled that dust into the cemetery where it had been sworn a dark figure was seen walking amid the markers, counting numbers on an abacus. The breeze whispered along Truth Street, past the accursed gaol and that house—that witch's house—from which sounds of infernal merriment and the scuttling of demons' claws could be heard, if one dared approach too closely.

Yes, it all was very clear now to the citizens, who had responded to this clarity of vision by fleeing for their lives. Seth Hazelton's house lay empty, the stalls of his barn bare, his forge cold. The hearth at the abandoned Vaughan house still held the perfume of baked bread, but the only movement in that forsaken domicile was the agitation of the wasps. At the infirmary, bags and boxes had been packed in preparation for departure, the glass vials and bottles nestled in cotton and waiting for . . .

Just waiting.

They were almost all gone. A few stalwarts remained, either out of loyalty to Robert Bidwell, or because their wagons had to be repaired before a trip could be undertaken, or because—the rarest cases—they had nowhere else to go and continued to delude themselves that all would be well. Exodus Jerusalem remained in his camp, a fighter to the end, and though the audience at his nightly preachings had dwindled he continued to assail Satan for the appreciation of his flock. Also, he had made the acquaintance of a certain widow woman who had not the benefit of male protection, and so after his feverish sermons were done he protected her at close quarters with his mighty sword.

But lanterns still glowed in the mansion, and light sparkled off four lifted wineglasses.

"To Fount Royal," Bidwell said. "What it was, I mean. And what it might have been." The toast was drunk without comment by Winston, Johnstone, and Shields. They stood in the parlor, in preparation to go into the dining room for the light dinner to which Bidwell had invited them.

"I deeply regret it's turned out this way, Robert," Shields said. "I know you——"

"Hush." Bidwell lifted the palm of his free hand. "We'll have no tears this evening. I have travelled my road of grief, and wish to go on to the next destination."

"What, then?" Johnstone asked. "You're going back to England?"

"Yes, I am. In a matter of weeks, after some business is finished. That's why Edward and I went to Charles Town on Tuesday, to prepare for our passage." He drank another sip of his wine and looked about the room. "My God, how shall I ever salvage such a folly as this? I must have been mad, to have dumped so much money into this swamp!"

"I myself must throw in my cards," Johnstone said, his face downcast. "There's no point in my staying any longer. I should say in the next week."

"You did a fine job, Alan," Shields offered. "Fount Royal was graced by your ideas and education."

"I did what I could, and thank you for your appreciation. As for you, Ben . . . what are *your* plans?"

Shields drank down his wine and walked to the decanter to refill his glass. "I will leave . . . when my patient departs. Until then, I will do my damnedest to make him comfortable, for that's the very least I can do."

"I fear at this point, doctor, it's the *most* you can do," Winston said.

"Yes, you're right." Shields took down half the fresh glass at a swallow. "The magistrate . . . hangs on from day to day by his fingernails. I should say he hangs on from hour to hour." Shields lifted his spectacles and scratched his nose. "I've done everything I could. I thought the potion was going to work . . . and it *did* work, for a while. But his body wouldn't accept it, and it virtually collapsed. Therefore: the question is not *if* he will pass, but *when*." He sighed, his face strained and his eyes bloodshot. "But he *is* comfortable now, at least, and he's breathing well."

"And still he's not aware?" Winston asked.

"No. He still believes Witch Howarth burned on Monday morning, and he believes his clerk looks in on him from time to time, simply because that's what I tell him. As his mind is quite feeble, he has no recollection of the passage of days, nor of the fact that his clerk is not in the house."

"You don't intend on telling him the truth, then?" Johnstone leaned on his cane. "Isn't that rather cruel?"

"We decided . . . I decided . . . that it would be supremely cruel to tell him what has actually happened," Bidwell explained. "There's no need in rubbing his face in the fact that his clerk was bewitched and threw in his lot with the Devil. To tell Isaac that the witch did not burn . . . well, there's just no point to it."

"I agree," Winston said. "The man should be allowed to die with peace of mind."

"I can't understand how that young man could have bested Green!" Johnstone swirled the wine around his glass and then finished it. "He must have been either very lucky or very desperate."

"Or possessed supernatural strength, or had the witch curse Green to sap the man's power," Bidwell said. "That's what I think."

"Pardon me, gentlemen." Mrs. Nettles had come. "Dinner's a'table."

"Ah, yes. Good. We'll be there directly, Mrs. Nettles." Bidwell waited for the woman to withdraw, and then he said quietly to the others, "I have a problem. Something of the utmost importance that I need to discuss with all of you."

"What is it?" Shields asked, frowning. "You sound not yourself."

"I am *not* myself," Bidwell answered. "As a matter of fact . . . since we returned from Charles Town and I have taken stock of my impending failure, I am changed in a way I would never have thought possible. In fact, that is what I need to discuss with all of you. Come, let's go into the library where voices don't carry as freely." He picked up a lamp and led the way.

Two candles were already burning in the library, shedding plenty of light, and four chairs had been arranged in a semicircle. Winston followed Bidwell in, then the doctor entered, and lastly Johnstone limped through the doorway.

"What's this, Robert?" Johnstone asked. "You make it sound so secretive."

"Please, sit down. All of you." When his guests were seated, Bidwell put his lantern on the sill of the open window and settled himself in his chair. "Now," he said gravely. "This problem that I grapple with . . . has to do with . . ."

"Questions and answers," came a voice from the library's entrance. Instantly Dr. Shields and Johnstone turned their heads toward the door.

"The asking of the former, and the finding of the latter," Matthew said, as he continued into the room. "And thank you, sir, for delivering the cue."

"My God!" Shields shot to his feet, his eyes wide behind his spectacles. "What are *you* doing here?"

"Actually, I've been occupying my room for the afternoon." Matthew walked to a position so that he might face all the men, his back to the wall. He wore a pair of dark blue breeches and a fresh white shirt. Mrs. Nettles had cut the left sleeve away from the clay dressing. He didn't tell them that when he'd shaved and been forced to regard his bruise-blotched face and the clay plaster on his forehead, he'd been cured of unnecessary glances in a mirror for some time to come.

"Robert?" Johnstone's voice was calm. He gripped the shaft of his cane with both hands. "What trickery is this?"

"It's not a trick, Alan. Simply a preparation in which Edward and I assisted."

"A preparation? For what, pray tell?"

"For this moment, sir," Matthew said, his face betraying no emotion. "I arrived back here—with Rachel—around two o'clock. We entered through the swamp, and as I was . . . um . . . deficient in clothing and did not wish to be seen by anyone, I asked John Goode to make my presence known to Mr. Bidwell. He did so, with admirable discretion. Then I asked Mr. Bidwell to gather you all together this evening."

"I'm lost!" Shields said, but he sat down again. "You mean to say you brought the witch back here? Where is she?"

"The *woman* is currently in Mrs. Nettles's quarters," Bidwell offered. "Probably eating her dinner."

"But . . . but . . ." Shields shook his head. "She's a *witch*, by God! It was proven so!"

"Ah, proof!" Now Matthew smiled slightly. "Yes, doctor, proof is at the crux of things, is it not?"

"It certainly is! And what you've proven to me is that you're not only bewitched, but a bewitched *fool!* And for the sake of God, what's *happened* to you? Did you fight with a demon to gain the witch's favors?"

"Yes, doctor, and I slayed it. Now: if it is proof you require, I shall be glad to satisfy your thirst." Matthew, for the fourth or fifth time, found himself absentmindedly scratching at the clay plaster that covered his broken ribs beneath the shirt. He had a small touch of fever and was sweating, but the Indian physician—through Nawpawpay—had this morning announced him fit to travel. Demon Slayer hadn't had to walk the distance, however; except for the last two miles, he'd been carried by his and Rachel's Indian guides on a ladder-like conveyance with a dais at its center. It had been quite the way to travel.

"It seems to me," Matthew said, "that we have all—being learned and God-fearing men—come to the conclusion that a witch cannot speak the Lord's Prayer. I would venture that a warlock could neither speak it. Therefore: Mr. Winston, would you please speak the Lord's Prayer?"

Winston drew a long breath. He said, "Of course. Our Father, Who art in heaven, hallowed be thy name; Thy kingdom come; Thy will be done . . ."

Matthew waited, staring into Winston's face, as the man perfectly recited the prayer. At the "Amen," Matthew said, "Thank you," and turned his attention to Bidwell.

"Sir, would you also please speak the Lord's Prayer?"

"Me?" Instantly some of the old accustomed indignation flared in Bidwell's eyes. "Why should *I* have to speak it?"

"Because," Matthew said, "I'm telling you to."

"Telling me?" Bidwell made a flatulent noise with his lips. "I won't speak such a personal thing just because someone *orders* me to!"

"Mr. Bidwell?" Matthew had clenched his teeth. This man, even as an ally, was insufferable! "It is *necessary.*"

"I agreed to this meeting, but I didn't agree to recite such a powerful prayer to my God on demand, as if it were lines from a maskers' play! No, I shall not speak it! And I'm not a warlock for it, either!"

"Well, it appears you and Rachel Howarth share stubborn natures, does it not?" Matthew raised his eyebrows, but Bidwell didn't respond further. "We shall return to you, then."

"You may return to me a hundred times, and it won't matter!"

"Dr. Shields?" Matthew said. "Would you please cooperate with me in this matter, as one of us refuses to do, and speak the Lord's Prayer?"

"Well . . . yes . . . I don't understand the point, but . . . all right." Shields ran the back of his hand across his mouth. During Winston's recitation he'd finished the rest of his drink, and now he looked into the empty glass and said, "I have no more wine. Might I get a fresh glass?"

"After the prayer is spoken. Would you proceed?"

"Yes. All right." The doctor blinked, his eyes appearing somewhat glazed in the ruddy candlelight. "All right," he said again. Then: "Our Father . . . who art in heaven . . . hallowed be Thy name; Thy kingdom come; Thy . . . will be done . . . on earth as it is . . . is in heaven." He stopped, pulled a handkerchief from the pocket of his sand-colored jacket and blotted moisture from his face. "I'm sorry. It *is* warm in here. My wine . . . I do need a cooling drink."

"Dr. Shields?" Matthew said quietly. "Please continue."

"I've spoken enough of it, haven't I? What madness is this?"

"Why can you not finish the prayer, doctor?"

"I *can* finish it! By Christ, I can!" Shields lifted his chin defiantly, but Matthew saw that his eyes were terrified. "Give us this day our daily bread; and forgive us our . . . forgive us our trespasses . . . as we forgive those who . . . who trespass . . . trespass . . ." He pressed his hand to his lips and now he appeared to be distraught, even near weeping. He made a muffled sound that might have been a moan.

"What is it, Ben?" Bidwell asked in alarm. "For God's sake, tell us!" Dr. Shields lowered his head, removed his glasses, and wiped his damp forehead with the handkerchief.

"Yes," he answered in a frail voice. "Yes. I should tell it . . . for the sake of God."

"Shall I fetch you some water?" Winston offered, standing up.

"No." Shields waved him down again. "I . . . should . . . tell it, while I am able."

"Tell *what*, Ben?" Bidwell glanced up at Matthew, who had an idea what was about to be revealed. "Ben?" Bidwell prompted. "Tell what?"

"That . . . it was I . . . who murdered Nicholas Paine."

Silence fell. Bidwell's jaw might have been as heavy as an anvil.

"I murdered him," the doctor went on, his head lowered. He dabbed at his forehead, cheeks, and eyes with small, birdlike movements. "Executed him, I should say." He shook his head slowly back and forth. "No. That is a pallid excuse. I murdered him, and I deserve to answer to the law for it . . . because I can no longer answer to myself or God. And He asks me about it. Every day and night, He does. He whispers . . . Ben . . . now that it's done . . . at long last, now that it's done . . . and you have committed with your own hands the act that you most detest in this world . . . the act that makes men into beasts . . . how shall you go on living as a healer?"

"Have you . . . lost your *mind*?" Bidwell thought his friend was suffering a mental breakdown right before his eyes. "What are you saying?"

Shields lifted his face. His eyes were swollen and red, his mouth slack. Saliva had gathered in the corners. "Nicholas Paine was the highwayman who killed my elder son. Shot him . . . during a robbery on the Philadelphia Post Road, just outside Boston eight years ago. My boy lived long enough to describe the man . . . and also to say that he'd drawn a pistol and shot the highwayman through the calf of his leg." Shields gave a bitter, ghastly smile. "It was *I* who told him never to travel that road without a prepared pistol near at hand. In fact . . . it was my birthday gift to him. My boy was shot in the stomach, and . . . there was nothing to be done. But I . . . I went mad, I think. For a very long time." He picked up the wineglass, forgetting it was empty, and started to tip it to his mouth before he realized the futility of it.

Shields drew a long, shuddering breath and released it. All eyes were on him. "Robert . . . you know what the officers in these colonies are like. Slow. Untrained. Stupid. I knew the man might lose himself, and I would never have the satisfaction . . . of doing to his father what he had done to me. So I set out. First . . . to find a doctor who might have treated him. It took a search through every rumhole and whorehouse in Boston . . . but I eventually found the doctor. The so-called doctor, a drunken slug who tended to the whores. He knew the man, and where he lived. He had also . . . recently buried the man's wife and baby daughter, the first who'd died of fits, and the second who'd perished soon after."

Shields again wiped his face with the handkerchief, his hand trembling. "I had no pity for Nicholas Paine. None. I simply . . . wanted to extinguish him, as he had extinguished something in my soul. So I began to track him. From place to place. Village to town to city, and back again. Always close, but never finding. Until I learned he had traded horses in Charles Town and had told the stable master his destination. And it took me eight years." He looked into Bidwell's eyes. "Do you know what I realized, the very hour after I killed him?"

Bidwell didn't reply. He couldn't speak.

"I realized . . . I had also killed myself, eight years ago. I had given up my practise, I had turned my back on my wife and my other son . . . who both needed me, then more than ever. I had forsaken them, to kill a man who in many ways was also already dead. And now that it was done . . . I felt no pride in it. No pride in anything anymore. But he was dead. He was bled like my heart had bled. And the most terrible thing . . . the most terrible, Robert . . . was that I think . . . Nicholas was not the same man who had pulled that trigger. I wanted him to be a coldhearted killer . . . but he was not that man at all. But me . . . I was the same man I had always been. Only much, much worse."

The doctor closed his eyes and let his head roll back. "I am prepared to pay my debt," he said softly. "Whatever it may be. I am used up, Robert. All used up."

"I disagree, sir," Matthew said. "Your use is clear: to comfort Magistrate Woodward in these final hours." It hurt him like a dagger to the throat to speak such, but it was true. The magistrate's health had collapsed the very morning of Matthew's departure, and it was terribly clear that the end would be soon. "I'm sure we all appreciate your candor, and your feelings, but your duty as a doctor stands first before your obligation to the law, whatever Mr. Bidwell—as the mayor of this town—decides it to be."

"What?" Bidwell, who had paled during this confession, now appeared shocked. "You're leaving it up to *me?*"

"I'm not a judge, sir. I am—as you have reminded me so often and with such hot pepper—only a clerk."

"Well," Bidwell breathed, "I'll be damned."

"Damnation and salvation are brothers separated only by direction of travel," Matthew said. "When the time is right, I'm sure you'll know the proper road upon which to progress. Now: if we may continue?" He directed his attention to the schoolmaster. "Mr. Johnstone, would you please speak the Lord's Prayer?"

Johnstone stared intently at him. "May I ask what the purpose of this is, Matthew? Is it to suggest that one of us is a *warlock,* and that by failing to utter the prayer he is exposed as such?"

"You are on the right track, yes, sir."

"That is absolutely ridiculous! Well, if you go by that faulty reasoning, Robert has already exposed himself!"

"I said I would go back to Mr. Bidwell, and offer him a chance at redemption. I am currently asking *you* to speak the prayer."

Johnstone gave a harsh, scoffing laugh. "Matthew, you know better than this! What kind of game are you playing?"

"I assure you, it's no game. Are you refusing to speak the prayer?"

"Would that then expose *me* as a warlock? Then you'd have two warlocks in a single room?" He shook his head, as if in pity for Matthew's mental slippage. "Well, I shall relieve your burdensome worry, then." He looked into Matthew's eyes. "Our Father, who art in heaven, hallowed be Thy name; Thy kingdom come; Thy will be done on earth as it is in—"

"Oh, one moment!" Matthew held up a finger and tapped his lower lip. "In your case, Mr. Johnstone—your being an educated man of Oxford, I mean to say—you should speak the Lord's Prayer in the language of education, which would be Latin. Would you start again from the beginning, please?"

Silence.

They stared at each other, the clerk and the fox.

Matthew said, "Oh, I understand. Perhaps you've forgotten your Latin training. But surely it should be easily refreshed, since Latin was such a vital part of your studies at Oxford. You must have been well versed in Latin, as the magistrate was, if only to obtain entrance to that hallowed university. So allow me to help: *Pater noster: qui es in caelis; Sanctificetur nomen tuum; Adventiat regnum tuum*—well, you may finish what I've begun."

Silence. Utter, deadly silence.

Matthew thought *I have you.*

He said, "You don't know Latin, do you? In fact, you neither understand nor speak a word of it. Tell me, then, how a man may attend Oxford and come away an educator without knowing Latin."

Johnstone's eyes had become very small.

"Well, I'll seek to explain what I believe to be true." Matthew swept his gaze across the other men, who were also stricken into amazed silence by this revelation. He walked to the chess set near the window and picked up a bishop. "Reverend Grove played chess, you see. This was his chess set. Mr. Bidwell, you informed me of that fact. You also said the reverend was a Latin scholar, and liked to infuriate you by calling out his moves in that language." He studied the bishop by the lamplight. "On the occasion of the fire that burned down a house that same night, Mr. Johnstone, you mentioned to me that you and Mr. Winston were in the habit of playing chess. Would it ever have happened, sir, that—this being a town of rare chess players and even more rare Latin scholars—Reverend Grove challenged *you* to a game?"

Bidwell was staring at the schoolmaster, waiting for a response, but from Johnstone there was no reply.

"Would it have happened," Matthew went on, "that Reverend Grove assumed you knew Latin, and spoke to you in that language during a game? Of course, you wouldn't have known if he was speaking to you or announcing a move. In any case, you wouldn't have been able to respond, would you?" He turned toward Johnstone. "What's wrong, sir? Does the Devil have your tongue?"

Johnstone simply stared straight ahead, his fingers gripping the cane's handle and the knuckles bleached.

"He's thinking, gentlemen," Matthew said. "Thinking, always thinking. He is a *very* smart man, no doubt of it. He might actually have become a real schoolmaster, if he'd chosen to. What exactly *are* you, Mr. Johnstone?"

Still no response or reaction.

"I do know you're a murderer." Matthew placed the bishop back on the table. "Mrs. Nettles told me she recalled Reverend Grove seemed bothered about something not long before he was killed. She told me he spoke two words, as if in reflection to himself. Those words were: *No Latin.* He was trying to reason out why an Oxford man didn't know the language. Did he ask you why, Mr. Johnstone? Was he about to point out the fact to Mr. Bidwell, and thus expose you as a fraud? And that's why Reverend Grove became the first victim?"

"Wait," the doctor said, his mind fogged. "The Devil killed Reverend Grove! Cut his throat and clawed him!"

"The Devil sits in this room, sir, and his name—if it *is* his real name—is Alan Johnstone. Of course he wasn't alone. He did have the help of the ratcatcher, who was a . . ." He stopped and smiled thinly. "Ah! Mr. Johnstone! Do you also have a background in the theater arts? You know, Mr. Bidwell, why he wears that false knee. Because he'd already visited Fount Royal in the guise of a surveyor. The beard was probably his own, as at that point he had no need for a disguise. It was only when he verified what he needed to know, and later returned, that a suitable masking was necessary. Mr. Johnstone, if indeed you were—are—an actor, did you perchance ever play the role of a schoolmaster? Therefore you fixed upon what you already knew?"

"You," Johnstone said, in a hoarse whisper, "are quite . . . raving . . . mad."

"Am I? Well, let's see your knee then! It'll only take a moment."

Instinctively, Johnstone's right hand went down to cover the misshapen bulge.

"I see," Matthew said. "You wear your brace—which I presume you purchased in Charles Town—but you didn't put on the device you displayed to the magistrate, did you? Why would you? You thought I was long gone, and I was the only one who ever questioned your knee."

"But I saw it myself!" Winston spoke up. "It was terribly deformed!"

"No, it *appeared* terribly deformed. How did you construct such a thing, Mr. Johnstone? Come now, don't be modest about your talents! You are a man of many black facets! If I myself had wished to make a false knee, I might have used . . . oh . . . clay and candle wax, I suppose. Something to cover the kneecap, build it up and make it appear deformed. You chose a time to reveal the knee when I was unfortunately otherwise occupied." He swung his gaze to Dr. Shields. "Doctor, you sell a liniment to Mr. Johnstone for the supposed pain in his knee, don't you?"

"Yes, I do. A hogsfat-based liniment."

"Does this liniment have an objectionable odor?"

"Well . . . it's not pleasant, but it can be endured."

"What if the hogsfat is allowed to sit over heat, and become rancid before application? Mr. Winston, the magistrate mentioned to me that you were repelled by the odor. Is that correct?"

"Yes. Very quickly repelled, as I recall."

"That was a safeguard, you see. To prevent anyone from either looking too closely at the false knee, or—heaven forbid—touching it. Isn't that true, Mr. Johnstone?"

Johnstone stared at the floor. He rubbed the bulge of his knee, a pulse beating at his temple.

"I'm sure that's not very comfortable. Is it intended to force a limp? You probably really *can't* climb stairs with it on, can you? Therefore you removed it to go up and look at the gold coin? Did you mean to steal that coin, or were you simply surprised at being caught in the act? Did your greedy hand clutch it in what was for you a normal reaction?"

"Wait," the doctor said. He was struggling to keep up, his own brain blasted by the rigors of his confession. "You mean to say . . . Alan was never educated at Oxford? But I myself heard him trading tales of Oxford with the magistrate! He seemed to know the place so well!"

"*Seemed to* is right, sir. I expect he must have played a schoolmaster's role in some play and picked up a modicum of information. He also knew that by passing himself off as having an Oxford education, the town would more readily dismiss the efforts of the man who served as the previous teacher."

"But what about Margaret? Johnstone's wife?" Winston asked. "I know her bell seemed cracked, but . . . wouldn't she have known if he wasn't really a schoolmaster?"

"He had a wife?" This was the first Matthew had heard of it. "Was he wed in Fount Royal, or did he bring her with him when he arrived?"

"He brought her," Winston said. "And she seemed to despise Fount Royal and all of us from the beginning. So much so that he was obliged to return her to her family in England." He shot Johnstone a dark glance. "At least that's what he told us."

"Ah, now you're beginning to understand that what he told you was never necessarily the truth—and rarely so. Mr. Johnstone, what about this woman? Who was she?"

Johnstone continued to stare at the floor.

"Whoever she was, I doubt she was really wed to you. But it was a clever artifice, gentlemen, and further disguised himself as a decent schoolmaster." Matthew suddenly had a thought, a flashing sun of revelation, and he smiled slightly as he regarded the fox. "So: you returned this woman to her family in England, is that correct?"

Of course there was no answer.

"Mr. Bidwell, how long was it after Johnstone came back from England that the ratcatcher arrived here?"

"It was . . . I don't know . . . a month, possibly. Three weeks. I can't recall."

"Less than three weeks," Winston said. "I remember the day Linch arrived and offered his services. We were so glad to see him, as the rats were overrunning us."

"Mr. Johnstone?" Matthew prompted. "Had you, as a thespian, ever seen John Lancaster—and that was his true name—performing his act? Had you heard about his magnetism abilities while your troupe was travelling England? Perhaps you'd already met him?" Johnstone only stared blankly at the floorboards. "In any case," Matthew continued with authority, "you didn't go to England to return that so-called wife to her family. You went to England to seek a man you thought could help carry out your scheme. You knew what it would take. By then you had probably decided who the victims were going to be—even though I think your murder of Reverend Grove had more to do with hiding your falsehood than anything else—and you needed a man with the uncommon ability to create perceived truth from wholesale illusion. And you found him, didn't you?"

"Mad." Johnstone's voice was husky and wounded. "Mad . . . goddamned mad . . ."

"Then you convinced him to join your mission," Matthew went on. "I presume you had a trinket or two to show him as proof? Did you give him the brooch? Was that one of the things you'd found during those nights you posed as a surveyor? As you declined Mr. Bidwell's offer of a bed and pitched your tent right there beside the spring, you could go swimming without being discovered. What else did you find down there?"

"I'm not . . ." Johnstone struggled to stand. "I'm not staying to hear this madman's slander!"

"Look how he remains in character!" Matthew said. "I should have known you were an actor the first night we met! I should have realized from that face powder you wore, as you wore it the night of the maskers' dinner, that an actor never feels truly comfortable before a new audience without the benefit of makeup."

"I'm leaving!" Johnstone had gained his feet. He turned his sallow, sweating face toward the door.

"Alan? I know all about John Lancaster." Johnstone had been about to hobble out; now he froze again, at the sound of Bidwell's quiet, powerful voice.

"I know all about his abilities, though I don't understand such things. I *do* understand, however, from where Lancaster took his concept of the three demons. They were freaks he'd seen, at that circus which employed David Smythe's father."

Johnstone stood motionless, staring at the door, his back to Matthew. Perhaps the fox trembled, at this recognition of being torn asunder by the hounds.

"You see, Alan," Bidwell went on, "I opened a letter that Matthew had left for the magistrate. I read that letter . . . and I began to wonder why such a demon-possessed boy would fear for my safety. *My* safety, after all the insults and taunts I hurled at him. I began to wonder . . . if I had not best take Mr. Winston and go to Charles Town to find the Red Bull Players. They were camped just to the south. I found Mr. Smythe, and asked him the questions that were directed in that letter."

Johnstone had not moved, and still did not.

"Sit down," Bidwell commanded. "Whatever your name is, you bastard."

Nineteen

Matthew and the others now witnessed a transformation. Instead of being cowed by this command, instead of slumping under the iron fist of truth, Alan Johnstone slowly straightened his spine. In seconds he seemed an inch or two taller. His shoulders appeared to widen against the fabric of his dark blue jacket, as if the man had been tightly compressing himself around his secret core.

When he turned toward Matthew again, it was with an unhurried grace. Johnstone was smiling, but the truth had delivered its blow; his face was damp, his eyes deep-sunken and shock-blasted.

"Sirs," he said, "dear sirs. I must confess . . . I never attended Oxford. Oh, this is embarrassing. Quite so. I attended a small school in Wales. I was . . . the son of a miner, and I realized at an early age . . . that some doors would be closed to my ascent, if I did not attempt to hide some . . . um . . . unfortunate and unsavory elements of my family. Therefore, I created—"

"A lie, just as you're creating now," Matthew interrupted. "Are you incapable of telling the truth?"

Johnstone's mouth, which was open to speak the next falsehood, slowly closed. His smile had vanished, his face as grim as gray stone.

"I think he's lived with lies so long they're like a suit, without which he would feel nude to the world," Matthew said. "You did learn a great deal about Oxford, though, didn't you? Did you actually go there and tour the place when you returned to England, just in case you needed the information? It never hurts to add details to your script, does it? And all that about your social club!" Matthew shook his head and clucked his tongue. "Are the Ruskins even really in existence, or is that your own true name? You know, I might have realized I had proof of your lies that very night. When the magistrate recited the motto of his own social club to you, he spoke it in Latin, believing that as a fellow Oxford brother you would need no translation. But when you recited back the motto of the Ruskins, you spoke English. Have you ever known the motto of a social fraternity to be in *English?* Tell me, did you make that motto up on the spot?"

Johnstone began to laugh. The laughter, however, was strained through his tightly clenched teeth, and therefore was less merry than murderous.

"This woman who was purported to be your wife," Matthew said. "Who was she? Some insane wretch from Charles Town? No, no, you would have had to find someone you at least imagined you could control. Was she then a doxy, to whom you could promise future wealth for her cooperation?"

The laughter faded and went away, but Johnstone con-

tinued to grin. His face, the flesh drawn over the bones and
the eyeholes dwindled to burns, had taken on the appearance of a truly demonic mask.

"I presume you made quick work of the woman, as soon
as you'd left sight of Charles Town," Matthew ventured.
"Did she believe you were returning her to the dove roost?"

Johnstone suddenly turned and began to limp toward
the door, proving that his kneebrace enforced the fiction of
his deformity.

"Mr. Green?" Matthew called, in a casual tone. The doorway was presently blocked by the red-bearded giant, who
also held at his side a pistol. "That weapon has been prepared for firing, sir," Matthew said. "I don't for an instant
doubt your ability to inflict deadly violence, therefore the
necessary precaution against it. Would you please come
back to your chair?"

Johnstone didn't respond. Green said, "I 'spect you'd
best do as Mr. Corbett asks." The air had whistled through
the space a front tooth used to occupy.

"Very well, then!" Johnstone turned toward his tormentor
with a theatrical flourish, the death's-head grin at full force.
"I shall be glad to sit down and listen to these mad ravings,
as I find myself currently imprisoned! You know, you're all
bewitched! Every one of you!" He stalked back to the chairs,
taking a position not unlike center stage. "God help our
minds, to withstand such demonic power! Don't you see it?"
He pointed at Matthew, who was gratified to see that the
hand trembled. "This boy is in league with the blackest evil
to ever crawl from a pit! God help us, in its presence!" Now
Johnstone held his hand palm-upward, in a gesture of suppli-
cation. "I throw myself before your common sense, sirs! Before your decency and love of fellow man! God knows these
are the first things any demon would try to destr—"

Smack! went a book down onto Johnstone's offered palm. Johnstone staggered, and stared at the volume of English plays that Matthew had devoured, and that Mrs. Nettles had returned to the nearby bookcase.

"*Poor Tom Foolery,* I believe," Matthew said. "I think on page one-seventeen or thereabouts is a similar speech, in case you wish to be more exact."

Something moved across Johnstone's face in that instant, as he met Matthew's gaze. Something vulpine, and mean as sin. It was as if for a fleeting space of time the animal had been dragged from its den and made to show itself; then the instant passed, and the glimpse was gone. Johnstone's countenance had formed again into stone. Disdainfully, he turned his hand over and let the book fall to the floor.

"Sit down," Matthew said firmly, as Mr. Green guarded the doorway. Slowly, with as much dignity as he could cloak himself, Johnstone returned to his chair.

Matthew went to the fanciful map of Fount Royal that hung on the wall behind him. He tapped the spring with his forefinger. "This, gentleman, is the reason for such deception. At some time in the past—several years, I believe, before Mr. Bidwell sent a land scout to find him suitable property—this spring was used as a vault for pirate treasure. I don't mean just Spanish gold and silver coins, either. I mean jewels, silverware, plates . . . whatever this pirate and his crew managed to take. As the spring was likely used by this individual as a source of fresh water, he decided to employ it for a different purpose. Mr. Johnstone, do you know this individual's name?" No response. "Well, I'm assuming he was English, since he seemed to prefer attacking Spanish merchant ships. Probably he attacked a few Spanish pirates who were themselves laden with treasure. In any case, he built up a wondrous fortune

. . . but of course, he was always in fear of being attacked himself, therefore he needed a secure hiding-place for his loot. Please correct me, Mr. Johnstone, if I am mistaken at any of these conjectures."

Johnstone might have burned the very air between them with his stare.

"Oh, I should tell you, sir," Matthew said, "that the vast majority of the fortune you schemed to possess is now lost. In my investigation of the pond, I found an opening to an underground flow. A small opening but, regretfully for you, an efficient one as to the movement of water. Over a period of time, most of the loot went down the hole. I don't doubt that there are a few items of value remaining—some coins or pieces of pottery—but the vault has been emptied by the one who truly owns it: Mother Nature."

He saw now a flinch of true pain on Johnstone's face, as this nerve was so deeply struck. "I suspect you found some items when you posed as the surveyor, and those financed your schoolmaster's suits. A wagon and horses, too? And clothes for your cardboard wife? Then I presume you also had items to finance your passage back to and from England, and to be able to show Lancaster what was awaiting him. Did you also show him the blade that was awaiting his throat?"

"My God!" Dr. Shields said, aghast. "I . . . always thought Alan came from a wealthy family! I saw a gold ring he owned . . . with a ruby in it! And a gold pocket watch he had, inscribed with his initials!"

"Really? I'd say the ring was something he'd found. Perhaps he purchased the pocket watch in Charles Town before he came here, and had those initials inscribed to further advance his false identity." Matthew's eyesbrows lifted. "Or was it a watch you had previously murdered someone to get, and those initials prompted your choice of a name?"

"You," Johnstone said, his mouth twisting, "are absolutely a fool."

"I have been called so, sir, but never let it be said that I am *fooled*. At least not for very long. But you *are* a smart man, sir. I swear you are. If I were to ask Mr. Green to sit in your lap, and take Mr. Bidwell and Mr. Winston for a thorough search of your house, would we find a sapphire brooch there? A book on ancient Egypt? Would we find the ratcatcher's five-bladed device? You know, that was a crowning move! The claw marks! A deception only a talented thespian could construct! And to create a *ratcatcher* out of John Lancaster . . . well, it was an inspiration. Did you know that he had experience with training rats? Had you seen his circus act? You knew Fount Royal was in need of a ratcatcher . . . therefore, instant acceptance by the town. Was it you or Lancaster who created the poppets? Those, too, were very convincing. Just rough-edged enough to appear real."

"I shall . . . lose my mind, listening to you," Johnstone said. He blinked slowly. "Lose my mind . . . altogether."

"You decided Rachel was perfect witch material. You knew, as everyone knows, what occurred at Salem. But you, with your sterling abilities to manipulate an audience, realized how such mass fear might be scripted, act upon act. The only problem is that you, sir, are a man who has the command of a crowd's mind, yet you needed a man with the command of the *individual* mind. The point being to seed this terror in Fount Royal by using selected persons, and thus to ruin the town and cause it to be abandoned. After which you—and Lancaster, or so he believed—might remove the riches."

Johnstone lifted a hand and touched his forehead. He rocked slightly back and forth in his chair.

"As to the murder of Daniel Howarth," Matthew said, "I suspect you lured him out of the house that night to a pre-arranged meeting? Something he would not have mentioned to Rachel? She told me that the night of his murder he asked her if she loved him. She said it was rare for him to be so . . . well . . . needful. He already had fears that Nicholas Paine was interested in Rachel. Did you fan those flames, by intimating that Rachel might also have feelings for Paine? Did you promise to meet him in a private place, to exchange information that should not be overheard? Of course he wouldn't have known what you were planning. I'm sure your power of persuasion might have directed Daniel to any place you chose, at any time. Who cut his throat, then? You or Lancaster?"

When Johnstone didn't answer, Matthew said, "You, I think. I presume you then applied the five-bladed device to Daniel's dead or dying body? I'm sure Lancaster never would have imagined he'd meet his end the same way. He panicked when he learned he'd been discovered, didn't he? Did he want to leave?" Matthew smiled grimly. "But no, you couldn't have that, could you? You couldn't let him leave, knowing what he knew. Had you always planned to murder him, after he'd helped you remove the treasure and Fount Royal was your own private fortress?"

"Damn you," Bidwell said to Johnstone, his face reddening. "Damn your eyes, and heart, and soul. Damn you to a slow death, as you would have made me a murderer too!"

"Calm yourself," Matthew advised. "He *shall* be damned,

as I understand the colonial prison is one step above a hell-hole and dungheap. Which is where he shall spend some days before he hangs, if I have anything to do with it."

"That," Johnstone said wanly, "may be true." Matthew sensed the man was now willing to speak. "But," Johnstone continued, "I have survived Newgate itself, and so I doubt I shall be much inconvenienced."

"Ahhhhh!" Matthew nodded. He leaned against the wall opposite the man. "A graduate not of Oxford, but of Newgate prison! How did your attendance in such a school come about?"

"Debts. Political associations. And friends," he said, staring at the floor, "with knives. My career was ruined. And I did have a good career. Oh . . . not that I was ever a major lamp, but I did have aspirations. I hoped . . . at some point . . . to have enough money to invest in a theater troupe of my own." He sighed heavily. "My candle was extinguished by jealous colleagues. But was I not . . . credible in my performance?" He lifted his sweat-slick face to Matthew, and offered a faint smile.

"You are deserving of applause. From the hangman, at least."

"I take that as a backhanded compliment. Allow me to deliver one of my own: you have a fair to middling mind. With some work, you might become a thinker."

"I shall take such into consideration."

"This beast." Johnstone put his hand on the convexity on his leg. "It does pain me. I am glad, in that regard, to get it off once and for all." He unbuttoned the breeches at the knee, rolled down the stocking, and began to unstrap the leather brace. All present could see that the kneecap was perfectly formed. "You're correct. It *was* candle wax. I spent a whole night shaping it before I was satisfied with the damn thing. Here: a trophy." He tossed the brace to the floor at Matthew's feet.

Matthew couldn't help but think it was much more palatable than the trophy of a carved-out, horrible-smelling bear's head he'd been presented with at the celebration last night. Also a much more satisfying one.

Johnstone winced as he stretched the leg out straight and briskly massaged the knee. "I was suffering a muscle cramp the other night that near put me on the floor. Had to wear a similar apparatus for a role I played . . . oh . . . ten years ago. One of my last roles, with the Paradigm Players. A comedy, actually. Unfortunately there was nothing funny about it, if you discount the humor of having the audience pelt you with tomatoes and horseshit."

"By *God*, I ought to strangle you myself!" Bidwell raged. "I ought to save the hangman a penny rope!"

Johnstone said, "Strangle yourself while you're at it. You were the one in such a rush to burn the woman." This statement, delivered so offhandedly, was the straw that broke Bidwell's back. The master of dead Fount Royal gave a shouted oath and lunged from his chair at Johnstone, seizing the actor's throat with both hands.

They went to the floor in a tangle and crash. At once Matthew and Winston rushed forward to disengage them, as Green looked on from his position guarding the door and Shields clung to his chair. Bidwell was pulled away from Johnstone, but not before delivering two blows that bloodied the actor's nostrils.

"Sit down," Matthew told Bidwell, who angrily jerked out of his grasp. Winston righted Johnstone's chair and helped him into it, then immediately retreated to a corner of the library as if he feared contamination from having touched the man. Johnstone wiped his bleeding nose with his sleeve and picked up his cane, which had also fallen to the floor.

"I ought to kill you!" Bidwell shouted, the veins standing out in his neck. "Tear you to pieces myself, for what you've done!"

"The law will take care of him, sir," Matthew said. "Now please . . . sit down and keep your dignity."

Reluctantly, Bidwell returned to his chair and thumped down into it. He glowered straight ahead, ideas of vengeance still crackling like flames in his mind.

"Well, you should feel very pleased with yourself," Johnstone said to Matthew. He leaned his head back and sniffled. "The hero of the day, and all that. Am I your stepping-stone to the judicial robes?"

Matthew realized Johnstone the manipulator was yet at work, trying to move him into a defensive position. "The treasure," he said, ignoring the man's remark. "How come you to know about it?"

"I believe my nose is broken."

"The treasure," Matthew insisted. "Now is not the time to play games."

"Ah, the treasure! Yes, that." He closed his eyes and sniffled blood again. "Tell me, Matthew, have you ever set foot inside Newgate prison?"

"No."

"Pray to God you never do." Johnstone's eyes opened. "I was there for one year, three months, and twenty-eight days, serving restitution for my debts. The prisoners have the run of the place. There are guards, yes, but they withdraw for their own throats. Everyone—debtors, thieves, drunks and lunatics, murderers, child fuckers and mother rapers . . . they're all thrown together, like animals in a pit, and . . . believe me . . . you do what you must to survive. You know why?"

He brought his head forward and grinned at Matthew, and when he did fresh crimson oozed from both nostrils. "Because no one . . . *no one* . . . cares whether you live or die but yourself. *Yourself,*" he hissed, and again that vulpine, cruel shadow passed quickly across his face. He nodded, his tongue flicking out and tasting the blood that glistened in the candlelight. "When they come at you—three or four at a time—and hold you down, it is not because they wish you well. I have seen men killed in such a fashion, battered until they are mortally torn inside. And still they go on, as the corpse is not yet cold. Still they go on. And you must—you *must*—sink to their level and join them if you wish to live another day. You must shout and shriek and howl like a beast, and strike and thrust . . . and *want* to kill . . . for if you show any weakness at all, they will turn upon you and it will be *your* broken corpse being thrown upon the garbage pile at first light."

The fox leaned toward his captor, heedless now of his bleeding nose. "Sewage runs right along the floor there. We knew it had rained outside, and how hard, when the sewage rose to our ankles. I saw two men fight to the death over a pack of playing cards. The fight ended when one drowned the other in that indescribable filth. Wouldn't that be a lovely way to end your life, Matthew? Drowned in human shit?"

"Is there a point to this recitation, sir?"

"Oh, indeed there is!" Johnstone grinned broadly, blood on his lips and the shine of his eyes verging on madness. "No words are vile enough, nor do they carry enough weight of bestiality, to describe Newgate prison, but I wished you to know the circumstances in which I found myself. The days were sufficiently horrible . . . but then came the nights! Oh, the joyous bliss of the darkness! I can feel it even now! Listen!" he whispered. "Hear them? Starting to stir? Starting to crawl from their mattresses and stalk the night fantastic? Hear them? The creak of a bedframe here—and one over there, as well! Oh, listen . . . someone weeps! Someone calls out for God . . . but it is always the Devil who answers." Johnstone's savage grin faltered and slipped away.

"Even if it was so terrible a place," Matthew said, "you still survived it."

"Did I?" Johnstone asked, and let the question hang. He stood up, wincing as he put weight on his unbraced knee. He supported himself with his cane. "I pay for wearing that damn brace, you may be sure. Yes, I did live through Newgate prison, as I realized I might offer the assembled animals something to entertain them besides carnage. I might offer them plays. Or, rather, scenes from plays. I did all the parts, in different voices and dialects. What I didn't know I made up. They never knew the difference, nor did they care. They were particularly pleased at any scene that involved the disgrace or degradation of court officials, and as there are a pittance of those in our catalogue, I found myself concocting the scenes as I played them out. Suddenly I was a very popular man. A *celebrity,* among the rabble."

Johnstone stood with the cane on the floor and both hands on the cane, and Matthew realized he had—as was his nature—again taken center stage before his audience. "I came into the favor of a very large and very mean individual we called the Meatgrinder, as he . . . um . . . had used such a device to dispose of his wife's body. But—lo and behold!— he was a fan of the stagelamps! I was elevated to the prospect of command performances, and also found myself protected from the threat of harm."

As Matthew had known he sooner or later would, Johnstone now swivelled his body so as to have a view of the other men in the room. Or rather, so they would have a full view of the thespian's expressions. "Near the end of my term," Johnstone went on, "I came into the acquaintance of a certain man. He was my age or therebouts, but looked very much older. He was sick, too. Coughing up blood. Well, needless to say a sick man in Newgate prison is like a warm piece of liver to wolves. It's an interesting thing to behold, actually. They beat him because he was an easy target, and also because they wanted him to go ahead and die lest they fall sick themselves. I tell you, you can learn quite a lot about the human condition at Newgate; you ought to put yourself there for a night and make a study of it."

"I'm sure there are less dangerous universities," Matthew said.

"Yes, but none teaches as quickly as Newgate." Johnstone flashed a sharp smile. "And the lessons are very well learned. But: this man I was telling you about. He realized the Meatgrinder's power in our little community, yet the Meatgrinder was . . . well, he'd rather kill a man than smell his breath, shall we say. Therefore this sick and beaten individual asked me to intercede on his behalf, as a gentleman. He actually was quite educated himself. Had once been a dealer in antiques, in London. He asked me to intercede to save him further beatings or other indignities . . . in exchange for some very interesting information concerning a waterhole across the Atlantic."

"Ah," Matthew said. "He knew of the treasure."

"Not only knew, he helped place the fortune there. He was a member of the crew. Oh, he told me all about it, in fascinating detail. Told me he'd never revealed it to a soul, because he was going to go back for it someday. *Someday,* he said. And I might be his partner and share it with him, if I would protect his life. Told me that the spring was forty feet deep, told me that the treasure had been lowered in wicker baskets and burlap bags . . . told enough to put a sea voyage in the mind of a poor starving ex-thespian who had no prospects, no family, and absolutely no belief in that straw poppet you call God." Again, Johnstone displayed a knife-edged smile. "This man . . . this crewman . . . said there'd been a storm at sea. The ship had been wrecked. He and five or six others survived, and reached an island. Pirates being as they are, I suppose stones and coconuts did the job of knives and pistols. At last, one man survived to light a fire for a passing English frigate." Johnstone shrugged. "What did I have to lose to at least come look for myself? Oh . . . he had an inscribed gold pocket watch hidden in his mattress that he also gave to me. You see, that man's name was Alan Johnstone."

"What's *your* name, then?" Bidwell asked.

"Julius Caesar. William Shakespeare. Lord Bott Fucking Tott. Take your pick, what does it matter?"

"And what happened to the real Alan Johnstone?" Matthew inquired, though he already had an idea. It had dawned on him, as well, that the turtles—reed-eaters by nature—had probably loved feasting on all those baskets and bags.

"The beatings ceased. I had to prove my worth to him. He survived for a time. Then he grew very, very ill. Sick unto death, really. I was able to get the coordinates of the waterhole's latitude and longitude from him . . . something I'd been trying to do for a month or more without seeming overly demanding. Then someone told the Meatgrinder that very night . . . someone . . . a little shadow of a someone . . . that the sick man coughing up all that blood over there in the corner . . . well, it was dangerous to everyone. Such disease might wipe out our little community, and we were so fond of it. By morning, alas, my partner had set off on his final voyage, alone and unlamented."

"By Christ," Matthew said softly, his guts twisting. "Little wonder you decided to invent the witchcraft scheme. You're on regular speaking terms with Satan, aren't you?"

Johnstone—for want of a better name—laughed quietly. He threw his head back, his eyes gleaming, and laughed louder.

There was a faintly audible *click*.

And suddenly, moving with a speed that belied his stiff leg, Johnstone lunged forward. He pressed against Matthew's throat the pointed edge of a five-inch blade that had been concealed within the cane's shaft.

"Be still!" Johnstone hissed, his eyes boring into Matthew's. Bidwell had stood up, and now Winston and Dr. Shields rose to their feet. "Everyone, be still!"

Green crossed the threshold, pistol in hand. Johnstone reached out, grasped Matthew's shirt, and turned him so the thespian's back was to the wall and Matthew's back was in danger of a pistol ball should Green lose his head. "No, no!" Johnstone said, as if scolding a wayward pupil. "Green, stand where you are."

The red-bearded giant halted. The blade pressed perilously near entering the flesh. Though he was quaking inside, Matthew was able to keep a calm mask. "This will do you no good."

"It will do me less good to be sent to prison and have my neck stretched!" Johnstone's face was damp, a pulse beating rapidly at his temple. Blood still stained his nostrils and upper lip. "No, I can't bear that. Not prison." He shook his head with finality. "One season in Hell is enough for any man."

"You have no choice, sir. As I said, this will do you no—"

"Bidwell!" Johnstone snapped. "Get a wagon ready! *Now!* Green, take the pistol by the barrel. Come over here . . . slowly . . . and give it to me."

"Gentlemen," Matthew said, "I would suggest doing neither."

"I have a knife at your throat. Do you feel it?" He gave a little jab. "There? Would you like a sharper taste?"

"Mr. Green," Matthew said, staring into the wild eyes of the fox. "Take a position, please, and aim your pistol at Mr. Johnstone's head."

"Christ, boy!" Bidwell shouted. "No! Green, he's crazy!"

"No further play at heroics," Johnstone said tightly. "You've strutted your feathers, you've shown your cock, and you have blasted me with a cannon. So spare yourself, because I'm going out that door! No power on earth will ever send me back to a goddamned prison!"

"I understand your rush to avoid judgment, sir. But there are the two men with axes waiting just outside the front door."

"What two men? You're lying!"

"You see the lantern on the windowsill? Mr. Bidwell placed it there as a signal to tell the two men to take their positions."

"Name them!"

"Hiram Abercrombie is one," Bidwell answered. "Malcolm Jennings is the other."

"Well, neither of *those* fools could hit a horse in the head with an axe! Green, I said give me the pistol!"

"Stay where you are, Mr. Green," Matthew said.

"Matthew!" Winston spoke up. "Don't be foolish!"

"A pistol in this man's hand will mean someone's death." Matthew kept his eyes directed into Johnstone's. Bloodhound and fox were now locked together in a duel of wills. "One bullet, one death, I assure you."

"The pistol! I won't ask again before I start cutting!"

"Oh, is this the instrument?" Matthew asked. "The very one? Something you bought in Charles Town, I presume?"

"Damn you, you talk too fucking much!" Johnstone pushed the blade's tip into the side of Matthew's neck. The pain almost sent Matthew to his knees, and it did bring tears to his eyes and make him clench his teeth. In fact, his whole body clenched. But he was damned if he'd cry out or otherwise display agony. The blade had entered only a fraction of an inch, deep enough to cause warm blood to well out and trickle down his neck, but it had not nicked an artery. Matthew knew Johnstone was simply raising the stakes in their game.

"Would you like a little more of it?" Johnstone asked.

Bidwell had positioned himself to one side of the men, and therefore saw the blood. "For God's sake!" he brayed. "Green! Give him the pistol!"

Before Matthew could protest, he heard Green's clumping boots behind him and the pistol's grip was offered to Johnstone. The weapon was instantly snatched into Johnstone's hand, but the blade remained exactly where it was, blood-deep and drinking.

"The wagon, Bidwell!" Johnstone demanded, now aiming the pistol at Matthew's midsection. "Get it ready!"

"Yes, do get it ready." Matthew was speaking with an effort. It wasn't every day he talked with a knife blade in his neck. "And while you're at it, fix the wheels so they'll fall off two hours or so down the road. Why don't you take a single horse, Johnstone? That way it can step into a rut in the dark, throw you, and break your neck and be done with it. Oh . . . wait! Why don't you simply go through the swamp? I know some lovely suckpits that would be glad to take your boots."

"Shut up! I want a wagon! I want a wagon, because *you're* going with me!"

"Oh *ho!*" With an even greater effort, Matthew forced himself to grin. "Sir, you're an excellent comedian after all!"

"You think this is funny?" Johnstone's face was contorted with rage. He blew spittle. "Shall you laugh harder through the slit in your throat or the hole in your gut?"

"The real question is: shall *you* laugh, when your intended hostage is on the floor and your pistol is empty?"

Johnstone's mouth opened. No sound emerged, but a silver thread of saliva broke over his lower lip and fell like the undoing of a spider's web.

Carefully, Matthew took a backward step. The blade's tip slid from his neck. "Your problem, sir," he said as he pressed his fingers to the small wound, "is that your friends and associates seem to have short spans of life. If I were to accompany you in a wagon, my own life span would be dramatically reduced. So: I dislike the idea of dying—*greatly* dislike it—but since I shall certainly die *somewhere* if I follow your wishes, it would be better to die *here*. That way, at least, the sterling gentlemen in this room may rush you and end this hopeless fantasy of escape you have seized upon. But actually, I don't think anyone would mind if you were to run for it. Just go. Out the front door. I swear I'll be silent. Of course, Mr. Bidwell, Mr. Green—or even Mrs. Nettles, whom I see there in the doorway—might shout a warning to the axemen. Let me think." He frowned. "Two axes, versus a knife and one bullet.

Yes, you might get past them. Then you could go to . . . well, where *would* you go, Mr. Johnstone? You see, that's the thorny part: where *would* you go?"

Johnstone said nothing. He still pointed both the pistol and knife, but his eyes had blurred like a frost on the fount in midwinter.

"Oh!" Matthew nodded for emphasis. "Through the forest, why don't you? The Indians will grant you safe passage, I'm sure. But you see my condition? I unfortunately met a bear and was nearly killed. Then again, you do have a knife and a single bullet. But . . . oh . . . what shall you do for food? Well, you have the knife and bullet. Best take matches, and a lamp. Best go to your house and pack for your trip, and we'll be waiting at the gate to give you a fine farewell. Run along, now!"

Johnstone did not move.

"Oh, my," Matthew said quietly. He looked from the pistol to the blade and back again. "All dressed up, and nowhere to go."

"I'm . . . not . . ." Johnstone shook his head from side to side, in the manner of a gravely wounded animal. "I'm not . . . done. Not done."

"Hm," Matthew said. "Picture the theatre, sir. The applause has been given, the bows taken. The audience has gone home. The stagelamps are ever so slowly extinguished. They gave a beautiful dream of light, didn't they? The sets are dismantled, the costumes folded and retired. Someone comes to sweep the stage, and even yesterday's dust is carried away." He listened to the harsh rising and falling of Johnstone's chest.

"The play," Matthew said, "is over." An anxious silence reigned, and none dared challenge it.

At last Matthew decided a move had to be made. He had seen that the knife's cutting edge had small teeth, which would have severed arteries and vocal cords with one or two swift, unexpected slashes. Especially if one came up behind the victim, clasped a hand over the mouth, and pulled the head back to better offer the throat. Perhaps this wasn't the original cane Johnstone had first brought with him to Fount Royal, but one he'd had made in either Charles Town or England after he'd determined how the murders were to be done.

Matthew held out his hand, risking a blade stab. "Would you give me the pistol, please?" Johnstone's face looked soft and swollen by raging inner pressures. He seemed not to realize Matthew had spoken, but was simply staring into space.

"Sir?" Matthew prompted. "You won't be needing the pistol."

"Uh," Johnstone said. "Uh." His mouth opened, closed, and opened again. The gasping of an air-drowning fish. Then, in a heartbeat, the consciousness and fury leapt into Johnstone's eyes once more and he backed away two steps, nearly meeting the wall. Behind him was the fanciful map of Fount Royal, with its elegant streets and rows of houses, quiltwork farms, immense orchards, precise naval yard and piers, and at the town's center the life-giving spring.

Johnstone said, "No. I shall not."

"Listen to me!" Bidwell urged. "There's no point to this! Matthew's right, there's nowhere for you to go!"

"I shall not," Johnstone repeated. "Shall not. Return to prison. No. Never."

"Unfortunately," Matthew said, "you have no choice in the matter."

"Finally!" Johnstone smiled, but it was a terrible, skull-like grimace. "Finally, you speak a misstatement! So you're not as smart as you think, are you?"

"Pardon me?"

"A misstatement," he repeated, his voice thickened. "Tell me: though I . . . know my script was flawed . . . did I at least play an adequate role?"

"You did, sir. Especially the night the schoolhouse burned. I was taken with your grief."

Johnstone gave a deep, bitter chuckling that might have briefly wandered into the territory of tears. "That was the only time I *wasn't* acting, boy! It killed my soul to see the schoolhouse burn!"

"What? It really mattered so much to you?"

"You don't know. You see . . . I actually *enjoyed* being a teacher. It was like acting, in a way. But . . . there was greater worth in it, and the audience was always appreciative. I told myself . . . if I couldn't find any more of the treasure than what I'd discovered . . . I could stay here, and I could be Alan Johnstone the schoolmaster. For the rest of my days." He stared at the pistol in his hand. "Not long after that, I brought the ruby ring up. And it set me aflame again . . . about why I was really here." He lifted his face and looked at Matthew. He stared at Winston, Dr. Shields, and Bidwell all in turn.

"Please put aside the pistol," Matthew said. "I think it's time."

"Time. Yes," Johnstone repeated, nodding. "It *is* time. I can't go back to prison. Do you understand that?"

"Sir?" Matthew now realized with a surge of alarm what the man intended. "There's no need!"

"My need." Johnstone dropped the knife to the floor and put his foot on it. "You were correct about something,

Matthew: if I was given the pistol . . ." He paused, beginning to waver on his feet as if he might pass out. "Someone had to die."

Suddenly Johnstone turned the weapon toward his face, which brought a gasp of shock from Bidwell. "I do have a choice, you see," Johnstone said, the sweat glistening on his cheeks in the red-cast candlelight. "And damn you all to Hell, where I shall be waiting with eager arms.

"And now," he said, with a slight tilting forward of his head, "exit the actor."

He opened his mouth, slid the pistol's barrel into it, squeezed his eyes tightly shut, and pulled the trigger.

There was a loud metallic *clack* as the wheel-lock mechanism was engaged. A shower of sparks flew, hissing like little comets, into Johnstone's face.

The pistol, however, failed to fire.

Johnstone opened his eyes, displaying an expression of such terror that Matthew hoped never to witness its like again. He withdrew the gun from his mouth. Something inside the weapon was making a chirrupy cricket sound. Tendrils of blue smoke spun through the air around Johnstone's face, as he looked into the gun's barrel. Another spark jumped, bright as a gold coin.

Crack! went the pistol, like a mallet striking a board.

Johnstone's head rocked back. The eyes were wide open, wet, and brimming with shock. Matthew saw blood and reddish-gray clumps of matter clinging to the wall behind Johnstone's skull. The map of Bidwell's Fount Royal had in an instant become gore-drenched and brain-spattered.

Johnstone fell, his knees folding. At the end, an instant before he hit the floor, he might have been giving a final, arrogant bow.

And then his head hit the planks, and from that gruesome hole in the back of it, directly opposite the only slightly tidier hole in his forehead, streamed the physical matter of the thespian's memories, schemes, acting ability, intelligence, pride, fear of prison, desires, evil, and . . .

Yes, even his affinity for teaching. Even that, now only so much liquid.

TWENTY

In the distance a dog barked. It was a forlorn, searching sound. Matthew looked over the darkened town from the window of the magistrate's room, thinking that even the dogs knew Fount Royal was lost.

Five hours had passed since the suicide of Alan Johnstone. Matthew had spent most of that time right here, sitting in a chair by Woodward's bed and reading the Bible in a solemn circle of lamplight. Not any particular chapter, just bits and pieces of comforting wisdom. Actually, he read most of the passages without seeing them, and had to read them again to glean their illumination. It was a sturdy book, and it felt good between his hands.

The magistrate was dying. Shields had said the man might not last until morning, so it was best that Matthew stay close. Bidwell and Winston were in the parlor, talking over the recent events like survivors of a soul-shaping battle. The doctor himself was sleeping in Matthew's room, and Mrs. Nettles was up at this midnight hour making tea, polishing silver, and doing odds and ends in the kitchen. She had told Matthew she ought to do some small labors she'd been putting off for a while, but Matthew knew she was standing the deathwatch too. Little wonder Mrs. Nettles couldn't sleep, though, as it had been her task to mop up all the blood in the library, though Mr. Green had volunteered to put the brains and skull pieces in a burlap bag and dispose of them.

Rachel was downstairs, sleeping—he supposed—in Mrs. Nettles's room. She had come to the library after the sound of the shot, and had asked to see the face of the man who'd murdered Daniel. It was not Matthew's place to deny her. Though Matthew had previously explained to her how the murders were done, by whom, for what reason, and all the rest of it, Rachel yet had to see Johnstone for herself.

She had walked past Winston, Dr. Shields, and Bidwell without a glance. She had ignored Hiram Abercrombie and Malcolm Jennings, who'd rushed in at the shot, armed with their axes. Certainly she'd passed Green as if the red-bearded, gap-toothed giant was invisible. She had stood over the dead man, staring down into his open, sightless eyes. Matthew had watched her as she contemplated Johnstone's departure. At last, she had said very quietly, "I suppose . . . I should rant and rave that I spent so many days in a cell . . . and he has fled. But . . ." She had looked into Matthew's face, tears in her eyes now that it was over and she could allow them. "Someone that evil . . . that wretched . . . was locked in a cage of his own making, every day of his life, wasn't he?"

"He was," Matthew had said. "Even when he knew he'd found the key to escape it, all he did was move to a deeper dungeon."

Green had retrieved the pistol, which had belonged to Nicholas Paine. It occurred to Matthew that all the men he and the magistrate had met that first night of their arrival were accounted for in this room. "Thank you for your help, Mr. Green," Matthew had said. "You were invaluable."

"My pleasure, sir. Anythin' to help you." Green had taken to fawning at Matthew, as if the clerk had a giant's stature. "I *still* can't believe such a blow as you gave me!" He'd massaged his jaw at the memory of it. "I saw you cock the fist back, and then . . . my Lord, the stars!" He'd grunted and looked at Rachel. "It took a right champion to lay me out, I'll swear it did!"

"Um . . . yes." Matthew cast a quick glance at Mrs. Nettles, who stood nearby listening to this exchange, her face an unrevealing sculpture of granite. "Well, one never knows from where one will draw the necessary strength. Does one?"

Matthew had watched as Jennings and Abercrombie had lifted the corpse, placed it facedown on a ladder to prevent any further leakage, and then covered a sheet over the deceased. Its destination, Bidwell told Matthew, was the barn down in the slave quarters. Tomorrow, Bidwell said, the corpse—"foul bastard" were the exact words he used—would be taken into the swamp and dumped in a mudhole where the crows and vultures might applaud his performance.

To end up, Matthew realized, like the dead men in the muck at Shawcombe's tavern. Well: dust to dust, ashes to ashes, and mud to mud.

It was now the impending fact of another death that concerned him. Matthew had learned from Dr. Shields that the stimulating potion had finally reached the limit of its usefulness. Woodward's body had simply given out, and nothing could reverse the process. Matthew didn't bear a grudge against the doctor; Shields had done the best he could do, given the limited medicines at hand. Perhaps the bleeding had been excessive, or perhaps it had been a grievous error to make the magistrate attend his duties while so sick, or perhaps something else was done or not done . . . but today Matthew had come to accept the hard, cold truth.

Just as seasons and centuries must turn, so too must men—the bad and the good, equal in their frailty of flesh—pass away from this earth.

He heard a nightbird singing.

Out there. Out in one of the trees that stood around the pond. It was a noontime song, and presently it was joined by a second. For their kind, Matthew mused, night was not a time of sad longing, loneliness, and fear. For them the night was but a further opportunity to sing.

And such a sweetness in it, to hear these notes trilled as the land slept, as the stars hummed in the immense velvet black. Such a sweetness, to realize that even at this darkest hour there was yet joy to be known.

"Matthew."

He heard the feeble gasp and immediately turned toward the bed.

It was very hard now to look upon the magistrate. To know what he had been, and to see what he had become in the space of six days. Time could be a ruthless and hungry beast. It had consumed the magistrate down to bones and angles.

"Yes, sir, I'm here." Matthew pulled his chair nearer the bed, and also moved the lantern closer. He sat down, leaning toward the skeletal figure. "I'm right here."

"Ah. Yes. I see you." Woodward's eyes had shrunken and retreated. They had changed from their once energetic shade of ice-blue to a dull yellowish gray, the color of the fog and rain he had journeyed through to reach this town.

Indeed, the only color about the magistrate that was not a shade of gray was the ruddy hue of the splotches on his scalp. Those jealous imperfections had maintained their dignity, even as the rest of Woodward's body had fallen to ruin.

"Would you . . . hold my hand?" the magistrate asked, and he reached out in search of comfort. Matthew took the hand. It was fragile and trembling, and hot with merciless fever. "I heard it," Woodward whispered, his head on the pillow. "Thunder. Does it rain?"

"No, sir." Perhaps it had been the shot he'd heard, Matthew thought. "Not yet."

"Ah. Well, then." He said nothing more, but stared past Matthew toward the lamp.

This was the first time the magistrate had surfaced from the waters of sleep since Matthew had been in the room. Matthew had come in several times during the day, but except for a few brief murmurs or a pained swallow the magistrate had been unresponsive.

"It's dark out," Woodward said.

"Yes, sir."

He nodded. Around his nose glistened the pine-oil–based liniment Shields had smeared there to clear his air passages. On his thin and sunken chest was a plaster, also soaked in the liniment. If Woodward noticed the clay dressing on Matthew's arm and the bandage—of cloth, which Dr. Shields had applied after Johnstone's departure—on his clerk's forever-to-be-scarred forehead, he made no mention of it. Matthew doubted the magistrate could see his face as anything but a blur, as the fever had almost destroyed the man's vision.

Woodward's fingers tightened. "She's gone, then."

"Sir?"

"The witch. Gone."

"Yes, sir," Matthew said, and didn't think he was telling an untruth. "The witch *is* gone."

Woodward sighed, his eyelids fluttering. "I . . . am glad . . . I didn't witness it. I might have to . . . pass the sentence . . . but . . . don't have to watch it . . . carried out. Ohhhhh, my throat! My throat! It closes up!"

"I'll get Dr. Shields." Matthew attempted to stand, but Woodward steadfastly refused to release him.

"No!" he said, tears of pain streaking his cheeks. "Stay seated. Just . . . listen."

"Don't try to talk, sir. You shouldn't—"

"I shouldn't!" Woodward blustered. "I shouldn't . . . I can't . . . mustn't! Those are the words that . . . that put you . . . six feet under!"

Matthew settled into his chair again, his hand still grasping the magistrate's. "You should refrain from speaking."

A grim smile moved quickly across Woodward's mouth and then was gone. "I shall have. Plenty of time . . . to refrain. When my . . . mouth is full of dirt."

"Don't say such as that!"

"Why not? It's true . . . isn't it? Matthew, what a short rope . . . I have been given!" He closed his eyes, breathing fitfully. Matthew would have thought he'd drifted to sleep again, but the pressure on his hand had not relaxed. Then Woodward spoke again with his eyes still closed. "The witch," he whispered. "The case . . . pains me. Still pains me." His fog-colored eyes opened. "Was I right, Matthew? Tell me. Was I right?"

Matthew answered, "You were correct."

"Ahhhhh," he said, like an exhalation of relief. "Thank you. I needed . . . to hear that, from you." He squeezed Matthew's hand more firmly. "Listen, now. My hourglass . . . is broken. All my sand is running out. I will die soon."

"Nonsense, sir!" Matthew's voice cracked and betrayed him. "You're just tired, that's all!"

"Yes. And I shall . . . soon sleep . . . for a very long time. Please . . . I may be dying, but I have not . . . become *stupid*. Now . . . just hush . . . and listen to me." He tried to sit up but his body had shut that particular door to him. "In Manhattan," he said. "Go see . . . Magistrate Powers. Nathaniel Powers. A very . . . very good man. He knows me. You tell him. He will find a place for you."

"Please, sir. Don't do this."

"I fear . . . I have no choice. The judgment has been . . . has been passed down . . . from a much higher court. Than ever I presided over. Magistrate Nathaniel Powers. In Manhattan. Yes?" Matthew was silent, the blood thrumming through his veins. "This will be . . . my final command to you," Woodward said. "Say *yes.*"

Matthew looked into the near-sightless eyes. Into the face that seemed to be aging and crumbling even as he regarded it.

Seasons, and centuries, and men. The bad and the good. Frailty of flesh.

Must pass away. Must.

A nightbird, singing outside. In the dark. Singing as at full sunlit noon.

This one word, so simple, was almost impossible to speak.

But the magistrate was waiting, and the word must be spoken. "Yes." His own throat felt near closing up. "Sir."

"That's my boy," Woodward whispered. His fingers released Matthew's hand. He lay staring up toward the ceiling, a half-smile playing around the corners of his mouth. "I remember . . . my own father," he said after a moment of reflection. "He liked to dance. I can see them . . . in the house . . . dancing before the fire. No music. But my father . . . humming a tune. He picked my mother up. Twirled her . . . and she laughed. So . . . there *was* music . . . after all."

Matthew heard the nightbird, whose soft song may have reawakened this memory.

"My father," the magistrate said. "Grew sick. I watched him . . . in bed, like this. Watched him fade. One day . . . I asked my mother . . . why Papa didn't stand up. Get out of bed. And dance a jig . . . to make himself feel better. I always said . . . always to myself . . . that when I was old . . . very old . . . and I lay dying. I would stand up. Dance a jig, so that . . . I might feel better. Matthew?"

"Yes, sir?"

"Would it . . . sound very strange to you . . . if . . . I said I was ready to dance?"

"No, sir, it would not."

"I am. Ready. I am."

"Sir?" Matthew said. "I have something for you." He reached down to the floor beside the bed and picked up the package he had put there this afternoon. Mrs. Nettles had found some brown wrapping paper, and decorated it with yellow twine. "Here, sir." He put the package into the magistrate's hands. "Can you open it?"

"I shall try." After a moment of struggling, however, he could not succeed in tearing the paper. "Well," he frowned, "I am . . . lower on sand . . . than I thought."

"Allow me." Matthew leaned toward the bed, tore the paper with his good hand, and drew what was inside out into the lamplight. The gold threads caught that light, and shone their illumination in stripes across the magistrate's face.

His hands closed into the cloth that was as brown as rich French chocolate, and he drew the waistcoat to him even as the tears ran from his dying eyes.

It was, indeed, a gift of fantastic worth.

"Where?" the magistrate whispered. *"How?"*

"Shawcombe was found," Matthew said, and saw no need to elaborate.

Woodward pressed the waistcoat against his face, as if trying to inhale from it the fragrance of a past life. Matthew saw the magistrate smile. Who was to say that Woodward did not smell the sun shining in a garden graced by a fountain of green Italian tiles? Who was to say he did not see the candlelight that glowed golden on the face of a beautiful young woman named Ann, or hear her soprano voice on a warm Sunday afternoon? Who was to say he did not feel the small hand of his son, clutching to that of a good father?

Matthew believed he did.

"I have always been proud of you," Woodward said. "Always. I knew from the first. When I saw you . . . at the almshouse. The way you carried yourself. Something . . . different . . . and indefinable. But *special*. You will make your mark. Somewhere. You will make . . . a profound difference to someone . . . just by being alive."

"Thank you, sir," Matthew answered, as best he could. "I . . . also . . . thank you for the care you have shown to me. You have . . . always been temperate and fair."

"I'm supposed to be," Woodward said, and managed a frail smile though his eyes were wet. "I am a judge." He reached out for Matthew and the boy took his hand. They sat together in silence, as beyond the window the nightbird spoke of joy seized from despair, of a new beginning reached only at an ending.

Dawn had begun to light the sky when the magistrate's body became rigid, after a difficult final hour of suffering.

"He's going," Dr. Shields said, the lamplight aglow in the lenses of his spectacles. Bidwell stood at the foot of the bed, and Winston just within the door. Matthew still sat holding Woodward's hand, his head bowed and the Bible in his lap.

The magistrate's speech on this last portion of his journey had become barely intelligible, when he *could* speak through the pain. It had been mostly murmurs of torment, as his earthly clay transfigured itself. But now, as the silence lingered, the dying man seemed to stretch his body toward some unknown portal, the golden stripes of the waistcoat he wore shining on his chest. His head pressed back against the pillow, and he spoke three unmistakable words.

"Why? Why?" he whispered, the second fainter than the first.

And the last and most faint, barely the cloud of a breath: *"Why?"*

A great question had been asked, Matthew thought. The ultimate question, which might be asked only by explorers who would not return to share their knowledge of a new world.

The magistrate's body poised on the point of tension . . . paused . . . paused . . . and then, at last, it appeared to Matthew that an answer had been given.

And understood.

There was a soft, all but imperceptible exhalation. A sigh, perhaps, of rest.

Woodward's empty clay settled. His hand relaxed.

The night was over.

TWENTY-ONE

As soon as Matthew knocked on the study's door, Bidwell said, "Come in!"

Matthew opened the door and saw Bidwell seated at his massive mahogany desk, with Winston sitting in a chair before it. The window's shutters were open, allowing in the warm breeze and early afternoon sun. "Mrs. Nettles told me you wanted to see me."

"Exactly. Come in, please! Draw up a chair." He motioned toward another that was in the room. Matthew sat down, not failing to notice the empty space on the wall where the map of the Florida country had been displayed.

"We are taking account of things. Edward and I," Bidwell said. He was dressed in a cardinal-red suit with a ruffled shirt, but he had forgone the wearing of his lavish wigs. On the desktop was a rectangular wooden box about nine inches long and seven inches wide. "I've been trying to locate you. Were you out for a walk?"

"Yes. Just walking and thinking."

"Well, it's a pleasant day for such." Bidwell folded his

hands before him and regarded Matthew with an expression of genuine concern. "Are you all right?"

"I am. Or . . . I shall be presently."

"Good. You're a young man, strong and fit. And I have to say, you have the most determined constitution of any man I've ever met. How are your injuries?"

"My ribs still ache, but I can endure it. My arm is . . . deceased, I think. Dr. Shields says I may regain some feeling in it, but the outlook is uncertain." Matthew shrugged one shoulder. "He says he knows a doctor in New York who is doing amazing things for damaged limbs with a new surgical technique, so . . . who can say?"

"Yes, I hear those New York doctors are quite . . . um . . . radical. And they charge wholly radical prices, as well. What of your head wound?"

Matthew touched the fresh dressing Shields had applied just that morning. In the course of treatment, the doctor had been appalled at the Indians' method of tobacco-leaf and herb-potion healing, but also intrigued by the positive progress. "My scar, unfortunately, will be a subject of discussion for the rest of my life."

"That may be so." Bidwell leaned back in his chair. "Ah, but women love a dashing scar! And I daresay so will the grandchildren."

Matthew had to give a guarded smile at this flattery. "You leap ahead more years than I care to lose."

"Speaking of your years ahead," Winston said, "what are your immediate plans?"

"I haven't given them much thought," Matthew had to admit. "Other than returning to Charles Town. The magistrate gave me the name of a colleague in Manhattan, and said I would find a position with him, but . . . I really haven't decided."

Bidwell nodded. "That's understandable, with so much on your mind. Tell me: do you approve of where I placed Isaac's grave?"

"I do, sir. As a matter of fact, I just came from there. It's a very lovely, shaded spot."

"Good. And you don't think he would mind that he . . . uh . . . sleeps apart from the others in the cemetery?"

"Not at all. He always enjoyed his privacy."

"I shall endeavor, at some point in the future, to erect a picket fence around it and a suitable marker for his excellent service to Fount Royal."

Matthew was taken aback. "Wait," he said. "You mean . . . you're *staying* here?"

"I am. Winston will be returning to England, to work in the offices there, and I'll be going back and forth as the situation warrants, but I plan on reviving Fount Royal and making it just as grand—no, *thrice* as grand—as ever I'd planned before."

"But . . . the town is *dead*. There's hardly twenty people here!"

"Twenty citizens!" Bidwell thumped the desktop, his eyes bright with renewed purpose. "Then it's *not* dead, is it?"

"Perhaps not in fact, but it seems to me that—"

"If not in fact, then not at all!" Bidwell interrupted, displaying some of his old brusque self. He was aware of his slippage, and so immediately sought to soothe the friction burns. "What I mean is, I will not give up on Fount Royal. Not when I have invested so heavily in the venture, and particularly as I still fervently believe a southernmost naval station is not only practical, but essential for the future of these colonies."

"How will you go about reviving the town, then?"

"The same as I originally began it. With having advertising placards placed in Charles Town and other cities up the seaboard. I shall also advertise in London. And I am getting to it sooner than later, as I understand I will be having competition from my own family!"

"Competition? How so?" Matthew asked.

"My youngest sister! Who was sick all the time, and for whom I bought medicine!" Bidwell scowled. "When Winston and I went to Charles Town to find the maskers, we also looked in on the supply situation at the harbor. Come to find out there was a whole load of supplies there those dogs had hidden from me! Luckily, Mr. Winston convinced a watchman to unlock a certain door—and imagine how I near fell to the ground to see all those crates with my name on them! Anyway, we also procured a packet of mail." He made a queasy face. "Tell him, Edward! I can't bear to think of it!"

"Mr. Bidwell's sister married a land speculator," Winston said. "In the letter she wrote, she indicated he has purchased a sizeable amount of territory between here and the Florida country, and has hopes to begin a port settlement of his own."

"You don't say!" Matthew said.

"Yes, it's damnably true!" Bidwell started to hammer his fist on the desk, and then decided it was not proper for his new age of enlightenment. "It'll never work, of course. That swampland down there makes ours look like a manicured showpark. And do you really think the Spanish are just going to sit still and let a half-pint, weasly milksop of a land speculator threaten their Florida country? No! He has no business sense! I told Savannah when she married that man she'd weep a tear for every pearl on her dress!" He stabbed a finger in the air like a rapier's thrust. "Mark my words, she'll regret such a folly as she's about to enter into!"

"Uh . . . shall I get you something to drink?" Winston asked. "To calm your nerves?" To Matthew, he confided, "Mr. Bidwell's sister never fails. To antagonize, I mean."

"No, no! I'm all right. Just let me get my breath. Oh, my heart gallops like a wild horse." Bidwell spent a moment in an exercise of slow and steady deep breathing, and gradually the red whorls that had surfaced on his cheeks faded away. "The point of my asking you here, Matthew," he said, "is to offer you a position with my company."

Matthew didn't respond; in truth, he was too shocked to speak.

"A position of not small responsibility," Bidwell went on. "I need a good, trustworthy man in Charles Town. Someone to make sure the supplies keep flowing, and to make certain such dirtiness as has been done to me in the past is not repeated. A . . . uh . . . a private investigator, you might say. Does that sound at all of interest to you?"

It took a little while longer for Matthew to find his voice. "I do appreciate your offer, sir. I do. But, to be perfectly honest, you and I would eventually come to blows and our fight might knock the earth off its tilt. Therefore I must decline, as I would hate to be responsible for the death of mankind."

"Ah. Yes. Well spoken, that." Bidwell did appear much relieved. "I felt I should at least offer you a future, since my actions—and stupidity—have so endangered your present."

"I have a future," Matthew said firmly. "In New York, I believe. And thank you for helping me come to that conclusion."

"Now! That's out of the way!" Bidwell heaved a sigh. "I wanted you to see something." He pushed the wooden box across the desk toward Matthew. "We searched through the foul bastard's house, just as you suggested, and found all the items you said would be there. That five-bladed device was still nasty with dried blood. And we discovered the book on ancient Egypt, as well. This box was placed in the bottom of a trunk. Open it, if you please."

Matthew leaned forward and lifted the lid, which rose smoothly on a well-oiled hinge.

Within the box were three charcoal pencils, a writing tablet, a folded sheet of paper, a gum eraser . . . and . . .

"What he found in the spring," Bidwell said.

Indeed. The sapphire brooch and ruby ring were there, along with a gold crucifix on a chain, seven gold doubloons, three silver coins, and a little black velvet bag.

"You will find the bag's contents of interest," Bidwell promised.

Matthew took it out and emptied it on the desktop. In the sunlight that streamed through the window, the room was suddenly colored by the shine of four dark green emeralds, two deep purple amethysts, two pearls, and an amber stone. The jewels were raw and yet to be professionally polished, but even so were obviously of excellent quality. Matthew surmised they had been captured at sea from vessels shuttling between tropical mines and the marketplace.

"The folded paper is also worth a glance," said Bidwell.

Matthew unfolded it. It was a drawing, in charcoal pencil, of a good-sized building. Some time had been spent in attending to the details. Present were bricks, windows, and a bell steeple.

"It appears," Bidwell said, "the foul bastard . . . intended to build his next schoolhouse of a less flammable material."

"I see." Matthew gazed at the drawing—a sad sight, really—and then refolded the paper and returned it to the box.

Bidwell put the gemstones back into the bag. He

removed from the box the pencils, the writing tablet, the eraser, and the drawing of the new schoolhouse.

"I own the spring, of course," Bidwell said. "I own the water and the mud. By the rights of ownership—and the hell I have gone through—I also claim for myself these gems and jewelry, which came from that mud. Agreed?"

"It makes no matter to me," Matthew answered. "Do with them as you please."

"I shall." Bidwell placed the little bag into the box, beside the coins, the brooch, the ring, and the crucifix and chain. He closed the lid.

Then he pushed the box toward Matthew. "It pleases me . . . for you to take this to the person who has suffered far more hell than I."

Matthew couldn't fathom what he'd just heard. "Pardon me?"

"You heard correctly. Take them to—" He interrupted himself as he snapped the first charcoal pencil between his hands. "—her. It is the very least I can do, and certainly it can't bring back her husband or those months spent in the gaol." In spite of his good intentions, he couldn't help but regard the box with a wanton eye. "Go ahead. Take it"—the second pencil was picked up and broken—"before I regain my senses."

"Why don't you take it to her yourself! It would mean much more."

"It would mean much *less*," he corrected. "She hates me. I've tried to speak to her, tried to explain my position . . . but she turns away every time. Therefore you take the box." *Snap*, died the third pencil. "Tell her you found it."

Realizing that indeed Bidwell must be half-crazed with humanity to let such wealth slip through his fingers, Matthew picked up the box and held it to his chest. "I will take it to her directly. Do you know where she is?"

"I saw her an hour ago," Winston said. "She was drawing water." Matthew nodded; he had an idea where she might be found.

"We must put ourselves back in business here." Bidwell picked up the drawing that Johnstone had done—the bad man's dream of an Oxford of his own—and began to methodically tear it to pieces. "Put ourselves back in order, and consign this disgraceful . . . insane . . . blot on my town to the trash heap. I can do nothing more for the woman than what I've done today. And neither can you. Therefore, I must ask: how much longer shall you grace us with your presence?"

"As a matter of fact, I have decided it's time to get on with my own life. I might leave in the morning, at first light."

"I'll have Green take you to Charles Town in a wagon. Will you be ready by six?"

"I shall be," Matthew said. "But I'd prefer you give me a horse, a saddle and tack, and some food, and I'll get myself to Charles Town. I am not an invalid, and therefore I refuse to be carted about like one."

"*Give* you a horse?" Bidwell glowered at him. "Horses cost money, aren't you aware of that? And saddles don't grow on trees, either!"

"You might wish for saddle-trees, sir!" Matthew fired back at him. "As that might be the only crop your farmers can grow here!"

"You don't concern yourself with our crops, thank you! I'll have you know I'm bringing in a botanist—the finest money can buy—to set our growing affairs straight! So stick that in your damned theory hole and—"

"Excuse me, gentlemen!" Winston said calmly, and the wranglers fell quiet. "I shall be glad to pay for a horse and saddle for Mr. Corbett, though I think it unwise of you, Matthew, to travel unaccompanied. But I wish to offer my best regards and hope that you find much success in the future."

"Write him a love letter while you're at it!" Bidwell steamed.

"My thanks, sir," Matthew said. "As for travelling alone, I feel confident I won't be in any danger." The demise of Shawcombe and Jack One Eye, he suspected, had made the backroads of the entire Southern colonies at least safer than Manhattan's harbor. "Oh. While I am thinking of it: Mr. Bidwell, there is one final rope that remains unknotted in this situation."

"You mean Dr. Shields?" Bidwell crumpled the torn pieces of Johnstone's drawing in his fist. "I haven't decided what to do with him yet. And don't rush me!"

"No, not Dr. Shields. The burning of the schoolhouse, and who was responsible for the other fires as well."

"What?" Winston blanched.

"Well, it wasn't Johnstone, obviously," Matthew explained. "Even someone so preoccupied with his own affairs as Mr. Bidwell can understand *that*. And, in time, I'm sure Mr. Bidwell might begin to wonder, as well he should."

"You're right!" Bidwell agreed, his eyes narrowing. "What son of a bitch tried to burn down my town?"

"Early this morning I had a thought about this burning business, and I went to Lancaster's house. The place is still a wreck, as you're aware. Has anyone else been through it?"

"No one would go within a hundred yards of that damn murder house!"

"I thought not, though I did appreciate the fact that the corpse has been disposed of. Anyway, I decided to search a little more thoroughly . . . and I discovered a very strange bucket in the debris. Evidently it was something Johnstone didn't bother himself with, since it simply appears to be a regular bucket. Perhaps he thought it was full of rat bait or some such."

"Well, then? What was in it?"

"I'm not sure. It appears to be tar. It has a brimstone smell. I decided to leave it where I found it . . . as I didn't know if it might be flammable, or explode, or what might occur if it were jostled too severely."

"Tar? A brimstone smell?" Alarmed, Bidwell looked at Winston. "By God. I don't like the sound of *that!*"

"I'm sure it's worth going there to get," Matthew continued. "Or Mr. Winston might want to go and look at it, and then . . . I don't know, bury it or something. Would you be able to tell what it was if you saw it, Mr. Winston?"

"Possibly," Winston answered, his voice tight. "But I'll tell you right now . . . as you describe it, the stuff sounds like . . . possibly . . . infernal fire, Mr. Bidwell?"

"Infernal fire? My God!" Now Bidwell did hammer his desk. "So that's who was burning the houses! But where was he getting the stuff from?"

"He was a very capable man," Matthew said. "Perhaps he had sulphur for his rat baits or candles or something. Perhaps he cooked some tar and mixed it himself. I have a feeling Lancaster was trying to hurry the process of emptying the town without telling his accomplice. Who knows why?" Matthew shrugged. "There is no honor among thieves, and even less among murderers."

"I'll be damned!" Bidwell looked as if he'd taken a punch to his ponderous gut. "Was there no end to their treacheries, even against each other?"

"It does appear a dangerous bucket, Mr. Winston," Matthew said. "Very dangerous indeed. If it were up to me,

I wouldn't dare bring it back to the mansion for fear of explosion. You might just want to bring a small sample to show Mr. Bidwell. Then by all means bury it and forget where you turned the shovel."

"Excellent advice." Winston gave a slight bow of his head. "I shall attend to it this afternoon. And I am very gratified, sir, that you did not leave this particular rope unknotted."

"Mr. Winston is a useful man," Matthew said to Bidwell. "You should be pleased to have him in your employ."

Bidwell puffed his cheeks and blew out. "Whew! Don't I know it!"

As Matthew turned away and started out with the treasure box, the master of Fount Royal had to ask one last question: "Matthew?" he said. "Uh . . . is there any way . . . any possible way at all . . . that . . . the fortune might be recovered?"

Matthew made a display of thought. "As it has flowed along a river to the center of the earth," he said, "I would think it extremely unlikely. But how long can you hold your breath?"

"Ha!" Bidwell smiled grimly, but there was some good humor in it. "Just because I build ships and I'm going to station a grand navy here . . . does not mean I can *swim.* Now go along with you, and if Edward thinks he's going to convince me to give you a free horse and saddle, he is a sadly mistaken duke!"

Matthew left the mansion and walked past the still waters of the spring on his way to the conjunction of streets. Before he reached the turn to Truth, however, he saw ahead of him the approach of a black-clad, black-tricorned, spidery, and wholly loathsome figure.

"Ho, there!" Exodus Jerusalem called, lifting a hand. On

this deserted street, the sound fairly echoed. Matthew was sorely tempted to run, but the preacher picked up his pace and met him. Blocked his way, actually.

"What do *you* want?" Matthew asked.

"A truce, please." Jerusalem showed both palms, and Matthew unconsciously held more securely to the treasure box. "We are packed and ready to leave, and I am on my way to give my regards to Mr. Bidwell."

"Art thou?" Matthew lifted his eyebrows. "Thy speech has suddenly become more common, Preacher. Why is that?"

"My speech? Oh . . . that!" Jerusalem grinned broadly, his face seamed with wrinkles in the sunlight. "It's an *effort* to keep that up. Too many *thee*s and *thou*s in one day and my lips near fall off."

"It's part of your performance, you mean?"

"No, it's real enough. My father spoke such, and his father before him. And my son—if I ever have a son—shall as well. Also, however, the widow Lassiter detests it. Gently, of course. She is a very gentle, very warm, very giving woman."

"The widow Lassiter? Your latest conquest?"

"My latest *convert,*" he corrected. "There is quite a difference. Ah yes, she's a wonderfully warm woman. She ought to be warm, since she weighs almost two hundred pounds. But she has a lovely face and she can surely mend a shirt!" He leaned in a little closer, his grin lecherous. *"And* she has quite the roll in her skirt, if you catch my meaning!"

"I would prefer not to, thank you."

"Well, as my father always said, beauty is in the eye of the beholder. The one-eyed, stiff beholder, I mean."

"You are a piece of work, aren't you?" Matthew said,

amazed at such audacity. "Do you do all your thinking with your private parts?"

"Let us be friends. Brothers under the warming sun. I have heard all about your triumph. I don't fully understand how such a thing was done—the Satan play, I mean—but I am gratified to know that a righteous and innocent woman has been cleared, and that you are also found guiltless. Besides, it would be a damn sin for a looker like that to burn, eh?"

"Excuse me," Matthew said. "And farewell to you."

"Ah, you may say farewell, but not goodbye, young man! Perchance we'll meet again, further along life's twisting road."

"We might meet again, at that. Except I might be a judge and you might be at the end of a twisting rope."

"Ha, ha! An excellent joke!" Now, however, a serious cast came over the wizened face. "Your magistrate. I—honestly—am very sorry. He fought death to the end, I understand."

"No," Matthew said. "In the end he accepted it. As I did."

"Yes, of course. That, too. But he did seem a decent man. Too bad he died in a hole like this."

Matthew stared at the ground, a muscle working in his jaw.

"If you like, before I leave I might go to his grave and speak a few words for his eternal soul."

"Preacher," Matthew said in a strained voice, "all is well with his eternal soul. I suggest you go give your regards to Mr. Bidwell, get in your wagon with your witless brood, and go to—wherever you choose to go. Just leave my sight." He lifted his fierce gaze to the man, and saw the preacher flinch.

"And let me tell you that if I but see you walking in the direction of Magistrate Woodward's grave, I will forget the laws of God and man and do my damnedest to put my boot so far up your ass I will kick your teeth out from the inner side. Do you understand me?"

Jerusalem backed away a few steps. "It was only a thought!"

"Good day, goodbye, and good riddance." Matthew side-stepped him and continued on his way.

"Ohhhhh, not goodbye!" Jerusalem called. "Farewell, perhaps! But not goodbye! I have a feeling thou shalt lay eyes on me at some future unknown date, as I travel this ungodly, debased, and corrupted land in the continual— continual, I say—battle against the foul seed of Satan! So I say to thee, brother Matthew, farewell . . . but never goodbye!"

The voice—which Matthew thought could strip paint off wood if Jerusalem really let it bray—was fading behind him as he turned onto Truth Street. He dared not look back, for he didn't care to become a pillar of salt today.

He passed the gaol. He did not give the odious place a single glance, though his gut tightened as he stepped on its shadow.

And then he came to her house.

Rachel had been busy. She had pulled into the yard much of the furniture, and a washtub of soapy water stood at the ready. Also brought into the cleansing sun were clothes, bedsheets, a mattress, kettles and skillets, shoes, and just about everything else a household contained.

The door was wide open, as were all the shutters. Airing the place out, he thought. Intending to move in again, and make it a home. Indeed, Rachel was more like Bidwell in her tenacity—one might say foolhearted stubbornness—

than ever he'd imagined. Still, if elbow grease alone could transform that rat-whiskered shack to a livable cottage again, she would have a mansion of her own.

He crossed the yard, winding between the accumulated belongings. Suddenly his progress was interrupted by a small chestnut-brown dog that sprang up from its drowsing posture beside the washtub, took a stance that threatened attack, and began to bark in a voice that surely rivalled the preacher's for sheer volume.

Rachel came to the threshold and saw who her visitor was. "Hush!" she commanded. "Hush!" She clapped her hands to get the mongrel's attention. The dog ceased its alarms and, with a quick wag of its tail and a wide-mouthed yawn, plopped itself down on the sun-warmed ground again.

"Well!" Matthew said. "It seems you have a sentinel."

"She took up with me this morning." Rachel wiped her dirty hands on an equally dirty rag. "I gave her one of the ham biscuits Mrs. Nettles made for me, and we are suddenly sisters."

Matthew looked around at the furniture and other items. "You have your labors ahead of you, I see."

"It won't be so bad, once I finish scrubbing the house."

"Rachel!" Matthew said. "You don't really plan on staying here, do you?"

"It's my home," she answered, spearing him with those intense amber eyes. She wore a blue-printed scarf around her head, and her face was streaked with grime. The gray dress and white apron she wore were equally filthy. "Why should I leave it?"

"Because . . ." He hesitated, and showed her the box. "Because I have something for you. May I come in?"

"Yes. Mind the mess, though."

As Matthew approached the door, he heard a *whuff* of wind behind him and thought the mighty sentinel had decided to take a bite from his ankle. He turned in time to see the brown dog go tearing off across the field, where it seized one of two fleeing rats and shook the rodent between its jaws in a crushing deathgrip.

"She does like to chase them," Rachel said.

Within the bare house, Matthew saw that Rachel had been scraping yellow lichens from the floorboards with an axeblade. The fungus and mildew that had spread across the walls had bloomed into strange purple and green hues only otherwise to be seen in fever dreams. However, Matthew saw that where the sunlight touched, the growths had turned ashen. A broom leaned against the wall, next to a pile of dust, dirt, rat pellets, and bones. Nearby was a bucket of more soapy water, in which a scrub brush was immersed.

"You know, there are plenty of houses available," Matthew said. "If you really insist on staying here, you might move into one only recently abandoned and save yourself all this work. As a matter of fact, I know a very comfortable place, and the only labor involved would be clearing out a wasp's nest."

"*This* is my home," she answered.

"Well . . . yes . . . but still, don't you think—"

She turned away from him and picked up a rolling pin that lay on the floor near the broom. Then she walked to a wall and put her ear against it. Following that, she whacked the boards three times and Matthew could hear the panicked squeaking and scurrying from within.

"Those defy me," Rachel said. "I've run out most of them, but those—right there—defy me. I swear I'll clean them out. Every last one of them."

And at that moment Matthew understood.

Rachel, he believed, was still in a state of shock. And who could fault her? The loss of her husband, the loss of her home, the loss of her freedom. Even—for a time at least, as she prepared herself for the fires—the loss of her will to live. And now, faced with the daunting—and perhaps impossible—task of rebuilding, she must concentrate on and conquer what she perceived as the last obstacle to a return to normality.

But who, having walked through such flames, could ever erase the memory of being singed?

"I regret I have nothing to offer you," she said, and now that he was looking for it he could see a certain burnt blankness in her eyes. "It will be a time before my cupboard is restocked."

"Yes," Matthew said. He gave her a sad but gentle smile. "I'm sure. But . . . nonetheless, it *will* be restocked, won't it?"

"You may put faith in it," she answered, and then she pressed her ear to the wall again.

"Let me show you what I've brought." He approached her and offered the box. "Take it and look inside." Rachel laid down the rolling pin, accepted the box, and lifted its lid.

Matthew saw no reaction on her face, as she viewed the coins and the other items. "The little bag. Open that too." She shook the gems out into the box. Again, there was no reaction.

"Those were found in Johnstone's house." He had already decided to tell her the truth. "Mr. Bidwell asked me to give them to you."

"Mr. Bidwell," Rachel repeated, without emotion. She closed the lid and held the box out. "You take them. I have already received from Mr. Bidwell all the gifts that I can stand."

"Listen to me. Please. I know how you must feel, but—"

"No. You do not, nor can you ever."

"Of course you're right." He nodded. "But surely you must realize you're holding a true fortune. I daresay with the kind of money you could get in Charles Town from the sale of those jewels, you might live in Mr. Bidwell's style in some larger, more populous city."

"I see what his style is," she countered, "and I detest it. Take the box."

"Rachel, let me point out something to you. Bidwell did not murder your husband. Nor did he create this scheme. I don't particularly care for his . . . um . . . motivations, either, but he was reacting to a crisis that he thought would destroy Fount Royal. In that regard," Matthew said, "he acted properly. You know, he might have hanged you without waiting for the magistrate. I'm sure he could have somehow justified it."

"So *you're* justifying *him,* is that right?"

"Since he now faces a guilty verdict from you in a tragedy for which he was not wholly responsible," Matthew said, "I am simply pleading his case."

Rachel stared at him in silence, still holding out the box to him. He made no move to accept it.

"Daniel is gone," Matthew told her. "You know that. Gone, too, are the men who murdered him. But Fount Royal—such as it may be—is still here, and so is Bidwell. It appears he intends to do his best to rebuild the town. That is his main concern. It seems to be yours as well. Don't you think this common ground is larger than hatred?"

"I shall take this box," Rachel said calmly, "and dump it into the spring if you refuse it."

"Then go ahead," he answered, "because I do refuse it. Oh: except for one gold piece. The one that Johnstone stole from my room. Before you throw your fortune and future away to prove your devotion to Daniel in continued poverty and suffering, I *will* take the one gold piece." There was no response from her, though perhaps she did flinch just a little.

"I understand Bidwell's position," Matthew said. "The evidence against you was overwhelming. I too might have pressed for your execution, if I believed firmly enough in witchcraft. And . . . if I hadn't fallen in love with you."

Now she did blink; her eyes, so powerful a second before, had become dazed.

"Of course you recognized it. You didn't want me to. In fact, you asked me to—as you put it—go on about my life. You said—there in the gaol, after I'd read the magistrate's decree—that the time had come to embrace reality." He disguised his melancholy with a faint smile. "That time has now come for both of us."

Rachel looked down at the floor. She had taken hold of the box with both hands, and Matthew saw an ocean's worth of conflicting tides move across her face.

He said, "I'm leaving in the morning. I will be in Charles Town for a few weeks. Then most likely I will be travelling to New York. At that time I can be reached through Magistrate Nathaniel Powers, if you ever have need of me."

She lifted her gaze to his, her eyes wet and glistening. "I can never repay you for my life, Matthew. How can I even begin?"

"Oh . . . one gold coin will do, I think."

She opened the box, and he took the coin. "Take another," she offered. "Take as many as you like. And some of the jewels, too."

"One gold coin," he said. "That's my due." He put the

coin into his pocket, never to be spent. He looked around the house and sighed. He had the feeling that once the rats were run out and her home was truly hers again, she might embrace the reality of moving to a better abode—further away from that wretched gaol.

Rachel took a step toward him. "Do you believe me . . . when I say I'll remember you when I'm an old, old woman?"

"I do. And please remember me, if at that point you're seeking the excitement of a younger man."

She smiled, in spite of her sadness. Then she grasped his chin, leaned forward—and kissed him very softly on the forehead, below the bandage that covered what would be his grandchildren's favorite story.

Now was the moment, he realized. It was now or never.

To ask her. Had she actually entered that smoke-palled medicine lodge? Or had it been only his feverish—and wishful—fantasy?

Was he still a virgin, or not?

He made his decision, and he thought it was the right one.

"Why are you smiling that way?" Rachel asked.

"Oh . . . I am remembering a dream I think I had. One more thing: you said to me once that your heart was used up." Matthew looked into her dirt-streaked, determined face, forevermore locking her remarkable beauty of form and spirit in his memory vault. "I believe . . . it is a cupboard that only need be restocked." He leaned forward and kissed her cheek, and then he had to go.

Had to.

As Matthew left the house, Rachel followed him to the door. She stood there, on the threshold of her home and her own new beginning. "Goodbye!" she called, and perhaps her voice was tremulous. "Goodbye!"

He glanced back. His eyes were stinging, and she was blurred to his sight. "Farewell!" he answered. And then he went on, as Rachel's sentinel sniffed his shoes and then returned to its ratcatching duties.

Matthew slept that night like a man who had rediscovered the meaning of peace.

At five-thirty, Mrs. Nettles came to awaken him as he'd asked, though the town's remaining roosters had already performed that function. Matthew shaved, washed his face, and dressed in a pair of cinnamon-colored breeches and a fresh white shirt with the left sleeve cut away. He pulled up his white stockings and slid his feet into the square-toed shoes. If Bidwell wanted back the clothes he had loaned, the man would have to rip them off himself.

Before he descended the stairs for the last time, Matthew went into the magistrate's room. No, that was wrong. The room was Bidwell's again, now. He stood there for a while, staring at the perfectly made bed. He looked at the candle stubs and the lantern. He looked at the clothes Woodward had worn, now draped over the back of a chair. All save the gold-striped waistcoat, which had gone with the magistrate to worlds unknown.

Yesterday, when he'd gone to the graveside, he'd had a difficult time until he'd realized the magistrate no longer suffered, either in body or mind. Perhaps, in some more perfect place, the just were richly rewarded for their tribulations. Perhaps, in that place, a father might find a lost son, both of them gone home to a garden.

Matthew lowered his head and wiped his eyes.

Then he let his sadness go, like a nightbird.

Downstairs, Mrs. Nettles had prepared him a breakfast that might have crippled the horse he was to ride. Bidwell was absent, obviously preferring to sleep late rather than share the clerk's meal. But with the final cup of tea, Mrs. Nettles brought Matthew an envelope, upon which was written *Concerning the Character and Abilities of Master Matthew Corbett, Esq.* Matthew turned it over and saw it was sealed with a red blob of wax in which was impressed an imperial *B*.

"He asked I give it to ye," Mrs. Nettles explained. "For your future references, he said. I'd be might pleased, for compliments from Mr. Bidwell are as rare as snowballs in Hell."

"I am pleased," Matthew said. "Tell him I thank him very much for his kindness."

The breakfast done, Mrs. Nettles walked outside with Matthew. The sun was well up, the sky blue, and a few lacy clouds drifting like the sailing ships Bidwell hoped to launch from this future port. John Goode had brought an excellent-looking roan horse with a saddle that might not raise too many sores between here and Charles Town. Mrs. Nettles opened the saddlebags to show him the food she'd packed for him, as well as a leather waterflask. It occurred to Matthew that, now that his usefulness was done to the master of Fount Royal, it was up to the servants to send him off.

Matthew shook Goode's hand, and Goode thanked him for coming to take that "bumb" out of his house. Matthew returned the thanks, for giving him the opportunity to taste some absolutely wonderful turtle soup.

Mrs. Nettles only had to help him a little to climb up on the horse. Then Matthew situated himself and grasped the reins. He was ready.

"Young sir?" Mrs. Nettles said. "May I give ye a word of advice?"

"Of course."

"Find y'self a good, strong Scottish lass."

He smiled. "I shall certainly take it under consideration."

"Good luck to ye," she said. "And a good life."

Matthew guided his horse toward the gate and began his journey. He passed the spring, where a woman in a green bonnet was already drawing water for the day. He saw in a field a farmer, breaking earth with a wooden hoe. Another farmer was walking amid fresh furrows, tossing seeds from one side to the other.

Good luck, Fount Royal! Matthew thought. And good life to all those who lived here, both on this day and on the day tomorrow.

At the gate, Mr. Green was waiting to lift the locking timber. "Goodbye, sir!" he called, and displayed a gap-toothed grin.

Matthew rode through. He was not very far along the sunlit road when he reined the horse in and paused to look back. The gate was closing. Slowly, slowly . . . then shut. Over the singing of birds in the forest, Matthew heard the sound of the locking timber slide back into place.

He had a sure destination.

New York. But not just because Magistrate Nathaniel Powers was there. It was also because the almshouse was there, and Headmaster Eben Ausley. Matthew recalled what that insidious, child-brutalizing villain had said to him, five years ago: *Consider that your education concerning the real world has been furthered. Be of excellent service to the magistrate, be of good cheer and good will, and live a long and happy life. And never—never—plot a war you have no hope of winning.*

Well, Matthew mused, perhaps the boy of five years ago could neither plot a war nor win it. But the man of today might find a method to end Ausley's reign of terror.

It was worth putting one's thoughts to, wasn't it?

Matthew stared for a moment at the closed gate, beyond which lay both an ending and a beginning. Then he turned his mount, his face, and his mind toward the century of wonders.

Visit
❖ Pocket Books ❖
online at

www.SimonSays.com

Keep up on the latest new
releases from your favorite
authors, as well as author
appearances, news, chats,
special offers and more.

SIMON & SCHUSTER
A VIACOM COMPANY
www.SimonSays.com

Pocket
Books